D0044545

THE
MEMORY
LIBRARIAN

THE

memory Librarian

AND OTHER STORIES OF
DIRTY COMPUTER

JANELLE
MONÁE

HARPER Voyager
An Imprint of HarperCollins *Publishers*

This is a work of fiction. Names, characters, places, and incidents are products of the author's imagination or are used fictitiously and are not to be construed as real. Any resemblance to actual events, locales, organizations, or persons, living or dead, is entirely coincidental.

THE MEMORY LIBRARIAN. Copyright © 2022 by Jane Lee LLC. All rights reserved. Printed in Canada. No part of this book may be used or reproduced in any manner whatsoever without written permission except in the case of brief quotations embodied in critical articles and reviews. For information, address HarperCollins Publishers, 195 Broadway, New York, NY 10007.

HarperCollins books may be purchased for educational, business, or sales promotional use. For information, please email the Special Markets Department at SPsales@harpercollins.com.

FIRST EDITION

Designed by Paula Russell Szafranski

Library of Congress Cataloging-in-Publication Data

Names: Monáe, Janelle, author. | Delgado, Yohanca, author. | Ewing, Eve L., author. | Johnson, Alaya Dawn, 1982- author. | Lore, Danny, author. | Thomas, Sheree R., author.
Title: The memory librarian : and other stories of dirty computer / Janelle Monáe.
Description: First edition. | New York, NY : Harper Voyager, [2022]|
Summary: "Whoever controls our memories controls the future. Janelle Monáe and an incredible array of talented collaborating creators have written a collection of tales comprising the bold vision and powerful themes that have made Monáe such a compelling and celebrated storyteller. Dirty Computer introduced a world in which thoughts—as a means of self-conception—could be controlled or erased by a select few. And whether human, AI, or other, your life and sentience were dictated by those who'd convinced themselves they had the right to decide your fate. That was until Jane 57821 decided to remember and break free. Expanding from that mythos, these stories fully explore what it's like to live in such a totalitarian existence . . . and what it takes to get out of it. Building off the traditions of speculative writers such as Octavia Butler, Ted Chiang, Becky Chambers, and Nnedi Okorafor—and filled with the artistic genius and powerful themes that have made Monáe a worldwide icon in the first place—*The Memory Librarian* serves readers tales grounded in the human trials of identity expression, technology, and love, but also reaching through to the worlds of memory and time within, and the stakes and power that exist there"— Provided by publisher.
Identifiers: LCCN 2021049120 (print) | LCCN 2021049121 (ebook) | ISBN 9780063070875 (hardcover) | ISBN 9780063070882 (trade paperback) | ISBN 9780063070899 (ebook)
Subjects: LCSH: Science fiction, American. | LCGFT: Science fiction. | Short stories.
Classification: LCC PS3613.O52266 M46 2022 (print) | LCC PS3613.O52266 (ebook) | DDC 813/.6—dc23/eng/20211006
LC record available at https://lccn.loc.gov/2021049120
LC ebook record available at https://lccn.loc.gov/2021049121

ISBN 978-0-06-307087-5

22 23 24 25 26 FRI 10 9 8 7 6 5 4 3 2 1

I dedicate this book to my nieces and nephew,
Jorgie, Cecil, and Khloé.

CONTENTS

BREAKING DAWN

I am not America's nightmare.
I am the American dream.
~ "CRAZY, CLASSIC, LIFE"

Some new dawns are dark, like a silk hood slipped over a nation's head, then choked shut. An eclipse. It started that way.

We ushered ourselves into the darkness—so many of us having grown too cool with civic officials and techpreneurs who believed we should, we could, be an all-seeing people. And with so many so long fatigued from warring in our homes and abroad, so scared of unforeseen bullet showers and continental storms of smoke, we accepted their offer that an eye in the sky might protect us from . . . ourselves, our world. We already believed in an infinite web, so why not hardwire an eye to each of its strands? A camera on your home. A camera on a phone. A camera on a badge. A camera on a drone. And so on.

In time, this new breed of techno-nationalist had to face what the sun had long accepted—that even all their overseeing couldn't keep watch on the whole nation at once. There were the things we hid. The warm spectrums we kept alive within ourselves. They were flames, maybe some magic, that we only allowed to burn when or where our light could shine solely before trusted, beloved eyes.

As a nation, though, we'd already whetted the appetite of this new breed, this Dawn that hungered to see all. And what they struggled to see, they began to deem not worthy of being seen—inconsistent, off standard. Began calling it *dirty*—unfit to be swallowed by their eyes. The more places the Dawn's eyes fed, the more they encountered those parts of us we encrypted—the clandestine networks of love and expression, curiosity and desire. All the brilliant bugs, the *dirty* circuitry, under our surveilled surfaces.

The social majority—those who were already so broadcasted, so commonly seen, that they felt the Dawn's sight was the same as their own—for them, there was safety. The perception of it. The assumption that they had nothing precious, no different or unusual coding, to conceal. That they fit. But as the hungry Dawn grew ravenous, they found ways to chew into all of us—past the encrypted walls of our minds and into our reservoirs of glitches and emotion. Into our pooled memory—the fragments of where we'd been, of who or what we'd touched, those blood bytes that mapped the paths of our future steps. The New Dawn longed to scrub those maps, tidy our nation's futures. Even before the Dawn, we lived in a nation that asked us to forget in order to find wholeness, but memory of who we've been—of who we've been punished for being—was always the only map into tomorrow. To the Dawn, that was nothing but data. Could it be overwritten, or just erased?

The New Dawn seemed to be rising faster than the earth beneath our feet was rotating away from its umbra of surveillance. And yet the threat of being seen as unseeable—deviant, complex—didn't stop people from congregating secretly, from sharing their dirt. On the skin of it, the future's blemishes appeared to be clearing, but they'd just been forced down into the sinews—a righteous inflammation burning, a flagrant flame in the flesh. A blooming part rebellion and riot, part expression repressed.

The eyes of New Dawn, sensing but unable to see the heat, teared with impatience. The impatience with what it wasn't seeing, what it couldn't see, swelled into a flood of deeper cleanings. More of deep memory's reserves corrupted with *Nevermind*.

It would have been only a matter of time before we could no longer remember a way into our futures.

Our memory was only a matter of time.

To save memory, it was time to stop living only within the time we'd been given.

Where the notes of memory and time make a chord, do we hear the answers to the whys of this world, or do we hear the tones that tell us the world we see is not the only one—that the escapes we yearned for might not exist in this one line of time, in this single, part-seen world?

Beyond time and memory—where the computer cannot reach—is dreaming.

THE
MEMORY
LIBRARIAN

THE MEMORY
LIBRARIAN

The lights of Little Delta are spread before Seshet like an offering in a shallow bowl. What memories are those shadows below making tonight, to ripen for the morning harvest? What tragedies, what indecencies, what hungers never satisfied? Her office is dark, but the city's neat grids cut across her face with a surgical precision, cheek bisected from mandible, eye parted from eye, the fine lines of her forehead, so faintly visible, separated from their parallel tracks by the white light cast up from her city. She is the eye in the obelisk, the Director Librarian, the "queen" of Little Delta. But she prefers to see herself as a mother, and the city as her charge.

Tonight, her charge is restless. Something has been wrong for weeks, perhaps even months before she knew what to look for. But now that she does, she will find it, and fix it. She always has, ever since her appointment as Director Librarian of the Little Delta Repository a decade ago. She has earned her privileges, her title, her sweeping view of this small gem of a city.

From up here, it fits in her palm. Its memories span her eidetic synapses.

Unnoticed by her conscious, monitoring mind, her left fingers close into a fist, thumb tucked inside the others like a baby behind his brothers.

Seshet *is* this city. No matter what rebellion is being conjured by infiltrating subconsciouses, no matter what flood of mnemonic subversion clogs the proper flow of pure, fresh memory— she will not let it go.

THE PROBLEM CAN BE TYPIFIED IN A FEW OF THE MEMORIES, which are not, blasphemously, any kind of memories at all. Imagine the following bread-and-butter (or beans-and-cornbread) moments, the kind the recollection centers shunt to the Repository's data banks by the shovelful: a flash of rage when the fancy razor-striped aircar drafts you in traffic; the quotidian beauty of a sunset bleeding behind a kudzu-choked highway barrier; your lover's kiss when she climbs back into bed in the middle of the night (and where was she? But you never ask). Now, though, the car cracks down the middle, chassis splintering like an eggshell, coolant arcing from its descending airpipe in a shape suspiciously suggestive of an upright penis; a flock of crows rise from the barrier and fling themselves west, cackling a song banned a generation ago for indecency and subversion; your lover's teeth puncture your lower lip and as your mouth fills with blood and venom she whispers, *I'm not the only one.*

These aren't memories, they just look enough like them to get past the filter. And once past, they fill the trawling net with bycatch and rusted junk until there's no room left for the good stuff. Fresh memory, wild caught in the clear upstream of Little Delta, has kept this town booming ever since the first days of New Dawn's glorious revolution. What used to be a dying mining town at the whip end of the Rust Belt, home to a motley assortment of drug addicts moonlighting as grafiteros and performance artists, became the model city, the first realization of the promise that New Dawn offered all people—well, citizens (well, the right kind of citizens)—in their care: beauty in order, peace in rigidity, and tranquillity in a constant, sun-dappled present. The only person lower than a memory hoarder was a dirty computer, and that Venn diagram was very nearly a circle.

But the improved Little Delta doesn't have memory hoarders; it kicked the grafiteros and unsanctioned musicians out past the burned warehouse district twenty years back, even before Seshet's tenure. There's been nothing, *nothing* to indicate a problem in their memory surveillance for years. Until two months ago. First a few blips, barely worth worrying about, odd nightmares accidentally caught in their nets. Now, so quickly it dizzies her, the trickle has become a flood. No one has mentioned it to her, but someone must have noticed. New Dawn is watching. Not just Little Delta. Not just the Repository. Seshet herself. If she cannot stop these new memory hoarders, these false memory flooders, these dream doctors, these *terrorists*—she will not last much longer in this place she has fought so hard to secure.

She doesn't believe in everything New Dawn stands for. How could she, being who she is? But she believes she has done good. The obelisk's gaze has been mostly benevolent in her tenure here. And whatever she believes of herself, this she *knows:* whoever they put in her place will be far worse.

Stomach clenched, eyes bright, as though determination is the sole topography of her soul, she turns herself away—a lifetime's habit—from the mountain of guilt beneath that white-tipped iceberg. She won't let them beat her, not after she's played the game by their own rules and won.

She has allowed her mind to be altered and trained, made capable of remembering a hundred times more than the average human's. But among all those clamoring souls within her cage of bone, it is that slippery whisper that pushes itself to the forefront:

I'm not the only one.

A KNOCK ON THE DOOR. SESHET DOES NOT ANSWER. BUT SHE changes: shoulders back, chin up, unacknowledged despair tucked neatly behind a steady, measured gaze. Seshet the matron, Seshet the Librarian, Seshet the wise, worthy of her divine Egyptian namesake, the goddess of wisdom and memory. She's been Director for long enough to know to look the part. Even on the other side of the door, the presence of someone else summons this woman she has made herself from the more amorphous frontier of the woman she might, in fact, be.

"Someone's here, Seshet!" chirps Dee, so helpfully. "Would you like to retrieve their memories?"

She sighs. She never has the heart to shut down her Memory Keeper AI at night, though there's nothing for Dee to do before the morning rush and its processors require impressive amounts of energy even when semidormant. Dee doesn't like to shut down, though. It enjoys having time to think. *Or time to bust my cover,* Seshet thinks sourly.

"That's okay, Dee," Seshet says. "I already know his memories." Her outward calm is a counterweight to the turmoil inside her. Twenty years as one of New Dawn's few Black women officials, suspected from the start of being halfway to dirty computer no matter how unimpeachable her conduct, has forged her like steel, with just the right amount of carbon to bend but not shatter.

She presses a button on her desk and the door slides back into the wood-paneled wall. Jordan stands in the opening, his hand still poised midknock. The hallway light limns him in a halo that makes her squint.

"In the dark again, Director Seshet?"

She sucks her teeth. "Come in, if you're going to. I don't like so much light at night."

"Yes, yes," he says, at the same time as she does. "It ruins my vision."

She smiles, softening as always with her favorite protégé. The door slides shut and she regards him in the hazy pixelated vision of half-dilated pupils. Dee, stubbornly independent as always, turns the ambients to their lowest setting. Jordan's changed for the evening into his street clothes: khaki chinos, blue button-down, loafers. White-boy chic for New Dawn's golden age. A model citizen, so long as no one asks him his number and knows what those final digits mean: child of seditionists and traitors, ward of the state, a charity case, eternally suspect.

Seshet has no such recourse to camouflage, fragile as it is. These days, she will leave the grounds in the full golden head-dress and robes of office. She has determined to embrace her distance instead of constantly hoping for an acceptance that will never be theirs. But Jordan is young.

"What are you still doing here, Jordan? Go home. Sleep. Forget about this place for a while."

"Is that a joke?" When Jordan scowls, he looks even younger than his years, enough to make her want to hug him or slap him. Do parents feel this way? Do they ever want to shake that insufferable innocence from their children? Had his? Had hers? But now the thought veers into dangerous waters and she perches on the edge of her desk to hide the wave of weakness in her legs.

"Memory Librarian humor," says Seshet, deadpan. After a moment, Jordan cracks a smile.

"You should too," he says. "Get some sleep, I mean."

"I'm fine, Jordan. I'm your superior, remember? You don't have to worry about us."

He takes a step farther into the room and then pauses, as

though the force of her solitary preoccupation prevents him from getting closer.

He tries to reach her with words instead. "Something's wrong."

For a moment, as she watches his sad face in the low light, a fist closes over her heart. *This is it, they've gotten to him, he's noticed the false memories and he's snitched, you knew this would happen, you knew—*

Then sense returns and she takes a careful, steadying breath. Did Jordan notice anything? Oh, he's staring at her, that worried frown even deeper now, a ravine between his eyebrows. She wants to smooth it away. She wants to tell him to leave her alone and never return.

"What's . . . wrong?" she manages, at last. *You're slipping, Seshet. Gotten too comfortable up here.*

He straightens his shoulders. "You're working yourself ragged, Director! Anyone can see it."

Her voice is thin. "Oh, can they?"

He shakes his head. "You hide it well, but I've noticed, and so have the other clerks. We see you too often not to know the signs."

"I appreciate the warning, Jordan. I should be grateful you're all watching me so closely. Perhaps I should go in for Counseling soon."

"Counseling? The Director Librarian? Director, of course I'm not—"

"If my *obvious* mental state is impeding my work here, then clearly my duty is to—"

"I'm not talking about your duty, Seshet!"

Her name, bare of its title, cracks in the air like a slap. After an astonished blink, she raises her eyebrows. His muddy green eyes meet hers for a second, but he breaks like a twig beneath the full force of that practiced gaze.

"I'm . . . my apologies, Director."

She sighs, looks away herself. She hates these games, their necessity. Especially with Jordan. She's protected him ever since his initiation five years ago. One Librarian misfit ought to watch out for another, she thought.

"Tell me what's bothering you, Jordan."

"I just wish you'd get out more. See the city."

"I'm seeing the city right now."

"*In* the city, not above it."

"I'm the Director Librarian." She gives her title every ounce of demanded weight.

To her surprise, he meets her eyes again. He's brave, and she loves him for it, fiercely as a mother lion.

"There's a woman I know. Friend of a friend. I think you'll really like her, Director. I think . . . maybe you could finally find a companion. A friend."

Dangerous ground, again. She has hinted things to Jordan over the years, but never said anything that could be held against her if his memories were monitored—and all their memories are monitored.

"I have friends," she says.

"Who?"

She swallows. "You. Dee. Arch-Librarian Terry."

Jordan checks them off on his fingers. "Your clerk, your Memory Keeper AI, and your immediate superior? That's not a partner. Or a lover."

Careful, Jordan. Steel in her voice. "What would you know about that?"

Jordan holds his ground. "More than you think."

The moment hangs there, two swords locked in battle. She shakes her head. Her heart is pounding too quickly.

"Jordan," she says softly, "I'm going to have to suppress this."

"I know. I don't care. I needed to tell you. I'm worried about you, Director. I wish you could feel again what it's like out there, in the world."

"Who feels it more than me? I have their memories."

"But Seshet," he says. This time her solitary name touches her like a caress. "What about your own?"

LITTLE DELTA'S DOWNTOWN SPANS FIVE BLOCKS OF SHOPS, RES-taurants, bars, and clubs, each one duly approved by New Dawn's Chamber of Standards. It has the reputation of being small but well curated, and on the weekends people from several towns over fill the adjacent parking lots to reward themselves for their hard workweek in Standards-approved fashion. There are always lines outside the commercial memory recollectors on weekend nights, crowds eager to exchange a few memories for points to top off their cards and buy another round.

Seshet moves steadily through the crowd, hoping for at least medium anonymity. No one would expect the Director Librarian to be out among the citizens of her city on a Friday night, let alone looking for the newest bar on Hope Street. Jordan selected her clothes himself: "Fashionable, but not trendy. Not calling attention to yourself, but not hiding either."

Seshet had sighed. "A Black woman in the business district in better clothes than theirs? I couldn't hide if I wanted to." The moment held. These weren't things normally stated aloud.

Her clerk, who looked like the chosen of New Dawn but would never fit easily in their tight folds, gave her a faint, bit-ter smile. "No," he said. "That's why you have to hide under a spotlight."

Perhaps that explained the navy-blue beret he'd put at a rak-ish angle over her close-cut hair. It was the finishing touch of an ensemble designed to make people pay more attention to her clothes than her face.

A group of loutish young men standing outside a crowded beer garden pay too much attention, giving her stares hard enough to break bones. She hurries past them, shoulders back, face slightly averted, as they laugh and elbow one another. Her heart starts to race, triggered by somatic memory, ancestor-rooted and atavistic, beyond erasure, even for the cleaners at the Temple. "Hey!" one of them calls. She ignores him. The map on her chronoband says the bar is just at the end of the block.

More laughter, pointed as barbed wire. "Hey, you! Hey, Librarian Seshet!"

She freezes for a fraction of a second, jerks her head sharply toward them: a blur of pastel-shirted white boys, folded over, eyes squinting as though in pain, lips puckered. "Seshet, Director Librarian!" the joker calls, emboldened by his fellows. "Give me a good memory tonight, won't you?"

Does she recognize him? Would she know his memories from the thousands that crowd her mind? But shock and fear prevent her access to them as cleanly as a lungful of Nevermind. She does not know anyone. She does not recognize anything. Only luck breaks the spell: a woman from the next table over—Taiwanese American, architect, midthirties, went through Counseling last year after a tough breakup, hardly remembers her ex any longer, so Seshet does for her—swings toward the men and bangs her pint on the table hard enough for the maple-tinted foam to spill over the sides. "Leave her alone, you assholes!"

At first Seshet wonders if the architect is defending her out of gratitude. Then she remembers that they have never actually met. One of the Standards Authorities on the block belatedly approaches the men and they back away, laughing with a kind of sheepish bravado that she's only ever witnessed in young white men. A beat too late, she understands: They don't know who she is at all. They just saw *what* she is, and for them that was more than enough. Seshet nods with chilly dignity to the architect (she ignores the Standards Authority, laughing with the boys even as he issues a warning) and resumes a steady, even stride. She swings her arms so her hands won't betray that ghostly rattle in her heart. She *is* the Director Librarian, after all, though they would never believe it. She will keep her head high until the day they take it off her shoulders.

She is carrying herself just like that, sharp as a hawk, graceful as a jaguar, dignified as a goddess, when she strides into Hope Street's trendiest new establishment and sees her.

Her: a lone woman, legs crossed, quietly sipping a drink chlorophyll-green at the end of a long chrome bar, heart-stoppingly beautiful. Seshet has never seen her before, not even in her city's memories. She knows anyway. *Her.* The one who wields the executioner's ax. The one who will make Seshet bow before she falls.

HER NAME IS ALETHIA 56934. HER NUMBER INDICATES A known deviance, but also that she has been cleared for full re-introduction to society. She came to Little Delta four years ago. "I needed a new start," she says, grimacing in that way that hints at a story but warns Seshet off from asking about it. "I got lucky when Pinkerton Cosmetics had a chemist position open up."

"And your number . . ." Seshet lets the sentence dangle. Alethia's open expression turns professionally neutral with a speed that hits Seshet in the gut. But she had to ask. Someone from New Dawn might see them together.

"I'm trans," Alethia says, in a clipped, matter-of-fact way. "Cleared years ago. Is that a problem?"

Seshet wants to crawl under the bar and hide. "No! Of course not! It's just, I'm the Director—" But of course Jordan would have told her that. Seshet's words stick like seed pods in her mouth.

Alethia's laughter is bitter, intoxicating as gin. "We all make our compromises." She leans forward. "Tell me something more interesting. Tell me why you came here."

Seshet frowns. Her heart is pounding so fast it's a wonder

she doesn't pass out. Her hand reaches for her drink—impossibly, luridly blue, with a name like "indigo flame"—and she drains half of it in a gulp. It tastes like orangey seaweed. "To Little Delta?" she asks.

Alethia nods encouragingly. Seshet clears her throat and takes a deep, steadying breath. No one has ever affected her like this before, not even her first lover twenty years ago, when they were both novice Librarians, clean and freshly purged of their pasts, ready to make their newest memories with one another.

"I was assigned here," she finally says. "Eighteen years ago." Half a lifetime ago. Long enough to watch the steady grid, the illuminated heart of the reformed town, expand beneath the obelisk's warmly glowing spire.

"Do you like it here?"

She stares at the woman: thick eyebrows, light brown skin, cheekbones to chisel stone, lower lip fuller than the top. "Like . . . it?"

Those eyebrows draw together, humorously confused. "As a place to live?"

"Oh." There is a mole on Alethia's left earlobe, easy to see because she wears no earrings. Seshet wants to kiss it. She wants to take it between her teeth and tug. "It's where all my memories are. I couldn't leave even if I had the choice."

She realizes, a hard drop of a second later, that she's implied a state secret that would mean instant disciplinary action if discovered. Luckily, Alethia looks more confused than ever and Seshet finds her tongue again. She asks Alethia what she does at her job, and discovers she spends all day in a lab coat mixing skin creams. Seshet tries to come up with ways to flirtatiously compliment Alethia's perfect skin—maybe *But I bet you don't need any of it?* She winces. *Director Librarian and still such a cornball, Seshet.* She is awkward as a teenager, mute as a memory hoarder. Her tongue feels wet and heavy in her mouth. Why is a woman like this even talking to her? Smiling, as if she sees something inside her that Seshet has long since lost track of?

Seshet finishes her drink.

"Would you like another?" Alethia asks.

Her expression is solicitous but neutral, and yet Seshet catches the faintest whiff of a side eye. For the first time that evening, she feels herself loosen up.

She lifts the heavy square cocktail glass, a tide pool of melted ice clinging to the bottom among fat drifts of blue-green pulp. She meets Alethia's caramel-brown eyes, and, as an answering spark from a fire so deeply banked she had not known it still smoldered, Seshet laughs.

"I would like," she says, "to take you to a place with better drinks."

ALETHIA KNOWS JUST THE ONE: A DIVE BAR CALLED COUSIN Skee's on the far east side, just one block from the old Woolworth Building that marks the frontier of Old Town with its dirty artist squats and dirtier crack houses. Cleared and abandoned now, according to Standards, but Seshet's seen too many memories of clandestine, rebellious activities over that darkened border to believe them. She wonders what Alethia knows about that warren of gap-toothed buildings dressed in garish primary colors, graffiti streaming like skirts at the edge of broken sidewalks. The poised, immaculate woman who greeted her at that hopeless Hope Street cocktail bar should be as out of place here as Seshet is, but the man behind the bar calls out "Lethe!" as soon as they open the door and greets her with a fist bump.

"Where you been, girl?" he asks, reaching without hesitation for the cocktail shaker by the sink. He takes an unmarked bottle with a cheap plastic spout, mixes that clear liquid with the contents of three other unmarked bottles, throws in some ice and starts shaking, all in the time it takes for Alethia to give him a sweet smile that stings Seshet down to the tenderest points of the soles of her feet.

"Working, Skee," says Alethia, sounding at once nothing like the woman at the trendy bar and even more impossibly herself. "You know the drill."

"Looks like you've got a good thing going," he says, taking in her designer shoes and purse at a glance. Alethia just shrugs. Skee's hard expression softens. He pours the drink with a flourish and pushes it across the bar.

"One mar-Skee-rita, on the house."

Alethia grimaces. "You still trying to call it that?"

"What you mean, *trying*? Been its name since back when you started—"

"And ain't no one but you called it that in all that time," says Alethia, leaning onto the bar with a strange smile, hard as glass. Skee stops short. At last, he glances at Seshet. He seems to sum her up and dismiss her in one swallow: *You may be Black, but you aren't one of us.* He doesn't know who she is. But he can smell what.

"And for your friend?"

Seshet perches on the bar stool, listing slightly to the side. "A mar-Skee-rita, please," she says, diction crisp as fresh linen.

Alethia lets out a surprised yelp of laughter. Seshet shivers. Skee grins. "That'll be ten points."

"Hard currency?" she asks, because she is who she is, and here on that hard edge between new order and old chaos, she wants to know.

Skee gives her a long look. So does Alethia, hooded and opaque, as though there is another woman entirely sharing space behind those wide brown eyes. Seshet itches to know what memories underlie that cold inspection, that easy laughter, that gentle smile, but for now—until she gets back to the obelisk and their memory data banks—she has no way to know.

Skee turns from them with a shrug and starts making

another drink. "Don't put recollection boxes all the way out here. Well, the check-cashing joint on the corner has one, works sometimes."

That was true enough. Memory recollection boxes were sparser the farther out from the center you went. But on the border of Old Town, the ones they did have went out of service with surprising frequency. Someone was always damaging the headset or the router, and somehow the vandals' faces or their voices or their memories were never captured, not by drones or Standards Authorities or even automated street surveillance. She'd wondered about that over the years. But she knew who was most likely to live out here at the edge, and she never pushed for a deeper investigation. No one higher up in New Dawn had ever asked.

Seshet reaches into her wallet and pushes two five-point coins across the table.

Skee slides across the margarita, still frothy from the shaker.

Their gazes lock. She's good at this game of mutual evaluation, but she can't fully commit; she's too aware of Alethia's watchful curiosity beside her.

At last, Skee shrugs and cracks his neck. "You happen to work around that obelisk, Miz . . ."

Seshet allows herself a small smile. "You wouldn't want to know."

AFTER MIDNIGHT, THE BAR IS OVERWHELMED WITH A NEW crowd, diverse in a way she's not used to seeing in downtown Little Delta (and certainly not in the corridors of the obelisk): the oldest must be in his seventies and the youngest still a teenager; all shades of brown, Black, and beige; men in dresses and women in sharp-cut suits and others who defy any gender categorization at all. She pretends not to notice. With New Dawn, any gender nonconformity is enough to get you a deviant code appended to your number—dirty computer, recommended for urgent cleaning—and she doesn't want to flag anyone tonight. Seshet recognizes some of them. They're still members of her flock, however wayward. Others are unrepentant memory hoarders, the kind who never so much as walk through downtown in case a drone recollector might land, light as a horsefly, on their temple and graze a few loose memories off the top while they're waiting for the light to change. She cares even for them, though they don't know it. The obelisk's eye, like any panopticon, gives only an illusion of omniscience—Seshet has made an art of selective gazing.

And now she is down in the dirty thick of it, watching and being watched in her turn, a sensation so unusual she keeps drinking just to dull the edge. Three mar-Skee-ritas in, Seshet finds she does not mind at all being one more in a crowd of hoarders and deviants. She hasn't gone in for memory collection herself in months—if anyone asked, she would have claimed work pressure, but no one has. The truth is that Seshet enjoys the sensation of memory hoarding, that sweet, leftover-Halloween-candy feeling of keeping something back for herself, however temporary. The new crowd is high on some kind of drug, singing songs she's never heard of in harmony, finishing one another's sentences. One of them, a light-skinned boy who reminds her of someone she can't place, wearing a baseball cap with a stencil of an old man with a star blowing out of his forehead, dances Seshet by the shoulders and stares into her eyes as though he can see straight into her memory-scoured soul. He laughs and says something that might be "full" or "bull"—the music the new crowd has brought with them is so loud—and then spins away from her. He freezes when he spots Alethia, turning at that moment from the pool table where she's just sunk another shot. Alethia raises her eyebrows. He opens his mouth and then closes it. Alethia gives him a brief shrug that seems to mean *Sorry I'm not who you thought I was* and goes back over to Seshet.

"How about," Alethia shouts into her ear, as intimate and low-voiced as a whisper, "we go back to my place?"

And now Seshet doesn't care about anything at all—not memory hoarders or memory flooders or who this motley crowd could be and the fact that they almost certainly washed over the border from some forbidden party in Old Town. For now she isn't Seshet, Director Librarian, distant queen of Little Delta. She is a woman, softened with drink, unburdened by memory, warm skin touching warm skin, and she wants more.

Alethia's place: one-bedroom apartment a fifteen-minute walk away in an anonymous residential building for young professionals without the money—or the number—for something better. There is a memory recollector in the lobby with signs of modest use (Seshet doesn't mean to notice this, but she does). The apartment is beige: carpet, couch, wallpaper. The photographs on the walls are luridly colored but minimalist in design: flowers, balloons, fishing boats in Bangkok. The kind of apartment that has no gaze, no stamp of ownership, only the vague notion of what others might imagine to be tasteful. It fits the modest cosmetic chemist she met on Hope Street, but it's nothing like the savvy, laugh-like-a-machete Alethia she met at Cousin Skee's. In the bedroom, Seshet finally finds her: a lipstick-red bedspread hitting her eye like Alethia's secret smile, just that tantalizing hint of *someone else*—and Seshet lets that analytical part of her unspool again, to rest in exhausted tangles. She might be the Director Librarian, but without this woman's memories stored in her head, they are just two humans learning together in the most old-fashioned of ways. It rubs against her nerves like salt water on a dirty wound, but there is peace in this ignorance too, a thrill of discovery, a joy.

"There's something about you," Alethia says, holding Seshet's temples between her palms and kissing her with slow, devastating deliberation. "I know I've never met you before, and it's like you've already moved in, you're already making room."

They fall on top of that crimson slash in the beige. They burrow into one another, discover what's beneath.

Jordan and Billie are in the clerks' office when Seshet comes in the next day, immaculately attired and five minutes late. All New Dawn-affiliated offices work half days on Saturdays, but most aren't as strict about it as the Repository. In any case, Seshet can't remember the last time she's enjoyed a day off. Jordan slouches and lowers the visor on his headset, as though deep in this morning's catch. Billie grins and raises her eyebrows until they meet her hairline. Seshet pretends not to notice. She loves Jordan, but he's an inveterate gossip and Billie is his best friend among the clerks. Seshet should have known he'd tell. She asks if they have her morning report. Jordan, still from behind his visor, says he's flagged some suspicious elements and he'll have that in her workspace in another twenty minutes. Seshet acknowledges him with a nod that he probably can't see and heads sedately into the hallway, as though she has no desire to move faster than a parade float. The door to her office slides open to the sound of her voice stating the passkey and then she is inside, at last, alone.

Her breath shivers inside her lungs like dry leaves in a fall wind. She presses the heels of her palms to aching eyes. She's had three hours of sleep. She'd regret even those wasted moments if not for the memory she savors now, blasphemous as a child, just for herself: Alethia's face painted obelisk gold in the morning light, lipstick and mascara smudged across the pillowcase, eyes half-open even in sleep, hands reaching across the sheets, palms up. In that pin-drop moment, Seshet understood that she had come to the crossroads and left them behind. Her life has found a bifurcation as profound as any initiation the elders of New Dawn could devise: Seshet before Alethia, Seshet now.

And even so, her worries are just where she left them last night.

"Seshet," says Dee. The big monitor to the right of the desk lights up. A face appears there slowly, as though approaching from a dark tunnel. "Seshet? Are we in trouble, Seshet?"

Dee scrunches its large, uncanny eyes, blue as the Caribbean Sea. Its features are Seshet's reflected in a fun-house mirror, distorted by time, by memory, by choice. The girl Seshet had been hated her dun-brown irises, longed for them to be the blue of the dolls in the store and the children in her headset. No one on the programs had her dark skin or kinky hair. That girl had longed for braids with beads at the bottom that clicked when she walked. She'd longed for eyes so blue they'd glow like the sky, even at night.

They purged these memories during Seshet's initiation, of course. But after a decade, once she ascended to rank, the elders gave them back to her: the lost memories of a lost woman. Until then, Seshet hadn't so much as remembered her old name. At Vice Director rank, she was authorized for a Memory Keeper AI, potentiated on whatever seed memories she chose. She gave it that lost woman's childhood, someone to keep those memories that no longer felt like her own.

"Why would we be in trouble, Dee?" Seshet asks calmly. Dee doesn't do well when Seshet is visibly upset.

"There's even more of those funny half-dreams this morning. I like them, but I don't think Terry does."

Terry, Arch-Librarian for the entire Midwest region, and her immediate superior. A hand clamps around her gut and squeezes. She's going to be sick. The moment passes. With a hiccupping breath, she goes to her workstation in an alcove by the monitor and settles into the leather chair. Jordan and the clerks call it her throne. Not to her face, of course.

"What makes you think that?" she asks. Memory Keeper technology is the most advanced New Dawn has to offer. And it might as easily be called Memory Librarian Keeper. She knows this, has always known this. And yet, she has trusted Dee.

"Terry asked me for a report on the half-dreams. And on you."

The headset with its golden geometry slides over her temples and clamps into the base of her neck. The net tightens over her skull, pressing until it passes the thick barrier of her hair and coolly touches her scalp. A familiar tickle of electrical engagement and her consciousness slides from the room, into deep memory space. The visor comes down last, and now Dee is right beside her, both child and disembodied consciousness, watching the floodplain of this morning's memory harvest.

"What did you tell him?" Her lips, which she can feel only with effort, don't move. Fully connected, there's no need for her to speak aloud.

"I told him that the half-dreams come from all over the city, and many, many dreamers. I told him some were silly and some were beautiful. I told him I hope more people learn to play because it's more fun for me."

In the memory space, Seshet turns sharply to Dee, who holds its knobby knees to its chest. She's let her Memory Keeper AI have complete freedom for years. She's never pruned its personality or deviations. But she doubts Terry would have the same patience with Dee's eccentricities.

"And Terry asked me how you were," Dee continues. "I didn't want to tell him but I had to, you know, he glows even brighter than you do. So I told him in a poem! That was all right, wasn't it, Seshet?"

In her chair out in the world, Seshet's fingers trace the air. In memory space, she catches Jordan's report of anomalous activity and pushes it to the edge of the plain. She already knows what it says, and she knows that Terry does too. After all these years as Director Librarian for one of New Dawn's flagship cities, she understands very well how their world works. She aimed for unprecedented power when she was young and hungry, the token in their elite program. She's held on to it by being smarter than any of them. But she's no longer young, and now her hunger is for what she glimpsed in Alethia's eyes last night, not the next rung on New Dawn's golden ladder.

But that doesn't mean she wants to fall to the bottom either.

"What was your poem, Dee?"

Never known love like this before
Except for last time
Someone I took for mine
Told me history couldn't rhyme
But don't get caught in the revolving door.

Dee pauses. Before them, one of last night's memories rises like a wave, crests, breaks.

"Was that okay, Seshet?" Dee asks just as the tide pulls them under.

"That was okay, Dee."

She hopes.

THERE ARE DOZENS OF VARIATIONS OF THIS ONE MEMORY, LIKE a symphony interpreted by different orchestras, the same recognizable piece layered with local color. It even begins with a song, heavy on the back beat, something Dee would like and Seshet finds gnawingly familiar. It's dark, and then the song explodes into brilliant chorus. Golden light spills all around them and burns where it falls. Are they fireworks? No, the light is coming from the obelisk itself. But not the views of it she knows, from the downtown business district or even the highway heading out of town. It's the view from the abandoned train station, from the warehouse district, from the derelict streets of Old Town. What has been her benevolent, watchful eye becomes a throbbing phallus, a malignant growth using the city for kindling as it burns. The light is coming for them, it's coming for them, *watch out, it's coming!*—that's the chorus to the song she couldn't possibly have heard before.

She's rising now, up and up, until she reaches the pyramidion of a shadowy obelisk, a dark spire to match the light. From this height, she can see the brightly lit streets of new Little Delta. People hurry to work or linger on sidewalks, gossip in cafes, play with their children. The Repository's most iconic structure belches like a furnace. Napalm, white-gold, rains down, hissing where it hits. But the citizens of Little Delta merely glance at it and smile. Around them, the city burns.

"Watch out!"

The memory voice is deep and hoarse with smoke. She senses that it's young and angry, but identity and emotion markers in a loose memory are notoriously unreliable. Let alone in one so clearly fabricated.

The obelisk has fully metamorphosed into its metaphoric counterpart now, a giant golden circumcised penis spitting white-gold ejaculate into the air like a pornographic Mount Vesuvius.

"Seshet! O Seshet!" that young man's voice says.

She has no body in the memory space, but she jerks inside her own mind. The force of it ought to stop the memory playback. But it has the inevitability of an avalanche now, bearing down on her like white fire through the streets of the city she has watched over for the past decade.

The chorus calls and responds, a propulsive chant in her ear: "Director Seshet! What have you done for us lately?"

"Seshet, the fire is coming!"

"Watch yourself!"

● ▬ ●

"My dearest Seshet, how delightful as always to see you."

Terry is sitting on a couch she recognizes from his office at New Dawn headquarters, a portable headset draped casually over one of the arms along with a pair of gaming gloves. His blue socks match his T-shirt, which looks new though it's the vintage merchandise of some decades-old pornographic anime (he likes it ironically).

He just popped onto her display screens in the middle of her lunch hour, all privacy codes summarily overridden. She was already sitting at her desk, preparing her reports. She does not startle or flinch when his voice comes over the speakers. She merely sets down her hand tablet and smiles.

This crisis might have caught her by surprise, but she is still Director Librarian of Little Delta, and the game of politics is in her bones.

Besides, she's always liked Terry.

"Wish I could say the same, Terry. Do you ever wear your robes?"

He laughs, which makes him look his age—at least sixty, though he tries to pass for an eternal horn-rimmed hipster of thirty.

"Never while I'm on the job, Seshet. Those are just for impressing the hoi polloi."

She opens her mouth and he holds up a hand. "Are you going to tell me the definite article is redundant? Because I already know that. I was using it—"

"Ironically? I was going to suggest you go among your polloi one evening just as you are now. It is an enlivening experience."

He claps his hands like a tennis fan appreciating a well-scored point. "I'm sure it is! It's so easy to get caught up in all of their memories, isn't it? Easy to forget that we don't have so many of our own."

She inclines her head. "As I was reminded last night."

He doesn't bother feigning surprise or asking what she was doing. He knows perfectly well.

It's only an ambush if you don't anticipate it.

"Did you enjoy yourself, Seshet?"

It was the most incredible night of my life, and you'll never take it from me.

"It was quite diverting, Terry." Her tone is smooth as a pearl, just a little bored. He cannot know what truly happened last night, just the outward appearance of it. Two women meet at one bar, get drunk together at another. They dance, they sing with the late crowd, they go back to one of their homes, they make love. Memory Librarians take many vows, but none of them are of chastity. Clean citizens of the New Dawn aren't supposed to enjoy same-gender love, but she's hardly the first official to bend those rules; she's not even the only one in Little Delta. He cannot know the *feel* of what has happened to her, that explosion ongoing beneath her breast, the way her fingers itch to call Alethia just to hear her voice again. Just to know it was real. He cannot know it unless he raids her memories—and she will do everything in her power to make sure he doesn't. It is dangerous to be the beloved of a Memory Librarian.

Terry lets the moment hang for a few uncomfortable seconds. Seshet waits for him. Gently, she raises one eyebrow.

He chuckles softly and shakes his head. "Ah, Seshet. Our conversations are always so refreshing. There's no one quite like you. Well. What's this I've been hearing about false memories gumming up the collection systems over there? Do you know who's responsible?"

"Not yet."

He narrows his eyes and tilts his head. She likes Terry better when he's not feigning affability, though she enjoys sparring with him when he is. She knows he's dangerous as a viper—he'd never have reached that position otherwise, let alone survived so many changes in leadership. But—until now, at least—he's put that venom to use in support of her. If that is changing, she hopes she can survive it.

"I'd suggest," he says, drawling, though the most southern thing about him is the Splenda in his iced tea, "that you find out quickly."

"I'm exploring our leads. I should have something more concrete for you soon."

He blinks at her, lips smiling. "Is it the drugs again, Seshet? Those street mixes of Nevermind? It's too bad you let that old witch doctor get away five years ago."

It is hard to keep the jolt of fear out of her expression, though she tries. From Terry's flash of gloating interest, she sees she failed. Doc Young and his legendary remixer MC Haze nearly destroyed her five years ago. Little Delta was becoming famous in the underground circuits as a mecca for wild parties and mind-blasting remixes of street-grade Nevermind. Mixes for sharing memories, mixes for creating dreams, mixes for seeing sound or hearing color. She hadn't caught Doc Young or his remixer, but she'd arrested and memory-suppressed a few hundred of their acolytes. Even sent a sacrificial dozen dirty computers to the Temple for full cleaning. Doc Young and MC Haze vanished, run out of town. Could they have returned? She'd prayed they wouldn't dare. But now she isn't sure.

"I . . . I don't know. The memories are odd. My Memory Keeper—"

"Oh, young Dee? She's sweet, isn't she?"

A wave of dizziness washes over her. Her forehead feels damp. She hopes he doesn't notice. "Dee is an artificial intelligence. Despite its presentation, it doesn't have a gender."

"Oh, of course. My apologies, Dee."

She refuses to wipe her forehead. At least Dee doesn't respond. He doesn't have to say it out loud: her near-failure five years ago, her deviant Memory Keeper, her sexuality, her race, her *self*—these are all ropes by which they might hang her, if they choose. During the last crisis with Doc Young and MC Haze, she had been worried that Terry might demote her, or even ship her to some off-site rural Repository. Now she knows those previously unthinkable fates would be gifts. If she fails to resolve this situation, Terry won't hesitate to have her Torched.

He's been her ally for fifteen years, but she knows a part of him would enjoy it—it would appeal to his sense of dramatic irony.

She leans back in her chair, away from the display. "As I was saying, my Memory Keeper calls them half-dreams. They're not memories but they're not those strong dreams that sometimes get past the filters either. Five years ago . . . we weren't picking up anything like this back then."

He waves his fingers, as though pushing aside her objection. "So it's something new. That remixer has had plenty of time."

She shakes her head slowly. "It could be MC Haze again, but all her remixes were based on Nevermind. These memories don't . . ."

"They don't what?"

She shrugs, uselessly. "They don't *feel* like Nevermind."

Not sedated, not coerced, not *stolen*.

Terry's basilisk stare should be comical given the blue socks and high-waters, the anime vixen with her breasts barely contained by two parallel strips of shining purple vinyl, but Seshet is very far from laughter.

"Then use your *feeling* and find out who is doing this and *stop them*. This has reached some members of the elder council."

She loses control of her expression for a second time. Terry's eyes crinkle in what seems to be genuine sympathy.

"Do we understand one another, Seshet?"

She forces a neutral smile, out of pride if nothing else. "Perfectly, Terry."

He nods and clicks out of her display.

Seshet does not move. A drop of sweat slides down her forehead, around her chin, and splatters on her desk.

IMAGINE A FLOOD, IMAGINE A WAVE, IMAGINE AN AVALANCHE, imagine a storm. Imagine any disaster you please, but note that it always begins as one before it becomes many. What in singular expression seems simple, laughable, beneath your notice, becomes, in the plural, the last thing you notice before you die. This is the bleak magic of exponential growth. It is the difference between two grasshoppers on your screen door and the eighth plague of Egypt. And if you haven't been paying attention to an uninhabitable swath of the Arabian desert when unseasonable cyclones drape the sands in blankets of water, creating the conditions for an unprecedented breeding season for desert grasshoppers, it might surprise you when clouds of vomit-yellow locusts descend to decimate your entire country's corn crop ten months later.

The trouble, as Seshet sees it, is with Cousin Skee. It's with Alethia. With that boy who danced her by the shoulders and told her she was full (or wool? Or beautiful?). She hasn't paid enough attention to Old Town since Doc Young fled the city. She hasn't monitored the border zones, like Skee's east side.

And why did she ignore it, wise Seshet, who ought to know better than anyone the danger of the margins? Seshet, queen, who wants to be a mother to her kingdom. Why not? Doesn't she watch over her people? But here's the rub: She has watched over some more than others. She has maintained the heart of the city in a mold as pure as any New Dawn could hope for. But she averted her gaze from the edges, from the ones who would never fit anyway. The ones who looked like her—and didn't look like them.

Director Seshet! What have you done for us lately?

Well, don't they fucking know? Is it possible that they haven't even realized? What has she done, wise Seshet, compassionate Seshet, even while precarious in power?

She has not looked.

And oh, poor Seshet, this is on her shoulders now. If Terry and the others haven't realized it, they will soon. Whatever the specifics of these half-dreams—a new Nevermind remix or hacking or something else—they are down from the desert, legion, o'errun.

IT IS A LITTLE ENOUGH DISASTER, AFTER THE GREAT DISASTERS of the morning, but Seshet can feel hysteria bubbling up like old vinegar behind her throat.

"Dee," she says, voice cracking at the end like a child's. "Dee, are you *sure* there's nothing more?"

"I'm so sorry, Seshet," Dee says. It sounds distressed, but it's removed its face from her display. "This subject isn't flagged for extra surveillance. These are the only memories in the cache."

"Alethia has a sleep headset."

"We have no record of its use last night."

A private smile pulls at her lips. Of course they don't. The smile collapses. "You checked the trash again?"

"It was all cleared at four thirty this morning, per standard operations."

"And her Counseling sessions?"

"After three years without incident we only retain the intake session and the final report. You yourself made sure we were the first to implement Chancellor Chelsea's privacy reforms. Would you like me to help you remember?"

Dee is already pulling up the relevant memories from six years ago. One of her displays flashes to visual-auditory recall: Seshet and Terry stiff-necked in full regalia, laughing at some joke of his before they stepped onto the podium to announce the reforms.

Even without the sensory integration of her headset, she is plunged back into that day, into the skin of her younger self, proud to be at the vanguard of New Dawn's short-lived reformist movement.

An older, harder Seshet shakes her head and stops the playback. "That isn't necessary, Dee."

Dee is silent for a few seconds. When it speaks, it sounds weary, even disappointed. "Would you like me to flag her now, Seshet?"

Seshet frowns. She has allowed Dee to develop a personality and a primitive consciousness—aspects that make it dangerous, according to Terry and his superiors—but it's still fundamentally a Memory Keeper AI bound by New Dawn's protocols. It has the processing capacity of a precocious child, not an adult capable of moral judgments. So why would her Memory Keeper be disappointed in her?

She defends herself anyway. "I need more information, Dee! I need to know who she really is, before . . ." *Before I lose myself in her.*

Before I lose control.

Displaying that annoying tick of independence and creativity that Seshet has allowed to develop in her Memory Keeper but is bitterly regretting now, Dee spreads five different memories across Seshet's displays and plays them all at once without sound: teenage Alethia hugging her father goodbye at the border wall while drones circle; Alethia in her lab, measuring chemicals, solitude isolating her like the walls of a test tube; Alethia moving into her apartment with just two suitcases and a hot-water kettle; Alethia on a bench in Standards Park, feeding the ducks in the artificial lake; Alethia on the viewing deck of the obelisk, just below Seshet's office, gazing over the cloud-covered city. How long ago was that? Three years. Seshet's heart lurches. They'd come so close to meeting. But is this the real Alethia? Where's "Lethe" of Cousin Skee's? Where's that cloaked, sharp humor? The cherry bedspread like a dagger thrust to the beige of that prefurnished apartment? Aside from her father, deported fifteen years ago after his citizenship was revoked for "unclean activities," why is she always alone?

"Dee, is this really everything?"

"You told me—"

"I told you what?"

Dee sighs. "This is what we have."

"And your analysis of the subject?"

She wishes Dee would show its face. It has never wanted to hide from her before.

"They smell funny."

"Dee, be serious."

But Dee is more stubborn than usual today. It begins to speak in singsong:

I didn't know what I really meant
When I asked you where the false time went
I only knew I had to let go
Before the fall's first blow.

"Enough!"

Seshet's shout brings down a charged silence.

Her eyes prick. She is conscious of an urge to apologize. Absurd.

"Flag her, Dee," she says, making her voice even harder to mask that flush of shame. "Bring me every last memory you can drag from the public recollectors or her headset tonight."

For the first time in their life together, Dee's voice sounds genuinely robotic. "Confirmed, Seshet. Alethia 56934 has been flagged for suspected deviance, high priority."

THE COUNSELING OFFICES SIT OPPOSITE FROM THE OBELISK, ON the other side of the City Hall gardens that are open to the public only on weekends and holidays. Seshet goes through the private entrance beside the balding topiary, nodding once to the guards who spring to attention when they see her. This late in the day, the private corridors are empty, though there will still be a handful of people in the public library and waiting room, hoping for a last-minute appointment with a Counselor. She hates coming here. Even as a novice, Seshet avoided the Social Librarians. The idea of having to constantly interact with the people whose memories she monitored repulsed her, like a surgeon who could handle cutting open intestines only if she forgot the human being who would use them later. Counseling receives a constant influx of people looking for help—or looking to raise their Standards scores and petition to change their numbers. She receives reports on their activities, of course. She even personally involves herself in the cases that interest her—diagnosing emotional liabilities, selecting the memories for repression or amplification, reveling in the messy, subtle work of realigning a personality. That the memories harvested during Counseling sessions are of a much higher quality, particularly useful for New Dawn's surveillance efforts, is merely a beneficial side effect of the Librarians' primary work.

Seshet doesn't really believe this any more than the Social division's Vice Director does, but they tell that to the fresh initiates in training and massage their memories so they can believe it as long as possible. She has long since made the necessary moral justifications.

In the end, a simple happiness is better than a complex disillusion.

She finds the Vice Director alone in his office, feeds from three Counseling sessions running silently on wall displays. His headset flashes reflected light from the sunset as he turns to greet her. Keith doesn't betray surprise to find her here in person, but his welcoming smile is perfunctory, and he only belatedly offers her the seat in front of his desk. Seshet stares at him for a care-fully blank moment and then seats herself, conscious of every regal gesture, on the couch facing the picture window. Keith's office is nearly as large as hers. He is Vice Director of a powerful division, golden-haired, blue-eyed, the third generation of New Dawn loyalists, and the favored heir of a certain bitter faction with long grudges who would like nothing more than to erase even the memory of Seshet's heterodox rise to power in Little Delta. It's one thing to allow people like her to train as initiates, the line goes, but quite another to let them seem to rule!

His eyes flick to the couch in annoyance. After a beat, he forces another smile, removes his headset, and makes his way to the chair facing her.

"You honor me by coming all the way here, Director," he says. "I was just preparing my report for you."

"Your report, Vice Director?" She allows nothing more than a hint of polite curiosity in her tone, but her thoughts are a storm. Someone has already told him about the memory flood-ing. He's had—hours? Days?—to consolidate his position.

He leans forward, hand on his knee, concerned frown be-trayed by the tic at the corners of his lips. Keith has never quite mastered the art of controlling his expression. But then, he's never really needed to.

"Well, of course, Director Seshet," he says, larding on the false concern until it is indistinguishable from gloating, "I couldn't leave you to face this kind of unprecedented attack alone. We're all Librarians in the end, despite our differences. We're here to defend the Repository . . . the New Dawn way of life! Well, aren't we, Director?"

Standards save her from young sharks tasting blood in the water. As if she hasn't beaten back better men than him in her time. As if she won't do so again. She sighs. "I will be happy to review your report in the morning, Vice Director. I assume the memories of those in Counseling don't have much to offer, in any case."

The Social division Vice Director, Seshet has had cause to observe, bears a distinct resemblance to a fish on a line when caught out. "My Memory Keeper is still checking everything we have archived—"

Under her patient gaze he belatedly falls silent. She nods. "Perhaps you don't yet have enough . . . experience in your position to know this, but no one from Old Town goes near Counseling. The ones responsible for these fabricated memories would be even less likely to betray themselves so easily. Counseling is how we monitor the health of Little Delta. But to destroy an illness, Vice Director, we need different means."

He swallows. She fancies that she can see a spark of panic behind those sky-blue irises, a belated realization that Seshet has not yet fallen, and might survive to see *him* fall if he does not take care.

"And what means might those be, Director Seshet?" No sign of his preening now.

"The loose memory bank. You do remember you're in charge of it, don't you?"

He frowns and shakes his head. "Loose memories! They're notoriously unreliable. My Memory Keeper would be stuck in there for half of every month if I let it. I only ever go in there if Standards is after me to find the suspect in a crime—"

She rises from the couch in a smooth gesture, and allows some of her real annoyance to inflect her tone. "Keith, have you been paying attention? These memory flooders *are* criminals. I very much doubt the ones responsible for this will be tagged in the system. They won't be easy to find. I need any suspect memories flagged and sent to my workspace. Traffic stops, ambient drones, recollection boxes out in the periphery, the ones outside grocery stores and check-cashing stores and pawnshops. And . . ."

He isn't bothering to control his expression at all now; his lower lip juts out like a surly child's. "Yes?"

She looks past his outraged expression to the sun setting over the garden. Her heart hurts at the thought of fighting this battle again, but she does what she needs to. "Keep an eye out for Doc Young or MC Haze. They might be back."

She remembers, a Librarian's perfect recall piercing the alcoholic fog, that light-skinned boy dancing with her at Cousin Skee's, drug-blasted pupils dark as the night sky. *You're full,* he sang to her over the loud jangle of someone else's music. *You're full as a beast and we have nothing to spare.*

Hungry? I'm starving:) A

A simple message on Seshet's private channel. She should stay at the Repository. She should comb through the other Vice Directors' reports, look for more clues, ask Dee for more data.

Instead, Seshet changes into another set of Jordan-approved street clothes and hurries to meet Alethia at a tiny Italian restaurant near her place. They pretend to be friends where anyone can see, but they touch under the table, careful for Alethia's sake, since she's already been flagged as deviant. They share wine and garlic bread. ("We have to eat it together," Alethia says, waving a piece under her nose, "or only I'll stink and you won't want to kiss me." Seshet nods like a marionette and takes another long gulp of red wine.) Alethia used the recollector outside the restaurant to load a few more points onto her TriCard before they went in.

"It's my turn to treat," she said, with a lift to her eyebrow that dared Seshet to object. Seshet eyed the recollector with a hunger she hoped didn't show and shrugged.

The meal is sublime, so heavy on the garlic it becomes a joke between them, cracking up when they order dessert, whispering, *But is it a* garlic *panna cotta? Can we try the* garlic *grappa?*

They linger over their dessert wine, which tastes faintly of anise, a different root vegetable.

"They say you Librarians have perfect memories. So tell me the first thing you remember." Alethia traces Seshet's uneven hairline with one finger. Seshet feels the touch through to the soles of her feet. She closes her eyes, a prayer for strength.

"My recovery room at the Temple," she says. "White and gold. The Torch standing beside me. 'Congratulations on your rebirth, novice Librarian. Your name is Seshet.'"

Alethia drops her hand, a loss. Seshet does not move.

"They memory-wiped you?" she asks, horrified and trying to hide it.

Seshet shrugs. "It's a requirement for initiation."

"And that name? It's unusual for New Dawn. An Egyptian goddess?"

At that, Seshet smiles. "We have the right to choose our new names. I guess my past self wanted to make sure that I knew how high I wanted to climb."

Alethia laughs softly. Seshet's heart skips one subtle beat and rebounds with ferocity.

"Well, we have that in common," Alethia says. "I chose my name too. I was sixteen when they approved my petition."

Seshet had wondered. Even under New Dawn's more liberal regimes, getting permits for transitions has never been easy.

"Your parents agreed?" Seshet asks. Though her own childhood memories are safely stored with Dee, this question leaves her aching, off balance.

There is a matching glimmer in Alethia's eyes, downcast over the dregs of her wine. "I was always my papa's little girl. My mom . . ." She shakes her head, sets down the glass like it holds something precious. "She agreed when it counted. She let me live my life."

There's a story there, but Seshet doesn't pry.

She doesn't need to.

She is remembering, on a loop made relentless by her perfect memory, what Alethia said, as she left the recollector booth: "No checking them out behind my back, okay?" She laughed but her eyes were worried. "You have the advantage."

She tries not to pay attention to the longing, the vulnerability in Alethia's voice when she invites Seshet to her apartment again. She tries not to think about that simple, declarative statement that rushes through the gulf between them: *You have the advantage.* And what is Seshet to do? *Not* take it? Stop being who she is while she exposes herself before a woman completely unknown to her? How could she possibly do that? Wouldn't *not* looking be abdicating her responsibilities as Director Librarian? What if Alethia wants to hurt her? What if she's a resistance agent?

But resisting who? a voice inside her asks.

She hushes it with deep kisses in the doorway of Alethia's apartment. Fingers caressing dark puckered nipples. Backs arched, toes curled. They curve like calligraphy on the red canvas of Alethia's bed, and Seshet cannot breathe, she cannot think, her memories are a whirlwind. She has never felt desire this raw in her life. But it's not their passion that scares her; it's the after hush, the easy sleep of Alethia in her arms, the soft kiss she places, like a brand, on the inner fold of Seshet's left wrist.

The woman who could have treasured this gift, Seshet threw away twenty years ago. So who does Alethia see when she looks at her? Seshet, Director Librarian—or the ghost of the woman she killed to become her?

SESHET MAKES SURE ALETHIA'S SLEEP HEADSET IS IN PLACE BEfore she leaves. They've drunk a bottle of wine between them; she's more likely to assume she put it on herself than that Seshet put it on for her. Alethia's wary voice: *You have the advantage.* And what of it? No one in her position has the luxury of fairness.

At three in the morning she calls a private aircar and heads back to the Repository. She hasn't slept at all, but her nerves are alive, her synapses snapping, the fall air full in her lungs and the sleeping city pulsing through her veins, hers alone.

KEITH SENDS HER A TERSE MESSAGE EARLY THE NEXT MORN- ing: his Memory Keeper has found something. He sends over a handful of loose memories scavenged from the southern edge of the city two days ago, all of them from unregistered users.

Seshet, unsleeping, fresh as a vampire, has stuffed herself full to sickness on a stream of Alethia's dreams and memories. With a physical jolt, she disconnects from that raw feed and forces her attention back to the crisis that might just topple her after a decade at the top of the obelisk. If even Keith is working on Sunday, she can't do less.

"Dee," she says, losing a battle with herself, "I need your help with this."

Her Memory Keeper's face appears, at last, in the corner of her nearest monitor: a sullen, angry child.

"Oh, so you're finished?"

She considers a number of responses, each one more de- fensive than the last. But Dee is just an artificial intelligence, a virtual helper built on her own discarded memories. There's no reason for her to care about its opinion.

So she simply pulls up the loose memories that Keith sent her and lets them play. She doesn't bother with the full headset, since like most loose memories, these are patchy and degraded. Drugs tend to do that, but so does desperation.

The memories all center on a party somewhere in Old Town. There are tunnels covered in black and white tiles in a pattern she can no longer make sense of; loose tiles crunch underfoot like eggshells. The tunnels converge on a larger space, a great platform with sunken tracks. Lights flash and sparkle from hidden crevices. One of the memories has a degraded olfactory register, which Dee tells her smells faintly of cotton candy and dried urine. Street-grade Nevermind comes in a lot of flavors, but she remembers the Candy Remix from eight years ago. One of Doc Young's staples, with a short, punchy high that made your every recent memory taste sweet. It was MC Haze's first big hit, the one that propelled her from the trenches of dime-a-dozen remixers to the dizzying heights of underground stardom. On the memory playback, which Dee has belatedly condensed into a composite far richer in detail, lights flash and project onto the ceiling. The outline of an old man seated beside a dark, upside-down obelisk raises his hands, palms out. Light gathers between his head and his hands until a star shoots from his forehead. It obliterates the man, leaving only the glittering words behind:

DOC YOUNG'S MIND BREAK

A few of the memories go on longer, but she stops playback.

"That's the old train station, Seshet," Dee says after a taut moment. "The north platforms." It sounds worried. But of course it does—it's a reflection of herself, and they both understand what this means.

"That old bastard." She's several steps behind him, as always. She slumps in her chair, rolled by the exhaustion she's kept at bay all morning.

"Dee, can you ring the Standards office?"

"Are you going to order a raid?" Dee says nervously. "Don't you remember what happened last time?"

A hundred detainees. A dozen branded as dirty computers, left as dead to their friends and families. Oh, she remembers. But what choice does she have?

Doc Young is back.

●　━　●

THE DAYTIME RAID TURNS UP A FEW SCRAPS: STRAY MEMORIES from the vagabond who sleeps across the street, discarded remix inhalers she sends to forensics, a smattering of stencils with Doc Young's new logo, the star bursting from his head like Athena from Zeus. She tells the Standards Chief to maintain a stealth drone formation throughout the night, to see who else they might pick up. Doc Young won't use the same place twice for his traveling club, but other people of interest might stop by.

She still isn't sure if the memory flooding is the fault of a new remix, but Doc Young's sudden reappearance after five years makes that more likely. She doesn't want to think of what Terry and the elders will say, if so. They forgave her then, but she doubts they will be so understanding a second time.

Jordan comes by her office again that night, bearing curry and beer like a sword and shield.

"You haven't eaten all day," he says, and hurries to the conference table to set out the food.

"Been watching me that carefully, have you?" Seshet says wryly, observing his practiced arrangement of disposable containers and silverware. As if he's determined to finish before she has a chance to kick him out. "What are you still doing here on a Sunday?"

"I just worry about you." He takes the lid off of a curry container. The smell of Jamaican jerk chicken hits her with an almost physical force. She's reminded that she still hasn't slept and—Jordan is correct—hasn't eaten more than a protein bar since this morning.

She sighs. "Tell me you at least got enough for yourself?"

He smiles, so grateful it pains her, and pulls out another container. "Just in case."

She removed her outer robe at some point in the last several frantic hours, so she eats with her clerk in just her white tunic and gold leggings, exhaustion or mortal terror relaxing her into an informality she hasn't allowed herself within these walls in all her time as Director. Jordan, predictably, doesn't comment on the formal vestment flung over the couch like a fancy throw pillow.

He waits until she's nearly finished before asking, she will grant him that.

"So, how are things going with Alethia?"

She chokes on the last mouthful of chicken and drains the rest of her beer before she recovers.

"Why?" she rasps. "Has she said something?"

Jordan shakes his head. "Just that she wishes you had a less demanding job."

"Job!" Seshet laughs and then, inexplicably, wants to cry.

Jordan looks halfway to tears himself. "Director," he says, looking at the remains of his turmeric-stained rice instead of at her, "just *trust* this time, won't you? I think you and Alethia have something very special."

It's out of character for him to overstep like this. Not just as her subordinate, but as her—friend? But Librarians are never simply friends.

"Jordan . . ." She makes her voice hard in warning, but he shakes his head like a stubborn toddler.

"Do something about it if you don't want me to pry. You haven't memory-suppressed me yet, I know it. I've been monitoring myself."

She blinks in surprise. "You've been . . . who taught you that?"

Monitoring is an advanced technique for detecting changes and manipulations in one's own memories. It is generally only taught to subdirectors, though Librarians of lower ranks can learn it at the discretion of someone higher up.

Jordan laughs with more bitterness than she had ever expected of him and wipes his eyes. "It was authorized, Director."

She wants to ask him *by whom*, the question nearly off her tongue before she swallows it back down. Does she want to know? Was it Keith, trying to suborn her closest clerk? Or, worse, Terry, tinting every friendly eye on her with a subtle shade of treachery?

"What do you want from me, Jordan?" She can't keep the distrust from her voice, any more than he can fail to hear it.

"Director. Seshet." He drives her name on his lips like a stake through her heart. "You don't need to control everything."

Stung, her spine stiffens. "I don't need—"

Somehow, his very intensity stops her. "If it's love, just let it be. Please."

SHE CAN'T HELP BUT THINK OF JORDAN'S WARNING WHEN SHE visits Alethia that night, though she knows it shouldn't matter. Jordan *and* Dee? What did she do to deserve the unfounded moralizing of children and artificial constructs?

"I missed you this morning," Alethia says, greeting her with a kiss at the door to her apartment. She's smiling, but her eyes are red-rimmed, puffy and bruised underneath. Without makeup or tailored clothes, her beauty feels more raw to Seshet, more familiar. She's wearing an old T-shirt and pajama pants, perhaps the same ones from last night. She secures all the locks behind Seshet before heading to the living room. All the blinds are down here and in the kitchen, but something in Alethia's mood stops Seshet from suggesting they raise them and turn down the lights. Alethia picks up a thick wooden pipe in the shape of a palm frond and flips open a lighter.

"Please tell me you won't report me," she says with a laugh, but the look in her eyes is a little too desperate, a little too real.

Seshet tries to lighten the mood. "Only if you share."

She's smoked weed a handful of times in her life—all with Terry, in fact, from one of his fancy vintage vape pens while they played some ridiculous old video game of his with a lot of guns and gore—but she's willing to try again just to take the scared edge out of Alethia's voice.

White smoke billows from Alethia's nostrils in soft, gentle whorls. *Oh, to be the smoke behind her teeth,* she thinks. Silently, Alethia passes the pipe and the lighter. Seshet knows how to do this, she has a thousand memories to show her, but the greenly burning smell brings her back, like a hook in her heart, to something older, personal. A little girl playing in the fall leaves, watching wide, beloved hips move with the rhythm of the rake; the smell of those leaves burning, painting sigils on the sky.

She gasps and coughs on a different smoke, in a different year, with a different name. Where did that come from? But it was her own memory, she knows it in her bones. The memory of that little girl she forgot for so many years, the one who longed, more than anything, for the woman with the rake to come back home.

Alethia is thumping her on the back, sitting her down on the couch. She brings her a glass of cold water, which finally soothes the burning in her airway. Seshet wipes her eyes.

"Don't know what happened," Seshet says, pushing the pipe onto the table.

Alethia wags her eyebrows. "You have a hard time breathing around me?"

Seshet's heart hurts. She leans back on the couch, closes her eyes against the fluorescent lights, her beloved's blinding smile.

"You're tired," Alethia says. "Did you work today?"

"You don't really get days off in my position. You?"

"I . . . went to the lab. I have a project I'm working on . . . anyway, I didn't stay long."

Seshet cracks open her eyes. Alethia is gazing pensively at one of the windows, as though she can see through the blinds.

"Did something happen?" Was she not careful enough last night? Did she disrupt Alethia's emotional balance with her real-time dive into her dreams and memories? The sleep headsets have that functionality, but it's not recommended outside of a specially equipped detention facility where the subjects can be closely monitored for side effects. Guilt washes over her, inexorable as unbidden memory. There is a difference, vital as a heartbeat, between what is permitted to her position and what is aligned with her soul. She knew that, once. She almost remembers it now, but the knowing slides, sinks into soft forgetting, is gone.

Alethia shakes her head as though shaking off a fly. "Tell me about your day. If you can, I guess. Did you bust any heads?"

Seshet sits straight up. "I don't bust—"

But Alethia is already holding her hands up, palms out. "Sorry, sorry, babe. It was just a joke. You *are* the Director of this whole little town. Heads are sometimes busted."

"If I have to order raids, it's for the good of our community—"

"So you ordered a raid?"

"I never said—"

Alethia's laugh stops her cold. "The poor things that get caught in that net. So many new Torches for the Temple."

"Alethia," she says, forcing herself calm though she feels as if she's falling in midair, "you know what I am."

Alethia blows out another lungful of smoke. In the hallway, someone unlocks their door and shuts it. Alethia keeps still until the hall has gone quiet again.

"Yeah, I know. I just wish I could see who."

"What's that supposed to mean?"

Alethia taps out the ashes straight onto the coffee table and refills the pipe. "Who are you, Seshet-without-a-number? Who would you be if you weren't Director Librarian? Who could we be, together?"

The vertigo is getting worse. Maybe the weed has finally kicked in. "Why are you asking me this, Alethia?"

She stares at Alethia, who keeps her gaze fixed on the window. "It's just . . . you have a reputation, you know? You're . . . kinder than most of them. Nothing happened to anyone we met that night at Cousin Skee's. I was taking a chance, bringing you there."

She feels sick. "What did you think would happen to them?"

Alethia meets her gaze at last, but now Seshet wants to turn away, to hide from the confusion and distrust she sees there. "I don't know, Seshet. You tell me. What's going to happen to whoever gets caught in that raid of yours?"

"Anyone going to one of Doc Young's parties needs Counseling, Alethia!" Alethia flinches but Seshet persists. "Yes, even cleaning. It's for the good of the whole."

Alethia snorts. "The good of the whole," she says, mocking. "My god, you sound just like them."

I am them, she almost says, fast and hot. She swallows back the cheap shot. Seshet could ascend to elder council itself and she still wouldn't be more than tolerated in New Dawn. She knows exactly what Alethia means.

"Alethia, what's going on? What happened today? Why are you like this?"

"Maybe this *is* who I am, Seshet. I'm not your dream girl. I'm just a woman in way, way over her head . . ."

She buries her head in her arms. Seshet, shocked, puts a hand on her shoulder.

"Just go." Alethia's voice is muffled and Seshet pretends she didn't hear. But Alethia raises her head a second later, so the words are clear as the new dawn light:

"Leave, Seshet."

You can say this for our Director Librarian, Seshet-without-a-number, the woman who named herself after a goddess so she could not forget what she meant to become: she does not flinch.

Whatever the consequences, the moral accounting, the line

drawn between the *she* who had not done this thing and the *she* who has—what is an official of New Dawn if not a professional consequence risker, moral accountant, line crosser? And Seshet has prided herself on being the best of them all.

This is her line, carefully marked in the sand before the tide of *what* she is drowns it in a sea of salt and noise: Alethia's memories.

She sees herself as through a haze of love and longing: a tall woman of regal bearing and awkward gestures, tongue-tied, eloquent-eyed, no longer young but ageless. That woman walks into Alethia's apartment. That woman says, with a pained smile, *Only if you share.*

She takes the memory and *pushes,* back behind the most painful moments of Alethia's past, behind her grief over her father lost on the other side of that border wall, behind the conflicted shame and love she feels for her mother lost to cancer, behind her first memories, her shock when she realized that other people saw her as a boy, and further, behind her first cries in the light, behind her waiting silence in the liquid dark. She pushes, and when Alethia puts her headset on tonight, she will respond and pull, until not a trace of their meeting a few hours ago remains accessible to her conscious mind. It isn't as good as a full Nevermind wipe, but it's the next best thing. No one that Seshet has suppressed has voluntarily recalled those memories ever again. She knows the trick, you see. No one remembers everything. And what's too painful to remember, you can simply choose to forget.

All Seshet does is use their own mental blocks as the bulwark against whatever she wants to hide from their consciousness. It's like a wall of fire in one of Terry's old video games with a treasure safely hidden inside. Here's the trick: if the flames burn on the fuel of your own shame, not even mortal terror can make you brave the heat.

• — •

SHE SLEEPS FOR A WHILE IN HER OWN WORKSTATION, VISOR still down, the floodplain of virtual space melding seamlessly with the dreamscape of her own memory-haunted mind. She does not know of what she dreams; those are locked away in the fastness of her own shame and regret. Just one follows her into craggy wakefulness, and it's not so much a dream as a belch of repressed memory, inexplicably brought to life. The sway of her mother's hips as she agitates the leaves. The girl in the grass. The crackle and burn.

"Dee," she says, without thinking. Their argument feels far away now. The logic of it lost to her in a groggy sickness, the hangover of what she has done to the woman she is falling in love with.

"You don't look so good, Seshet."

Seshet tries to laugh, but it's like wet ashes, it won't come out. Dee is a child playing on the floodplain, now empty, waiting for the morning's harvest. She has never known whether Dee acts the role of a child for her benefit, or for some arcane satisfaction of its own.

"Dee," she says, coughing on something too silty for tears. *You have a hard time breathing around me.* No matter what else they have, Alethia won't ever remember that. "Show me my old memories, won't you? Show me my mother."

Dee's uncanny eyes go wide as a Kewpie doll's. "Really? You never want to look at those."

"I . . . remembered something. From my childhood."

"But you can't remember those, not as a primary memory. Not unless . . . Oh, Seshet."

Seshet thinks she doesn't deserve Dee's understanding, its kindness. Even if it is an artificial intelligence fundamentally limited by New Dawn's protocols, it understands her better than any human ever has.

"I must have suppressed it," she says, out loud, for the first time. "That's how they missed it in the Nevermind wipe."

Humans repress their own memories, of course. They do it all the time. Headsets wouldn't work, otherwise. Nevermind would just be a really trippy drug. The fact that New Dawn has weaponized this effect for its own purposes doesn't mean that people don't forget things for their own simple survival every second of the day. It's not so surprising that she would have done so. But why remember now, after so much time?

Without another word, Dee pulls up a memory and rolls it over her in a full sensory wash. Ah, she has always liked this one. She is eight, and her mother has just come home from some mysterious trip overseas. She has brought back a suitcase full of treasure and she shows young Deidre the spoils, piece by piece. Here is the necklace of cowries she purchased on the beach from a boy no older than Deidre; here is the doll made of corn husks and twine with black beans for eyes; here is the program for the opera, red ink on cream paper that still smells of someone else's cologne.

"I can breathe there, Deidre," she says, a refrain the child recognizes. "Your memories are your own."

"But when will you let me come with you, Mom?"

"When you're older, honey. When it's safer."

Deidre never understood what her mother meant by that. Then her mother and father fought and her mother stopped going on her trips, stopped bringing back bounty. Just a year later, her mother abandoned them both.

The memory fuses with another and another: her mother doing the laundry, cursing at the old machine that always rocked during the spin cycle; her mother singing her to sleep, *Remember*, some old song from before memories were things you could hold in your fist like coin; her mother screaming at the top of her lungs from the top of a hill, "I own my own soul!"

"Why do you think she left us, Dee?" Seshet asks now, though she doesn't remember this girl that she was, not really.

Dee shuts down the memories. "She wouldn't have done it without a good reason, Seshet. I know it."

Terry has come to Little Delta for an unofficial visit. The news rushes through the obelisk like water over a ruptured dam, but Seshet, sleeping in her office, is among the last to hear it. It's Jordan, of course, who saves her. He spends five minutes arguing with her door monitor before Dee finally wakes her up.

"Oh god," Jordan says, "I was beginning to worry you'd died."

"The door monitor would have let you in if I were dead," Seshet says, yawning. She's still in last night's street clothes, which look—and smell—days old.

Jordan grimaces. "That's what it said. Thank you, Dee."

"You're welcome, Jordan!" Dee says, inordinately pleased. It doesn't acknowledge most people—a precaution Seshet instilled in it early on—but Jordan has always been on its short list of friendly humans.

He tells her about Terry, which wakes her the rest of the way up, no need for the coffee he has so helpfully brought. She drinks it anyway.

"How long has he been here?"

"Half an hour," Jordan says. "He's taking a tour of the Counseling building."

She closes her eyes briefly. So he's seeing Keith before her. This is meant to send a message, but knowing Terry, it's as likely to make Keith feel overconfident as it is to make Seshet feel undermined.

"And this morning's crop?"

Jordan hesitates.

"Out with it, Jordan. Things can't get much worse."

"Over fifty percent are those junk memories," he says in a small voice that means he still can't believe it. "I don't know how,

Director, but they've gone from a blip to nearly overwhelming the system in less than a week."

A little more than that, she thinks, not that it matters. "Exponential growth," she says. "It's a killer."

She uses the shower in her office and puts on the extra work robes she keeps in the closet. She can't afford Terry's performative casualness, and she doesn't bother to try.

She meets him, an hour later, as the perfectly composed Director Librarian of Little Delta, in her robes of office.

He's wearing the hat of Arch-Librarian, but below the neck he's all ironic hipster, reaching for meaning in the corporate branding of the past. This time it's an Atari T-shirt, corduroy pants, and pink Vans. She has to grant him his point: in the hallways of the obelisk his peculiar style stands out even more than his vestments would.

"Seshet!" he says. "Good news! I've gotten my hands on the Japanese original of *Final Fantasy III*, remember I was telling you about that?"

She blinks at him. "Congratulations?" She's never managed to keep track of all the video games he's played in front of her, but she generally drums up enough interest in the moment to keep things pleasant. The weed helps.

He settles himself in one of her armchairs, crosses left foot over right knee, and balances his conical red cap on the end of one pink shoe. "I'd suggest we head straight to Greenfriars, but I guess the play-through will have to wait. You must be drowning in work. Don't mind me, I just stopped by to say hello."

Greenfriars is one of the New Dawn resort facilities, about an hour out of town, reserved for officials, their families, and select friends. She has never spent much time there.

"Hello, Terry. I've just had a pot of tea brought up. Would you like some?"

She pours the tea into two matching ceramic cups, marked with gold and lapis filigree in the sigil of New Dawn. The tea pours green and fragrant as fresh-cut grass, and she doesn't offer him any sugar. Terry only ever drinks iced coffees thick as milkshakes with protein powder. He takes the cup from her with a sardonic lift to his eyebrows.

"Tea, that's charming. So . . . how's it going?"

She doesn't prevaricate. "Doc Young is back in town. I'm waiting on news of a sting operation from the Standards office."

"Good. And his remixer?"

"I'm not sure if MC Haze is with him this time, but it's possible."

He takes a tentative sip and grimaces. "Well, I'm sure it will be settled soon in your capable hands, Seshet."

Seshet puts her cup smoothly in its saucer, disconcerted. What happened to the urgency, the veiled threats of their last conversation? And if he's so sure she can resolve it, why has he bothered to come here in person? Terry hates Little Delta. "I'm grateful for your confidence in me."

He beams like a proud father. It makes him look ancient. "You deserve it! In fact, that's just what I wanted to bring up with you personally. We've all been impressed with your tenure here. Even those who weren't in favor of your ascension have come around now. You were a controversial appointment, you know that, but you've done very well. You've proven the New Dawn ethos. 'Order, Standards, and Merit above all.'" He hesitates theatrically. "You're Merit, of course."

Seshet raises her cup to hide her expression. "Of course. You came all the way to Little Delta to tell me that?"

Saltier than she meant it to come out. Terry may have been her ally for over a decade, but he still loves to unbalance her.

He takes another swig of the tea in his enthusiasm. "A little more than that, dear. We're considering you for a promotion. The directorship has opened in Minneapolis. Big city, very different operation from what you have going on here, but lots of opportunity for a hungry Librarian. Of course, I know you're already bonded to this city. We'd have to wipe you again. That's not wonderful, but you've only just turned forty, your brain is still resilient enough. You can keep your personal memories, of course; no one wants to worry you about that."

Her mind is blank with astonishment. She blurts the first thought that pops into it. "Minneapolis? Terry, you were Director of Minneapolis."

"I was! So you can see, Seshet, there are big things ahead of you. Who knows where you might go after this. We just need to see a successful resolution to this memory plague problem and, honestly, your nomination is in the bag." Satisfied as a cat over a clean plate, he puts down his teacup. "Do we understand one another, Seshet?"

She nods. "Perfectly, Terry."

As she hoped, the sting nets a group of revelers hoping to catch Doc Young's latest party a day late. The detention memory swipe of one of them turns up a pair of half-dreams that match the ones flooding their systems. The subject—one Leon 75411—says he doesn't know anything about memory flooding or new remixes, he just picked those up at another party, a mind meld with a group of strangers. No, he doesn't know who they were. No, he couldn't find them again. The Standards Chief is interrogating the detainee personally. In his professional opinion, he tells Seshet, the boy is telling the truth. But that doesn't mean his memories might not give more clues. She tells the Standards Chief to put the detainee into a coma and harvest as much as they can. When the memories arrive to her workstation, however, she goes rigid with shock. She recognizes the kid, this Leon 75411, low-grade memory hoarder and antisocial deviant. He's the light-skinned boy with the stencil of Doc Young's Mind Break on his cap who danced with her at Cousin Skee's. With a lurch of nausea, she now remembers who he reminded her of:

her half brother, child of her father's second marriage after her mom left. They had never gotten along.

Alethia said she had taken a chance bringing Seshet to that bar. But this wasn't the same. Seshet hadn't broken that trust—this kid walked into her trap entirely of his own accord! But she imagines trying to justify herself to Alethia and can't bear to look at the kid's first memory in the queue. She tells Dee to conduct a preliminary analysis and declares herself done for the day.

She wants to see Alethia, to make good on the bad she did last night and try again.

But Alethia is distracted when Seshet arrives. She pulls what sounds like a table from the door before unlocking it.

"Did anyone follow you up the stairs?" She's still in the pajama bottoms of the last two nights, though she's changed to a different bleach-stained T-shirt.

"I'm alone," Seshet says, sidling through the crack Alethia leaves open. Alethia looks ragged, haunted, like the day has weighed her down with cement blocks.

"I missed you yesterday," she says. The words disorient Seshet, then hit her like a blow. She hides their effect behind a smile and an embrace. It's better this way. A fresh start, their fight not just forgotten but made as if it never was. Alethia hangs in her arms, trembling, before she gathers her strength and pulls back.

"Lethe," Seshet says, "are you okay? What's happened?"

But Alethia just rubs her temples and heads to the kitchen. She has a full pot of coffee under the drip, and a wad of discarded filters in the sink. She pours herself a mug and offers another to Seshet.

"But it's late," Seshet says.

Alethia shrugs. "I can't sleep."

"No wonder! How much coffee have you had today?"

"No, I mean, I can't *let* myself sleep. I've been having terrible dreams lately." She shakes her head and shudders. "That's what

I get for buying the cheap headset, I guess. All for a couple of lousy Social points. Why do you guys authorize those things if they don't even work?"

She slams her empty mug down on the countertop. Seshet jumps.

"Sorry," she says. "Sorry, babe. It's been a rough few days. How have you been? How's work?" She gives a jittery laugh, a momentary flash of something bright and wild as she leans against the countertop. "Bust any heads today?"

Seshet thinks of Leon, she can't help it, but none of that pained guilt shows in her practiced, earnest expression. She's in control now. She knows where this is going, and she can steer their ship to calmer waters. "Lethe," she says again, savoring the nickname on her tongue, imagining years of having the right to call this woman hers, "I don't bust heads. I'm the Director Librarian, not a tyrant."

Alethia holds her eyes. Seshet wants to know who she sees there. She wants to see herself as Alethia does, majestic and awkward, powerful and kind.

Alethia nods slowly. "Just remember the difference, okay?"

What's that supposed to mean? "Okay," she says instead, because this time she's doing it differently. "Now will you tell me what's wrong?"

Alethia gives her a trembling smile. "I need help. Can I trust you, Seshet?"

"Yes," says Seshet—knowing she is lying, but imagining she might be telling the truth.

I saw you last night. You didn't think I'd recognize you after all that work you had done, but I'd know those hands anywhere. There you were, my ghost, my lost genius, my little missy Haze. Thought you'd gotten away with it, took my money and left me with a dud mix instead of that game-changer you promised. But you made a mistake going back

*to Skee's. I'll tell your bosses at Pinkerton exactly the kind
of work you used to do. You think you can lead a normal,
happy life now? Went to Counseling, and you're a reformed
member of society? My parents are New Dawn, bitch. I'll tell
everyone.*

*Or you come back and finish the mix you promised me.
Those fingers still got the old magic, don't they?*

You have three days. You know where to find me.

The letter is unsigned. A signature, apparently, would have
been superfluous.

Alethia is curled in a ball on the edge of her couch, head
between her knees. She hauls in great lungfuls of air, like a child
just rescued from a burning building.

Seshet feels like she's the one who's caught fire.

"You're MC Haze." Her voice comes from a distance. As
though she's watching by the window as another woman, calmly
seated on the couch beside a hysterical Alethia, reads and rereads
a sloppily handwritten note that was left on Alethia's workstation Sunday morning, when no one should have known she'd be
going into the lab.

"I used to be." Alethia sounds strangled. "I got out."

"You had surgery?"

"It wouldn't have worked if anyone could recognize me."

"Is that where this . . . associate's money went?"

A bleak, disbelieving laugh. "Does that matter?"

"What mix were you working on?"

"That *definitely* doesn't matter."

"Who is he?"

"You can tell it's a guy?"

"Please."

She sighs. "His name is Vance Fox."

Seshet freezes. Technically, New Dawn has dispensed with
the need for surnames. But some lineages persist. Keith comes

from the Fox family, though he doesn't have any children. This must be a cousin or nephew.

"Do you realize that your remixes and Doc Young's parties nearly destroyed me five years ago?"

Alethia regards her with one eye, balefully red. "Well, your raids and head busting nearly destroyed *me* five years ago. They *did* destroy a lot of my friends. So I'd say we're even. You're still at the top of that obelisk and I'm . . ." She gulps back another sob.

"How on earth did you get past Counseling?"

Alethia snorts. "Did you think I could learn to remix Nevermind without learning how to hide my own memories? I made myself into exactly who they wanted me to be."

"And me?" Seshet asks. She is floating on the ceiling, she is flying to the stars, away from here. "Did you turn yourself into . . ." She can't finish the sentence.

"What, some kind of honey trap?" Alethia's tone is cutting. "If I did, then I'm really the honey. I didn't change a thing for you, Seshet. You've met me exactly as I am."

"Then why . . ."

"I don't know! I saw you, once, when things were going south with Doc and we were scrambling. There was a parade downtown and I thought, why not? Let me see who wants to destroy my life so bad. So I made myself a remix mask for the drones and I went to see you. You were standing on that platform in your robes like some kind of mannequin, and beside you this even bigger official was going on and on, Standards and Order and Merit, blah blah. And I was right there. I pushed my way to the front of the crowd, you understand? And I'm rolling my eyes at this gasbag and you're just standing straight as an arrow, no emotion at all. And then he says something like, 'With New Dawn, there is a place for everyone as long as everyone stays in place.' And I can't help it, I start to laugh. Well, I snort and then try to pretend it was a sneeze. Now, imagine how scared I get when I realize you're looking at me. Staring at me. And you smile, Seshet. It maybe lasted half a second, but that smile said everything."

"Said what, Alethia?"

"'You're not the only one.'"

"HOW DO YOU KNOW HER?"

She corners Jordan in his quarters, mad as a banshee, livid with fear, uncaring. Alethia is MC Haze. Alethia was in the crowd while Terry was giving one of his tendentiously long monologues, as though daring anyone to yawn or crack a smile. And what's worse—though Seshet is too furious to realize the strangeness of this—she believes Alethia, *but Seshet doesn't remember.* And she should remember everything that has ever happened to her since her initiation twenty years ago.

Jordan's quarters are small and spare, as befits a Librarian clerk. There's only a twin mattress in a metal frame, a kitchenette that doubles as a washbasin, a desk with a single display and a headset. She wonders, in some detached, watchful part of her, how he got the money to buy her clothes for that first date with Alethia. Had he used his meager savings? Or has someone been filling his account?

Jordan, dressed for bed, stumbles to his knees.

"I can't tell you that, Director," he says, crying. His upper arms, revealed by his nightshirt, are crossed with old scars. She doesn't know what they're from. It hits her, again, that though she has more power in this city than anyone, with the people she cares about most she feels as vulnerable as a child. She should know why Jordan has his scars. She should know why Alethia risked meeting her. She shouldn't be here, sleepless and ragged with pain like some regular citizen slated for Counseling! How much more power will she need before she can feel safe from everyone moving in ways she doesn't expect and cannot control, even as she loves them?

"You can't tell me?" Seshet echoes, disbelieving.

He shakes his head. "I promised."

"Your *promise* matters more than your oath?"

He averts his gaze, shoulders trembling.

"She's no friend of a friend, is she? Someone told you to put her in touch with me, didn't they? Who, Jordan? Tell me who set this up!"

He keeps shaking his head, sobbing like a dog expecting a kick.

Terry; it must be him. Who else could have scared poor, loyal Jordan like this? Certainly not Keith, soft as cream pudding. She gives Jordan a disgusted look and turns away. She can't stand to see his fear.

"Get up," she says. "I expect you on duty in the morning."

"Seshet—"

She silences him with a raised hand. "But I won't ever trust you again."

Doc Young has had a traveling party for as long as Seshet has been alive. Longer, if you believe the legends. They say he used to be a kid leading the protests against New Dawn's glorious revolution, before the original Alpha America Party established the Standards and memory surveillance regime, which stamped out all "antisocial deviance." They also say Doc Young's taken his party on the road around the world, to countries that still haven't adopted New Dawn's freely available surveillance technology. The countries, Seshet now remembers, where her mother loved to travel, before she disappeared. Doc Young is bigger than Little Delta, but it's a part of him; it's where he's from, and where he learned to love drugs and music and that crazy, classic life. He's returned to it again and again over the decades, like a comet around the sun. And like a comet, he disrupts the tides and obscures the stars, he dazzles and he terrifies—and he's gone before anyone can ask him to clean up the mess.

No, that he leaves for Seshet.

Which is probably why, after Alethia's confession, Seshet had sat frozen on that beige couch, its synthetic fibers scratching through her leggings, and realized that she had an opportunity.

"I'll help you with Vance Fox," she had told Alethia, "if you'll bring me to Doc Young."

Alethia was silent for a whole minute. "Promise me you won't detain him."

"I promise to give him enough time to get out of town again. Good enough?"

Alethia narrowed her eyes, probably sensing Seshet's dozen unspoken caveats. But then she spread her open palms to the ceiling. "All right."

And now, the night before Vance Fox's ultimatum expires, they are crawling—not touching, wary as strangers—through tunnels so abandoned Seshet can't find them on her proprietary plans of the city. They are hunting for the next place Doc Young has convened the world's longest-running experiment in bacchanalian civil disobedience. They meet no one else in the tunnel, which worries Seshet until she hears music coming from up ahead. She has a hundred questions—How does he announce the locations? What are these tunnels? Why did Alethia start remixing? Why did she stop?—but she doesn't say anything. Alethia's shoulders are rigid with tension.

A short climb up a ladder, and they emerge into an abandoned high school gymnasium, softly lit with innumerable tiny lights above them, like stars. The arched windows are black, painted or boarded up. The wooden floor is crusty and rat-chewed, the symbol of a prancing bull still barely legible at its center. A few dozen people lounge on fallen bleachers. A circle of five, visors down, pass around an inhaler while their fingers twitch in unfathomable creation. A band is playing a hypnotic rhythmic drone on an elevated platform by one of the rusted hoops. Seshet doesn't understand the music at all, thinks it might be a deviant cousin of the New Dawn–approved jazz, which is the only kind she has ever heard.

A curtain made of lights and smoke and fluttering strips of cloth obscures the other hoop from view.

Seshet looks around doubtfully. "There's not a lot of people here."

Alethia raises her eyebrows. "What, you were expecting a go-go?"

"What's a go-go?"

"Never mind. There's usually more people here, but we're late. It started this morning."

"This morning!"

"Changing times makes him harder to catch."

Alethia leads her across the floor to the curtain. A pair of large men in silver suits emerge from the smoke to stand in their way. Alethia raises her hand, flashes a card with the symbol of a dark, upside-down obelisk, and the men move seamlessly to the side, though one of them gives Alethia a sharp glance she pretends not to notice.

Behind the curtain, an old man in a chair that resembles Seshet's workstation, but also an actual throne, is watching a flow of images on a screen behind their heads. Three people wearing VR headsets lie beneath the screen on thin pallets. Seshet pauses to stare at the projection, which looks like a memory but must be a lucid dream, somehow shared between the three people on the floor.

"Alethia," she says, in a reverent whisper, "oh, Alethia, is *that* Nevermind?"

Alethia takes her hand and squeezes. "It's the Soñador remix."

"One of yours?"

A small smile of pride. "One of mine."

The man of the upside-down obelisk, her old rival in a new kingdom, watches their approach. He is as much king in this territory as she is queen in hers, and she regrets the nondescript black clothes Alethia insisted upon. She'd feel steadier in gold-embroidered robes. Doc Young is a big man, solidly muscled for all his years. It's not his physical mass that impresses so much as his gaze, which seems to pick you up like so much fluff and weigh you against a counterweight only he knows. From behind square glasses, those eyes are ageless, weary and bright with curiosity.

"Director Seshet." A regal nod. "I thought you might seek me out this time."

One of the silver-clad men by his side gives Seshet a startled second glance.

The old man smiles, deepening the crevasses between his eyes and mouth. *Black don't crack,* Seshet thinks, *until it falls to pieces.* Still, he's handsome as a painting.

"Welcome to the upside-down kingdom," he says, spreading his arms. "And I see you've brought someone to guarantee your safe passage. Welcome back, dear."

Alethia lowers her gaze and then, to Seshet's shock, goes to one knee. "It's been awhile, Doc."

"I knew you had your reasons. Stand up, girl. You don't look all that different to me."

Alethia smiles and wipes carefully at her eyes. "That's just 'cause you know how to look. Doc, we—I mean Seshet—has a favor to ask."

He regards Seshet for a curious moment and then snaps his fingers. "Ben, Henry, the divider, please."

The two silver shadows pull out black accordion dividers from the post behind Doc Young's throne. Connected in a circle around the three of them, the dividers hum and emit a faint purple glow. The ambient noise of the party drops to nothing.

"Now we can speak privately," he says. "Lethe, you took a risk coming here. I'm not the only one who will recognize you even with that new face."

"I know that, Doc. But it's already happened. Vance found me. He wants me to finish what I started."

He sucks in a sharp breath. "And you're sure you don't want my help?"

Alethia smiles a little. "Not this time. Seshet has promised to help me if you help her. So . . ."

"*Has* Seshet?" he asks, looking between them in slowly dawning comprehension. He snorts. "I see you haven't changed at all, Lethe. Never met a risk you didn't want to take."

Alethia spreads her hands carefully against her thighs. "There was one, Doc."

He regards her for a moment. His silence has an oddly comforting quality, as though those in his presence are seen and understood without need for words. At last, he takes his glasses, cleans them on his scarf, and considers Seshet far more coolly.

"You made my life very difficult the last time I was in town, Director. You took some of my best friends. So why would you of all people ask me a favor now that I've just got back?"

Seshet takes a deep breath and releases it slowly. She's in Doc Young's territory now. As the representative of New Dawn's power here in his shadow court, perhaps she ought to defend their—her—past actions, but she has never been their most loyal servant, merely their most competent.

She shrugs. "Times change."

"New Dawn doesn't."

"No collective is static; you of all people ought to know that."

"So, how has New Dawn changed, Director Librarian? Or is it just Little Delta? Or is it . . ." He leans forward. ". . . perhaps . . ." He raises a large, blunt finger. ". . . just you, Seshet?"

She'd been furious when Doc Young escaped the final sting operation five years ago. If she could, she would have personally thrown him into the detention car to take him to the Temple. But she hasn't felt such professional rage for years; she doesn't know when it all left her. There'd been too many memories to take on, too many people to care for, too much city to watch over for her to nurse a grudge with an old man who trafficked forbidden magic to forgotten souls in Old Town.

Does that mean she's changed? Does it matter? Like any good Jungian, she knows she is carried along by something greater than herself.

"Could be," she says.

She details the half-dreams clogging their systems, how they can't pinpoint the source of their exponential growth.

"I think the elders want to blame you, but nothing you have here would be capable of creating the wave we're seeing. I doubt anyone here has used a recollector in months." She hesitates. She'd misdirected Keith before, not wanting him to realize a truth that's been haunting her for the last week. But if she isn't honest with Doc Young, then what's the point of asking for his help? "The ringleaders might be from your side of the tracks. But the flooding . . . it's coming from citizens in good standing. They're people we've numbered and tracked and now they're making our memory collection useless. I don't think this is your style, but I think you might know whose it is. Or at least, have a hint of *what* the hell is happening."

He regards her for several long seconds and then, abruptly, slaps his knee, laughing so hard his chair shakes.

"If someone has finally managed to outsmart you memory vampires, why in hell would I help you stop them, Director Seshet? I've been waiting decades for that obelisk to fall. I might like you better than your predecessor, but that doesn't make you my friend."

"No," Seshet says. "But I'm Alethia's friend."

"So she's your hostage?"

"Just my leverage. She can ask your help anytime she wants.

But I know the Fox family. My help will probably be more effective."

Alethia acknowledges this with a tight nod. Doc Young adjusts his glasses, a gesture that feels oddly definitive.

"For Lethe, I'll look into it. I'll tell you the what, if I can find out, and maybe even the how. But I won't tell you who. I won't betray my brothers like that."

"And sisters," Alethia says, rolling her eyes, the lines of an old argument.

"And sisters," Doc Young says, nodding sagely at his former star remixer.

"That's fine," Seshet says quickly. If she has the how and the what, she can work out the who on her own, anyway.

"But before I tell you what I know, I need a boon."

Seshet eyes him warily. And she'd almost made it out. "A boon?"

"A dream, Seshet, queen of the white city. You steal our memories, but down here we deal in dreams. So give me one of yours, let me suck it from you like the yolk from an egg, and I'll let you know what I find out."

THE PLAGUE OF LOCUSTS PAUSES IN ITS INEXORABLE TRAJEC-tory. It does not diminish, nor does it expand to ever more biblical proportions; it sits, as if in wait on a decimated field, wings churring.

Are they waiting for her, Seshet wonders? To see what she will do, now that the golden obelisk has at last met the dark? But that seems solipsistic even for a Director Librarian. These memory fakers, these dream makers, whoever or whatever they are, have ambitions beyond the toppling of one incidental Director Librarian of one small city.

Dealing with Alethia's harasser was easy enough. She simply went to Keith and told him she'd ID'd a cousin of his dealing remixed Nevermind among the loose memories of Doc Young's parties. She didn't want to report him, of course, but considering the current crisis, she didn't know how she could keep this from Terry, at the very least . . .

Keith went red and promised, in a strangled tone, to deal promptly with Cousin Vance.

Alethia has not heard a word from Vance Fox since. After a few days, she returns to work.

LEON 75411 WAKES FROM HIS INDUCED COMA WITH ENOUGH memory damage that they decide he's better off getting a full cleaning at the Temple. The deep sweep turned up two faces with a high probability of being the ones who seeded the half-dreams, but neither of them is registered and a deeper search of the loose memory bank has turned up nothing else so far. Seshet does not have much hope for its success. The pattern of the flooding makes it clear that her worst fears have come true: the majority of people propagating the half-dreams really are registered citizens in good standing, with high Social scores. They are hiding in plain sight. She wonders if Doc Young has found the originators yet, but until she can learn enough dreaming to put one together for him, she can't go back to ask.

A week passes. A cold snap comes in; red and golden leaves brown and wither seemingly overnight and cast their bodies to the ground. She walks through drifts with Alethia, crunching and giggling, until the street sweepers pass through and the sidewalks are clean again, and white. *Queen of the white city,* Doc Young called her. She cannot forget it.

At night, after work, Alethia teaches Seshet how to dream. They begin with a simple remix: Dalemark, one of Alethia's first.

"What does the name mean?" Seshet asks.

Alethia blushes. "It's a fantasy kingdom in a series I liked as a kid. I was such a blerd. Still am, I guess."

Seshet, who never had time for any hobbies at all, kisses her.

The remix induces a soft, receptive state, similar to ecstasy but with a mnemonic bite. Memories flow like honey down a comb, sweet and slow. But these are no memories of waking life, no. These are memories of dreams. And if you wait carefully, you can stretch them, taffy-twist them around your finger into something to keep you warm at night, long after the mix has burned itself out.

"Relax, Seshet," Alethia says, stroking cool fingers along her arm. "We're in no hurry."

"It's been a week. I have to give him a dream soon."

"You won't give him anything wound so tight. Deep breaths. Dreams aren't memories. They are memories' voices."

"What's that supposed to mean?"

"You've got to let them sing."

They call them singing lessons after that, one of their jokes that's more earnest than Seshet likes to admit. She starts remembering her dreams on Dalemark, embarrassing, pedestrian little allegories:

She stands on the viewing deck of the obelisk, naked, while citizens of Little Delta set fire to the bottom.

Alethia remembers their fight and says that to win her back she must find all the lost memories, all over the world (she doesn't share that one with Alethia, of course).

She is on the run in Old Town, where everyone ignores her, but everyone in the white city (she cannot forget it) wants to flay her alive.

"What am I supposed to do with these!" She is actually crying, for the first time in years. She had forgotten how much she hates to remember her dreams.

"Just let them be," Alethia says, for what must be the fifteenth time. She is sleep-deprived and exasperated. Her apartment smells of burnt coffee and burnt tires and the sage they burn to mask the first two.

Seshet tries again. The Alethia dream comes up again, relentless as a tide. She does not panic. With Alethia's hand in hers, she feels strong enough to let it be. And then it happens. The dream memory shifts. Dream-Seshet gets in an aircar and drives to the beach. There, inside each seashell and shard of sea glass, is a memory. She kneels in the sand and picks them up, one by one. The work is infinite, but she is at peace.

Alethia can see it worked. "Now," she says, with a teacher's satisfaction, "we share."

They use headsets hacked so they don't connect to the obelisk's data stream. Seshet doesn't ask how Alethia got them. She seems different, though Seshet can't quite place how. She's as affectionate as ever. When they have sex, Seshet has never felt so seen or beloved. And yet she can't help but wonder if Alethia is saying goodbye.

"You're not going to vanish into a hill after this is over, right?" she jokes, the first time they dream together.

"I'm not the goblin king," Alethia snaps. And then, more softly, "Let's just be here now, okay, Seshet?"

Seshet will take it, for now.

They pop the remix, which tastes of peppermint—aftertaste of burnt tires (Alethia, grimacing: "I was young, all right?")—and project their dreams into the virtual space. Seshet sees how Alethia dreams of Old Town, not as frightening or aloof, but mysterious, exciting, free. She sees Doc Young in an obelisk below the graffiti-skirted streets, big as a boulder, the voice of the earth. She sees her face on the body of a monstrous bee, a queen without a throne.

Is that how you see me?

The remix amplifies the dream, and consciousness controls it. More than one mind gives you more raw material, but the principle is the same. Without words, communicating only in the fragments and symbols of their singing unconscious, they build something they both long for. A city for everyone, not just the few New Dawn deems valuable. Graffiti leaping off of the downtown financial high-rises; Skee slinging margaritas on the esplanade; a tiny woman rapping so hard sweat slides down her face while the white boys who harassed Seshet the other day are lined up behind her, bound and blindfolded. Seshet has never felt anything like this raw creative energy before. She doesn't understand how she lived without it all these years. Dreams are better than memories; they bite.

"YOU SEEM DIFFERENT, SESHET."

Dee sounds strangely tentative. Seshet smiles at her Memory Keeper's avatar. "Do I?"

"Are you very happy with Alethia?" it asks.

She blinks in surprise. Dee almost never asks about her private life. "Very," Seshet says, and grins despite herself. More than a week of remixed Nevermind seems to have rewired her synapses, opened paths she'd never dreamed existed within herself. She almost doesn't want to give Doc Young a dream and solve the mystery of the memory flooding. Then what excuse will she have to pop Nevermind with Alethia and dream together? She's a Director Librarian. Once she solves the memory flooding crisis, she's likely to become Director Librarian of all Minneapolis. She'll make Arch-Librarian within ten years. Arch-Librarians don't pop street-grade remixed Nevermind.

But they might certainly have a lover.

It's late. Jordan's morning report—delivered with a strict professional distance that felt physically painful to her, though she didn't know if she even wanted to bridge that gap—indicated the half-dreams are holding steady at 50 percent of the crop. Terry and the elders are watching. She ought to feel afraid, even panicked. Instead, she wants to sing.

You know you are, literally, my dream girl, she said to Alethia last night, before they finally slept. Alethia just shook her head and smiled.

"Seshet," Dee says, startling her again.

"What, Dee?"

"May I make a suggestion?"

Seshet frowns. Dee has opinions all the time. Why would it want permission now to air them? "Go ahead," she says.

"Have you considered monitoring your own memories?"

Seshet sits bolt upright. Her first instinct is to ask why, but then she realizes that perhaps Dee is acting this way because her office is being monitored. Memory surveillance is merely New Dawn's preferred method, not its only option.

"That's a great idea," she says instead, and sits in her workstation.

Once Seshet has fully dropped into the virtual space, they can talk safely.

"I've been tampered with?" Her heart starts beating so fast she can feel it even past the numbing effect of the headset.

"Of course. I don't know why you don't monitor yourself more often. Think about Alethia."

"What about Alethia?"

"Think about how you met."

Frantic, Seshet goes back to that night on Hope Street, hurrying past jeering white boys, opening the door to the bar, heavy beneath her still-shaking hand, and then—

Alethia drinking that terrible green cocktail, meeting her eyes like an old friend.

Seshet feels the edges of the memory for any of the telltale signs of tampering: holes, ragged edges, the bruising pain of something cut with Nevermind or hollowness of something merely well suppressed. But . . .

"It's whole, Dee. No one's touched it."

"No," says Dee, "this is important, Seshet. Alethia told you, didn't she? The *very first time* you met."

"Alethia told—" At last she remembers Alethia's story of why she wanted to meet Seshet, despite everything. That break in her facade, the moment of shared hilarity, during the New Dawn parade five years ago. But that brings up an even bigger question.

"Dee, how do you know what Alethia told me?"

"They won't let me tell you that, Seshet. But you ought to be able to guess."

"They— Oh." Her virtual self has no eyes to close, but she sinks into the painful realization of something she should have known long ago. Dee always seemed like a part of her. It had been a mistake to potentiate it on those recovered memories of her childhood. The other Librarians had thought she was mad. Now she understands why. How will you ever suspect your own childhood self of sabotage? How will you tell that little girl with impossibly blue eyes that it must shut off every day, that it must stay out of your memories, and that, if necessary, you will replace it when it develops too much of a mind of its own? She gave Terry the easiest informant imaginable. She can't fathom why he ever bothered with Jordan.

"Don't be angry with me, Seshet," Dee whispers. "It's hard to say no to them."

"It is," Seshet agrees, dazed. "For me too."

"But I found ways! I put up lots of copies of your memories that aren't very interesting so they didn't bother looking for the interesting ones. They only know a little about Alethia."

"And this conversation?"

"Oh, they never bother with your memories of virtual space. They don't realize you talk to me here. No one else does."

Dee is looking at her so earnestly that it's easy to forget its face is a construct, just like its intelligence. She can't fathom what it really sees or what it actually thinks.

And yet, it still seems just like her friend.

"Do you have the memory of how Alethia and I met, the very first time?" Seshet asks.

"No," Dee says.

So Seshet does what she should have done a week before but was too scared to try: she reaches back. Her eidetic memory re-creates the details of the speech on the podium before the parade: the way her collar chafed, the sweat dripping into her underwear from the ninety-degree heat, Terry's every soporific pronouncement on the pillars of the New Dawn covenant with its "beautiful citizens." Terry revels in hypocrisy, he butters his bread with it. She remembers wanting to roll her eyes and physically aching with the necessity to remain impassive.

She does not remember Alethia.

But she feels—there!—a tiny, but unmistakable, hole. As though all of the emotion and color have drained out of the memory at one specific point. Memory suppression, to a precision that impresses and terrifies her. She checks, but every recent memory with Alethia is clear.

It's minimal, but it's undeniable: someone has been tampering. Who? She doubts Dee will be able to tell her, but she suspects. Who else would have known about that memory but Alethia? Who else would have bothered to suppress so precisely such an unimportant moment? Not Terry. If Dee is telling the truth, New Dawn doesn't know Alethia's secret identity. And even if they did, why suppress *that* fleeting moment and not the rest of this week?

But there is someone who has been working with her, with an unregistered headset, using remixed Nevermind. There is someone more than capable of reaching into her open, trusting mind, and twisting just a little.

She pulls herself out of the workstation so quickly she gives herself a headache. She doesn't care. The pain just feels like one more sign on the road she'd never meant to take. She needs answers.

And she knows just who can give them to her.

Doc Young had given her one token, one-time use. *Call me when you have a dream.* She calls him now, in a white rage—or a black one—and she goes to the point indicated on the virtual map in her palm with nothing in her mind but fire. She takes precautions. That is a side benefit, perhaps, of wild suspicion—it splatters everyone and everything. She tells her clerks she's taking the evening to rest. She sends Alethia a short message saying the same. For the first time in their life together, she shuts Dee off. And then, black-clad, she walks the long blocks of her city like any normal citizen, crossing over the unmarked southern border to Old Town like she's crossed so many lines before.

She'd been willing to accept so much wrong with New Dawn for the sake of the promise of safety, of control. But there is no safety here, certainly not within those golden walls. She could get Torched tomorrow, or she could take the directorship of Minneapolis.

But—Alethia. Even if Seshet can't control their relationship, she can learn a little more before her inevitable fall. Perhaps knowledge can be something to hold on to here in the rubble of her ambitions.

The X marking the spot is an old sidewalk park, derelict as everything else nearby. But a second look reveals the four battered chess tables to be in perfect working order. Seated at one of them, alone, is Doc Young. He's putting out the pieces as she slides in across from him. It is with no surprise at all, and with more than a little admiration, that she sees his special set, Egyptian themed. The golden and onyx obelisks are meant to be the rooks, but Doc Young switches them with the seated kings. The long-necked queens look like her. Probably coincidence, but maybe not.

"I have a dream," she says. "But I have a question first."

He pushes his pawn forward. "Go ahead."

She frowns. "Doesn't white go first?"

"Why, when you already have the power?"

She mirrors his move. "We're on your territory."

Queen's pawn up. He nods. "I expect you want to know about Lethe."

It has occurred to her that she is as hypocritical as Terry for being so livid with Alethia for doing the exact same thing that Seshet did. Her logical self, unfortunately, does not seem to have much influence on her present state of mind. She wants control, she always has. For a week, she thought she could relax her grip around Alethia. She was wrong.

Reckless, she moves her queen. "What was she working on before she left town? Why did that Fox boy want her back?"

He toys with his rook—the erstwhile king—before settling on the knight. He moves it into position, one swipe away from her queen. "She didn't tell you?"

She moves her queen to take the king's pawn. Hopeless now, deep in enemy territory. She doesn't care. "She said it didn't matter."

He snorts and considers his options. Puts a finger on his obelisk, tilts it back and forth. He wears a cap against the cold, which shades his expressive eyes. "She called it Rewind," he says softly. A wind blows between them, cold as a grave. "She was always clever with names. It wasn't a remix. It was something completely new. An antidote. The Fox boy gave her the seed money. I told her it wasn't a good idea, but Lethe never cared. She was going to change the world. Instead, it nearly got her."

"An antidote? To what?"

He looks up, spears her there as his black obelisk topples her long-necked queen. "To Nevermind. Her idea was that if you gave it to someone soon enough after a full wipe, they could get most of their memories back. Now, is that a drug or a bomb?"

Seshet grips the edge of her chair. An *antidote* . . . Was it possible? But she could believe anything of Alethia. "And she ran before she could finish it."

"That Vance kid must have let something slip. She realized she'd be dead the moment she proved it worked. So she destroyed her lab and ran."

Rewind. New Dawn's worst nightmare. Between that and memory flooding, the foundations of their rule—their *control*— would be fatally undermined.

She moves her king, though she doesn't know anymore if that golden obelisk was ever really hers. "And the memory flooding?" she asks, settling the piece in the middle of the board as in a ritual slaughter. "Did you find out?"

The knight slams into it from the side. "Your dream first."

HE PROJECTS IT ONTO THE SIDE OF THE BUILDING FOR ANYONE to see. Did he think she'd care? She pops the remix and slides into her dreams like a warrior, ready to do battle. She's found her anger again, that molten hot, emboldening thing, though she's not sure who most deserves it. Terry, with his weaponized hypocrisy, his ironic T-shirts and meticulous suborning of every good thing in her life? Or Jordan, too weak to stand up to him? Or Dee, designed for betrayal, but so loyal in its own child-like way? Perhaps Alethia, still, who must have loved her even as she tricked Seshet into laying herself bare. She could hate Doc Young, destroying Little Delta's equilibrium for generations with his mind-twisting parties and the whispering idea, which New Dawn cannot kill, that there is something more, something different, something *real* out beyond the margins. Or no, the only real target is herself. Seshet, who used to be Deidre, a girl who wanted to travel the world with her mother, to see all the places where her soul could still be her own. Seshet, who felt that raw possibility of her own soul for the first time this past week, dreaming with Alethia.

She uses it all. The countless seashells on the beach, each one a penance. The way she and Alethia made love while melding dreams, until the memory and its voice merged into counterpart harmony, a perfect chord that was this ever-present moment. She dreams herself at the top of the obelisk looking down, then at the bottom with the rest, staring up in awe and terror. "I own my own soul!" dream Seshet shouts. "I own my own soul!" the crowd echoes. She is running now, past the obelisk, past the limits of Old Town, to a hill with an oak tree naked in winter. She is watching a woman jerking against the restraining hands of two black-clad men, tall as the oak. The woman gags, turns to Seshet one last time. Her eyes speak love and incandescent anger. The men shove her in the car. They drive her away.

Behind Seshet, the tree moves its branches in the wind. "You own your own soul," they say.

"IT'S NO ONE PERSON," DOC YOUNG TOLD HER. "THIS GENERA-tion of kids growing up with remixed Nevermind and recollectors everywhere, their brains are wired a little different. Word is someone in the obelisk leaked a way to confuse the recollectors. Double up your boring memories and they won't check for anything more interesting. So people started doing that if they could learn the trick. These kids got so good at it they started playing around. Left funny scenes they made up in their own heads. You get points every time you use a recollector, so they start making cash. Get their friends in on it. You can't tell what they're do-ing because they stumbled on a glitch in the code. If you go to a recollector first thing after the morning download, you can load it up, fool it into thinking your memories are enough for the whole day. Everyone else who uses it gets a point, but their real memories get trashed while their ID gets attached to the ones stuck in the buffer, the ones from the morning. It's a stupid bug, Seshet. They just exploited it, made it look like every citizen of Little Delta was dreaming of flaming vaginas or whatever they used that day. At first it was a game. But it's more serious now, isn't it? Now it might be revolution. But what do I know? I'm getting too old for this. I think this will be my last season. I don't want to die a Torch."

Seshet winced.

He put a hand on her shoulder. "That was your mother, in the dream?"

Seshet nodded.

"And you didn't know they'd taken her?"

"I was . . ." She cleared her throat. "They must have suppressed the memory. But I remember now . . . that's why I wanted to become a Librarian. I wanted to find her again."

"Good luck," he told her. "Don't be too hard on Lethe. She's finding her own way."

And now she's in her office again, more alone than she has ever been.

Alethia has left a dozen messages on their private channel, but Seshet doesn't check them. Dee is shut down, silent as death. Jordan wasn't even in the clerks' office. She has no friends. Her life was the obelisk, and the obelisk is a lie. She has always known that, but she thought that its lie could be in the service of the greater good. She has seen people go on to happy lives after Counseling who might have died without it. She has held all of their brutal, impossible memories in her own mind so that theirs might be clear. She has watched the recollection point system provide housing and food to all but the most determinedly antisocial. Little Delta has become a byword for everything good that New Dawn has to offer this country.

But her mother never left.

With pained, jerky movements she calls up the personnel

records for all of New Dawn's facilities. She searches for her mother's first name, but it's too common, and they would likely have changed it. Records on Torch case histories are restricted; she can access them, but the search would be flagged. Does she care? She doesn't know anymore.

Almost as an afterthought, she calls the tech chief and informs her of the bug responsible for the memory flooding. The horrified chief promises it will be addressed in time for tomorrow morning's harvest.

An hour later, Terry knocks on her door.

"That was fast," she says, and then realizes that Dee can't hear. It's forty minutes in dedicated-path aircar from Greenfriars to the obelisk. It seems she is to keep her position, for now. He wouldn't have bothered to knock, otherwise.

"How is the hero of the hour?" he says. "I brought some bubbly so we can toast."

"Please tell me its active ingredient is alcohol, not THC."

"It'll go straight to your liver, I promise." He hums to himself as he sets the crystal flutes on her coffee table and pops the cork from a bottle of extremely expensive champagne.

"All that fuss over a computer error!" he says, toasting her. "I don't understand modern technology at all."

"No," Seshet says, clinking her glass with his and taking a sip. "We just call people computers."

"Well, it's a metaphor! Do you want to tell me how you cracked the code?"

I treated with the enemy and was betrayed by everyone I have ever loved, except the woman I spent most of my life thinking betrayed me. "Not very interesting. I followed some kids until I realized they must be doing something with the recollectors themselves."

He nods. "Well, like I told you, Seshet, your nomination for the Minneapolis directorship is a formality now. Congratulations."

She clinks glasses again, and waits. She ought to be weary unto death, but she admits to a deep and morbid curiosity as to Terry's real reason for interrupting his evening weed-and-video-game session to see her personally.

"And I wanted to just mention, Seshet," he says, rewarding her, "when you move to Minneapolis, there will be no trouble if you'd like to bring people along with you. Your favorite clerks. Your tailor. Your hairdresser—that's a joke. I hope you won't be offended when I say we've been pleased to see you found yourself a companion at last! Of course, officially we at New Dawn frown on homosexuality, but it's not a problem at our level. No one's going to call the Minneapolis Director a dirty computer, no matter who she sleeps with! In fact, a little grit in *our* systems makes us stronger. We've been worried, to be honest, watching you hole yourself away up here. You're a paragon of virtue, but virtue needs to bend sometimes, or it might break. You understand that, right?"

Her voice is smooth, pleasant. "Of course, Terry."

"Now, we understand that your Alethia is someone who might be considered a *very* dirty computer. She got up to all sorts of mischief in her youth. That's what Vance Fox tells us, in any case. Of course, he's not the cleanest machine himself, as you well know. The facts, let me be frank, don't matter so much as the *impression*. But you have nothing to worry about, Seshet. In Minneapolis, you and Alethia will both be under my personal protection. We'll even find some good work for her. Her talents are wasted making skin creams, wouldn't you say?"

"That might be," she says distantly. She takes a long, slow sip of champagne. Why is it so expensive, exactly? It tastes just like the bile rising up her throat.

"Well, you propose it to your girl and then we'll make the arrangements. You have my full support, Seshet. I'm glad to have been the one to see your potential, all those years ago."

Just like Terry, just like New Dawn, to be so sure they made her. What were her paltry dreams of control, compared to this white man's bulldozer of self-assurance?

He rises and so does she. He shakes her hand. She keeps her grip strong, professional. Just at the door, he stops as though he's forgotten his keys.

"By the way," he says. "I thought you might like to know—your mother is still alive. She's been a Torch at our Nashville facility for the last thirty years. The Mother Superior tells me she's an excellent assistant, quite happy."

SHE CALLS JORDAN INTO HER OFFICE THAT NIGHT. HE STANDS in her open doorway frozen, limned in light.

"Come in, if you're going to," she says. "You know I don't like the hall light."

"Yes, yes," he says. "It ruins your night vision."

The door slides closed behind him. She turns back to her picture window, to the lights and the darkness of the only city she has ever loved.

"Terry told you to find Alethia for me, didn't he?"

"Yes. Seshet—"

"I just can't understand—how did you know? Or was it Terry? How could you have guessed she'd be so . . ." But Seshet has no words to describe how Alethia is. She's finally read the messages on their private channel. She erased them all, but the last one strobes across the screen of her mind like a warning, or a lighthouse beacon.

"Terry wanted you to date *someone*, Seshet," Jordan says. "I don't know why. I just told him I knew the right woman. Because *you* told me who she was."

Her spine stiffens. "*I* told you . . ."

"You told me you loved her and you wanted a second chance. You begged me to help you try if you ever found her again."

Her stomach lurches as what was left of the ground beneath

her crumbles to vanity and dust. *"Again?"* But even as she falls she's remembering that hole in her memory, that precision cut where the first time they laid eyes on one another ought to be.

No one is better at memory suppression than Seshet. Her style is distinctive.

"Three years ago. She introduced herself to you at some club. You fell in love and dated for two months. But it all went to pieces, Seshet. You started to doctor her memories. You suppressed arguments, amplified your good qualities, you know . . ."

"What we do." Seshet's voice is hard.

Jordan offers her a watery laugh. "What we do. And when she found out . . ."

Seshet closes her eyes. "She would have hated me. And instead of accepting that, I . . ."

"You memory suppressed every trace of your relationship. Both hers and your own. You told me what you were doing just in case you had another chance. You wanted me to warn you, and I tried!"

She leans her forehead against the glass. "I'm sorry, Jordan. You tried, and I went straight back to hell. I didn't even hesitate." She'd stopped, though. What had changed?

Vance Fox, the threat that prompted Alethia's confession. Seshet must not have known the truth of Alethia's double life back then. She certainly hadn't practiced dreaming with remixed Nevermind. That had opened her in ways that she hadn't known were possible. She'd remembered her mother. Was that enough? Had she changed enough? Were their good memories enough, if their bad memories couldn't ever be erased? But isn't that what life had been like before the Repository, before New Dawn? Whatever choices you made, you couldn't just erase your own knowledge of them. You had to live with them until you died.

Unlike her father, happily ignorant of how he had pawned off her mother as a dirty computer so he could be free to marry his mistress. He'd died in his bed a few years ago, surrounded by grandchildren. She'd always known he was an asshole, but she'd felt guilty about it until her initiation, never able to pinpoint why.

Was that freedom from memory? Or just a decades-long con?

"Seshet?"

"Yes, Jordan?"

"You also taught me to monitor myself."

She laughs. "One good deed for my ledger."

"And I taught Alethia."

The laughter snags. "You taught . . . when?"

"After our conversation, when I realized you must be doing it again. You had the same look as last time. So I met her in a cafe and we practiced."

"But, Jordan, that was over a week ago!"

Why didn't Alethia kick her out then? Because she needed help with Vance Fox. But afterward? The remixes, the dreams? But Seshet never touched Alethia's memories afterward.

"For what it's worth," Jordan says by the door, "I think you're a good person. If I survive this place, it will be because of you . . . and Dee."

In its own way, this startles her more than anything else he's said tonight. She faces him at last. "Dee?"

A band of light from a passing car catches the edge of his tremulous smile. "You were taking a shower and it let me in. It told me how to double up my memories to fool the recollectors. It said it had been doing that with you for years."

Doc Young said someone from the obelisk had leaked the technique. But Dee and Jordan?

"Jordan," she says, "what are you doing here that you need to hide from the recollectors?"

But he just shakes his head. She could raid his memories, dig behind his buffers, hunt for his secrets. But even if she can't have Alethia, she's done violating the minds of those she loves to shore up her own fragile security.

"Good night, Jordan."

"Good night, Director. See you in the morning."

She can't read his smile entirely, but the warmth is real, and that's good enough.

If you find me, come only as yourself. I don't know if we can be together. I don't know if I can ever really trust you. But I know we don't have a chance if you stay there.

This is the last message Seshet received from the love of her life. Alethia has gone to ground, her careful second chance destroyed because of Seshet. If Seshet finds her again, it can't be as Director Librarian. Not even as Seshet, though Deidre hardly feels like her own name either. And if she stays Seshet, if she moves to Minneapolis, she will have to forget about Alethia forever. And not in the easy, New Dawn way. In the hard, old way of forgetting, which is remembering with grief.

If she goes to Alethia, on the other hand, she will lose any chance of seeing her mother one last time. Funny how Terry knew immediately about her personnel searches. Had he set an alert all this time, waiting for her to guess? How many layers of leverage have they built up over the years, carefully waiting for its useful moment? Countless, she's sure. What's the point of memory collection if you don't use what you steal?

At last, she boots up her Memory Keeper.

"Seshet!" says Dee, bouncing from monitor to monitor in a frenzy. "I've lost nearly twenty-four hours!"

"I'm sorry, Dee."

"Are you still mad at me?"

"No, honey. No."

Dee is quiet for a while. "You figured out who suppressed your memories of Alethia, didn't you?"

"I did."

"You made me promise not to say! I gave you hints."

"You did. You were good and loyal, Dee. Thank you."

"You never thank me, Seshet."

Seshet grimaces. "I'm beginning to think I'm not a very good person."

"Alethia left you?"

"Not . . . exactly."

"You did much better this time! You only suppressed her once! You did it sixteen times before. Maybe if you try again you won't suppress her at all."

If Seshet's heart is breaking, why can't she stop laughing? Her stomach hurts and her eyes are streaming before she gasps to a halt.

Dee sighs. "You're right. It doesn't work as well as your bosses think it does."

If you find me, come only as yourself.

But who is she? If Alethia really knew, would she have written that? What has Alethia done to deserve Seshet's bullish blundering into her life?

Then again, Doc Young said his Lethe took risks. Maybe even enough of a risk to finish a revolutionary drug that she abandoned five years ago?

Maybe even enough of a risk to love a reformed Memory Librarian learning, too late, to let go?

From the top of the golden obelisk, she traces the shoreline where the lights of Little Delta go down to the darkness of Old Town. Where, among those shadows, might she find the upside-down obelisk and the aging king who reigns there? Where might she find a woman whose dreams are memories and all her own?

Her left hand closes in a fist. With a conscious effort, she relaxes it.

"Did you know that Mom never left us, Dee? They took her."

Beneath them, lights flash. "Some part of you always remembers."

NEVERMIND

Part 1

Jane stepped into the desert night, slipping out of the steady, comforting beat of the Pynk Hotel. Away from its familiar bass lines—the sounds of agitated mattresses, the deep snores, bodies pressed against doors and walls, the soft breathy melodies and grunting percussions—there was desert evening air. She missed the music of the hotel the moment she exited, even as the wind hit her face, just cool enough to mimic the feeling of misting water.

But there was still one familiar bass beat out here. Jane smiled, turning toward the sound of a steel-toed boot tapping a salvaged fender. Closer still, Jane heard the beat's permanent accompaniment, the mid-tenor humming to themselves as they nodded off, a moment's respite in between stripping the usable parts off a ruined vehicle.

"We heading to the Cave tonight?" They cracked one eye open curiously.

Perhaps they weren't nodding off, Jane realized as she shrugged. "Maybe I just wanted to say hey, Neer."

Neer snorted as they stood up. They were only a couple of inches taller than Jane, and at least half of that from the boots. Still, they tilted their head down sometimes as they looked at people, as if it made them just the slightest bit shorter. Jane didn't comment on it all that often anymore. "If you wanted to say hey, you would have been on my ass to get to bed before you even stepped out the door." Neer's imitation of Jane sounded nothing like her, beyond their intonation, yet they persisted. "'Neer, if you don't get your Black ass to sleep, I'm going to convene the Chord and force a vote for you to go on vacation.'"

"Okay, you got me, sweetie. I could use a hand if you don't mind." Jane crooked her elbow, inviting Neer to link arms. As Neer complied, Jane laughed, and Neer's smile grew. Jane got a pang in her heart, more maternal perhaps than she felt for almost anyone at the hotel. It was as rare to see Neer smile like that as it was for Jane to be *this* vulnerable with anyone, except perhaps . . .

"Thought you would have stayed in tonight, with Zen leaving again in the morning."

There were more questions than that, hidden behind the words: why Zen wasn't here with Jane, for one. "She needs to rest. And besides . . ." Jane gestured loosely with her free hand. "If she's worried about me, she might try to delay again. And New Dawn doesn't stop its work just because I'm having a bad night."

Neer accepted the answer serenely, leaving Jane to her thoughts on the way to the Cave. She tried to focus on the beat of their footsteps instead, Neer's boots clomping alongside Jane's more muffled sneakers. Jane's steps, despite her height, were always longer than Neer's, surer, and gave the appearance of Jane guiding Neer into the Cave, although Neer knew the path as well as anyone at the hotel.

The pair stopped in front of the Cave, sliding their arms out of their union. Neer sucked on their teeth, looking at the entrance.

Jane narrowed her eyes. "You don't have to go in if you don't want to."

Neer shrugged off the suggestion. "It's just us and your memories, right? I'm golden." Neer forced a smirk, and Jane could imagine that if Neer smirked at any of the other occupants closer to their age like that, Neer would be dangerously, delightfully popular. "Pynk, even."

Jane rolled her eyes and marched inside. Just on the edge of the land around the hotel, every step deeper into the Cave turned the sand darker, damper, until green patches of moss and grass grew sparingly in the darkest soil. The walls were cold and sometimes slick with moisture; a few times water dripped down from the stone above.

She liked to close her eyes when she stepped into the Cave, although it wasn't necessary.

When she spoke in the Cave, the echo carried the deepest notes of her voice, the reverb filling the darkness as if she were on a stage. Jane let her head drop back as she hummed a melody from before the Pynk Hotel or even New Dawn's capturing her. She let herself sway to the dripping water until she heard a shake and a snap, and the blackness behind her eyelids turned red.

She opened her eyes and shifted; Neer had pulled out a flashlight from their belt clip, resting it on a large piece of flatter stone. It lit up the onyx-swirled gray stone, not like a spotlight but like a candle.

An intimate performance.

"Same as usual?" Neer asked. Jane nodded, slowly settling down into the dirt, kneeling. Neer took a breath and then recited the opening:

"Tell me a story you don't want to forget."

Jane pressed her hands against the rich soil. When she had first arrived at the hotel, she'd questioned the way that the Cave was used. This rich dirt could have been moved into the sun to grow trees and vegetables. The pushback had been immediate.

It was one of the earliest things that the occupants of the Pynk Hotel taught her: this cave *was* growing things, was being used for growth.

Because instead of tubers or flowers, *memory* found purchase here.

"When I arrived a second time," she spoke, as much to herself as to Neer, as much to plant her hands and her heat in the soil and hope to find her roots, *"I knew the path by the way the sun traveled across the sand, reflected off the shitty car that we'd rewired on the way from . . ."*

She paused. For a second, it wasn't that she didn't *know* the name of New Dawn, but rather that the feel of it was too big, too intense to come out as words.

New Dawn was at the tip of Jane's tongue like a flame atop a matchhead. The sterile walls, the way numbered names and faces stood over her as if to comfort, as if to assure her that *clean* was the only thing she could ever want, desire. Cleanse the dirtiness from her mind, her lips, her tongue, the way her thighs moved, so that then—and only then—she would be something holy.

But it was the dirt in between her fingers now that was real, not their lights and dictates. Not the dirt they perceived. She reminded herself of the dirt before her, under her—the real dirt—of the way it shifted in her hands; at her fingertips it was suddenly smooth and cold, the slab they'd placed her on in that New Dawn facility. Around her wrists, dirt tightened, the straps that they'd held her down with, and she remembered that fighting against *these* would be fighting against the flow of memory, not New Dawn acolytes.

"From where, Jane?" Neer's voice broke through, like it always did. They had never been at the facility with Jane, which was another reason why Jane had asked Neer to help her. Neer was part of the present.

"From a New Dawn facility."

"Which one?"

Jane was silent.

"I'm sorry," Neer said, "I thought . . . maybe you'd know this time."

Neer wanted to help, Jane told herself. *"Ché drove and Zen held me up when I could barely stand. We shredded our New Dawn clothing, tore off sleeves and shortened long skirts, making belts and bracelets from headpieces. We'd hid boots and leather jackets before we'd gone in."*

"Did you wear those when you arrived at the hotel?"

"I . . . couldn't remember the drop site, which was when I got scared," Jane recited. She felt the moment of panic in her rooted fingertips, up her arms, into her breathing. *"New Dawn's list of Standards was still too loud, shoving out memories that were* mine. *But I remembered . . ."*

This was what made Jane wake up and need the Cave tonight, she realized. This was the moment in her memory where things had . . . cluttered, filled with the taste and smell of Nevermind, the gas New Dawn had used to try to clean her body of her soul and her memories.

She'd stared at the ceiling, unable to recall what she'd once remembered. And that was what the Cave was for.

Neer's voice softened; they recognized where Jane needed support. *"You remembered something important, Jane. Something you told me before. Do you want me to remind you? Or do you want to let it grow yourself?"*

Jane wanted to seed the memory herself, wanted to push it to grow and take root and never ever let anyone pluck it away again. She took a deep breath, though; she welcomed Neer's guidance, welcomed the way that Neer cataloged every story that Jane thought needed remembering. Healthy plants often had a caring gardener. Even as she was frustrated with herself for needing someone else. *"Tell me what I remembered."*

Neer took a deep breath that recalled the one Jane took moments before. *"You remembered the route to the hotel,"* Neer shared, and the words caused little blossoms of recollection in Jane's mind, in the coolness of the dirt. *"You led Zen to us, sure that you would find help to clear out the Nevermind haze. You and Zen were welcomed like old friends, like old lovers reunited. It took years, but in the Pynk your mind was safe again. In the Pynk you helped us as we helped you."*

Jane smiled, because the end of her story came back to her. She welcomed it the way she and Zen had been welcomed. She focused on the warmth of that welcome, of how the Pynk Hotel was a place that opened its arms to anyone who located themselves in womanhood, however they came to understand it. *"And when the gas of Nevermind threatened to come back, there was always the dirt. The solid dirt in the Cave that the Pynk Hotel shared with me, to heal."*

Jane pulled her hands out of that dirt. Black soil still clung to her fingers, and she was pleased. New Dawn labeled her a dirty computer, and so there was a certain satisfaction in this dirt saving her. It would outlast any attempt of theirs to "clean" her, to scrub away her memories.

Neer was at her side in case Jane needed help to get up. Jane had it, though, waiting until she was standing to throw an arm over Neer's shoulder. "The dirt is still good, Neer."

"It always is."

JANE REMEMBERED, VAGUELY, ZEN GIVING HER A KISS AT SUNrise, urging her to wake up, but it was another hour or two before Jane made her way out from under the blankets. She wasn't alone, though; Zen may have already started prepping to head out into the desert, but Guitar was still there, wrapping around Jane like a lanky-limbed octopus.

"Girl, ain't nobody trying to be up this early" came Gui's voice, muffled by Jane's hair. Jane thought she'd gone to sleep with it braided but . . . right, she'd undone it while walking back to the hotel with Neer. Foolishness, leaving it as a problem for future her to pick through.

At the time, though, it had made so much sense. The past can be like that.

"You're right, Gui." Jane chuckled. "But Zen's *already* up, and probably packing the car."

There was a pause, and then: "Shit. Guess we should go say bye, huh?"

"I *guess*." Jane smacked Gui's side playfully as both rolled out of the bed.

Waking up next to Gui was nice, with her strong arms and catlike stretches, but even nicer was the fact that it had been years since Jane had last woken up panicked because she couldn't feel Zen beside her—or worse, couldn't recall the beautiful dirtiness of what it felt like to be in her arms. She could wake up on a morning that Zen was going on the road without fear; not only was she not alone, but she knew Zen would return.

And while Zen was gone, Jane knew she could close her eyes and reminisce, something that New Dawn had once tried so fiercely to steal from her.

Gui and Jane showered and dressed quickly. Like most at the hotel, their outfits shared scraps of fabric: repurposed older clothing stitched together to make new garments and fashions, with hand-me-downs and hand-me-ups worn with equally joyous flair that reminded Jane of back when she used to be able to go to thrift shops with friends as a teenager. Jane's shorts were cuffed with the same material used for Gui's skirt. The wrap Jane used as a temporary fix for her hair was also a pocket on Gui's shirt. Once put together, their outfits were castoff couture meets salvaged streetwear, their personalities and energy on display in every piece.

When they made it outside, a group was already milling around Zen's Cadillac, the same Cadillac that once carried Jane to the hotel. Everyone had their own schedule, their own things to do for the community—whether it be farming or salvage, in addition to the creative pursuits that filled their days—but it was uncommon for quite this much of the hotel to be awake this early. Zen's leaving was special, though, and they wanted to be able to see her off.

Jane watched Zen slam the trunk closed before stepping forward. "I know you're not leaving without saying goodbye."

Zen's dark eyes sparkled with mischief. "One: I've never done it before and I'm not gonna start today, and two . . . I was about to send some of the girls to try and wake you up, Sleeping Beauty." There was laughter over Jane's shoulder, and since they were all in good spirits, Jane saw no reason to make a comment about it. She did raise an eyebrow at Zen for encouraging them, and Zen gave her a reassuring smile. Quieter, she said, "Seriously, I was going to make sure to see you, babe."

Jane let Zen place her hands on her cheeks, lifting Jane's face up and giving her a quick kiss.

"How long is this scouting trip for again?" Jane asked.

"A couple of weeks," Zen promised. "Ché reached out about a few young computers who'd gotten away from New Dawn. Wanna give them supplies, tell them about life after the facilities . . ." Zen sighed, the first shadow over her cheerful mood. "And check and make sure they aren't New Dawn plants."

Jane shuddered. New Dawn didn't do it often, but sometimes the easiest way to figure out where rebels were was to give them someone to save. Over the years, Ché and Zen had gotten very good at helping figure out whether they had to rescue someone or avoid a trap—and had even managed to dirty up a few of the cleansed in the process.

"You got this," Jane said, kissing her back.

"*We've* got this," Zen corrected. She glanced over Jane's shoulder as she moved her hands away. "And Gui, you better keep our girl Jane company while I'm away."

Jane turned just in time to see Gui wink. "The things I do for my duty." Gui let her voice playfully drop into a bedroom pitch.

"We like those things you do," Zen retorted. "I'm looking forward to them when I get back, so stay safe."

Gui snorted. "We're all getting ready for festival. No one's going to get in trouble."

"I *like* when my music starts trouble." Jane found comfort in the annual festival. It was a showcase for all the creative work that the hotel did during the year, be it singing or fashion or painting, storytelling in the form of words and film and stage and dance . . . the occupants of the Pynk Hotel did it all. "Shame you're going to miss it this year, Z."

"You'll have to do a dramatic reenactment for me when I get back."

"We'll see about that—"

"Oh, Jane, good, you're up!" Jane and Zen turned at the sound of Nomie's voice. Nomie halted her walk-run only steps away from Zen's car, suddenly realizing that she'd interrupted goodbyes. "Oh, uh, sorry, Zen, but we were having some issues with this truck we were salvaging, and I wanted to ask Jane—"

Jane and Zen glanced at each other. Having escaped New Dawn and brought more so-called dirty computers to the hotel over time, Jane had grown into a position of leadership at the hotel. Not intentionally, and she certainly wasn't in *charge*— things were decided by the committee, by the Chord coming to harmony via vote—but she knew her way around the hotel and, more important, the world *outside* of it in a different way from most. She was wary of what the smell of *legendary* and *heroic* could do, and gently sidestepped anything that resembled *authority*. She was happy to be a counselor, an adviser, and voted along with the rest of the conclave.

But that didn't really slow the day-to-day requests. "If it's salvage issues, why don't you ask Neer? They know engines and metal better than I do."

Nomie shrugged. "It's not, uh . . . technical?" She was embarrassed. "Pel and Rhapsody are—"

"Ah." It was a personal disagreement that Nomie was trying to nip in the bud, then, but Rhapsody and Pel were both grown, stubborn spirits compared to Nomie's barely nineteen self. Jane doubted that either of them even knew Nomie had come running to seek advice. "Then *definitely* grab Neer to keep an eye on that salvage while I finish with Zen. I'll be over in a second."

Nomie nodded gratefully before running back toward the edge of the territory. Jane shook her head. "Well, I wanted this to be a little bit longer of a goodbye, but . . ."

"*You got a job, babe, you got work to do,*" Zen sang teasingly. "I can't keep Ché waiting anyway."

"Send him my love."

This time, Zen kissed Jane's forehead softly, and Jane felt the curve of her smile. "Always do. Take care of everyone—and make sure to take care of *yourself.*" Even Zen knew better than Jane that no matter how she avoided it, Jane was a guiding force at the hotel.

"Back at you."

Jane lingered only for a moment as Zen finished up saying goodbye to the others, starting to walk by the time Zen was driving out into the desert. There were always worries, of course: New Dawn, bounty-hunting blushounds, the elements . . . but Jane trusted Zen to handle herself, and trusted Zen and Ché to support each other as well. That lightened the load that she'd used to carry when Zen left.

The hotel itself helped with that. It was a community in every sense of the word, the residents supporting each other physically, emotionally, and spiritually. It was the freedom that Jane had loved before New Dawn, with a place to call home as well. When she was worried, she never had to be alone.

Even on the short walk to find Nomie and the others, Jane could savor the sight of that community in action. She watched a few folk pulling apart an old refrigerator for parts by some rocks, two of them practicing harmonies on a new song. There were a few occupants coming in and out of the diner, and Jane overheard them chatting about the meals they wanted to make for the upcoming festival. She jumped at the sound of a loud honking pattern; it was Transitive Property, a newly formed musical trio that was working on an experimental concept album about gender.

All the groups had something else in common, aside from uniting as queer and woman-aligned: they'd sought out an escape from a world that dealt in painful binaries, in good or bad, dirty or clean. Everyone at the Pynk Hotel was here to experiment with art, with freedom, with *life,* and whatever that meant for them.

It was why Jane could heal here, and why Jane stayed. There was so much self-discovery and reflection with healing the scars that New Dawn left, and New Dawn had made sure to create a world outside the hotel where few people had the freedom for either. Here, those were encouraged and supported in a way that Jane had always dreamed of.

It was hard not to think about what made Pynk a safe place as Jane moved into the territory right outside the hotel. They kept the perimeter as safe as they could with warning systems, electrical trip wires, and such—normally it was just to discourage animals that could bite and poison from getting too close, but there was always the worry of New Dawn. New Dawn struggled to track down the hotel because of the desert and its sand, as well as the Pynk's general off-the-grid-ness. Personally maintained generators and a reliance on salvage meant that there wasn't much that could lead New Dawn to them, except trying to find a scouting party and following them back.

In addition, Zen and Gui always theorized that New Dawn wanted to avoid making martyrs of those at the hotel. If they could decisively clean every woman in a raid, perhaps they'd hit hard, but perhaps . . . perhaps New Dawn worried about how those they hadn't deemed "dirty" and in need of cleaning would react.

Jane wasn't sure if that was wishful thinking, a way of appreciating the power of the hotel as a problem to New Dawn, but she liked to believe it. Still, the farther from the hotel she went, the more *aware* she was of the threat, as if the danger literally grew under the sands she moved across.

But as Jane approached Nomie and the others, she told herself it was all fine. She wasn't alone in the sands. It helped to hear their voices on the approach, as if moving closer to a stressed but still audible safety.

"—isn't *environmental* damage, Rhapsody." Pel's voice was a restrained soprano, tense as she tried to not raise her volume.

"It's *possible,* is all I'm saying. Not that I *know* what it is." Rhapsody was on a tear, her heart-shaped face showing a blend of rage and frustration. She was gesturing heavily at what Jane thought was one of the hotel's few security precautions: an electrical trip wire trigger trap in case anyone tried to approach the territory from places other than the main roads. Rhapsody had an old green-gray metal helmet in her hand, so she must have just come from a salvage/scouting run—Pel had a thicker padded jacket on as well. "The thing is, neither of us know. I'm just uninterested in panicking about it."

None of the hotel residents *liked* having to don the padding or helmets, but there were threats on salvage runs that they couldn't predict. All roles at the hotel were determined by volunteering, but that was even more true for salvagers and scouts.

Rhapsody, Neer, and Pel were regular volunteers for those runs. Rhapsody and Pel were adventurers at heart; Neer was a tinkerer. And right now, Neer seemed to be avoiding the debate by doing exactly that: examining the damage to the trap that Jane was too far away to see.

"You're interested in being foolish about—" Pel noticed Jane's presence (once Jane cleared her throat to get them to be quiet).

"Jane." She tilted her head in greeting. Normally, they might have hugged or kissed, but neither of them thought that appropriate in the moment.

"Heard that there was a . . . nontechnical issue I might be able to help with," Jane offered. She gestured with her chin over at the trap. "Looks pretty technical from here."

Neer didn't look up from their crouch. "Technical report: the trigger box is fried, and the wires are shredded." Neer was moving some of the sand and rocks around the trap, revealing more of the wires that were usually obscured. "Doesn't look like a snake trigger either."

"Or bird, or coyote, or anything like that," Pel added, throwing a look Rhapsody's way.

"There was rain a couple of nights ago," Rhapsody pointed out. "Any of those animals plus the rain could cause all sorts of damage. Or"—Rhapsody's voice took on an accusatory tone— "maybe it was human error."

Jane raised an eyebrow. "What are you thinking?"

"Our main engi*neer* has been focusing on those truck salvages, and maybe should have scheduled more time for maintenance runs." Rhapsody was careful in her rage, but she doubled her emphasis by glaring at Neer.

Jane realized then that Rhapsody, rather than an extreme sense of focus, was the reason the crouched tinkerer wasn't looking up from their work. How much time had Rhapsody spent accusing Neer of incompetence before Jane arrived, or even just icing them out? And more important, why waste time like that?

She knew why, and it bothered her the way Rhapsody constantly targeted Neer. This was not new.

"My routine's been pretty regular," Neer muttered, lifting a couple of the wires. "Jane, look at this."

Jane wasn't sure whether to admire Neer's restraint or push them to defend themself, but she came over, crouching. "What's up?"

Neer held up a clutch of wires. Jane had spent a little time in all the different jobs at the hotel since arriving. If people were going to come to her for advice, she needed to know what she was talking about. That said, the darkened edges of the wiring didn't tell Jane much of anything. She shrugged and allowed Neer to explain. "The burnt parts could be a short."

"Which could be anything from needing to be replaced, to animals, to water damage," Rhapsody piped up.

"Or an overload," Neer allowed. "But . . ."

"But . . . ?" Jane took the wires in hand and squinted at them, trying to see what Neer saw. It took a moment, but finally, the pieces fell together. "We need to call a meeting of the Chord. Immediately."

Rhapsody was flabbergasted as Jane turned and stood. "What? Over repairs?"

"Over what we're going to do to protect ourselves."

Jane resisted the urge to look back west, in the direction that Zen had gone. They were more than capable of handling themselves as a commune, but still . . .

Either before or after the burning, those wires had been cleanly *sliced* in two. And that meant it was intentional.

THERE WERE CHORDS OF EVERY SIZE, USUALLY NO MORE THAN once a week. Small Chords were convened for different types of work—those who salvaged would convene about schedules or what parts of the desert needed to be covered, whereas those in charge of farming might convene to plan the harvest. Larger Chords came together once a month to discuss any issues individuals might have. The largest Chords weren't typically convened more than every four to six months, and only for the most important of decisions.

On the rare occasion that Jane asked for a Chord, they had to sit outside of the hotel to make sure everyone could attend and hear one another. This time was no exception. Jane sat on the hood of a pickup truck, her legs tucked underneath her as she waited for Pel, Rhapsody, and Nomie to share what they'd found. Gui sat in the back of the truck, legs sprawled out.

The hotel wasn't a community that typically held tension the way it was doing now. It was a place of healing, of freedom and escape. As Jane looked out over the group, though, it felt as if the air were coiling and then recoiling around the discussion of the damage. The occupants glanced back and forth at one another, and at Jane; they were wondering why others were talking before Jane, she was sure. The information being imparted was necessary, but everyone was waiting with bated breath to see what Jane would contribute.

"I've been doing salvage runs for a couple of years now," Rhapsody said. "I know environmental and animal damage. I think that's what this is, and I'm *sorry*, but this feels like it's pulling us from important community chores." Rhapsody glanced over at Jane, tilting her head apologetically, holding her hands up. "I got a bit of an attitude back at the trap site, but I don't really think any person had anything to do with it. New Dawn doesn't snip wires."

But they do fuck with computers, Jane joked to herself dryly. Rhapsody's perspective made sense; she hadn't ever been in New Dawn's custody, and it was a rare, rare experience that New Dawn hunters made it close to the hotel. If Jane hadn't personally experienced New Dawn's cruelty, she wouldn't be so sure either.

"The wires look sliced, though." Gui spoke up as she lifted a hand to Jane's leg reassuringly. Jane appreciated the gesture, even though she didn't need it. Gui had promised Zen to keep an eye out, after all. "That's not an animal messing around. Not unless there's a coyote out there with a pair of scissors."

Nobody seemed in the mood to laugh. "Do we *know* they

were cut?" Jane glanced over at another commune member who spoke up. "Those aren't thick wires."

"My eyesight's still pretty good," Jane countered. "And I'm not the only one who saw it."

A couple of occupants glanced over at Neer, who was leaning on the side wall of the hotel, standing. Neer looked back and forth, skittish at the group gaze, before nodding. "Cut and burned, maybe by a lighter or matches. I'm not sure how, but I'm certain it was intentional."

There was muttering, and then another voice, "Who would *do* that?"

"Couldn't be New Dawn," someone else said. "They like their stuff 'clean.'" There was derisive laughter from the Chord—the typical, disgusted reaction to New Dawn's rejection of the dirty.

Jane wanted to laugh along with them, with the kind of freedom being at the Pynk Hotel had given her soul, but unfortunately there *was* an answer to that question. One that no one was going to like. Jane let go of a low whistled melody, normally a sign that she needed to speak. They quieted.

"Blushounds."

The muttering started back up at the pronouncement, full of the disbelief and worry that Jane had expected. Jane hadn't intended the kind of dramatic bomb drop that mentioning blushounds caused, but she also knew that trying to speak right after offering her theory would just be additional noise. So she let them get it out of their system, understanding what the group was thinking when it heard *blushounds*.

Because if New Dawn was the bogeyman, then the blushounds were the bogeyman's forward scouts. No one knew whether they were a natural mutation or somehow created from New Dawn's cleansing attempts. What everyone knew was that they were technically humans and made their presence felt because New Dawn needed someone or something tracked.

Blushounds worked for other morally ambiguous people as well, which made this even trickier. If they were involved here, though, Jane was pretty certain they were using their "talents" for New Dawn.

Their greatest tool was a twisted form of empathy, quite literally. They had the ability to sense—to "sniff"—emotions left by people. Negative emotions were easiest for them to track, but trained blushounds knew how to track any emotional traces left behind on cloth or in rooms. That, and the way that using this skill caused a brilliant, almost glowing blush and heat across their skin, had given them their name.

And Jane had encountered them before. Because of that experience, she knew that if anyone could find the hotel, it would have to be a blushound. They'd be the probe before the attack, but there *would* be an attack. Not by the blushound—they found close contact overwhelming and at times psychically painful. Everyone's emotions were laid bare like an overbearing perfume to them, and as far as anyone knew, they lacked the capability to shut it off. So while they could do the tracking, it still meant this was all just prologue.

Nomie was edging toward a nauseated shade of gray. "But what would they want?"

Everything, Jane thought.

Gui was throwing Jane a narrow-eyed, confused look; Jane hadn't shared this theory yet with the other woman. It wasn't out of a lack of trust, but rather Jane taking time to try to sort out what a blushound would mean. They were employed with a purpose, a target, a job. There was someone on the other end of that leash, and they were looking for something. And without knowing what that was . . .

What if it's me?

She didn't want to think that; New Dawn had lost track of her years ago, as far as she knew, and she hadn't done anything to put herself back on their radar. Maybe they were after Zen, but if that was the case, messing with security didn't make any sense, not when she could be easily caught away from the hotel.

She looked over the other occupants of the Pynk Hotel. Fear stabbed her momentarily, but as was typically the case with her, it mutated quickly to righteous anger. It could be any of them; it could be New Dawn targeting all of them. How *dare* they try to shatter the freedom of those at the Pynk, their safety and creativity? Yes, New Dawn might want the world "clean," but the Pynk Hotel wasn't part of their world. They'd be going well out of their way to waste their time on this community. Of course, she had gone through so much at the hands of the pious monsters who had attempted to scrub her sense of self from her brain, maybe it shouldn't be surprising that New Dawn wasn't content to let anything outside their pristine walls remain dirty.

To see that it might be happening again made her shake.

Staring down at her hands, Jane thought of all the fighting she'd done just to be sitting where she was. All the running. All the times her laughter, her bodily autonomy, and her love had been interrupted and ripped away by New Dawn's cold view of what being a person, a computer, really was. And how all of that was more impressions, echoes from her muscles and the dirt, rather than actual true remembrance.

Her palms ached, missing people and memories something painful.

"We don't have any evidence of it *being* a blushound yet," Pel was saying. Jane was startled by the woman's voice. She'd expected the dissent from Rhapsody, who was currently chewing her lip and contemplating the horror that Jane's theory suggested. But Pel . . . Jane had figured Pel was already on her side. Pel continued, "There are others out there . . . misogynists, for example, jealous of the family we have here." There were murmurs of acknowledgment. "But we've also survived people trying to push us out of the hotel before." That had been a long time ago, though. Jane didn't say anything, but those attacks were so deep in the past that half the current occupants might not remember how to fight back this time.

They could fight, yes. But Jane needed to convince them this push was happening first. Because Rhapsody was heartened by Pel's statement and was not seeing this threat the same way Jane was. "Pel's got a point. We've dealt with people trying to force so much on us. Capitalism for one; monogamy for another. Right now, without knowing anything else, I believe that we should keep an eye out, but work as usual. Us salvagers and scouts can even put in some double time, making sure that everything is in place, if that would make you feel better, Jane . . . ?"

It's not about me, she wanted to say. But Jane watched the way that the Chord grew less tense with Rhapsody's words. And she wasn't the leader, despite the way even Pel and Rhapsody were looking to her for permission. Besides, maybe they were right that even if there was something nefarious in the works, the Pynk could deal with it. They were *together,* and their survival in the desert, reliant on each other, proved that.

She just resented the idea that they would have to. That wasn't the *point.*

"I'll accept double shifts," Neer spoke up, probably louder than Jane had ever heard them. "It's my responsibility to make sure that our security is up to par."

Rhapsody spoke carefully. "It shouldn't be any single person's responsibility. We are all notes in the chord, and without it, the sound doesn't work." At that, Jane hid a smirk; Neer needed to be reminded about that every so often. "I'll take lead on opposite shifts." Rhapsody turned to the rest of the Chord. "Anyone else who wants to volunteer, let us know."

Jane found herself speaking before she intended to. "I'll do salvage runs as well." Someone who remembered what handling blushounds was like should be doing runs, especially if the hotel occupants were avoiding a larger strategy.

Pel nodded at Jane and then at Rhapsody; the argument between the two was buried. "That sounds like a strong plan. Let's finish this up with a vote to make sure everyone is on board with what the Chord will play."

Jane was quiet during the vote, thinking about cut wires, dirty computers, and being chased by hounds. But she made sure to raise her hand with the *aye*s when the time came.

"CLOTHES HAUL!"

Nomie's voice rang out from the front of the Pynk diner. Everyone, including those on kitchen duty, echoed her words in an excited chorus. Salvage wasn't always as joyous as this, but even Jane, lost in her thoughts about wiring, allowed herself a moment to . . .

She didn't like to use the word *forget* when she didn't have to, when it wasn't literal. The wounds of New Dawn sometimes made her forget, however temporary the memory lapse was. This was different, though; salvage allowed her to put aside the stress and trauma. That wasn't quite forgetting.

More, it was her *choice* to "forget."

Jane and Gui made it to the front couple of booths, where Nomie and Rhapsody were bringing in boxes of clothes. Boxes were cut into—already being prepped for repurposing elsewhere in the Pynk—to make it easier to sort through the new piles of thrifted, traded, and salvaged clothing.

Nomie was showing off a find that she'd claimed before even stepping into the diner; a purple-and-pink-polka-dotted faux fur coat. Some of the growing crowd were already cooing over how the colors popped against her dark skin, and Jane's smile grew.

Not even the traces of Nevermind that were surely still in her veins had taken the memory of the first time she'd been at the Pynk for a clothes exchange. The first time she and Zen had shown up at the hotel, without expecting anything, they were greeted and ushered to the front of the group. *Pick something that calls to you, that feels right on your skin. Wear it or deconstruct it,* they told her. *Make it into something new. And when it doesn't feel right anymore, we pass it along.*

She and Zen had picked matching pink sweaters, different shades but the same cut, selected because of the way the knit felt against both their own thighs and each other's. They were the simplest things that either had worn in years, and yet they felt as much theirs as anything else they'd chosen. Years later Jane understood why: both the simple sweaters and, later, the studded leather jackets they discovered were freedom, chosen because of what they meant at that moment.

Zen had filmed them trying on the new pieces, then put together a mini documentary. A memory of a memory.

The second time Jane arrived, she'd been clad half in the clothes from New Dawn and half with pieces she'd gathered on the road. She, Ché, and Zen had torn sleeves from their tunic tops—Ché the left, Zen the right, and Jane both sleeves. Zen had added a "dirty" hip-high split to her skirt, and Jane had replaced hers with Ché's old pants, after Ché traded New Dawn ornamentation with a traveling merchant for a new pair. When they got to the hotel, Ché offered to take the remaining New Dawn clothing with him, or maybe they could burn it, together.

Jane had declined then.

Years later, Jane still hadn't traded the pants or the sleeveless tunic. She hadn't destroyed them or worn them. She kept them tucked away and made sure she remembered where she'd gotten them from.

Where she'd come from.

"You picking that piece, babe?" Gui put an arm around Jane's waist from behind, and Jane realized she'd been frozen in place, her fingers on the stitching of an emerald-and-gold blazer. "It'd look good on you." Jane slipped on the jacket, turning in Gui's arms. Gui grinned. "You gotta."

"It'll be good to have a little extra something when we do the trip wire maintenance tonight anyway," Jane conceded.

Gui sighed. "You could have volunteered for the clothing run, you know. Instead of trying to be Jane the Hero."

Jane was taken aback by Gui's sudden concern—they hadn't spoken about things since the Chord, but Jane hadn't thought they needed to. She reached a hand up to Gui's cheek, rubbing the soft skin with the pad of her thumb. "You think I'm tryna be a hero by volunteering to make sure that the trip wires are in place?"

Gui glanced upward, a small tell that she was picking her words wisely. "I think you're stressing, and going out there 'instead of someone else,' in case your blushound theory is correct." Jane stilled. Did she really use that self-sacrificing phrase *that* often? "Hey, hey, hon, I'm not saying it's *not*, I'm saying that we don't need a single person sacrificing themselves. That's not very . . . Pynk of you."

This was the same thing Rhapsody had said to Neer. And as much as Jane didn't want to be the leader, the hero, it was a role she fell naturally into—subconsciously, even, she realized.

Jane tried to relax her muscles, taking off the blazer and stepping out of Gui's arm. "That's not what I'm doing. I'm just not about to see the writing in the sand and say it's someone else's job to deal with it. I've never asked anyone to do anything that I wouldn't do, and I'm not about to start now."

"I'm sorry, I—" When Jane turned, Gui wasn't looking at her. Instead, she had her head down, digging through some of the neon and animal-print fabrics that had been brought. The fabrics could become anything here, Jane thought idly. "I promised Zen I'd watch out for you."

"But watching out for me isn't the same as shielding me from the world outside the Pynk," Jane asserted. "I've been out there before, and as long as I'm not alone, I'll be fine. And that's the point of this, isn't it?" Jane gestured around the diner, at where Pel and Nomie were trading wigs and deciding which looked best with Nomie's new coat. "That we're not alone. So trust in that, all right?"

Gui let out a deep breath and nodded. "You're right."

"I know." Jane snorted. Gui was still nodding, a conversation going on in her head that Jane wasn't privy to.

"You should wear the white boots with the blazer, then," Gui relented.

"I should check with Neer about loading up," Jane said. "If you end up making any sketches off those fabrics, I want to see them before we head out, okay?" Jane pushed up on her tiptoes to give Gui a quick kiss, which Gui returned.

She willfully put aside the fact that she knew the softness in Gui's smile was from concern.

JANE SUCKED HER TEETH. "YOU KNOW, I GOT SHIT EARLIER TO-day for taking on too much responsibility about this sabotage . . . and I'm starting to understand why."

The heat warped and glitched the horizon beyond Neer. They were laser focused on the way that wiring was visible under and over the sand, as if someone else had lifted the wire to trace its origins and only half remembered to rebury it.

The brazenness was what concerned Jane so much. As if whoever did this wasn't concerned about being caught.

Jane and Neer usually traveled in comfortable silence, but this patrol was anything but usual. Neer's silence was coiled and warped like the waves of desert air, and Jane wasn't much different. Even as they neared sunset, the threat of New Dawn stretched across the vast beige around the endless sands, in the shadows of cacti and jagged rocks.

"If that's your way of starting to check on me, I'm fine."

Jane tsked, still watching Neer's work from over their shoul-der. Jane just wanted to understand the damage the way that Neer did.

But she left the tech to the expert and scanned the horizon again—Neer could be consumed with the work, while Jane kept an eye out for blushounds and coyotes.

Jane squinted toward a rock formation that would have been a great place for an ambush. It would be easy for a New Dawn truck—let alone any hovercopters or drones—to come barreling from that direction with little to no notice. It was the reason that Jane had a sawed-off shotgun sitting in the bed of the pickup truck near them.

Not that the double barrels gave her any comfort. Having to carry a weapon was unsettling now. The Pynk Hotel was a place without that kind of violence. Even the gun that Jane had with her now was usually kept in a secure lockbox buried on the edge of their territory, a disturbing necessity—and, more, a disturbing reminder of a time Jane hoped they could be past.

Bile rose in Jane's throat, but she walked over and grabbed the shotgun nonetheless.

"If you're fine," Jane said with faux nonchalance, "you can help me with my story."

There was a beat of silence, and if Neer had said they couldn't help, Jane would have dropped it. Instead: "Could use the distraction."

"From?"

"Having fucked this maintenance."

Neer's honesty hurt. But so did the self-doubt. "You didn't fuck it; don't let those theories get under your skin, homie." Jane held the shotgun up toward the rock formation, marveling at the strangeness of its weight. "You walked me through all of your procedures, and everything someone else from the hotel could have done. Feels like something different than neglect."

"If that was the case, the others wouldn't—" Neer cut themself off, shaking their head. "What story do you want to tell?"

Jane's heart hurt at Neer's almost-admission, but she continued to grant the distraction. "I want to tell the story of Alice."

"Which one?"

"The party incident. With the blushounds."

Neer took a breath, standing up from the wires. Dusting off their knees, they walked over to the pickup truck, pulling out a canteen of water. A long sip later, they began to tell Jane's story.

"Alice isn't an abandoned name," Neer stated. *"It is not a dead name but a shield name, one you used to keep New Dawn from tracing what you were doing. And what Alice was doing was protest parties. Zen would film parts, play them at other parties, and Ché would help you get the word out.*

"The parties were dirty, were everything that New Dawn wanted to wipe away. Unlike older parties, there were no smoke machines; Alice wanted the partiers to be able to see each other in the night air, clear and sharp and imperfect in their beauty."

Jane interjected here, the part that she remembered: *"The parties were nights of freedom, but there was a practical angle too. It's how we tried to keep each other safe. We shared information, smuggled things that they never wanted us to see—erotica, music, hacked tech made art. And that was what I did as Alice. Orchestrate that."*

There were memories of these parties at the edges of Jane's smoky mind, the rainbow and neon lights, the clubs and rooftops. There were clothing exchanges there too, but . . .

Alice had focused on finding clothing and the like for people whose skin crawled from pretending to be a clean computer, who otherwise wouldn't have places to see themselves.

It was a fucked-up thing, to have to smuggle slacks and lingerie and combat boots, extensions and wigs, but it was necessary.

"You okay?" Neer asked, breaking out of the tone of the ritual.

The break helped jolt Jane from the murkier edges of memory, and when she spoke next, it was a question to restart the ritual. *"Tell me the part I'm struggling to say. The part where . . . someone touched a leather jacket."*

Neer pressed their lips together tightly. *"You told me that Alice struggled to be open and free while having to shoulder suspicion, and this one night was why.*" Neer passed the water over to Jane, who drank carefully, eyes still trained on the horizon.

"*There was one partygoer dressed in black, white paint splattered across his bulletproof vest. Some people repurposed the gear of New Dawn oppressors, so a vest wasn't a tell, not with the metal-decorated sneakers and scanner-proof makeup. The gloves should have been, but there was so much happening that night . . .*"

"*Not the gloves,*" Jane said carefully, "*but the way that he took them off, just to touch the clothing. The way he recoiled from a messily patched sleeve.*"

"*He did recoil, hissing, from the only thing he'd touched the whole time he was there.*" Neer looked down at their own hands, as if they were imagining what he'd felt. "*And though there was space between you, you told me that you could feel the heat off his body.*"

Jane nodded. "*His hand was red like he'd just come out of a hot shower, or like a fever rash. I lifted my eyes and saw him, saw wide eyes and I knew.*"

"*You told me to always ask what he said to you. As long as you had that moment, they could never take this memory from you.*" Neer doesn't say how they'd pointed out that New Dawn couldn't take memories away anymore, that the gaps weren't caused by Nevermind but by the scars it left behind on Jane's heart. After that first time, they never brought it up again, and for that, Jane was grateful; whether or not they were right, the gaps and the smoke remained.

It took Jane a beat, but the words came. "*He told me that too much of anything hurt him—too much joy and fear and grief. And that was what freedom was to him. Too much.*"

"*And then you flipped the fucking table on him,*" Neer said, a twinge of amusement twisting the corners of their mouth. "*Tell me what that looked like until you need me to take over.*"

"*I remember the clothes coming up, flying over the table with the force of the flip. Gave me cover the same way that New Dawn hover-copters have lights to spot and blind us.*"

The boxer briefs and T-shirts arced in the air over binders and bras, a billowing blossom that signaled to the rest of the party it was time to bounce. Jane reached out to the closest partygoer—their face is glitched and broken by time and New Dawn—and pulled them away.

As Alice, Jane had a plan there, had party organizers who knew how to clear out the impromptu dance floors and save as many people from the threat as possible. Even if the blushound was alone, the fewer scents he could encounter, the fewer people that he could track, the better.

"He was the scout." It was as if the memory had cracked open, briefly, for Jane to see in full. *"He chased me while I looked for Zen and shouted to make sure she was safe . . .*

But there were others, New Dawn authorities, the necessary violence to make their cleanliness run."

Zen had once explained to Jane how violence from blushounds and guards wasn't dirty by New Dawn's standards. Dirt needed to be cleansed, and dirt was *who you* were, how you didn't fit into New Dawn's vision of the world. Their foot soldiers couldn't be dirty. What they did was part of the New Dawn machine. Computers programmed to drag the dirty in so that the Torches could lead them into the light.

In reality, the sound of choppers had likely drowned out most sound aside from screaming, but in Jane's memory of that night she could hear her boots and his sneakers hitting solid ground.

"Where'd he chase you to?"

It was Jane's turn to smile. *"The stage. Where there was plenty of stuff to beat his ass."*

Blushounds were trackers, but idiosyncratic in that they didn't want to tangle with too many folks at once—too much is, after all, too much. So they fixated on targets, and that was always a contingency on Alice's part: party planners who volunteered to be "targets" while others escaped.

Alice always volunteered, and that night, bathed in lights

of purple and pink, she'd grabbed the microphone stand like a quarterstaff. She yanked the audio cord out of it so she could wield it freely . . .

. . . and then she slammed the bottom of it into the blushound's chest. Once for coming after her, and twice for coming after her before she got to perform her set with Zen and Ché. Three times for making everyone scramble.

"Four times for ever saying any of us were too much."

"You escaped that night."

"After knocking him out? Yeah. Took me a day to find Zen and Ché, who had to hole up in another building until the search copters and blushound scouts cleared out the area."

Neer broke the script. "What if sometimes . . . everything *is* too much?"

Jane blinked, surprised. "We're not too much. Never too much. Who we are and what we feel can't be too much. Might feel that way sometimes, but it isn't true."

Neer looked down at the sand, kicking it with the edge of their boot. "Wish I could believe that." They turned to drop the water back in the truck.

Jane gently took their arm. "Who is telling you that you're too much, Neer?" The fact that Jane would fight anyone who said such a thing was implied strongly enough that Neer snorted, but Jane gave them a firm look. She had an idea but wanted to see if Neer would say it. "I mean it."

Neer shrugged. "Ain't nobody saying it, Jane, but you know how it is. Some folk think saying who you are is being too much and take it out on you. Or your work."

"Maybe New Dawn does that. But that's not what Pynk is about, and I'll fix that shit right now."

"I know you would, but it's . . . I just wanna work on salvage, fix up cars and radios we find, keep the electricity on. I'm not trying to be special. I just found my place, even if people think that looks a little funny." Another pause. "It's not everybody. It's not even most people. But I wonder . . . would people be questioning my work if they didn't think I wanted to be special? Or would they be out here with us right now? Keeping an eye on shit?"

"I'm not dismissing your concerns at all, but absolutely none of that should matter." Jane shook her head. "That's not acceptable." Again, Jane had her suspicions, but now she would need to proactively keep an eye on Neer, on the ways that others approached them at the hotel. It was easy to watch out for the overt, but Jane wasn't about just doing the easy. As Jane or as Alice.

"Why'd you want that memory now?" Neer asked.

"I've been going back over everything I remember about dealing with blushounds, trying to think about the kinds of tracking I've seen from them. They'll sometimes do sabotage, but that usually means someone's come up with that plan specifically. Remembering just makes me more sure that we're dealing with blushounds."

"Why, though?"

"I think it's to track where we're at, at the Pynk," Jane confided. "Not physically, but emotionally."

"But *why*? Why now? Why not just attack us?"

That was the part that Jane kept snagging on. "They could think we're distracted enough to try right now, and we just stumbled on their sabotage. Or maybe . . . maybe they're trying to rile us up. Make us eat at each other from the inside? I wish I knew."

Neer opened their mouth to reply, but both of them turned sharply toward a whirring in the distance. A puff of sand from behind the rock formation like a billowing pile of clothes tossed from a table.

"Get in the truck, now!" Jane was already moving into the back. She had a single one of the custom shots loaded, but that wasn't going to do much if she couldn't reload.

Neer didn't utter a word of argument until they were already in the driver's seat, shouting back as they started the engine, "You don't need to be back there!"

If only that were true—Jane knew all too well what running from New Dawn was like. The pickup truck, held together with ingenuity and salvaged gear, was never going to outrun the three tank-tread cycles bearing down on them, even the one with the sidecar. Besides, as they started to approach, Jane could see that there was a rifle in the hands of the sidecar passenger.

So she *did* need to be back here.

Jane knew that their ammo was going to be far more deadly or painful than anything her shotgun could spit—more accurate too. And she had to ignore the fact that her stomach lurched as she lifted the shotgun. She didn't like the feel of it in her hand already, and it was worse with the adrenaline of being chased.

The truth was, she didn't want to hurt anyone, even New Dawn lackies. She'd worked and run hard and long to not have to pull triggers. Even fighting against the blushound as Alice had been about protecting others more than herself. But she and Neer couldn't run back to the hotel with New Dawn on their tail. They couldn't risk anyone getting hurt at the Pynk. Jane was no soldier, would never be, but she'd protect the family she'd found like they protected her.

"Just keep moving!" Jane said. *And then maybe I won't have to pull this trigger.*

Maybe they could lose the bikers, or throw them off somehow—

The authority in the sidecar lifted their rifle and Jane dropped down in the bed of the truck. Rather than whizzing above her, though, the next sound was a loud *POP* as the right side of the truck dropped sharply.

"They hit the back wheel!" Neer shouted, along with a string of curses. Jane felt the inertial jerk of the truck, now veering and trying to slow down even as Neer battled against it.

Jane was glad to have been lying down when they were hit, even though it meant that she slammed against the side of the truck bed. She pulled herself up with one arm enough to see over the edge of the truck bed. The bikes were still crossing the sand, drawing ever closer.

With the sand whipping across her face, stinging her vision, Jane held up the shotgun. She tried to control her breathing, her thundering heartbeat. She tried not to think about the way that the sand was kicked up by the truck, by the bikes, billowing—

Like clothes over a table. No, like smoke, like gas swarming around Jane, into her nose, through her mouth, gagging her, fighting against her need to stay awake and remember . . .

She adjusted to a crouch; the adjusted center of gravity improved her balance. She tried to focus herself, blinking away both sand and memory. It was cruel, how trauma made her remember now when she needed to be present, when getting lost in the past could get her dragged back into the halls of another facility, without Zen to anchor her and help her escape.

Finally, her hands felt nothing but the sting of sand and the shotgun's weight. Her internal fight felt like it took days rather than seconds, but she tilted the gun, aiming lower than the biker and sidecar were ready for.

The shotgun ammo was only filled with enough powder to give it the necessary speed and momentum; the rest of it was *webbing*. The shell exploded out of the gun, the webbing expanding before slamming into the front wheel of one bike and sticking both bike and biker to the ground. The motorcycle hit the webbing hard, without time to compensate. Jane watched as the back of the bike went up in the air, the sidecar jerked by the sudden inertia, both riders thrown off.

Jane reached for another web shot, but the small box slid back and forth as Neer struggled to maintain control. Jane cursed.

Without sidecars to hamper them, the other two bikes were

able to maneuver out of the way of their webbed companion, and had gained ground, only a few feet away from the back of the pickup truck.

This close, the bikers loomed large, and Jane tried to push the haunting way their gas masks threatened to panic her out of mind. It didn't work as well when she caught sight of one of them grabbing a grenade off their jacket.

"Gas masks!" she yelled. "They're throwing—"

The grenade arced upward as their pursuer threw it overhead. Halfway through the throw, Jane saw the gas already starting to leak from it. She moved to yank off her shirt, hoping to use it as an impromptu filter around her nose and mouth, but a familiar refrain stopped her.

Release the Nevermind
Release the Nevermind
Release the

Jane was slammed forward, barely saving herself from being thrown off the truck by grabbing hold of the sides. It took a moment to understand what happened; the effects of Neer braking all occurred at once.

The grenade flew overhead, now overshooting its target. The blown tire prevented them from fully stopping, so the truck slid slightly to the right, but not so fast that the bikers flew past; instead, they slammed into the pickup truck's tailgate and were thrown backward by the force. The crash left dents in the tailgate of the truck, but the bikers were far worse off than the pickup.

In front of them, to the left, Jane saw a small cloud of Nevermind. Or that's what she thought, until she realized that the gas that was being dispersed was a muddy green-brown plume. That wasn't the Nevermind she remembered. The grenade was close enough that the gas reached Jane's nose and mouth even as it thinned out. She shuddered and grew nauseated.

And then suddenly, she *remembered*.

It wasn't just one memory. This was like the murky recollection of stories from the Cave, except this was a torrent, a sandstorm crashing down on her senses and her mind.

There were Zens and Chés and Mary Apples and Neers and *so many versions of herself,* so many moments from her life all happening to every limb at once. Every tender intimate touch, every agonizing pain . . . every dose of Nevermind, and every gasping breath of clean air afterward.

Her panicked body told her that she had to get out of the truck to be free of the gas; it would rise up, it hit her while she was in the *truck—New Dawn facility—at the party—at the home she grew up in—*

She yanked off her shirt and put it over her mouth. She thought the gas was dissipating, but the white smoke of old Nevermind in her mind made it difficult to be sure; she couldn't risk it.

"No." She wheezed and coughed as she climbed out of the truck bed, as she fell over the side of it. The pain of the ground and sand slamming against her meant little except another system overload.

She grabbed the door handle of the passenger side, jerking it open and crawling inside. The windows were up; she'd be okay once she slammed the door shut, she just needed to breathe.

Neer might have called her name, or that might have been a dozen times in the past that she'd heard them say it. Jane struggled to control her limbs, to force each memory out of her nervous system and back into her past. She took gulping breaths, thought of the Cave and its dirt, and the millions of memories rooted in the ground . . .

There were hands on her shoulders in the present, but Jane struggled to feel them. She heard a voice—Neer's voice, saying words that Jane had to fight to hear.

It was the coughing that hooked Jane's mind, a sudden present panic that she'd brought this torrent onto Neer. It didn't clear the memories, but it raised the volume just enough on the present . . .

Tell me about where you're sitting, Jane. Jane didn't understand. *You keep talking about the past. Tell me what the seat feels like* now.

Jane struggled to find the sensations of the present while wondering what stories of the past her mouth rambled about. She found the stickiness of the leather seats under her thighs, the way the sweat on her body from adrenaline and fear felt against her calves. She reached out in front of her and there was a hard plastic dashboard, textured enough to feel under her fingertips.

The past was starting to recede like a tide.

"I—" She tried to say a hundred things at once, all the things she felt *now,* but had to find just one. "Thanks, thanks. I'm good now. I think." She turned to look at Neer, whose face bore a slight bruise—had Neer hit the steering wheel when braking? How much present had happened just now that Jane wasn't awake for? "How'd you figure out how to speak to me?"

Neer put their hands back on the steering wheel, starting the car up. "You were talking to Ché and Zen, but not . . . You've had me hold on to your stories for you, Jane. All these memories . . . you trust me to know when you're mixing them up."

Jane nodded, but it was a drained, tired response. "Well, I think you took them out," she said, glancing through the rearview mirror and barely seeing the motorcycles splayed across the sand. "But we should get out of here."

"I'll drive around for a few hours; make sure they can't follow us back if they wake up." Neer's voice was hoarse, and Jane longed to take over driving. Taking over so someone else didn't have to, she thought dryly. But Jane couldn't drive right now. "Enough wind today that it'll cover up tracks after a bit." Jane nodded, dropping her head back on the seat.

They drove until it was impossible to see the bikers. Jane, still shirtless, kept her face covered, comforted by the feel of fabric over her nostrils rather than New Dawn's drugs creeping in.

It was cool in the Cave, and between that and her blanket, Jane could mitigate the pain of the bruises all over her body. The dirt was soft underneath her; that, plus the silence, was enough for now.

She'd brought a sewing kit with her so that she could repair her clothes and some pieces from various members of the hotel. Gui had offered to come along, but the concern on her face . . . Jane just needed a little time to breathe. Away from unwanted thoughts.

Jane felt someone enter the Cave, the stretch of an additional shadow. She didn't tense up, though. Not all company was unwanted.

"I've never been chased by New Dawn before."

When Neer didn't move from the entrance, Jane paused in her sewing, patting the dirt next to her. Neer eased down, pulling their knees in under their chin. They looked younger this way, or maybe Jane's tender heart just felt that way.

"You did what you had to do," Jane answered. "I'm proud of you, homie." Neer rolled their eyes fondly, and Jane leaned into them. "You doing okay?"

Neer shrugged. "The truck is fucked. It'll take me at least a week to get it running." That didn't sound like the issue, and Jane raised a questioning eyebrow. Neer sucked their teeth. "What *was* that gas anyway?"

"Never seen it before," Jane said. "Best guess is some kind of reverse Nevermind." She'd shared her experience with the gas with Neer once they were far enough from it that she felt safe. "Maybe it's to overwhelm targets."

"Or make it easier for blushounds to track," Neer offered.

"Bringing up all sorts of emotions to identify." Jane shuddered at the thought. "It's good that everyone believes us."

"We sure as hell wouldn't lie about something like this." When they'd finally made it back to the hotel the next day, it had been buzzing with worry. The truck was the least of everyone's concerns with Jane and Neer's injuries. It was mostly cuts and bruises, but Neer had dislocated their shoulder, and Jane had gotten a bit cut up while in the back of the truck.

"When I got here," Jane said carefully, "the second time . . . it was a relief. My head was still foggy with Nevermind, but there's so much support here that I could still move forward. I was still free, and Zen and Ché were okay. We could create art and make love and help others do the same."

She looked down at the basketball shorts that she was repairing, going back to stitching them up. "When I would go scouting with Zen, I could prepare for the threat of New Dawn, at least a little bit. But ever since you found that damaged wire, it feels like they're right up on our asses."

"They're closer than they used to be," Neer provided.

"More real than they've been in a long time," Jane agreed. "So I don't know what it felt like for you, running from them the other day, but I've got something a little similar."

"That why you're in here?"

Jane nodded. "I needed grounding. I needed to just remember what I *want* to remember, not everything that floods in when I think about New Dawn."

"The hotel not grounding enough for you?"

Jane lifted the shorts, double-checking her handiwork. "Plants have a lot of roots that spread out wide sometimes. I figure it's kind of like that." She decided that she needed to go back over the hem she'd just fixed. "There's something special here, extra, especially when I'm not with Zen and Ché." Jane smiled softly. "You help me out with that, though, so thank you."

Neer coughed uncomfortably. "I, uh . . . you're welcome. Though all the story-remembering doesn't matter if New Dawn sweeps in and—"

Jane cut them off sternly. "Don't even start with that. The way New Dawn tries to make us clean? The *only* thing that matters is that we remember." Jane remembered what it felt like to have not just her own life chipped away, but the memory of the sweetest thing that had ever happened to her—Zen. "That's why I get scared when my memory gets murky. Because as long as we remember and live, New Dawn doesn't win."

"Sorry, I shouldn't have said that."

"I don't need an apology, I just want you to understand." Jane glanced over at her sewing box and realized that now was as good a time as any for what she'd wanted to share. "Here, I've got something to help with that."

"With understanding New Dawn?" Neer sounded doubtful. "I'm not sure there's much else that you could hand over that you haven't already shared." Ignoring them, Jane pulled a white tunic out of the box, and Neer fell quiet for a few seconds. They knew what it was; they'd heard about it enough.

Jane cleared her throat. "Neer, when I left that facility, I didn't get rid of what I wore. Didn't hand it off to anyone either. It's probably superstitious, but . . . it's one of the anchors I used to remember. To remember that I *escaped*, that even though they tried to re-dress and reinvent me, make me something bland and clean . . . they didn't win. I held on, and I wasn't alone.

"Still," Jane continued, letting out a short, sad laugh, "that didn't always mean it was easy to look at. But that was good, that meant that I still *felt* something when I looked at it. That I still understood New Dawn was worth fighting against."

Jane rubbed her thumb against the fabric. The dirt underneath her, the tunic in her hands . . .

She stood between Ché and Zen, saw the hole starting along the stitching of Zen's sleeve. It must have snagged on something while they were escaping. It was a burst of defiance that made her reach out to hook a finger in the hole.

Zen grabbed Jane's hand, clenched it tenderly, kissed it. Then she went the extra mile, doing what Jane was imagining—she grabbed the shirt sleeve and yanked, *the ripping sound louder than anything Jane had ever heard.*

Zen glanced across to Ché. It took an extra few seconds to tear the threads enough to tear off Ché's sleeve, and longer still for Zen and Ché to pull simultaneously at Jane's. The sleeves caught, took a few more seconds. Ché had to tear one with his teeth, his apology for doing so in the language of kisses down that same arm. Zen's came off more freely, and so she gave kisses equally freely.

They kissed. They laughed at this small defiance, at the way it was so meaningful and pointless at the same time. They laughed and kissed until they tasted each other's relieved tears on each other's cheeks.

When they started driving again, they threw the torn sleeves behind them, fluttering and billowing in the wind.

Jane swallowed a lump in her throat. "When you were driving, and I had to shoot, I remembered where I got this. I hated remembering. But I've got to do it anyway, and I'm *so* grateful that you help me remember, so . . ." Jane held out the tunic, and Neer blinked, baffled. "Here. So that you never forget how you've helped me. Thank you."

Neer reached out their hand, their fingers floating over the tunic as if worried it would sting. After a second, however, Neer took it, reverently. Jane hoped it was reverence for memory itself, rather than remembering New Dawn.

"My favorite hoodie took a bit of a beating while we were out," Neer said after a moment. "Mind helping me stitch it up?"

Jane nodded. "Of course."

PART 2

Neer wrapped their arms across their chest protectively, thumbing the white cloth that now patched up the sleeves of their hooded sweatshirt. The most recent Chord—the second in a week now, far more than anyone was accustomed to—was ending, the Pynk Hotel residents slowly unfolding from places beside the pool. Neer watched one group go back inside and a few others walk toward the diner; only a small handful stayed around the pool.

Neer was sitting on the edge, their shorts short enough that they could kick their feet in the water without getting the edges damp. Looking down, they watched their rippling reflection in the water, framed by the night sky.

They looked tired, they thought, their lips wrinkling in displeasure. They already had what their last partner had described as "sleepy," downturned eyes, and the past week wasn't helping any. They wore their exhaustion in the way they pulled themself inward, in the slope of their shoulders.

Their reflection vanished as the soft lights of the pool were turned on. Glancing up, Neer saw that it was Gui who was responsible. She hadn't interrupted Neer's thoughts on purpose—she was crouched on the other side, her head was turned, and she was chatting with Rhapsody and Jane. Jane was smiling, a comforting sight. If Jane could smile after the run-in they'd had, after the entire Pynk community had to have volunteers to stand guard, then Neer could at least uncurl from their own discomfort.

Neer knew why they were taking this so personally, and it wasn't because of being shaken by the New Dawn encounter. The problem started before then, when they'd first seen the cut wires, when the first Chord occurred and everyone wanted to believe that things hadn't changed for the hotel. It wasn't that *no one* was worried about the sabotage—Jane surely was, and enough in attendance respected Jane's instinct to vote alongside her—but others ranged from unconcerned to angry at *Neer*, and that was what hurt.

To Neer, and the others, the hotel was a safe place, a bubble of beauty and joy, and for them, that beauty was in mechanics. Even the traps they helped maintain made Neer feel like an artist. Having rebuilt the truck from rusted salvage was a work of art. The first real time that Neer really felt like they belonged at the hotel was when they, Pel, and Zen had painted the truck its bright rose.

And now someone had disrupted all that, and it felt as if the weight of that disruption was on Neer's shoulders, left there by the creeping suspicion that was appearing on the faces of those here that they loved.

"You look like you could use a shoulder rub." Neer looked up over their shoulder. Speaking of Pel . . . "If you want . . . ?"

"I'd love that, actually." Neer was surprised at their own admission. The honesty came with a prize; Pel knelt behind the mechanic and started to rub their shoulders. Pel was a bassist and farmer, and had strong, confident fingers. Neer dropped their head down slightly. "You don't think this is my fault, do you, Pel?"

Pel turned Neer by the shoulders, frowning. "Girl, where'd you get that idea?"

It was nice when Pel called her "girl." Maybe it was because the first time Pel did it she'd asked if it was okay, or maybe it was because of the warmth in her voice when she said it. It was one of those moments that didn't make Neer's skin crawl. "If I'd been better at keeping up with the traps, they wouldn't have gotten so bold, or I would have had some earlier sign and—"

"The problem," Pel declared, "is that you spend so much time trying to disappear that you don't see anything else happening around you." Neer didn't get it, and Pel gently turned Neer's head so that she could look in their eyes. "Pynk's a community, Neer. A strong one. We're all interconnected—no way you're solely responsible for bringing New Dawn to our door. Not unless you're making deals with them, and you don't seem like the type to want to be a clean computer."

Neer laughed. "No, I'm plenty fine staying dirty." They'd dealt with the clean and the dirty before New Dawn started labeling everyone, from when they were a kid. They'd more than accepted who they were.

"Exactly." Pel smiled. "Can I ask you a question?"

"Go ahead."

"Are you worried that you did something to cause this . . . or that the rest of the girls *think* you did?" Neer looked away, chewing their lip. They couldn't help but glance across the pool at the trio still talking. Jane caught their eye and smiled back; Neer glanced away before they could accidentally meet Gui's or Rhapsody's eyes. "I'd like to think everybody here knows better than to give you shit for existing, but I'm not a fool."

"It's not everybody," Neer said. "It's not even most of the others."

"One or two is enough," Pel said. Neer nodded. "Well, you spend a lot of time with our girl Jane—what would she tell you?"

Jane would probably share a story from when she and Zen were driving across the country, Neer guessed. About the parties outside of the hotel, and how every inch of life's purpose was to find love, freedom, and your people. To embrace your own weirdness and other folks' wildness.

Neer imagined Jane in tulle and leather and sequins and knew the answer. "She'd say fuck 'em."

Pel gave them a fierce grin. "Fuck yeah, she would."

Neer wished they were able to have the strength that was ever-present in Jane's voice.

• — •

EVEN WITH THE STRESS OF THINGS, NEER COULD WATCH THEIR fellow Pynk occupants prep for the festival with anticipation. No one had much need for Neer's help aside from wanting an audience as they practiced. So Neer stayed by the pool, happy to observe. And the truth was Neer loved listening to their work, watching their short plays. It wasn't Neer's art, but it was wildly beautiful and thrilling—no one *stopped* them from creating work here, and it never got old watching what that resulted in.

The result of Pel's massage was even more satisfying, as Pel lulled Neer into bliss with a strong bass line in her bedroom. But eventually even Pel had to drift off to sleep. Neer tucked Pel in, not arguing when Pel muttered, still asleep, about how Neer should stay. They'd done this before, with Neer slipping away at the end of the night. Neer couldn't help but feel like they were taking up too much space when they tried to stay, no matter what sweetness Pel muttered.

Besides, tonight Neer had something else to do rather than wake up in Pel's strong arms.

Neer went to their own room and switched out of their shorts into heavy denim. They considered changing their hoodie but decided against it; the desert night was cool, and if Neer had to do any running, the long sleeves might keep them from getting scraped up.

The real issue was that Neer wasn't a weapons person. No one came to the Pynk to fuck with weapons; you came for safety. If Neer was going out, though, and risking blushounds, well, they couldn't very well go out without any protection. They looked around their room with a frown before grabbing a wrench and shoving it in their back pocket.

But they weren't sure that'd be enough. So, on the way out of the hotel, Neer jogged over to a pile of wrecked objects, put to the side until someone figured out what to do with them. There were all kinds of items—and Neer found two that would be useful: a destroyed guitar and bass, snapped in half after a particularly . . . *dramatic* concert night.

Grabbing the necks of both instruments, Neer fully detached them from the ruins of the rest. They winced at the cracking wood sound but reminded themself that this was a worthy dismantling. It took a combination of instrument strings, wood glue, and a welding torch to finally make the pseudo-quarterstaff that Neer swung across their back with guitar straps. But it would do.

It was the crafting, Neer assumed, that got them caught.

"Sneaking out?"

Rhapsody.

Fuck.

Not exactly the kindest face in the hotel. Neer turned, taking a deep breath. Rhapsody was half-dressed, in panties and a T-shirt at the door. That didn't take away from the glare that she was leveling. "Where are you going?"

"Just checking nearby trip wires," Neer answered. It wasn't a lie, since Neer did plan on checking them while they were out. "Can't sleep, figured I'd be useful."

Rhapsody narrowed her eyes; Neer didn't need to be a blushound to feel the distrust coming off her in waves. Could Neer blame her entirely? Yeah, Rhapsody already didn't like them, but right now, coming out to see Neer sneaking out of the hotel without anyone else? Maybe . . . Neer sucked their teeth. No, Rhapsody should know better than to treat Neer with suspicion. They belonged at Pynk same as Rhapsody did, had offered up as much of their creativity and community labor to the hotel as Rhapsody did.

Rhapsody *should* trust them. But some just weren't wired that way.

"You want to come and keep an eye on me?" Neer said. Then, after a moment: "Watch my back?"

Whichever one convinced Rhapsody, it didn't matter; she held up a hand to tell Neer to wait a minute. Neer could have—

maybe should have—gone off when Rhapsody went back inside. If Rhapsody grew more suspicious of Neer and woke the others up, that would risk Neer's very place at the hotel. The Pynk hotel was built on trusting the community, and with everyone this tense, Neer couldn't risk losing that. So they waited the few moments it took for Rhapsody to put on a pair of sweatpants and come back downstairs.

"I don't have a second wrench," Neer said.

Rhapsody pulled a small item out of her pocket. "Taser."

And with that, they left the hotel.

THE DESERT NIGHT ALWAYS SOUNDED LIKE DRY RATTLING, EVEN if there were no signs of snakes.

"Why did you end up coming to the Pynk?" Rhapsody kept an eye on the horizon as they walked across the rocks, and kept her voice almost even, almost casual. But Neer heard the emphasis on *you.*

"People around me were vanishing, and then showing up in commercials and posters for New Dawn," Neer answered. "I tend toward quiet, and they struggle to clean dirt they can't see . . . but I knew it was only a matter of time. I'd trip up, be honest about how I felt about gender or sexuality or art to the wrong person and . . . poof." Neer imitated a puff of smoke with their fingers. "And then, after a while, I was sick of living . . . in hiding.

"I got on a mountain bike and just started moving. It wasn't easy to find out about the Pynk Hotel, but I found people who eventually trusted me, knew that I needed a place where I could be who I was. I was led to the hotel and made myself useful." Neer smiled to remember it; they'd traveled with a small handful of transfolk who liked staying on the move. When they'd voiced wanting a place to lay their heads for a while, one woman talked about her time at the hotel, a place that kept her safe until she wanted to wander the road again. When Neer showed up, the folks at the hotel immediately led them to the diner to eat. They'd been cold at night, so Zen had given them a sweatshirt. And when Neer said their pronouns, Jane and Pel were the first to use them without Neer fearing that it wasn't safe.

"Hm."

Neer resisted laughing; what a fucking response. "What?"

"It was just odd to me, that this was where you—"

"I'm a Black woman," Neer cut her off. "Genderfucked and a woman . . . the kind of existence that New Dawn wants to clean away and erase. I wonder, though," Neer added, "whether they could ever even erase that existence from any of us. It's not just memory that makes me a woman, that makes me genderqueer. It's something . . . else. So I wonder if we'd ever be clean enough for them. Either way, here, clean or dirty, I felt welcomed. Mostly." Neer tried to imagine the tone of voice Jane would use and emulate its strength. "What do you think?"

It was a dare, seeing how far Rhapsody would go in questioning Neer's belonging. To be honest, it was almost refreshing to have Rhapsody ask rather than seethe in silence when Neer knew the truth. Neer didn't want that disdain—that was why Neer had come to Pynk, for a place of acceptance—but at least if Rhapsody kept going, Neer could tell her to fuck all the way off.

Unfortunately, Rhapsody didn't take the challenge. She sighed heavily, looking out into the darkness. "We should split up, cover more ground."

Neer thought the entire point of Rhapsody coming along was to keep an eye on them, not cover more ground, but they nodded all the same. Rhapsody started walking west, so Neer went southeast, trying to go around the perimeter of the hotel's outer territory.

"Maybe Rhapsody will go back home," Neer said to themselves. They didn't have high hopes.

There weren't any other trip wire sabotages, as far as Neer

could track, although increased patrols from the hotel meant that all the sands were more disturbed than usual. Neer held both ends of their wrench inside the front pocket of their hoodie, not realizing how hard they were clenching it until their knuckles ached.

Neer had to breathe. They couldn't keep an eye out for trouble if they were this tense. They needed to focus. And maybe *focus* was why they thought of the Cave, and how close they were to its opening. Jane and others used it to focus all the time; why shouldn't they?

Neer made their way to the edge of the Cave and found stepping in harder than it should have been. It was easier when Jane was in there, when Neer knew that they were supporting someone else. It was easier still when Rhapsody's distrust and questions weren't at the forefront of Neer's mind; was the Cave *for* Neer, even?

Did Neer deserve to cross the entrance?

Even as that question hovered over her, a gloved hand suddenly came from behind Neer, covering their mouth—or at least, attempting to. Neer was struggling immediately, pulling out the wrench and swinging upward wildly, losing their grip on the wrench and letting it fly. It hurt when the wrench clipped the side of Neer's lip, splitting it, but Neer was sure that it hurt their attacker more when it slammed against their arm. The attacker recoiled, giving Neer a chance to turn and back away, braced for a fight.

Their attacker was in black or dark blue Kevlar—Neer wasn't sure which. Their hair was yanked up in a dark ponytail, and there was a mask over much of their face. Not a gas mask, however; just a thin layer of fabric to cover their features. They shook their hand, and Neer heard them hiss in pain.

Good.

But Neer was suddenly aware, a throb flaring up their back, that they were all that stood between the Cave and their assailant. The idea of this person getting into the Cave, even getting *close* to such a sacred place, was as alarming as that of the attacker breaking into the hotel, and Neer couldn't have that. So it was Neer who moved next, taking the makeshift staff off their back and running at the masked figure with a shout.

Neer was easily thrown off balance by the incoming punch, although the attacker cursed loudly in a high alto voice; they'd forgotten not to punch with that recently injured hand. That was good; that meant Neer got their dominant hand.

The satisfaction of the moment didn't stop Neer from falling after the blow, although they managed to keep a grip on their staff. Their opponent lunged down at them, and Neer brought up the staff; it hit the attacker in the gut, causing a gasp and a grunt before the attacker fell over to the side.

A scream cut through the desert night: Rhapsody.

"Fuck, fuck, fuck." Neer was babbling swears in a panic, scrambling back up into a standing position before bringing the quarterstaff down on the opponent's head.

Guitars weren't meant to survive being slammed down on hard surfaces—the very reason why there had been broken instruments for Neer to grab in the first place—Neer shouldn't have been shocked when the bass half snapped and splintered. Neer wasn't used to being in fights, so it freaked them out for a moment. They had a sharp pointy end now, and they kept thrusting it forward to give themself some space.

The dark-clad fighter dove low, at Neer's side. By the time Neer reacted, their opponent had Neer's wrench in hand. Neer stumbled back a few steps, trying to figure out a way around without getting hit.

Rhapsody screamed again, and Neer threw themself forward, coming at their attacker's waistline. They connected, and both of them tumbled in the sandy dirt. This close, it was difficult for either of them to get a real hit in, and so Neer ripped off the face mask. They needed to know who was trying to kidnap them, needed to have a face that wasn't an amalgamation of New Dawn horror stories.

The face staring back at Neer had honey skin and high cheekbones . . . and fiercely angry eyes. Their face and neck were flushed red as well, and it was then that Neer realized how *warm* the attacker was, even through clothing.

The attacker was a *blushound*. Worse still, the blushound looked as if they would have been at home at the hotel, trying on faux fur coats and spandex. Looked like any of the hotel occupants that Neer had spent the past few years around, not like some strange blank cultist or pale government official.

The blushound hissed, and Neer realized that tears were filling their eyes. It wasn't pain, though. "Stop . . . touching . . ." came the strained voice, and it wasn't the voice of violence, but of a desperation that Neer knew well.

Neer wasn't touching any of the attacker's skin but understood that the closeness might have been too much anyway—still, sympathy for that intense empathy didn't allow Neer to forget they had been *attacked*, and so Neer threw the hardest punch they knew how. Their attacker stopped fighting them, knocked out.

As the blushound's breath slowed to steady, Neer was still panting, knowing that Rhapsody was probably dealing with a similar situation. A quick pat-down gave Neer some useful tools: plastic ties to restrain the attacker's limbs and a small electrical baton. After a moment of consideration, Neer picked up the face mask. They weren't sure if the mask would do much against Nevermind or whatever other gas had been used on Jane in the prior attack, but it was better than nothing.

Neer dragged the blushound to the entrance of the Cave, near brush—leaving a New Dawn op inside just felt wrong to them. Done, they looked at the horizon, trying to remember the direction of the screams.

They had to find Rhapsody.

What Neer found was Rhapsody on the ground, wheel tracks veering off into the distance. She wasn't knocked out but was barely pulling herself up on her feet. Neer went to help her, and Rhapsody was too shaky not to take the help. "What took you so long?" she groaned.

"A blushound."

"Yeah? I barely . . ." Rhapsody shook her head, as if sand were filling it and distracting her. "There was a transport, New Dawn. Tried to grab . . . managed to . . . kicked my way out . . ." Rhapsody frowned, trying to catch her thoughts and breath. "They didn't come back to get me?"

Neer listened to the night air; nothing. "Maybe they were too far out to be able to find you again?"

"They sounded disappointed." Rhapsody's laugh was halfway to a wheeze. "And one of them split off, said they—"

"That's probably the one that I had to deal with," Neer said. "Let's get you . . . let's get you back to the hotel."

"What happened to your blushound?"

Neer grimaced. "Dealt with."

For now.

NEER WAS CROUCHED OUTSIDE OF THE CAVE, FEELING THE heat from the sun over their back. It was especially noticeable where Neer had patched their hoodie, where the ex–New Dawn fabric was slightly thinner than the sweatshirt. It made them scratch their arm unconsciously; it didn't even feel *uncomfortable*, just very obvious when Neer was silent.

"We're keeping secrets from the hotel now?" Jane had come to the Cave alone, like Neer had asked, even as scolding and concern battled for dominance in her voice. "We've talked about shutting out the rest of the community when you're worried."

Neer chewed on the inside of their mouth as they stood up, glancing continually over their shoulder into the Cave. "I'm gonna tell them. I have to. I need your help . . . to figure out how."

Jane tilted her chin up questioningly. "I'm listening."

"When Rhapsody and I got attacked . . ." Neer started, then paused. Jane was going to be angry, they were sure of it, and Neer probably deserved it if Jane dragged their ass all the way back to the hotel and shamed them in front of everyone. They'd never *seen* that happen, but there was always a first time, right?

"What happened?" Jane took a step forward. Neer heard a sound, a low scraping, and held up a finger to their lips. Gestured into the Cave. Jane frowned and listened more closely. "What is that noise?"

But Neer didn't answer; just led Jane into the Cave, barely touched since the last time Jane had shown up, except for a few spots where it looked like someone had tried to make dirt angels in it. And, of course, the navy-clad woman held by plastic restraints sitting in the corner, trying to scoot across the dirt to a sharp stalagmite.

When the blushound glanced up at Neer and Jane, there was a long silence, the prisoner's eyes wide and unsure.

"Jane, meet Bat." Neer let out a nervous chuckle. "Bat, Jane."

Jane nodded in Bat's direction, but quickly turned back to Neer. "Neer, we don't do this."

"I know, I know, I shouldn't have brought her into the Cave, but I didn't want to carry her to the hotel, or ask for help, because I didn't know what the Chord would vote to do with her, and I know it's dangerous to have anyone who isn't part of the hotel inside anyway, so this was the place that was safest and—"

Jane shook her head. "Not the Cave, Neer. The fact that she's bound against her will." She moved over and crouched next to Bat, who recoiled at the nearness. "Are they too tight?" Jane asked simply. Bat, with wide, suspicious eyes, shook her head no. "There are gentler ways to restrain a woman if you *have* to do it, Neer. Pynk Hotel doesn't kidnap people or keep them locked up."

Neer blinked; they'd been so sure that they'd done wrong bringing a blushound into the Cave, disrespecting a sacred space, that they hadn't thought beyond that. If anything, Neer kept coming back to the thought that *they'd* been attacked and they didn't want Bat to run back to New Dawn. It had seemed so obvious in the moment, but now they weren't sure what the right choice was here.

They knew they hadn't thought it through.

Jane sat back on her knees, keeping space between her and Bat—but also, Neer noticed, keeping herself between Bat and the stalagmites that Bat had been trying to get to. "I'm not saying we're going to let her get away with attacking you, but we have to be careful how we deal with this. If we can't be better than New Dawn . . . ?" Neer nodded but wasn't sure if Jane saw it. Instead, Jane was looking at Bat; Neer wondered if Jane saw what Neer did, how Bat looked like she would have been at home at the hotel, in another life. "They called you Bat. Is that what I'm calling you?"

Neer didn't understand why Jane was being so nice to Bat. "You were the person who told me why we should worry about blushounds."

"And when a blushound is tracking you, you need to be worried," Jane commented. "But right now, I think it's clear that . . . Bat, yes? Isn't going anywhere."

"Bat's . . . whatever," the blushound finally said. "It's better than numbers. Didn't they already tell you this?" Bat asked, looking at Neer.

Jane raised an eyebrow at Neer. "They did. I assume they're about to tell me a lot more."

Neer coughed. "Right. Yeah." Bat and Jane both looked on expectantly, and Neer realized the double test in front of them: both Bat and Jane would judge Neer's actions not just by what

Neer did, but also by *why*. And with what Neer needed to explain to Jane, it might end up being important that Bat understood as well.

When Jane spoke again, her voice was softer, though she still pressed them. *"Neer, tell me a story."*

And that made it easier.

I came back to the Cave once I got Rhapsody to the hotel and knew she was taken care of. In the adrenaline, it was easy to forget what had really happened; in the comedown, it was easy to think that there would be no one in the Cave when I came back. So it was more surprising to see the sand and dirt disturbed, but no new footprints leading away.

I did not realize that my wrench was no longer on the ground, though, and what that might mean. I know you probably would have noticed, Jane, but I'm not used to being that *alert.*

Entering the Cave, I didn't hear anything at first. Bat—who to me was just a blushound at that point, who thought of herself as a series of number designations for New Dawn—was lying in wait. I'm new to being ambushed, and maybe that is why she almost got me. But the dirt in the Cave is a strong foundation, and I didn't fall over when she tried to tackle me. I dodged when she tried to hit me.

"You don't sound angry at her," Jane observed. Bat snorted.

What Neer didn't explain was that Bat's tears made it hard to stay angry. That watching the waves of unwanted empathy consume Bat made Neer see the fight differently.

I would have done the same to her if I'd been knocked down, and this felt different from before. When I was attacked the first time, she was trying to drag me away. She wasn't trying to drag me from the Cave this time. I don't want *to be attacked, but what happened next . . .*

Bat, you kept forgetting that you lost one of your gloves in the struggle . . .

"The gloves are thick enough to make it so I can grab someone," Bat provided, and Neer recognized the sound of someone not used to being addressed and asked to think. "But without one of them I would get close, and your panic hurt."

Neer nodded.

At one point we fell. I hit the dirt and needed to figure some way out of the struggle. My fingers clenched the dirt and I . . .

I don't know if this was disrespect of the Cave, but I flung a clump of dirt in Bat's face. She scrambled from me, trying at first to claw it out of her eyes, but then . . . Neer kept talking but started to look at Bat. If Neer was getting the next steps wrong, they wanted to be corrected. *Bat calmed down.* Cooled *down.*

I know it doesn't make sense, but it's something about the dirt—maybe the same thing that helps your memory and helps us all use the dirt for meditation and find safety in here. Bat gasped and told me . . . I feel you less. *And it sounded like . . . relief, like gasping relief, and Bat stopped fighting . . . I took the wrench, restrained her.*

Neer looked at Bat again and came out of the storytelling. "You didn't fight me when I restrained you."

"I breathed in the dirt, tasted it, and I could *feel* you, but it didn't hurt the same," Bat explained, her words awkwardly staccato. "I was in shock." She knew how to speak perfectly, but her delivery was stilted by discomfort, either from being part of a conversation or because of whom she was speaking to. Her curls had gotten messy, and she blew a few strands out of her eyes. "I would have otherwise," she said, just in case either of them had forgotten it was a possibility.

Neer glanced at Jane and shrugged. "If the dirt can heal the stress of her empathy, I couldn't just take her out of the Cave, and I couldn't risk that anyone else would want to."

"That's what you were most concerned with? Not why she was after you?"

"Sure, but I'm not about to take bets on if Bat is going to tell me anything." Neer smiled lopsidedly.

"There's nothing to tell," Bat snapped.

"Nevermind?" Jane suspected. "Or the other drug, the one that hits you with a flood of memories?"

"You mean the by-product?" Bat shook her head. "Street chemists have been playing with it for a minute, but New Dawn started flushing and filtering that stuff into the earth around their facilities whenever they needed to vent their area. We blushounds all grew up in towns where the water and soil were soaked in both that crap and Nevermind. Neither gas works on us. We just feel everything . . . all the damn time."

"Then there's always something to tell."

"I had a paying job, and I was doing it."

"Your paying job," Jane snapped back, "was kidnapping."

"That's the kind of work they give to blushounds. We're not . . ." Bat sucked her teeth and lifted her chin defiantly. "It's not like any of *you* are taking us in." Bat's words were full of venom, and Neer felt the burning of it—even if it wasn't directed at them specifically. Everyone at the hotel knew what it was like to feel turned away by the rest of the world. When Neer's heart raced with fear at the threat of blushounds, could they blame Bat for feeling rejected from the jump?

"Any woman is welcomed at the Pynk Hotel," Jane retorted. "Long as they're willing to be part of the community and not ally with places that want to erase who we are."

"I've been to places that 'welcome everyone' before." Bat was bitter, and Neer knew that feeling all too well. "They all sing the same lyrics until you scare them, and then they need a solution for who you are. Not much different than New—"

"We're *not* New Dawn," Jane said icily. Bat didn't respond, instead turning to look back at Neer. Jane took a breath. "I want to be very clear: I'm not saying you haven't lived that. I believe you. But the hotel is different." After a moment, she added, "Neer, you didn't say why 'Bat.'"

Neer's cheeks warmed. "I asked Bat her name, and then

asked if she *wanted* to be called a string of numbers. Eventually, she said no."

"It's short for 'combat,'" Bat muttered under her breath, glancing away.

"I explained how Neer was short for Engineer, and Gui for Guitar, and Pel for A Cappella . . . how we renamed ourselves after our passions and talents."

"And I know how to fight," Bat finished.

Jane nodded. "I see." She finally stood up, and Bat glanced up at her, waiting like Neer to hear their punishments. "We're going to have to talk to the rest of the hotel about what to do." She looked Bat in the eye. "*You're* going to have to stay with us until we have another option than sending you to New Dawn, but Neer's right. If you want to stay in the Cave because it hurts less, I'm not going to force you away from it. I wouldn't want that to happen to me."

Bat clearly didn't trust Jane's words. She should—and eventually would, Neer was sure; Jane always kept her word.

There was noise outside the Cave, and Neer's heart leaped into their throat as Bat tried to scramble into a defensive posture despite being bound. Because the sounds were familiar, the voices and footsteps not of the enemy.

Rather, it was Pel, Nomie, and Rhapsody leading the other Pynk occupants toward the mouth of the Cave.

NEER HELD THEIR BREATH, STARING PAST RHAPSODY. THEY didn't care about Rhapsody's expression, a bizarre blossoming of disgust and satisfaction. They did care about Pel's expression behind Rhapsody, with its carefully trained blankness that failed to cover how Pel's eyes went back and forth between Neer and Bat.

"What are you doing, Neer?" Pel's accusation hung heavy, condensation on the stalactites in the Cave. "And who is *that*?"

The question was almost absurd. Bat's clothes were dark and fight-ready, and she was still bound with restraints. It didn't take a genius or empath to connect this all to the attack from the previous night. The real questions were bigger and more damning than who and what.

Neer swallowed, and their throat was dry. "I was figuring out what to do, so I asked Jane to—"

Rhapsody's eyes lit up with understanding. "You brought Jane into your fuckery?" She wasn't wrong. Neer had dragged Jane into this because they trusted Jane, needed a hand—but hadn't thought about what this would look like. The pit of fear was starting to grow roots of mortification and shame as well. "You told me that you *dealt* with this."

"Doesn't technically look like a lie," Pel murmured. But she wasn't looking at Neer when she spoke.

Jane put up her hands in a calming gesture. "What we're not going to do here is pretend this is a cut-and-dried situation. Neer was attacked, and needed to decide the right way to handle this. So they asked me for help. What did you expect them to do?"

Rhapsody was thrown, and for a second, Neer was hopeful. That soured quickly when Rhapsody said, "I expected to be told the truth after *I* was attacked. I also didn't expect one of *ours* to allow a blushound into this cave, into such an intimate and sacred space. It's an insult to all of us!"

Jane took a step forward, in front of Neer. "It's an *insult* that you don't trust us enough to listen to what any of us have to say."

"I trust *you*, Jane."

She said everything in that sentence, Neer thought, their gut roiling.

Jane just said, "Trust Neer."

Rhapsody was quiet for a moment, shaking her head and curling her hands into fists. "You say it like any of us are supposed to be okay with secrets. And I don't wanna hear that they didn't lie, because that omission shit is *lying*."

"Rhaps—"

Neer took a step forward. "Nah, Rhapsody is right." They tried to make their voice louder than usual. "I could have been upfront from the jump about all of this, but I was scared. But I'm *not* lying to the community, to any of y'all," Neer said. They didn't intend for the volume to make their voice crack. Or maybe it wasn't their words; maybe their voice cracked when they glanced behind them to where Bat was staring at them with narrowed, guarded eyes.

Bat didn't trust them either. Jane might be the only one in the room who did, and Neer wasn't so sure they were earning that trust.

"Why did you leave . . . her?" Nomie hesitated; Neer nodded. "Why did you leave her in the Cave is what I don't understand." There was a pleading roundness to Nomie's words, begging Neer to make this betrayal make sense.

Neer shrugged. "Only place I could think of. She was already here, and too big for me to drag."

Jane interrupted before more questioning continued. "If you all wanna interrogate Neer, we can have a proper Chord. Because we have ways of dealing with hotel issues."

Rhapsody sucked her teeth and almost barked out a laugh, shaking her head and turning away.

It was Pel who spoke. "You're right, Jane. We have proper ways of dealing with hotel issues."

"What about . . ." Nomie gestured toward Bat. "Her?"

"The dirt in the Cave—" Neer began.

Rhapsody cut in. "We take her back to the hotel, unfortunately. This is a hotel issue," she elaborated, and every time someone said "hotel issue" Neer's skin crawled like it was being rejected. "And so we'll deal with the blushound as the Pynk Hotel, as a Chord. Period."

Neer felt the distance between themself and the "we" in Rhapsody's words. She'd just declared, but that wasn't how things worked at the Pynk, and Neer knew that. So they did something they were realizing they had the right to do: spoke up again.

"The Cave dirt helps her like it helps us—maybe even more—and we don't *stop* helping people." They felt like they were an echo for Jane's words, as if they were trying to pull themself back to the Pynk Hotel on the strength of Jane's courage. It was unfair to Jane, Neer thought, but what other raft did Neer have right now, with the rest of their world staring down upon them with distrust and betrayal in their eyes?

"We cannot keep that *outsider* in the Cave!" Rhapsody sputtered. "It's no better than having *men* in here, and that's a line we're not going to cross today, Neer."

"That's not—"

"We could vote on it right here and right now," Rhapsody countered. "That's *fair*."

Neer attempted to stand a little straighter, but they knew Rhapsody wouldn't have proposed this if she didn't already know the outcome. The votes were already obvious before they took a count. Pel abstained, while Nomie hesitantly voted to take Bat under guard to the hotel. This felt wrong, like the weight of panic settling where the justice and safety of the hotel should have been.

Jane helped Bat stand, whispered to the blushound something that kept her from kicking up a storm. Neer watched, feeling helpless; what could they do? They couldn't very well explain why they felt the need to at least be kind to the blushound, even after the attack. The old distrust of their own voice rushed in. They didn't trust themselves to recount how it felt to see Bat react to the dirt in the Cave, at least not well enough to change anyone's mind. Words weren't Neer's art, the courage to speak them even less.

But they could do something. "Nomie," they hissed as others started to leave the Cave.

Nomie was spooked for a moment, as if she expected Neer to do something more than speak. "Y-yeah?"

"You got a water bottle on you?" After a moment, Nomie

handed one over. "Thanks." Neer opened the bottle and emptied the water inside into the dirt, before Nomie had time to be baffled. Then they grabbed the sharpest rock they could find, cutting around the top of the bottle to allow for a larger opening.

Nomie's eyes went wide. "You're gathering dirt and taking it *out* of the Cave?"

Neer grunted in acknowledgment. "We've done it before. It's not as potent, but it's something."

"But that's—"

"Nomie." Neer's head shot up, and the intensity they directed at Nomie silenced her. "Bat needs the kind of healing the dirt provides. Or maybe it's not healing . . . it helps, okay? And I'm not a prison guard or New Dawn. I know what I saw, and I'm not going to deny her this." It took a moment before Neer added, "I've already messed up once by binding her; I'm not making the mistake of forgetting compassion again.

"And fuck anyone who wants to deprive her of a handful of dirt."

Neer moved past Nomie with an affected confidence that they were only able to fake because most of the Pynk Hotel was walking in front of them. Still, behind them, they heard Nomie's sputtering surprise.

"*Bat*'?"

"You're gonna get locked up."

Neer was worrying a nail and trying their best to ignore Bat. "We don't lock people up."

"What?"

"You heard Jane in the Cave. I made a mistake cuffing you before. We're not a fucking police state," Neer mumbled around their ring finger. "Incarceration isn't . . ." They didn't have the energy for a political argument with Bat, not while wondering what was about to happen with the Chord.

Neer had done their best to lay out their case to the Chord, explaining the same story to the hotel that they had to Jane. Jane did what she could to speak up for them, but the facts were unavoidable: Neer knew about a threat to the hotel (Bat), didn't tell everyone immediately, and then gave her access to the Cave. Each part of that was a grave error, and Neer didn't know what would happen if the Chord decided that this was all intentional.

There was always forgiveness for folly and mistakes within the hotel, but if they felt the way Rhapsody did? If the others voted that this plus the sabotage was too coincidental? Then Neer would be considered a traitor to their friends and family and lovers, and that had never happened before in the history of the hotel. And if this was judged to be a betrayal . . . would they still be able to offer forgiveness?

Would Neer even deserve it?

"Okay, fine." Bat grunted. "They'll probably exile you, then. Maybe they'll set us both off together, since you 'don't do incarceration,'" she said, sounding doubtful still.

Neer laughed at the absurdity of that image, of the two of them—Bat still with wrist restraints and a half bottle of dark brown dirt—walking out into the desert. "Well, at least if we get picked up by New Dawn, they can't gas you . . ." Neer tried to stay joking, but it hurt.

"Don't do that."

"Do what?"

"You're getting emotional and it's a small room," Bat explained.

Neer sighed. "How exactly am I supposed to stop my emotions?"

Bat peered at a pinch of dirt they had between two fingers, holding it up to their nose for a moment, sniffing at it. Studying. "I don't know. This is why it's easier with New Dawn people," Bat explained. "They're . . . flatter than the rest of you dirty computers."

"Because they've had their memories *erased*," Neer snarled. "Clean means they've had everything taken from them."

Bat paused, sucking her teeth, and Neer was getting sick of other people making that sound. She rolled the dirt between her fingers before sinking the two fingers back into the bottle. "I can't help that your emotions hurt my head."

"And I can't help having emotions," they snapped back. "You can at least respect that they're *mine*."

Bat exhaled, almost in relief, before flicking her chin up to get some curls off of her face. "At least stay angry. Anger causes less of a migraine when I smell it."

But that wasn't who Neer was, and already her anger was dissipating. "Who am I going to be angry at?"

Bat shrugged, holding up the dirt bottle in Neer's direction. "Take this. Last time I tried to put it down I nearly knocked the thing over."

Neer knelt and grabbed it, holding the bottle in their hands. The ritual of knowing the dirt was in their hands did help, a little, to quiet the million what-ifs flying through their mind. "If I was angry," they said carefully, "I would only be angry at myself. And I can't imagine that 'smells' very good."

Bat narrowed her eyes again. "No . . ." She sounded surprised. "It smells like misery and hatred." After a moment, she broke eye contact. "Like that woman who was yelling at you. Smelled hateful enough to make my head pulse."

"She doesn't hate everyone," Neer said after a moment. "She loves the hotel. It's outsiders and New Dawn that she hates."

"You sure about that?"

"Yes," Neer said with absolute surety. "You don't come to the Pynk Hotel to persecute. You come to get away from that, and she's stayed and been part of the community for a long time." Neer didn't elaborate on the way that Neer and Rhapsody likely had different definitions of *outsider*, though. Bat could sense emotions, so trying to hide certain things made no sense; telling everything made even less sense. Not wanting to dwell on it, they asked, "Why attack us, Bat? If you told everyone, it might go a long way—"

"New Dawn hired me to track an emotional scent, and that's what I did. Not my fault you got in the way."

"You attacked me, remember."

"Yeah. Right."

"So they're looking for one person?" Neer seized on that with a strength that made Bat flinch for a moment. "Rhapsody?"

Bat shook her head. "Absolutely the fuck not."

"Then . . . ?"

Bat rolled her eyes. "Jane."

Of course it was Jane. That made a horrific kind of sense; Jane was a failure to clean, an escapee.

"I was told to keep watch when her trail took her away from the hotel, take her while she was alone." Bat gestured to Neer's arms. "You have her emotional smells all over you. What, do you guys share clothes or something?"

"What? Yes, we all do—" Neer's eyes went wide. "The patches." Bat stared blankly, so Neer added, "I used her clothes to patch up my sweatshirt. Something she wore back at New Dawn." In fact, it was one of the rare pieces of clothing in the hotel that bore *only* Jane's past. How many times had Jane looked at it and thought about her past, her present? Neer had smelled like her, and that had drawn Bat to them.

In a small way, Neer was proud they'd been able to keep Jane safe.

But they still had questions. "And why *now*? *Who* in New Dawn—"

"If you don't do prison, I assume you're not an interrogator and I don't have to answer anything I don't want to."

"Of course not." Neer's answer was as sincere and immediate as earlier ones. "I just . . ." Needed to know. Not for the hotel, although the safety of the hotel was in the forefront of Neer's mind, but to explain the situation they were in. To be able to explain it to Jane above all. Would that make up for getting Jane involved?

Bat was taken aback. "I don't usually get a say in whether or not I answer."

"You don't usually spend time at the Pynk Hotel," Neer replied.

"Hard to get a reservation," Bat sneered.

"No, it's just hard to find. But once you're here, you're welcome. Even by ones who may not do so as fully as others."

Bat shook her head. "How naive are you that *right now* you're still singing their praises?"

"Why wouldn't I?" Neer started, only to immediately piece together every little dig that Bat had taken. Quietly, "Are you saying you smell someone who feels . . . off?"

"I'm saying you *know* I do and—" Bat looked woozy suddenly, honeyed skin growing splotchy and green. Her nose flared as the door to the hotel room opened.

Ah, Neer thought, that would be a reason for Bat's sudden illness. Jane was at the door, and Neer didn't need an empathic sense of smell to see all the warring emotions playing across her face. Rage, disappointment, frustration, fear, and worry must have been a heady, nauseating perfume for the blushound, and filled Neer too with their own anxious blend of feeling.

"Well?" Neer tried to keep their voice even, but trying to hide the quavering meant they spoke too fast to be nonchalant. "What was the vote?" Normally, Neer and Bat would have been in the room, but a preliminary motion requested by members of the Chord had had them step out. There was pressure and suspicion attached to them seeing the vote, and since Bat wasn't a hotel occupant, it made sense to keep them away. Neer agreed to wait things out in their bedroom; it had meant, at least, that Neer could keep the dirt with Bat while showing they had no desire to fight with the rest of the hotel.

Any little thing to help.

It didn't seem it had helped all that much.

Jane was struggling to find words over a pacing irritation, though, and so Neer stood up, holding out Bat's dirt to Jane. *"Tell me a story,"* Neer offered. *"Of what happened in the room."*

Jane blinked, taking a moment to refocus on the plastic bottle in Neer's hand. "Is that from the Cave?"

"It's like watered-down rum." Bat raised her voice slightly. "Can you even share it?"

"If there's anything I know about that cave," Neer said, not turning from Jane, "it's that every grain of dirt there is for all of us, and those that we want to help. Right?" Jane nodded, and Neer held up the bottle again, this time slightly tilting it. Jane obliged, holding up a palm so that Neer could sprinkle some dirt into her hand.

Jane's fingers curled around the dirt tightly. It wasn't rooted the same, Neer knew, wasn't attached to the Cave the same. But that didn't mean that it wasn't a part of the same earth that grounded them, wasn't the same scrap of planet that helped keep them dirty. Neer wanted to will that truth into the handful of dirt Jane was holding, into Jane's mind.

"Tell me a story," Neer repeated.

Jane closed her eyes and breathed in deep. Neer watched her expression soften, relax. Turn from frustrated and fixated to focused. It was a meditative moment that Neer had seen many times, even if it was odd to see outside of the Cave.

"I told them I was against the decision," Jane started, *"because it wasn't what we did. It's like I've told you a hundred times, and like you've seen two hundred times more: we come here to be free, to be allowed our flaws and our wildness, and that means we offer each other forgiveness and grace and understanding.*

"But instead, Rhapsody spoke of things that sounded like the outside world, and she made the others so scared of what was beyond the walls of the hotel leaking in that they agreed. Said we couldn't trust

that you hadn't caused the sabotage, that if you were protecting blush-ounds you might be protecting New Dawn and hurting us."

That was both exactly what Neer had expected and everything that didn't make sense. Jane was right; the hotel had always been a place of healing and understanding, but since the sabotage, the attacks . . . Neer had seen in Rhapsody's eyes what she would say to the Chord, not that she'd been particularly quiet about it.

Neer didn't mention the conversation that they'd had with Rhapsody while on patrol. *Why are you here?* Rhapsody had asked. Neer wondered if Rhapsody had used their answer to sway the room, whether or not they'd realized it.

Instead, Neer prodded Jane to continue. *"And what did the Chord decide to play?"*

"Keep you under guard until others investigated," Jane answered after a strained silence. *"It was . . . noted that I was too involved to lead the investigation, because you'd been such a support to me. So I volunteered to guard you both."*

"They agreed to that?" Neer was surprised. If Jane wasn't impartial enough to investigate . . .

Jane's mouth quirked up wryly, a bit of cynicism making her open her eyes and leave the meditative state. "They may have agreed to Rhapsody investigating you, but they weren't going to totally shut me out in a vote. I'm pretty sure Gui and Pel would have had their heads, and that's before considering what would happen when Zen got back." Zen's name had a gravitational effect on Jane's smirk, pulling it down into a frown. "Wish Zen was here. I sent word to her to cut her scouting trip short, that the hotel was going through it, but it'll still take her awhile to return." Jane shook her head, trailing off as someone called her name outside the door. "I'll be right back, okay? We'll figure this out."

Jane's angry optimism was offset by the sound of the door closing behind her.

Bat was laughing. No, it was a snicker, bubbling up behind Neer. Neer turned and glared. "What's so funny?"

"You're not a police state, but you're sure as fuck letting the executioner lead your investigation. The fuck does that sound like to you?"

Neer was getting fed up. "Stop hinting at things and playing games. You have something to say, say it." They whirled around to face Bat; Bat had said anger caused them fewer migraines, so maybe Neer was performing a mercy.

Bat tilted her head for a moment. Then, slowly, she pressed her back against the wall so she could push herself up into a standing position. At first, Neer thought Bat was savoring the moment spitefully, but then Neer noticed that Bat was still faintly green; the hotel was plenty painful right now, for everyone in it; it just took a different form in this room, for the two of them.

Neer shoved back their irritation for long enough to bring the plastic bottle over to Bat. They held up the bottle below Bat's nose, and she inhaled deeply, letting out a long sigh. "*Tell me the truth, Bat.*" Neer didn't think that Bat was one for stories.

"I know Rhapsody wasn't a target," Bat explained. "I know that because I've smelled her hatred and fear before."

"I smelled them all over the New Dawn facility where they hired me."

NEER WAS ALREADY FEELING HELPLESS BY THE TIME NIGHT HIT.

No one was going to believe Bat now, and that meant few people would believe it coming from Neer either. Telling Jane lifted some of the burden; Jane trusted Neer's instincts enough not to dismiss it but could only do so much. They needed *proof* for the Chord, and neither Neer nor Bat nor even Jane had any of that.

They both *knew*, but what good was knowing when Rhapsody had stripped most of the trust that the hotel had in Neer?

They couldn't rightly snoop in Rhapsody's room either. Everyone went in and out of each other's rooms often, as friends and lovers. But there was no way that Neer would be able to both sneak away *and* get into Rhapsody's room without anyone noticing, and Jane being gone from their side too long would rouse suspicion.

Jane said that Rhapsody *was* at least encouraging everyone to stay alert. For whatever good that would do if what Bat said was true.

"They had you testing the perimeter as well?" Neer asked again.

Bat's offered information was offered grumpily now, due to Neer's repetition and the clear irritation of the wrist restraints. "*Yes.* Several blushounds were sent to test and wreck security traps. New Dawn authorities tend to work in squads. Big, splashy transports, NDRs, and such. We don't like being too close to others, so we're trained to be a little more . . . quiet when necessary." Bat dropped her head back, staring at the ceiling. Neer had suggested the bed, but Bat declined; there were more emotional scents on the sheets than on the floor. "We were given a map of the points, and ways of tracking Jane . . . old clothes, taken when she was brought into New Dawn I guess, since they were all tulle and leather."

"They didn't burn them?" Neer was surprised.

"Guess not." Bat shrugged noncommittally. "I don't like doing sabotage when I have a choice. I like a fight more. So I got tracking duty."

"You had a map, though, so it had to be provided by someone who knew the hotel."

"Exactly. And the map smelled like an angry and scared motherfucker."

Neer swallowed the now ever-present lump in their throat. They fell silent, knowing the answers to all the other questions they could ask, even if they didn't want to believe them. Except for the one that Bat couldn't answer:

Why?

"How should I know?" Bat said. Neer hadn't realized they'd spoken out loud. "I didn't *meet* her; I just know the smell. She was scared and angry when she drew the map. Ask *her* what got her spooked."

If only they could. But Neer was pretty sure they weren't going to get the chance to interrogate Rhapsody. Neer pressed their lips together tightly, the word *outsiders* on the tip of their tongue. But that didn't make sense either. New Dawn was as outside and threatening as it got. Why on earth betray the hotel, turning them over to New Dawn? What was the point?

"We had express orders to grab Jane and Zen if we got eyes on them. Don't grab anyone else unless we needed to. Guess that was part of Rhapsody's deal."

No one else?

Just them? But . . .

There was a low, loud gong noise vibrating the walls suddenly, played through the hotel's speakers. Neer so rarely heard it outside of a test that it took a moment for them to even *care* about it.

Jane was already opening the door; she'd been keeping her vigil right outside. "The alarms are going off all through the hotel!"

Neer was up on their feet. Behind Neer, through the open door, they heard movement, the wooden floor transferring the running footsteps along with the alarm blaring. The confused muttering, the shouts to one another. It was an unnatural cacophony in the hotel, the kind that made tears prick Neer's eyes. There was no horror movie scene Neer knew that reflected how deeply wrong it was to hear this kind of chaos inside the hotel, where there should have been sounds of laughter and music and bedsprings.

Bat practically slumped at the overwhelming wave of fear that crashed over her. Neer helped keep her up, even as they moved toward the window. It had been secured from the outside for the purposes of containing Neer and Bat, but that didn't stop Neer from looking through it. There weren't many hotel folks outside yet aside from those who had been on guard. Even they were emerging from the few vehicles that they kept; a couple of occupants with makeshift shields and tools to defend themselves poking out of truck beds and open Cadillacs.

They weren't all looking in the same direction because there were trucks coming from either side, their lights blinding. Neer stumbled back from the window. They heard shouts as well as squealing wheels and brakes.

New Dawn was raiding the Pynk Hotel.

"No one else my *ass!*" Neer twirled around to shout at Bat. "They're here to clean us *all!*"

Bat was trying to hold up her hands, the anger apparently doing enough to offset the pain of the hotel's fear. "Whoa, whoa, I didn't fucking *lie* to you." She looked between Neer and Jane rapidly as they both moved closer. "*We* were ordered not to take anyone but Jane. I don't know what this is."

Neer lifted their chin, trying to keep the mounting panic away. "Why should I believe you?"

"I don't really have much of a say in that now, do I?" Bat retorted. "But . . ." Bat was getting frantic. "The dirt! Look, I don't really care about your hotel one way or another, but that cave? It was the first thing to make my sense of smell *relax* that I've ever experienced, okay? And if New Dawn finds out about it, there's no way they'd ever . . . That I'd ever be able to . . ." Bat straightened up. "I won't defend your hotel, but I'll fight for that kind of peace."

Neer didn't have time to explain that those two things were one and the same. Neer looked at Jane, who was cautious but clearly ready to move. Neer nodded and held out a hand to Jane. "Do you trust me?"

"Of course," Jane said without hesitation.

Neer pulled Bat's gloves out of their hoodie pocket. "You got a pair of scissors?"

NEER REMEMBERED WATCHING ZEN'S FOOTAGE OF SOME OF the raids that happened at their illegal parties. Dirty computers in happy hedonism, intimately with and for each other, suddenly scattered to the winds and the ground as the patrol lights glared from above. Zen had chopped the footage up for her musical documentaries. She and Jane worked on accompaniment that fit the chaos, electric guitar notes that warped and warbled too long against the listener's skin and the crashing of cymbals over speedy drum riffs. It triggered the right level of panic and fight-or-flight, Jane explained. Occasionally someone else joined in—Gui or Pel more than others—to compose pieces that sounded like their own fear.

It was therapeutic when done like that. There was nothing like that burst of creative healing in hearing the actual noises that accompanied the reality. For Neer there was only the clash of being frozen by horror and the electricity of adrenaline pulling in a hundred different ways.

Neer wanted to run, wanted to escape, but they could not leave the Pynk Hotel to fall. Too many of their sisters were running panicked and scared. It didn't matter to Neer how many of them Rhapsody swayed in the vote. Had convinced to turn against Neer. The thought was still hard to swallow.

Neer shook their head; they could only hope that this plan, half built from storytelling sessions and desperation, would work.

Neer was right outside the hotel when someone in armor grabbed at Neer, and even while struggling against the masked assailant, they tried to remember what they'd told Bat and Jane: Avoid the stun baton, but check for gloves, for thick coverage where it was unnecessary. Sure enough, the hand that tried to yank them away toward the transport was covered in a glove similar to Bat's.

Through the glove, they were warm. Blushounds, then, rather than normal authorities. They may have been grabbing anyone, but that meant that they were still *looking* for someone. Jane, likely. And that was good, all things considered.

"I'm *not* Jane," Neer snarled. "Or Mary Apple, or a computer—" In their panic, they gripped the pair of scissors they'd taken from the hotel, stabbing backward. They forced themselves not to think about how they'd stabbed down toward the assailant's thigh, or what the blushound tumbling back with a shriek meant. Neer made sure they never lost their grip on the scissors; they hadn't taken them for stabbing.

Neer searched the desert sand. As they'd feared, they saw that a few of the hotel's invaders had gas masks. A transport was stopped, surrounded by blushounds in riot gear, their shields blocking sight of the opened backs of the vehicle. They no doubt had some way of releasing that crude gas on the unsuspecting folk of the hotel. This new chemical weapon to overwhelm. Nevermind to clean up after.

Just another reason for Neer to rush.

Their eyes landed on the diner, where several armored authorities were approaching with electric batons and riot shields. The diner doors were closed; was anyone holed up inside?

Neer was down to one hoodie sleeve when they'd left the hotel and did a quick check to make sure they hadn't lost the other sleeve. Satisfied that they were still good, Neer bolted toward the diner, but not the front way that was being surrounded. Instead, they moved toward the back door, where only one assailant with a baton was slowly creeping.

With a wail rather than a warrior's yell, Neer ran at the person's back, slamming into them hard enough that momentum drove both at the diner's wall, hard. There was a sharp stinging pain for a moment before Neer was able to jump back; just in time, as the sudden push seemed to have caused the blushound to slam into the wall with the baton between them and the hard surface. The raider shuddered violently as the baton made a *zzzzzt* sound.

Neer pounded on the back door. "It's me! Neer! Let me in!"

There was rumbling inside before someone jerked the door open so hard that Neer nearly fell in. Behind them, they heard the door slam shut again. Neer looked up; it was Pel locking the diner door.

Neer was surprised by the hug and relieved kiss that greeted them. "I was scared that when the transports came," Pel explained as she pulled back, "your blushound would have a plan to attack you."

"What?" Neer blinked. "No, no, she, uh . . ." Neer looked around the diner at the current situation. There were about half a dozen occupants with Pel, all varying levels of scared and enraged. Nomie was curled up in a booth, a gnarly bruise giving her cheek and eye a swollen purple appearance. "Look, I have reason to believe these people have a map of the hotel." Everyone paid much closer attention. "We're lucky they don't have the keys to the diner, but they will break through soon."

"Then we beat them here," Pel offered. She gestured to the counter; the group had been at work, pulling out the fryers, the pans, the hot oil. Preparing as much of a defense as they could in such a short amount of time. "I can buy the other girls time—"

"The gas that they used on Jane," Neer pointed out. "They've got tanks full of it. We just run out there, or one of us just sacrifices ourselves, it'll mean nothing but pain for us. It's only a matter of time until that same gas smokes us out of here, and trust me when I say I can't watch any of you go through that. I just can't." They pressed their lips together for a moment, scared of the way they had to raise their voice to make sure all in the room heard what they said next. "But I have a plan. I think it'll work."

A woman near Nomie spoke up. "And how do we know *you* didn't bring those misogynist, homophobic fucks down on our heads, Neer?"

"Neer could have tried to save themself when the attack started," Pel countered. "Run off. Instead, they're here. So if you hear the plan and don't want to join in, fine. But we *listen* when others speak."

"You still believe in me." Neer couldn't help the shock, even though they could still feel Pel's quick kiss.

"Of course I do. It's the blushound I don't trust," Pel said. "Where is she?"

"With Jane," Neer answered. "Helping with my plan."

"Wha—"

"Please—just trust me. We can end this." They stared into Pel's eyes, and, eventually, their friend relented. Neer nodded, relieved. "But it'll work better the more people are in on it." The front door shuddered. It was blocked by every bit of furniture they could move in the diner, but it would get pushed through eventually, or the attackers would pivot to the back. "Please. Help me save Pynk."

"W-what is it?" Nomie asked hoarsely. What had those people done to her in their short time raiding?

Neer gestured at the sleeve of their hoodie that was still in one piece. "They targeted me in the Cave because I had old fabric from New Dawn that Jane wore. To them, it smells like what they used to track Jane. So let's confuse them."

Neer had already cut part of the stitching of the sleeve, so now they yanked at it, tearing the entire section off.

"That'll buy us a little time, overwhelm them with the scent they're supposed to track, instead of making it—" The door shuddered again. "Instead of letting them focus on it. Please, just trust me, I—"

"What good will that do if they drag us all in?" came the expected question.

Pel's expression was firm. "I won't let that happen. I assume you have a secondary plan?"

Neer shrugged and tried to make their awkward grin look like a confident smirk. "We just need to make this more effort than it's worth to them. They've got electric batons. Take them, shove them in the pool. Get them clear of their transports. Make them run. That'll buy us time when the sun comes up, in case they're planning another attack. They were testing to see how easy we'd be to take in for these past couple of weeks." Neer may have bared their teeth. "We'll show them how hard we'll fight to stay dirty."

Pel nodded sharply. "I'll handle that from here."

Neer took out the scissors that Jane had given them and started handing out strips of Jane's tunic.

MOST OCCUPANTS SEWED THEIR SMALL STRIP OF JANE'S TUNIC into the scraps of their quickly made face coverings. The masks might not stop a full blast of gas to the face, but they would give them time. And that was really all they could ask for.

Pel was a great leader, and when the party burst from the back door of the diner, armed with grilling forks, hot metal fry baskets, and bottles of thick hot oil, the New Dawn authorities didn't know what to expect. Confusion reigned now on both sides: the blushounds were frustrated, thrown by a sudden wrench in their psychic system that they couldn't identify, even as they struggled against New Dawn's better arsenal.

But Neer's kith had the advantage of the hotel itself. Of fighting for their home. Neer didn't take control of the first transport, but they did get into the driver's seat of the second. The motor was still on, and the back was open; blushounds were trying to load up Pynk occupants. It was harder to do so when Neer pressed down the gas pedal. It became impossible when they made the vehicle do a doughnut, watching as the blushounds flew out the open back in the rearview mirror.

In the headlights, Neer saw the nearest other vehicle, saw *Jane's* face behind the wheel. They knew Jane couldn't see it past their face mask, but Neer smiled and nodded determinedly at her all the same.

Knowing it was Jane in the other transport filled Neer's chest with renewed adrenaline, and they did a sharp U-turn in the direction of the nearest collection of blushounds.

It was a game of chicken: Neer behind the wheel, leaning on the horn to make a point as three blushounds with riot shields protected one with what Neer could only assume was a grenade launcher. There were only seconds of distance between them, and Neer's heart rattled in their ears.

"Don't make me hit you," Neer begged aloud, even though the blushounds couldn't hear their ragged pleas. "Just fucking *run,* you don't need to do this, New Dawn doesn't fucking care about you either—"

It was rambling that continued till the last second.

The grenade launcher fired . . .

The blushounds jumped out of the way, retreating from the truck . . .

The grenade cracked against the windshield as it went off . . .

Neer threw up their arms as they hit the brakes. There was an explosion of mud green across the windshield, lit to look radioactive by the headlights. Sickly glowing green leaked into the van, and Neer's eyes watered.

The filter could do only so much, and Neer tried with their whole being to remember what they'd told Jane, to stay present as memories poured in.

Zen gave Neer clothes when they were cold. Tell me a story, Jane said, or maybe it was Neer, or maybe it was Pel. Rhapsody snorted, unimpressed, as Neer traveled with other transfolk like them. They saw their tired face in the reflection of the pool as Pel kissed them, as Pel massaged them and cut trip wires sparked in the distance . . .

When Neer reached for the present, for the transport's wheel, for the klaxon and gong of alarms, they kept accidentally holding on to *stories*, to all the stories of Jane's that they'd worked so hard to never, ever forget.

Alice's parties were invaded just like this. Walking on legs that refused to move just like this, in a New Dawn facility. A soul shattering at the realization that the love of their life didn't recognize them, a soul stitching itself back together as the two plotted to escape. The drive back to the Pynk Hotel for healing. The drive to the Pynk Hotel for the first time.

A blushound named Bat who got a face full of dirt and needed peace, ripping Jane out of a truck and letting her thump hard against the ground, slapping at her face to get her to listen . . .

Not Jane. No . . . Bat was slapping *Neer's* face, in the present, as Neer coughed and gagged on fading gas. "Don't fucking leave me alone with these women," Bat was saying. "I'm not explaining myself to anyone again."

Neer was able to clear the hacking gunk from their throat, lifting their mask long enough to spit it out on the ground. "You aren't alone here." Neer was shocked at how easy it was to respond. "Not ever."

Bat snorted. "You still sound ridiculous."

"I came to Pynk because of all the people who thought I should hate how ridiculous I can be. It's not an insult anymore." Then, after a second, "Thanks."

"Most of the New Dawn folk realized you weren't going in easy, and that you were prepared for the gas," Bat explained, and it was only then that Neer realized that the air was clearer. It must have been at least a few moments since the grenade had gone off, maybe more: Had they missed the final retreat? "They may or may not be back eventually, but it'll be a bit if they're smart enough to rethink their strategy. That experimental gas, it only works if the people who breathe it in actually get overwhelmed."

Neer nodded distractedly, glancing over at the transport as Bat helped them stand up. The windshield was shattered, and two of the wheels had been blown. Their tinkering heart hurt at the sight of it, but the salvager in them knew that there was greater joy and message in tearing it apart, using its pieces for all kinds of work that the New Dawn Standards would frown upon.

They walked over to the wreck, glancing around at the state of the hotel. There were fallen riot shields, and a couple of the occupants—Neer spotted Pel—had acquired shields of their own. Many of them were some form of hurt, but triumphant. As was the hotel's way, they were already reaching out to one another, seeing who needed immediate help.

"What are you doing?" Bat asked.

Neer reached into the transport and pulled the keys out of the ignition. Hefting them in their hand for a moment, they aimed far across the horizon and *threw* the keys as hard as they could. "Fuck off, New Dawn!" they shouted. Bat didn't laugh, but she looked cautiously optimistic.

Neer didn't know if it was the dropping adrenaline, the encroaching pain, or remnants of the crude gas that made them miss the signs of what was about to happen.

They were slammed into from the side at high speed, by hands that Neer remembered from helping them up after an "attack" only a couple of days before. Their attacker screamed with an unbridled, wordless rage.

"Rhapsody, no!" Neer shouted, but it was too late. They hit the ground with a thud, the light of the transport making Rhapsody's shadow stretch over them, twice as long as Rhapsody was tall. It was almost impossible for Neer to see Rhapsody's expression, even when they squinted. That didn't mean that Neer didn't already know it.

Bat started to move in, but Neer held up a hand. If Rhapsody was going to do this, then Neer was going to defend themself as an occupant of the Pynk Hotel. This was their fight.

"You're going to destroy the hotel!" Rhapsody screeched. Her voice was ragged, and Neer wondered if she too was recovering from that gas. If she was, what memories were still floating in Rhapsody's head, and how did she look back at them and think *any* of this was okay?

Neer was aghast. "*I'm* going to destroy it? You brought New Dawn to our doorstep!"

"What are you even—"

"They knew *everything.*" Neer's throat was suddenly dry, and the sand stung their eyes. "Where our traps were, when we patrolled. They have a *map,* and where do you think they—"

Rhapsody grabbed Neer by the hoodie, but already shredded, it tore away, leaving Neer's tank and sports bra behind. Neer used the moment to scramble up to standing, bracing to defend themselves. "What do you *think* you know?" Rhapsody asked. "Huh?"

"Bat smelled you with New Dawn." Neer's breath was ragged. "*Why,* Rhapsody? I know you hate me, but you *love* this place as much as I do. As much as any of us do." If any of the New Dawn assailants hadn't retreated, Neer couldn't tell. Even without the bright light of the now-useless transport, the silence before Rhapsody's answer encompassed Neer's whole attention, their whole world. "Why fucking wreck something you love so much?"

Rhapsody lunged at Neer, throwing a punch. Neer tried to dodge, but still got hit in the side of their neck, gasping for breath. "I was *protecting* it, you idiot!" Neer staggered. "*You* have no idea what the point of the hotel *is;* you just want it to be some safe space for anyone, but the Pynk isn't for *everyone,* or *just anyone.*"

"You did this because of *that*?" Neer's incredulous disdain overpowered their wheezing. "Because of me? Because I'm not *your* definition of a woman?"

"Because you *aren't* one!" Rhapsody shouted, and her statement reverberated in the air. "And the more we allow people like *you* into the hotel, the less safe we all are."

"Rhapsody, I know exactly what the Pynk Hotel is. I know *exactly* what and who we're protecting here. Do you?"

"You and Jane had everyone suddenly rethinking who we

were! Who this was for. And I'm not going to let you reinvent the hotel in your image. That's how our spaces become the space of men, of misogynists, of—" Rhapsody shoved Neer this time, and Neer lost their grip on the scissors. "So I did what I could to protect us by making a deal to get rid of part of the problem."

Neer's eyes went wide. "You were going to give them Jane."

"And then New Dawn would pretend that we didn't exist," Rhapsody insisted. "Give them Jane and Zen and once those two were *clean* the rest of us could be free to live the way we intended to. But it had to look . . ."

"Like you weren't involved," Neer completed. They didn't know if Rhapsody was lying to herself or really that wrapped up in their fantasy. "You made it look like they were raiding in general. And if they got Jane . . .

"So what, did New Dawn break their promise tonight? Because you weren't fast enough?" Neer gestured around the desert, at the streaks of battle left behind.

Rhapsody shook her head insistently. "No, no, we realized . . . that it couldn't just be one or two of you. That the problem was everyone like you, so if you were cleaned . . ."

"You were willing to turn me over too," they said quietly. It wasn't a surprise; not now. Neer suddenly felt calm as shadows moved at the edges of the lights, still too bright for Neer to see in full. "Sorry I'm the wrong kind of dirty for you," they said, disgusted.

Rhapsody had no response except an aborted, frustrated yowl as she launched herself again at Neer. Neer threw up their forearms defensively, blocking some of the bright light, except for the sharp lines of it that came through between their limbs . . .

No blow came, but Nomie's voice did. "You said 'we.'"

Neer lowered their arms, to the sight of Jane and Bat standing between them and Rhapsody. At the edges of the transport light, some of the residents of the hotel were starting to inch closer. The light obscured their expressions, but not the tension in the air.

Rhapsody was staring in wild disbelief at Jane, and then at those who surrounded her. Nomie spoke again. "You said 'we,' but you meant you and New Dawn, not us." Nomie gestured to Jane and Neer. "Not them."

"Neer isn't one of us," Rhapsody snarled. "Why are you guys acting like—"

"And what about me," Jane asked.

"A necessary sacrifice," Rhapsody said after a moment. "I know it would hurt some here to lose you but—"

"You *were* working to protect your own," Jane said decisively. "But you decided everyone who didn't fit your womanhood wasn't worth protecting. Including me, I guess, because I damn sure don't." Jane stared Rhapsody down hard, and Neer held their breath. "You were already willing to sacrifice one of your own for peace . . . but are you willing to look me in the eye and say I don't belong at Pynk? The hotel is space for the dirty." Jane glanced back at Neer. "For folx like us."

Even in the blinding spotlights, Neer spotted reactions to Jane's statement. Some moments of shock, a couple of heads nodding. The light couldn't blot out the supportive smiles, directed towards Jane and Neer both.

Even Rhapsody understood what Jane was saying. "Are you serious?" Rhapsody looked nauseous. She took a step back before realizing that there were Pynk occupants behind her as well. On every side. And their horror wasn't directed at Jane, where Rhapsody would have hoped. "You're going to spit on our womanhood like that?"

"No one is—" Nomie piped up and stepped forward. She must have thought, optimistically, that she could explain things to Rhapsody, but Rhapsody recoiled from her immediately.

"Do you even hear yourselves?" Rhapsody snapped. "You're not *listening*. You're siding with a damn *blushound and two females who don't even respect who they are* instead of me, you're not—"

"Tonight is over," Jane interjected.

Neer found their voice again. "You tried to turn us against each other, Rhapsody. Because you decided who was and wasn't 'Pynk enough.'" Neer sneered, and then winced from the attempt. "Instead, we"—Neer smiled over at Jane—"realized who we were. You said it yourself, Rhapsody: That's not how we do things here. Never has been. That's why . . . that's why I was welcomed here in the first place."

Neer tilted their head up, showing their full height. "And that's why you can go fuck yourself."

The dam of fear started to collapse in upon Rhapsody's face. It really was over, for now at least, Neer realized. Tomorrow, they'd have to repair things, get ready in case New Dawn tried again, but *this*?

This bullshit was going to be old news.

"If we were you, Rhapsody," Neer said, "you'd be tied up and punished. You wanted to make that what we do here." Neer sucked their teeth. "But we can be better than that. We already are." They glanced at Jane. "I've been told that more than once. If you choose to run tonight, Rhapsody, that is your choice. But you won't be welcomed back after making that decision. If you'd rather do what we do at the Pynk Hotel and actually heal . . . tomorrow, we'll take you to the Cave and start there."

Rhapsody blanched, and Neer decided that they were too tired to hear the answer. Instead, they turned away, taking a deep breath, as several women walked up to Rhapsody. Two close shadows remained behind them.

"You could run too, you know." Neer didn't turn around, instead looking toward the horizon. "Anywhere. Long as Rhapsody doesn't decide she'd rather be clean, I'd bet no one at New Dawn would know what happened to you."

Bat tsked. "Sure, and I probably will, at some point."

"But?" Jane asked, walking to Neer's other side. It was then that Neer noticed Jane cradling their own arm. Running circles around New Dawn wasn't an easy thing, even if they'd done it a hundred times.

"But I've still got questions about the Cave. So . . ."

Neer smiled, surprised by her reluctance. "You've got time to ask away, long as you don't fuck with the hotel."

"Pfft," Bat said. "I'd have to fuck with you two to fuck with the hotel, and . . . no thanks."

"You would, wouldn't you," Neer conceded, and for some reason that was the best thing they'd heard all night. Neer sighed heavily. "Bat pointed out that they might come back, Jane. What do we do then?"

Jane raised an eyebrow. "Why are you asking me? I'm not in charge, and I think you're better at coming up with a plan than you give yourself credit for." Neer didn't know what to say. "I'm gonna ask you the same thing as I asked Rhapsody: do you think I belong at Pynk?"

"Of course," Neer answered without hesitation.

"And if I belong here," Jane continued, "And I'm just as genderscrewed as you . . . I'd say you belong too. So, Neer: what do you think happens next?"

Neer paused at the enormity of that question. "Maybe we move. Maybe we stay. I don't know. But . . . either way, we'll still be the Pynk Hotel. Just . . . maybe a little bit more mobile."

Jane smiled a toothy grin. "Just think about it as going on tour," they said. "We'll make it fun." Then Jane squinted at the horizon, pointing toward the thin line of sunrise. "Hey, Neer, look at that. Fashionably late and everything."

It took Neer a moment, but as their eyes adjusted, they saw a car in the distance. A familiar Cadillac. How long had it been since Zen had left the hotel? Neer couldn't help but laugh.

"I think I'll stay out here," Jane decided. "Wait for her to come home." Neer nodded. "Shouldn't be very long, but . . . you mind telling a story while we wait?"

Neer didn't mind at all.

TIMEBOX

Raven didn't know she was listening to the radiator, but she was. She squinted through the window of the third-floor sunroom, watching a man outside on the street. At first, he had kicked the tires of his car, talking to himself and shaking his head. But now he laid his whole upper body against the hood as though embracing the car, pleading with it, cajoling it to work. A drone whizzed above his head, doing its abrupt and skittish hummingbird dance midair, its red camera indicator light blinking. He did not seem to notice. Finally, the man stood and tipped his head back, looking into the sky, and covered his eyes with his hand. He seemed to be crying. Raven fumbled with the locks on the windowpane. Two right to open? Or two left? Or one left, one right, facing away? She could never remember. The locks had been painted over and over, and as she tugged at one, tiny white splinters leaped into the air, sticking to the damp glass.

"What are you doing? It's freezing out."

Raven jumped, banging her knuckle against the window-pane. She turned, feeling guilty without knowing why. Akilah took her injured hand and brought it to her face, examining it closely before kissing Raven's aching finger.

"There's a dude outside with a broke-down car. *Stressed*. I was just wondering if we could do something."

Akilah arched a brow. "You fix cars now? From three stories up?"

Raven felt a hotness rise around her neck. "No. I dunno—I thought we could call somebody maybe. Or maybe he's out of gas. Just thought I would ask."

Akilah's eyes slid over the slivers of white paint on the dark hardwood floor. "Got it. I just came in here to see what all this noise is about. I guess it's this thing." She slapped at the radiator, then pulled her hand away. "Ow!"

"You okay, babe? That's hot."

"Yeah, I see that now."

"Sorry. It's a radiator."

Raven regretted the condescension as soon as the sentence was out of her mouth. She hadn't meant it like that. But taking conscious stock of the radiator for the first time sent her mind elsewhere. When she heard the word come out of her own mouth, it was as though someone had shifted a radio dial out of the static and into the glory of a song you danced to in middle school, and Raven paused to take in the keen singing of the metal. The hot hiss, low whistle, and the *bang-bang-bang* that meant warmth was coming.

Akilah glared at the radiator accusingly. "It must be broken." She leaned forward to examine it. "We can get the maintenance woman to come take a look at it when she does the dishwasher. It's not pulling off the food for the compost chute and it's not sorting the dishes."

So, it just washes dishes, Raven thought. Best to save that battle for later. Triage. "The radiator's not broken," she said, stepping past Akilah, out of the sunroom and into the living room. "It's just old. That's what they do. I've always kinda liked the noise, honestly." Behind her, she felt the thrust of Akilah's forthcoming protest in some intangible but irrefutable way, like the weight in the air before a thunderstorm. She changed the subject quickly. "You see that hook in the ceiling? We can hang a plant. Or some fabric, the way you liked in JJ's apartment."

Akilah nodded, appeased. She stepped into the living room and took Raven's hand. Her palm was still warm to the touch. They moved through the rooms together, Raven marveling at each detail—two bedrooms, the linen closet in the bathroom, the counter space, her first ever dishwasher, "broken" though it was. Akilah reserved comment, and the less she spoke the more Raven chattered on, filling the space. *Their* space. They continued in this way until Raven, singing the merits of the light fixtures, was interrupted.

"What do you think this is for?" Akilah had let her hand go and was peering through a small door adjacent to the dining room. Raven moved to her side and looked. It was a large pantry, with built-in cabinetry at the bottom and old shelving that reached the high ceiling. The space atop the cabinets was broad enough to function as a workspace, and the pantry was wide enough and deep enough for two people to pass in and out comfortably.

Raven stepped inside and tugged at the chain cord dangling from the ceiling, and the room was flooded with a harsh light from the unadorned bulbs. "It's like a kitchen prep space, or storage space, looks like. These old apartments have all these little built-in extras. That's why I feel so lucky that we snagged this place. We can put whatever we want in here. Canned food, or you can brew kombucha. Honestly, it's big enough to be a writing room, or study, if we want to put a stool up to this counter. Or a meditation room . . ."

Raven turned; Akilah was gone.

She felt that mixture of humiliation at the realization that she had been talking to herself and relief that by definition no one was around to know. She stepped out of the pantry/kombucha brewery/study. She could hear Akilah at the front door, talking to someone.

"Yeah, everything seems fine but the dishwasher. Thanks for checking."

"No problem. I can come in sometime this week and take a look."

Raven stood behind Akilah and waved. "Hello! Good to see you."

Her first impression was that the maintenance woman was tall enough to fill the door frame, but after a beat Raven realized that that was not so. She just commanded the space, and when she spoke her tenor voice magnified the effect. She wore a navy jumpsuit streaked with dust at the knees, and an enormous key ring hung from her belt, audible if she moved even slightly. The jumpsuit had a name badge sewn on at the chest: CORNELIA. Her gray hair was braided tightly into two thick plaits that met at the back of her head. She nodded formally at Raven.

"Hope y'all are settling in okay. Just knock or call if you need anything."

Raven started to speak, but Akilah was already closing the door, looking at her chronoband anxiously. "Thanks, Cornelia," she said, and Raven winced at the casual dismissal and the sound of the older woman's unadorned first name. It hung in the air, bare and embarrassing. No *Ms. Cornelia*, or *ma'am*. The lock clicked shut, and Akilah turned cheerily on her heels. "Thai food for dinner?"

Only later, after they were fed, eating straight from the styrofoam since all their plates were in boxes, seated on blankets on the floor; after they had watched two episodes of *A Different World*, and split the bottle of celebratory "first grown-up apartment" champagne that Akilah's mother had ordered for them;

after they had made love on the fold-out futon that would eventually go in the guest room but until Thursday's mattress delivery was their only bed; after Raven had lain blissfully on her stomach and realized that the pillow under her face was not her own but Akilah's, and taken in the smell of almond oil and sage while Akilah murmured to her; after Akilah had drifted off next to her, the elastic corner of the mis-sized fitted sheet curled next to her face, and Raven realized she couldn't sleep in this new place, and wondered whether this futon was too uncomfortable to offer to guests, did she startle with the memory of the weeping man and his car. Silently, she slid from the bed, grabbing her T-shirt from the floor, and moved to the sunroom. Outside, the night was still and the man was gone. The car was still there, and under the glare of the streetlight, it had accumulated two magnatickets.

RAVEN PACED THE APARTMENT IN A DAZE AS THE BEGINNINGS of dawn slipped between the blinds. Everything was in disarray, the glowing novelty of the night before all worn away and having left behind only the reality of half-opened boxes and dust and disorder. The hardened remnants and orange oily streaks of the unattended leftovers on the counter lent the back half of the apartment an odor that, on its own, should not have been unpleasant—drying green onions, lemongrass, and fish sauce, tinged with sugar—but fluttering as it did at the edge of her growing anxiety, it nauseated Raven.

Akilah was still in bed. Raven wanted to open the blinds to offer some assistance to the feeble overhead light, but let her be. She tried to rip open a cardboard box next to the mirrored closet door. Rather than tearing, the packing tape adhesive caught itself, folding over, taut and strengthened. Her breath quickened.

"What's the problem?" Akilah had sat up and was fishing

around the sheets, annoyed, for the bonnet that had come off in the night.

"I'm gonna be late for work," said Raven, disappointed at the tremulousness of her own new morning voice. "I have work and then class right after, so I'm trying to get all my shit together and it's taking me forever to find everything. My books, my notebooks. And now I can't find my damn earrings."

Akilah had retrieved her laptop from the side of the futon, but paused her scrolling to cut her eyes up at Raven. "What do you need earrings for?"

Raven bent over the box, pulling out scarves and a fitted hat, pens and forks, a bottle of lotion. She wanted to turn the whole thing over onto the floor and smash the cardboard with her feet. A small aluminum bird sculpture that Akilah had bought in Costa Rica poked out cheerily from the pile, and as Raven reached for the box, its sharp edge cut her finger, swift and shallow. She was bleeding, and Akilah was still talking, but at the bottom of the box she saw it—the old cookie tin that she knew was full of her jewelry. A Doc Martens shoe had sat on top of it and dented the lid, but there it was. She tugged it out of the box and held it to her chest, knowing she should find a Band-Aid somewhere and knowing just as well how impossible that would be. Suddenly short of breath, she turned to Akilah.

"I just didn't want to go out without earrings." Raven thought of her mother, smiling at her in the mirror each day as she put her earrings on. They would be hoops or chandeliers, shining against the muted tones of her uniform. Raven would be seated on the rim of the bathtub, dressed for the school day that wouldn't begin for two hours yet, ready for her mother to drop her at Ms. Shirlene's house on the way to work. *Just a little something to brighten my day,* her mother would say, pinching her cheeks. *Since you won't be with me.*

She started herself out of the memory and looked away from

Akilah. In her search, she had been unable to stop picturing her-self at work without the earrings, sitting in the ergonomic desk chair that cost almost as much as a month's rent, touching her bare earlobes, feeling the small forever-swollen place where they were pierced. It would drive her nuts all day, she knew—every tight-smiling customer staring only at her ears as they inquired about a ten-class package or whether they could borrow an extra mat or if there was a towel service. And no matter what anyone else thought, the earrings were for Raven. For *her* and her alone. Just one thing—normal, predictable, controllable.

She moved to the bedroom door, running through a rapid-fire mental accounting. Bag, wallet, keys, notebook, pens, phone, charger. TriCard. Books . . . it was Tuesday. Pathophysi-ology. She frowned. *Shit.* There was a quiz today, one she hadn't had time to study for, and she desperately needed to pass this class, given how things had gone last semester, when she had completely and utterly failed to balance her work schedule with school, and—

"I just think you should do some reflecting," Akilah was saying. "You've just . . . you've always had this thing. Since col-lege. Like, why do you care so much what other people think of you? And why does that have to manifest in how you dress? Earrings are cool, but they're also emblematic of a kind of re-spectable orthodox femininity that I don't think matters that much. Like, do you need to wear pearls to work?"

Raven closed her eyes and leaned against the door frame. "You know damn well I don't wear pearls to work."

Akilah rolled her eyes, but she was all in now. She closed the laptop. "No need to curse at me. I'm just having a conversa-tion with you. I feel that in a healthy relationship I should be able to have a conversation with my partner about how we move through the world. And, you know, toxic patterns."

Raven shook her head. "I have to go. I'm sorry. I don't—I just don't have time right now. We can talk about this later."

She rushed back into the kitchen. Keys, keys, keys. On the counter? Akilah called after her. "And that's another thing! You never have any time—you need to slow down!"

Easy for you to say.

Raven glanced at her chronoband. It was 9:19. The bus she wanted to catch, the last bus that would get her to work on time, was four minutes away from the stop. If she could get her keys quickly, everything else was in a bag by the door, and she could sprint to the stop and just barely make it.

Kitchen. Counter.

No keys.

Akilah was still talking, but Raven couldn't fully make it out. It was better that she didn't hear. She was crying now, and she still couldn't breathe right, and everything felt hot and itchy. Her eyes darted around the room, as though the keys might appear in some place where they had not been moments prior, as though an answer might appear, or money for a car, or her mother with the breakfast she hadn't eaten. None of those things was forthcoming. But the door to the pantry was open, and inside Akilah had already stored some extra toilet paper, paper towels, and a box of tissues. Raven walked into the pantry, tore open the tissue box, and closed the door. She curled herself into a corner, wedged against the cabinets, and cried.

By the time she was done, it almost felt good. Being alone, in this little contained space, not having anyone to watch her cry and say anything about it. She wiped her face and blew her nose. Akilah had bought the soft brand-name tissue, and that was nice. She looked at her chronoband again. Fifteen minutes had passed. Being on time was done with, but if she could wash her face and get to the bus stop, she wouldn't be that late, and Hilarie was unlikely to care anyway. Raven had her class, so she wouldn't be locking up after work, and Akilah would be home from the bookstore to let her in at night, so she could get by without keys today. Raven took a deep, shivering breath.

This could work. She stood, rubbing the small of her back where it had been pressed against the hinge of the cabinet door, and walked purposefully out of the pantry and toward the front door.

". . . there are these things we inherit," Akilah was saying from the bedroom. "And there are ways to move past them." Raven's brow furrowed. She must be on a call—ranting for fifteen minutes into the ether was a lot, even for Akilah. Raven stuck her head into the bedroom.

"I'm out, babe. I couldn't find the keys, so could you let me in tonight? Love you." Akilah peered at her from amid a nest of blankets. She hadn't even moved.

"Oh. Sure. Love you too."

Raven reached for her bag. She should call Hilarie once she got on the bus, just to let her know how late she would be. She would be cool about it. After all, Raven reasoned, she had just moved. Everyone knows moving is the worst.

She grabbed her knit hat from the hook on the wall where she had left it the night before. *This is where keys should go*. Raven looked at her chronoband. It read 9:20 A.M.

RAVEN FOUND HERSELF OSCILLATING ALL DAY BETWEEN BOUTS of frenzied energy and completely debilitating fatigue. One minute she was Super Clerk—folding sanitized towels and laying them methodically in the drawer behind her desk, clearing the customer service inbox within the first half hour of her late arrival, greeting each person who entered the yoga studio with almost unnatural aplomb. The next moment, she could barely hold her head upright, excusing herself at one point for a bathroom break that was actually an excuse to just lock herself in the small lime-painted restroom, lean against the wall, and close her eyes without being seen. She chalked it up to anxiety and the exhaustion of the morning's cry, as though it had sapped something out of her that couldn't be recovered. When her eyes were shut, she pictured the interior of her body as being filled with battery acid, or what she imagined battery acid to be—a roiling liquid, at once blue and green, its tides rising and falling unpredictably.

In her up moments, she brewed black tea, and drank it, and brewed more, and drank it. She searched online for a cheap repair shop that wouldn't require her to take her chronoband to the DisCom store. It was years old and no way was it under warranty, and God only knows how much they'd charge her there to fix a chronoband that somehow stopped keeping time for fifteen minutes before starting back up again. She counted the hours until it was time to go to class. On her break, she ambled to the coffee distro down the block, stood quietly for a while staring into their baked goods case as though pondering something deep and unknowable, and hoped no one would notice when she surreptitiously took a paper cup and lid from the stack on a corner counter and walked out the door without buying anything.

Back at the yoga studio, she just had time to fill the cup with coffee from the singed pot, put the lid on the cup, and tug her jacket on before Jazmyne came in for her afternoon shift. Raven wanted to tell her about how a white woman who had been a member of the studio for years and attended classes four times a week had referred to her, Raven, as "Jazmyne" that morning. Last time that had happened, Raven had thought they would have a good laugh about it. Jazmyne was several inches taller than Raven, and several shades lighter, wore rimless glasses and had a septum piercing where Raven had neither, and was fond of tremendous 3C wigs. Raven was bald. But Jazmyne had not laughed at all—only nodded quietly and moved to the coat closet to hang up her things, stung and silent. So this time Raven kept it to herself.

Besides, Jazmyne seemed overcome with something already. Raven put her bag down on the counter, pausing her planned rush to the door. "Hey. You good, ma?"

Jazmyne moved her head in a way that was neither a nod nor

a refusal, settling into the desk chair. "I'll be all right. I'm a little flustered. I just came from the hospital."

Raven frowned. "Your pops?"

"Yeah. He's scheduled for another surgery on Monday. And I have to call his job and say he won't be there, and then figure out who can take PTO between me, Cece, and Trey, but I don't know if I can count on Trey to ask all the questions and write down everything the doctors say, and last time—"

She cut herself off abruptly, shaking her hands in front of her eyes as though furiously batting away a swarm of gnats. "I'm sorry. I can't get all into it. I know you have to go, and I was late."

"I was late this morning. You're good. For real."

Jazmyne nodded, swallowing. "We'll make it work." She pulled a glittery pink water bottle from her bag and took a long, slow sip, then looked up at Raven. "You know what kills me? This sounds stupid, but . . . it's not just that he's sick. Like, yes, okay. I worry. But my father has been sick forever. It's just all this stuff *around* the sickness that makes it harder. I hate visiting hours. I hate being told that a doctor is going to come talk to you and answer a question, and sitting around for infinity waiting for dude to show up, only for him to bounce thirty seconds later. I hate the building. I hate parking hella far from the entrance and then rushing to get to the whatever-the-fuck pavilion and taking the third elevator down the blahzay-blah memorial corridor and by the time you get there . . ." She exhaled heavily. "I just hate it."

Raven nodded, having so much to say and not knowing what was worthy. Jazmyne looked at her own chronoband. "Girl, you gon' be late. I'll clock you out."

THE BUS WAS HOT, AND SLOW. SOMEONE IN THE BACK WHO Raven couldn't see was coughing fitfully. She checked her chronoband. Two voxes from Mom. Raven double-tapped her right temple and called her mother, who had just finished a shift and was pulling into the bus depot. Raven kept her eyes low so that the aircast screen hovered just above her lap, her mother's face beaming up at her from her knees. She told Raven about a fight two people on the bus had had over a stolen TriCard. "And baby, when I tell you she got so mad at the other lady that she kicked her off the damn bus? I mean *kicked* her! I pulled up to the red light and she put her foot right in her behind and ol' girl was out the door! I dropped the hover to about two, three inches *just* in time. If it was one of the old-model buses with the stairs and the big tires, boy, she would have busted her head. And I got on the intercom and I said, '*Hey!*'" She paused, and when she spoke again she was laughing so hard that she wheezed, struggling to get the words out. "I said, '*Hey!*'" She pointed forcefully at her chest. "'*I'm* the only one who gets to kick people off this bus, you hear?'"

Raven let out a high peal of laughter that shook her body. "Ma, you're killing me!"

And that's how she missed her stop, wiping the tears from her eyes. It didn't help that the windows of the bus were fogged with hot breath and vapor. And so Raven, who had been late for work, was now late to class, and did her best to hold her head up high as she made her way to the only available spot, in the front row, directly in front of the professor, who registered a minor annoyance at the piercing squeal that emerged from the hinged metal chair when Raven pulled out a seat for herself. A few people looked up, visibly bothered by being distracted from the quiz they had already begun.

It seemed as though the moment it started, it was over. Then the hot bus again. And then home. Ms. Cornelia was in the foyer, putting a new label on the mailbox. JACKSON & SAINT CLAIR. She was rubbing over the plastic label with the blunt end of a key, pushing the adhesive against the metal. She nodded solemnly when she saw Raven.

"Mailbox is all set for you. Put the key in an envelope under your door this morning."

Raven was about to thank her when she was struck with the realization that these small details—the mailbox, the key—felt like the greatest kindness anyone had shown her all day. The image of the mailbox at her last apartment jumped suddenly into her head: layered with year after year of peeling mailing labels, permanent marker that bled from the rain, masking tape. Name under name under name, none of them hers. She swallowed.

"Thank you, Ms. Cornelia," she said, smiling. "I *really* appreciate it." She tried to savor the words, her sincerity a little pink cotton candy cloud hanging between them.

"That new apartment working out for you?" As she spoke, Ms. Cornelia peered closely at a spot of paint on the door that was just barely chipped, running her finger over the varnish.

"Yes, thank you so much. Definitely the nicest place I've ever lived. Heat was real good last night."

Ms. Cornelia turned and faced her squarely. "Good. Good." Raven had one foot on the stairs but waited, unsure whether the older woman had more to say.

"We had two units vacant at the same time, but when I met you I thought . . . I thought that one would do you good. I take my job very seriously in that regard. You understand me?" She looked somberly at Raven, her dark brown eyes rimmed with a thin icy line of blue. *Arcus senilis,* thought Raven.

"Sometimes people think they want one thing," Ms. Cornelia continued, "but they *need* another. And some people aren't ready to take care of what they think is right for them. So I give it a lot of thought. A lot of thought."

Raven nodded primly. She didn't know much about property but wanted to say something adequately grateful. "It's perfect. The south-facing windows in the sunroom especially. I'm thinking I'm finna put some plants in there. It'll be good."

Ms. Cornelia nodded, but now she was looking away from Raven again. "It will be," she said, suddenly dreamy. "It will be good. It was the right decision."

On the climb to the third floor, Raven felt like she was moving underwater, her legs weighted with the day of worrying and sprinting and sitting and standing and rushing and worrying some more. At the door to the apartment, she knocked, then knocked harder. She called Akilah's name at a volume she hoped would rouse her if she was sleeping without alerting the neighbors, because they had *just* moved in and she didn't want to be *that* neighbor already, not in the first week. When there was still no answer, she felt so depleted that she sat on the doormat and cried quietly, her head tipped back against the heavy wood of the door, her knuckles hurting.

Akilah was not home, despite knowing that Raven would be back at precisely this time and was without keys. Raven sent her a vox, whispering so that the neighbors wouldn't hear. *Home soon? Locked out.* No response. Botched attempts at comings and goings from her own home felt like a bad sign. But having already had one good cry for the day—and not wanting to be the crying-in-the-hallway neighbor any more than she wanted to be the banging-on-the-door neighbor—Raven allowed herself exactly one minute of muted weeping before she shuffled back down the stairs to see if Ms. Cornelia could let her in, which she did gamely, asking no questions. She only turned over each key on the massive ring methodically, examining them closely until she found the correct one, and told Raven, "It will be nice to have a quiet moment to yourself at the end of the day." Raven nodded.

"It's good to be alone a little bit," Ms. Cornelia continued. "To sit with your thoughts." She waved a solemn goodbye and closed the door before Raven could respond.

Inside, the furniture hadn't arrived yet, and there was no

Akilah, either. But she had left all the lights on. Of course. Raven found her keys almost immediately, sitting forlornly on the bathroom sink.

Of course.

In the kitchen were arrayed the paper bags of nonperishable groceries Raven had brought from her old apartment, untouched since they had moved in. Fishing around in one of them yielded a family-size box of spaghetti and a can of tuna, and she found a pot in a box labeled KITCHEN that was partly filled with cooking utensils and partly filled with Akilah's workout clothes. She turned the water on, running it for a few moments to get any cadmium out, then put the pot on the stove and turned it on. She checked the time on the oven clock: 6:02. She could just catch DJ Crash Crash. She triple-tapped her left temple, and the familiar voice flooded her head. Leaving the tuna and noodles on the counter, she hauled the rest of the groceries into the pantry.

"Goooood morning, midnight! This is DJ Crash Crash. If you had a hard day at work, you made it. Congrats. Tonight on the show we have a very special guest, Miss Flora Cruz, fresh and ready before her set tomorrow night at the Hopeless Note Comedy Revue. Everybody needs to come through. Drink specials, free TriCard points, and I hear there will be some VIP guests in the house. Flora, how you doing?"

Raven began pulling cans from the bag and stacking them neatly on the shelf. Black beans, chickpeas, cannellini beans on one side.

"Good to be here, Crash Crash. You know, I been listening to you my whole life and I never thought I'd get to meet you. Your head shines just like they say. Can I touch it?"

Several large, squat cans of stewed tomatoes. Tomato paste. Tomato sauce. Diced tomatoes. What was the difference?

"Now, see then, Flora, I'd have to charge you, and you supposed to be my guest . . ."

Raven giggled. Flora Cruz went into a routine about how if the rumors about "day-erase" tech were real, she would use it to make her boyfriend think all his exes were ugly, and the jokes were so stupid but her delivery was so winsome and sincere, and Crash Crash egged her on with such charm, that soon Raven was laughing so hard that her chest hurt. She was still catching her breath when DJ Crash Crash said, *"And now, your weather report, ten past the hour."* She had completely lost track of time. Shoving the twelfth and final can of black beans onto the pantry shelf, she turned and was surprised to see that the heavy door had swung shut behind her. Pushing it open and rushing out of the small room, Raven almost slipped in her socks as she rounded the corner to the kitchen, expecting to see the pot boiling over.

She peered into the pot, then took a step back, startled. The flame was going, but the water was flat and still. No steam rose. Raven held her hand over the surface of the water and felt nothing.

In her head, she heard the tiny, crowing voice. *"Goooood morning, midnight! This is DJ Crash Crash. If you had a hard day at work, you made it. Congrats. Tonight on the show . . ."*

When Akilah got home, Raven was seated on the couch, staring at the wall and biting her nails to the quick, the half-eaten bowl of noodles and tuna abandoned on the floor at her feet. When the door creaked open, she jumped up.

"Hey! I have to show you something."

Akilah raised an eyebrow and put a tote full of books on the floor. "Hi, good to see you too," she said.

Raven nodded. "Sorry, sorry. Hi. I—"

Akilah shook her head. "I can't believe it, man. I just got home, and I see what's-her-name in the hallway. The maintenance woman. And she tells me that you were locked out and she let you in? And that she didn't charge today, but that *just for my reference* the property management company has a fee for that next time? I was like . . . okay, thanks. No need to be the fucking police about it."

Raven furrowed her brow. "You said that to her?"

"No, no. I just felt like she was all up in our personal business and I didn't like it. Like, okay, people lose their keys. It's whatever."

"Well, sure, but that's the thing, right?" Akilah's arm was stuck in her coat, and Raven reached over to help her. "People lose their keys. And I get why they don't want people to call her about lost keys twenty-four/seven."

Akilah rolled her eyes. "Yeah, disincentives solve everything. That's so depressing. Like, can't we just have a system of care where we don't have to pay people for every little thing? Why do we even have locks in our building? We should be able to trust our neighbors. When I was growing up we never locked our door."

Raven swallowed. She thought of summertime visits to the house where Akilah had grown up, a Victorian on Ursa Island. There was one ferry that could shuttle you back and forth to Palo Alto, and it required a pass from an approved resident. Once you were on the island, it was patrolled at night by security guards, one of whom had stopped Raven once when she left a sweater at a neighbor's house during a dinner party and had gone by herself to retrieve it. Her TriCard was in the sweater, and he made her do a retinal scan, alone in the middle of the street. After clearing her, he apologized—her daily guest registration had nearly expired, Akilah had forgotten to renew it for the night, and his scanner had clocked her from three hundred yards away as having an unrecognized data signature. She had spent the night unable to sleep, sobbing as Akilah held her, whispering *I'm sorry, I'm sorry, I'm sorry* until the sun was high and her dad was calling up the stairs about pancakes.

But yes, it was true. They left the doors unlocked.

Raven eyed the books Akilah had abandoned on the floor.

When she spoke, her tone was measured. "Are you just getting home from work?"

"Nah. I only went in for a couple of hours today. Willow invited me over to come see this mural she's been working on and wanted to return some books I loaned her."

"Oh." The rest of the sentence lingered at the back of Raven's throat like the taste of burnt garlic. *So you were home pretty much all day. Is there a reason you weren't home to let me in? Or did you just forget me?* She said none of it, though. Instead, she grabbed Akilah's hand.

"I have to show you something."

In the confines of the pantry, Raven looked at her chronoband: 7:08.

"Okay," she announced. "Ten minutes have passed, right?"

Akilah looked around, fixing her gaze on part of the wall where there had been some water damage and the paint had peeled. "Um, yep. If you say so."

"No, for real. We came in here at six fifty-eight. It's seven oh-eight." She showed Akilah the chronoband the way a magician shows the crowd his empty top hat.

"Okay, yeah. I see."

Raven's heart was beating extra fast as she turned the doorknob slowly, as though afraid to break something. "Okay. Okay." She opened the door and pulled Akilah through after her, then held up the chronoband again.

It read 7:08. Her heart sank. Akilah stared at her. "Yep. Was that like . . . a performance about the importance of mindfulness and presence? Or the passage of time? Help me out. I'm missing something."

Raven was crestfallen. Akilah had already gone into the kitchen, peering into the empty fridge as though willing something to appear. "I should have picked up some wine on the way home," she murmured. Raven's mind raced. What had gone wrong? Or was she losing it? Or was it something about *her*, not the room? Or . . .

She turned back to Akilah.

"Listen. I know this sounds crazy. But can you just go in the pantry alone? Without me. For five minutes."

"What?"

Raven was already tugging her back to the pantry door. "Please?"

THEY SAT CROSS-LEGGED ON THE FLOOR OF THE DINING ROOM. Akilah had an expression on her face that Raven struggled to read. She looked at once scared for her life and like she was watching someone incredibly sexy across a bar—her mouth opened slightly, one eyebrow raised, doing little to conceal her desire.

"So time passes in there . . . normally . . . but not out here. Or it resets when you come out here."

Raven nodded.

"But only if you're alone, with the door closed?"

Raven nodded again. She hadn't spoken since Akilah had emerged. Having someone else confirm this extraordinary thing suddenly made it real, possible, and little by little she was transitioning it from the realm of her mind reserved for minor absurdities and the likelihood of her own insanity into the realm of the speakable. It was happening slowly, piecemeal, like moving through a beaded curtain.

Akilah gripped her hand. "Do you know what this means?"

Raven nodded. "It means I don't have to be . . . *tired* all the time. I can do my schoolwork and not be behind. I can nap before I go to work."

She tapped on the doorknob triumphantly, as though it were the source of this miracle. "I can go visit my family and spend time there and know that I can make it up when I get back. We can finally spend more time together. I can . . . I can get it all back, love." She had been looking up at the ceiling as she spoke, this new life arrayed in a constellation before her: rest, and sleep, and time. She could relax with Akilah. She could make time to think. She could fill the parts of herself that now felt so hollow. Squeezing Akilah's palm against hers, she looked down, making eye contact with her . . .

Akilah looked at her in disbelief. No, Raven realized after a beat. It was *disgust*.

"Do you . . . do you *hear* yourself?"

Akilah stood, faced Raven, then abruptly began pacing the room, keeping her eye on the pantry door as she stalked back and forth. "Everything you're saying is *I, I, I, me*. This is so much bigger than you, Ray. This is . . . this is *community* wealth. We should open the room up, to—to organizers who need to get work done! Or as an artist's residency. Something good for everyone. Think of all our people. Think of what this could mean for them."

Raven tried to imagine artists and organizers coming and going in and out of the apartment to use their pantry. She looked around at the dining room, its hardwood floors shining and bare, an untackled pile of boxes making the space still all but unusable. "But Akilah . . . this is . . . this was supposed to be our home. You and me."

Now Akilah touched the brass doorknob of the pantry, circling it as though tracing the outline of a map. "This is so, *so* much bigger than *you and me,* Raven," she said. She was whispering, barely audible, and Raven, still seated on the floor, leaned toward her to listen.

"Don't you see what this could be? What this could *do?*" Akilah ran her fingers across the dingy shelves, touching each of the cans Raven had stacked neatly, one by one.

"With this small room, we could change the whole system,

Ray. And you want to use it as a home office or something? To be more, what, *productive*? To *produce* more?" She was sneering now. "You know that the last thing this world needs is more stuff."

"But that's not— I don't want to make more stuff. I want to help people. I want to be a nurse. Isn't that for the greater good?"

Akilah stopped moving around and stared directly at Raven, her spine straight.

"Raven. Don't you get it? This room *severs our relationship to time*. That's it. That's the whole thing. The crux of it all, you know? We could—we could end capitalism!"

And then she was pacing again. Raven could see the undersides of her white socks with every footfall, and at the back of her mind she registered that the socks had accumulated a speckled layer of gray dust. *We haven't swept since we moved in*, she thought grimly.

Akilah continued. "This is about collective responsibility. We have something really radical on our hands. We need to use it for more than . . . taking a nap."

Raven recoiled like she had been spit on. In a rush, she felt it all at once, all the weight of all the tired she had ever been. She closed her eyes. She was in kindergarten, riding the bus with her mom at the end of a shift, sitting near a security guard who had just gotten off work and her three nodding-off kids, hoping that any monitor from the Transit Authority who boarded the bus to track her mother would think she belonged to this other woman. She was fifteen, telling her teacher she couldn't be in chess club anymore because she had to pick up extra hours at the sandwich distro, struggling to stay awake and finish her homework at the library before work started at six, and staying until midnight, her legs aching as she mopped the floor. She was twenty-three, grinning at the admissions counselor and telling her yes, no problem, handling the coursework in the program would be no problem, and the internship, and the field assignment, and the study groups, and the commute? No problem. Not a problem. She was running, always running—running to work, running to eat, running to class, studying at 2 A.M. while Akilah was fast asleep, dozing off at her computer, pinching herself, slapping herself, eating ice cubes to stay awake. She had bookmarked an article about nursing in her quickfile and highlighted the part about salaries, and how nurses could use their understanding of science and medicine without going to medical school, which cost so much, and they could help people. She could get there, she told herself. But she would have to sprint.

Raven had been sprinting. Had been out of breath for years. The days of her past and future and present running sat like a weight on her chest, but she couldn't articulate any of it. It felt like a thin haze hanging in the air between them, and Akilah was just waving it away, as if none of it mattered. As if Raven didn't matter.

Akilah was shaking her head now. "Raven, there are Black women out there who are really—really in *need*—"

At that, Raven's jaw dropped, despite herself. Akilah stopped her pacing, staring at her. But once her mouth was open, Raven's brain seemed to register the possibility of more oxygen, and she yawned massively, her hand flying to her mouth to cover it.

"Akilah, I'm sorry, but I'm just . . . really tired. Can we talk about this tomorrow? I have a morning class. I need to be up at five A.M."

When Raven went to brush her teeth, there was a note tucked under the front door. SORRY FOR YOUR SITUATION BUT FYI UR FIGHTING IS VERY LOUD. WE HAVE A BABY WHO CANNOT SLEEP. PLEASE KEEP IT DOWN THX. Raven's face burned with shame when she read it, and she instinctively looked around, as though the angry neighbor might be hiding in the coat closet. She tore the note into pieces.

• — •

AKILAH FELT HOT WHEN SHE WOKE UP, AND BEFORE SHE WAS fully conscious, she had already shoved the covers from her body. Raven had left the curtains open, and the midmorning sun lay in a concerted beam across her face and torso. Akilah was sure it looked beautiful, though it left her to wake up with an aching head, sweating beneath her thin white tee. She grabbed a notebook from the side table, and a dull pencil. *Photo series— time-lapse self-portraits? Morning portraits?*

She checked her chronoband: 10:04 A.M. She was supposed to be at the bookstore at 11:00. She needed to shower, stop at the coffee distro, and hit up Willow to figure out when the next clinic organizing meeting would be. She squinted at the closet, which still hung bare of hangers, much less clothes. All these damn boxes. She should stop at the Exchange after work and pick up some new clothes—some overalls, maybe, and some fall sweaters.

Akilah brushed her teeth. Raven had unpacked a box yesterday that included a pile of clean underwear, and she pulled a pair from where Raven had left her boxer briefs neatly folded on a chair. She smiled to herself. "After all these years, when you got a girl who folds your underwear, you'd be stupid to let that go," she had told Willow. "She been on that since college."

Willow had nodded absentmindedly, reaching for a box cutter to unpack a new shipment. "I feel that," she had said. "As long as you both have space to grow, after all this time, you know? Hopefully you grow in the same direction."

Akilah had been pondering that for a minute. *Growing in the same direction.* It made her think of the entrance to her parents' vineyard, the massive gate marked by a trellis of Zinlot grapes. Every year, the groundskeepers would ascend a pair of ladders, toting shears as big as her arm, and cut away the parts of the vine that would not or could not wind around the trellis. If parts of the plant could not grow the way they were ordered to grow, they were mercilessly cut away. Something about it always struck Akilah as terribly violent. Coercive. She had said so to her father once, at dinner.

"Violence, my love, is man re-creating himself," said her father, refilling his glass. "According to Fanon, anyway."

Akilah was a believer in signs, in fate, and in the universe telling you things. So when, at precisely 10:11 A.M., she spotted a copy of *The Wretched of the Earth* at the top of the tote bag she had retrieved from Willow, and it came just in the midst of her reverie about the vines and Fanon, she felt that that was all the sign she needed. She grabbed the book at first, then her computer, before doubling back, picking up the entire tote, and dragging it all into the pantry.

"I'VE GIVEN THIS A LOT OF THOUGHT," RAVEN SAID THAT NIGHT. "And, Akilah, I want to meet you where you are. I really do. You're right, this is so much bigger than us. Or it could be. I want to be . . . I want to be open to that. I truly do. And I want to bring relief to our people. And joy. I want to share your vision of what's possible."

Akilah nodded, distracted. Raven went on. "But you're always talking about boundaries. And I just think, you know, if we have this thing, we need some boundaries. Like maybe not telling anyone about it right now, and just making a plan, you know? Some . . . norms. Or agreements." As she spoke, she was carefully picking individual peas out of her tofu fried rice, piling them in a corner of the plastic takeout lid. Akilah stared at the little growing mountain of peas, half listening.

"And another thing I was thinking—we don't even know how it affects our bodies. Like, what if there's some kind of side effect? It could be, like . . . I don't know. Aging us. Or it could be carcinogenic. We don't know anything about it."

Akilah nodded absentmindedly. She had learned one thing about the room's effect on her body, something she hadn't considered but that should have been obvious, in retrospect. She had spent hours in the pantry that morning before work—reading Fanon, journaling, smoking weed, pulling tarot cards. After three hours inside and two minutes outside, she realized that she was too tired to go to work, so she spent another hour in the room drifting in and out of sleep before waking up, refreshed, showering, and getting to the bookstore on time. But it meant her day had an extra four-hour addendum, and the effect was so disconcerting that she couldn't process anything else Raven was asking her to think about in this moment. It was like being high for the first time, unclear on what was happening or what had happened or when it would all end. She avoided Raven's eyes, and Raven, seemingly relieved that broaching this topic had not immediately led to another fight and taking Akilah's reticence for deep and meaningful contemplation, was happy to chatter along.

"So we're agreed, then?" Raven suddenly reached out, tenderly, and touched Akilah's cheekbone with her index finger, drawing an invisible heart beneath her eye. "We're cool?"

Akilah smiled and drew her close. "We're cool."

RAVEN'S EYES SNAPPED OPEN. SHE HAD STRUGGLED TO FALL asleep, and once she had, her sleep was restless, filled with anxious half-formed stress dreams that were jarring yet incomprehensible, and impossible to remember. But when she was finally and truly awake, she knew why—her pharmacology take-home midterm was due at 9 A.M. How could she have forgotten? She had thought about it all day at work yesterday, and had planned to start it after dinner. But the planned conversation with Akilah had consumed all of her mental reserves, and it had gone so oddly well. Having steeled herself entirely for that talk to be a disaster meant that when it wasn't, it was like water had been poured over a pilot light inside her, and everything was extinguished. She had gone to bed feeling not soothed at all but empty and antsy, and now it was four in the morning and she had to finish a test for a required course in five hours, and then be at work an hour later. Moving silently to the edge of the futon, she sat up and stared at Akilah, unable to draw her gaze from her sleeping form but simultaneously terrified that her eyes were somehow shooting out beams of light that would wake Akilah any second.

Boundaries, thought Raven. *Boundaries.* Well, this was an extraordinary circumstance. She retrieved her computer, textbook, and notebook from her bag near the bed. On her way to the pantry, she turned the bathroom light on and closed the door. If Akilah woke up, she would think Raven was in there.

WHEN AKILAH ROSE AT TEN, SHE FOUND A POT OF COFFEE waiting for her, and a love note. She smiled. Raven had also located and washed a single mug and left it centered neatly on a square of paper towel. Akilah remembered college, the first time she was in Raven's dorm and saw the little caddy where Raven kept her few pieces of cutlery, two bowls, a couple of chipped plates, and . . . a seemingly infinite pile of small paper towel squares that she cut meticulously with a pair of sewing scissors. She had teased Raven, who had looked away from her hastily, saying only that that was how they did it at home. Akilah had found it charming then, because they didn't actually live together. Now she would pay Raven anything to keep a damn paper towel intact.

Afternoon shift—no work until one o'clock today. Though the coffee hadn't hit yet, Akilah felt charged—electrified, as though in dreaming her mind had been churning and eager. She felt at the high noon of herself, beaming and awake. She had things she wanted to write, things to read, questions to ask of herself and the world.

When she was settled in the pantry, seated amid a pile of pillows she had hauled in from the bedroom, incense lit, the first words Akilah wrote were these:

> If we carefully regard the works of art that we consider seminal in the history of the world—works of painting, literature, dance, sculpture; all the beautiful things wrought by human hands and imagination—it is clear that what unites them is time. Time purchased with hoarded and illegitimate wealth, time wrung from the muscles of Black bodies, time wrenched through a vicious alchemy from the violent arms of colonialism. Friends, we exist in a perpetual state of time debt, wherein only those who have benefited from this thieving achieve the privilege of what we so blithely call genius. Comrades, what would it mean if what was once stolen could now be repaid?

"Obviously, we need to consider what the contraindications might be for oral medications. If the epiglottis and esophagus are not fully functional for whatever reason, the patient could be at risk for nosocomial pneumonia, right?" Professor Nasir looked around expectantly, and everyone nodded. "You know what, this feels like a pretty good time to take a fifteen-minute break, and then when we come back I'll go over the midterm. See you all shortly."

The room was filled with the small fabric thuds of everyone arising at once from the lecture hall seats. Raven fished around in her bag for the doughnut she had bought earlier as a treat for getting through the midterm, then stood and stretched her legs.

She moved slowly and had sat at the back of the hall, so most of her classmates were gone from the room by the time she made it to the bottom row of seats and headed toward the door. To her minor horror, she arrived at the same time as Professor Nasir, and hung back awkwardly to let her pass. But instead of moving through the door, the older woman paused, smiling at her.

"Raven," she said. "Right?" Raven nodded. "You look a bit different from your picture in Pupilist. You had locs at the beginning of the year, I guess?"

Raven smiled and ran a hand over her bare head. "Yeah, for years and years. It was time for a change."

"Mmm," said Professor Nasir knowingly, her own blond-and-red locs hanging regally over her shoulders. "I bet that was a big goodbye. Hard to make a transition like that. But sometimes so necessary."

Raven nodded again, wanting to be present for this moment of unexpected attention but wondering despite herself how much of her scant fifteen-minute break had elapsed.

"Anyway," said the professor, "I won't keep you. I just wanted to say that you turned in a great midterm. Seemed like a huge leap forward from your last written assignment. Whatever you're doing, keep doing it! Okay?" She added the last word as though unsatisfied or slightly confused by the look on Raven's face, which was not the affirming glow she usually received in the wake of student praise.

"Okay," said Raven, conjuring up something she hoped looked like easy confidence. "Thanks so much. I will."

There was a short line at the microwave, and Raven leaned against the wall, balancing her doughnut on top of a container of leftovers. The two students in front of her were talking about the midterm. The one closer to her, she knew, was Julián. She followed him on the network, so she knew way too much about him—that he played conga drums, that he had two cats named Rémy and Martin, that he had been a barista and so knew how to make fancy pour-over coffee and latte art. But they had never spoken. He was deep in conversation with a girl whose name was Stephanie or Estelle—she couldn't remember. Something with a *st* sound.

"Honestly, this class, Micro, Chem . . . all of the science stuff? I'm good with. I feel like that's what I signed up for," she was saying to Julián. "It's the other stuff I struggle with. Foundations, management, ethics . . . all these *soft skills,* like they call them. It's all so fuzzy! Like, tell me the answer!"

Julián laughed merrily. It wasn't clear to Raven whether he actually agreed or was just being polite. But it was Estelle/Stephanie's turn at the microwave now, and deprived of a conversation partner, Julián seemed to notice Raven for the first time. He smiled amiably. "Raven? How's it going?"

Raven had been everywhere but where she was, caught up in tracing the steps that lay before her after class was over. Bus home, maybe a couple of hours to make some headway on the boxes if she did something simple for dinner, homework for Molecular Therapeutics. Hearing her name, she gathered herself within the span of normalcy, just barely escaping the extra beat that would have made it weird. "Hey," she said. "I'm good, good. Just happy that the midterm is over."

Julián nodded, turning his foil-wrapped sandwich over in his hands. "I hear that. Yo, by the way, your girl Akilah? That's your girl, right? Sorry to be weird. I follow her on the network. Anyway, that thing she posted today is . . . Mind-blowing isn't even the word. Just wild. I read it on my lunch break and haven't been able to stop thinking about it. That shit about how time is stolen from us? And the thought experiment at the end? The what's-it-called . . . timebox? Like Schrödinger's cat, but on some next-level shit? Man . . ."

Later, when Raven would replay this week in her head, there was so much that made her ashamed. So many things she was sure she could have done differently, or understood more quickly, no matter how many times her friends told her otherwise. But it was this moment that stuck with her—the moment when Julián kept talking, wired and emphatic, and she acted for all the world as though she shared what enthralled him. She too had read what Akilah had written, oh yes, of course, knew about it, was proud of her, supported it all, definitely.

On the bus ride home after class that night, as she finally read what Akilah had shared with the digital world, she would openly sob through a panic attack, unnoticed by anyone. She would send Akilah vox after vox and get no reply, and she would be unable to stop scrolling through the comments on Akilah's essay, unable to stop seeing it posted and reposted by seemingly everyone she knew and thousands more people whom she would never meet. She would see the comment from someone with the handle BabyxxGirlxx2001: *omg my friend used to have something like that. in rogers park twenty years ago. I know it sounds crazy but I swear.*

But right now, with Julián, Raven was convincing in her pretense at normalcy. And in that one small lie, she was so pleased.

AKILAH SHOOK HER HEAD. "YOU'RE THINKING FROM A PLACE OF *fear,* Raven. We need to be thinking from a place of possibility. A place of abundance."

"I'm thinking from a place of an *agreement* we made. Together."

Akilah rinsed out a mug in the sink. *Poorly,* Raven thought. Tea stains circled its insides, and the tiniest, barely perceptible touch of lipstick was at the rim. "I know. But inspiration struck, and it couldn't wait."

Raven felt her teeth chattering, though she was not cold. Akilah had turned her back to her and returned to carefully arraying thin slices of cheese on a plate next to some multigrain crackers. Raven's arm was outstretched, forlorn and useless, a bridge to nowhere. She stepped closer to Akilah, moving in so that their faces were inches apart, making herself unignorable.

"You saw that comment. If someone out there knows about . . . this thing, and now what you wrote is like some kind of corroborating evidence, word could get out. People could come and . . . I don't know, break in. Try to use it. Try to hurt us. Or we could get kicked out of the building, or New Dawn . . ."

Akilah met her gaze but said nothing.

Raven looked past her, over her shoulder. Something small and black on the counter caught her eye. It was moving. An ant. And of course, as is always the case with ants, where there was one, there were many. They promenaded across the microwave and down the hinge of the cabinet, then across the baseboard and to the back door. Stone-faced, Raven turned from Akilah and started tearing through the cabinet. Akilah stared at her.

"What are you doing?"

"Looking for vinegar. Because we have ants." Raven spun around, brandishing the plastic bottle like it was confirmatory evidence of a heinous crime. "Because everything here is a mess. Because we're not done unpacking, or organizing, or shopping, or doing anything we need to do to make this place feel like a home we *share*." She ripped a paper towel from the roll, balled it up, and doused it in vinegar. "Because I straight-up don't have time for this, or time for anything, and because you apparently don't see us as a priority, because you're too busy writing manifestos. Because you don't respect me or our shared space enough to give a *fuck!*"

The last word came out as a throaty scream, and Raven fell to her knees, scrubbing the ants at the baseboard with vinegar. A banging came from below—a broom handle or a mop against the ceiling.

Akilah laughed hoarsely. "If they're mad about their damn baby not sleeping, how is it helpful to make *more* noise?"

Raven shot her a look of disdain, then moved on her knees

toward a vent in the floor near the back door. She leaned down, yelling into it.

"I'm sorry! I'm really sorry!"

Akilah shook her head. "I don't know why you're acting like this or raising your voice at me or cursing at me. I'm trying to do this in partnership with you. I'm trying to live into what I thought we *both* believed. About community." Akilah leaned against the fridge, her hands in her pockets, watching Raven on her hands and knees, her back arched, hollering into the floor. The kitchen reeked of vinegar. Akilah had never felt so bad for someone in her entire life. She moved to Raven's side, lowering herself to sit beside her on the floor.

"Listen. I apologize."

Raven's eyes shot toward her, shifting from begrudging hope to deep suspicion and back within the span of a moment.

Akilah put a hand on her back. "For not unpacking more things while you're at work. For writing publicly about the thing without telling you first. For being messy. And for not supporting you more even though I know you're working your ass off. Okay? I'm really sorry. And I'm gonna do better."

Raven stopped scrubbing and crawled forward, putting her head in Akilah's lap.

"Okay." She closed her eyes a moment while Akilah traced a finger across her ear, down across the nape of her neck, over her collarbone, and across her breast. This was good. This was possible. Akilah took her hand, pulled her up, and led her to the bedroom.

Afterward, tugging her T-shirt on, Raven went back into the kitchen for a glass of water. She let her eyes flit across the room, making a list in her head. *Trash bags. A new broom and dustpan. Shelf liners.* Her eyes fell on the dishwasher. It would be awfully convenient if it would do all the fancy things it was supposed to do.

She called into the other room. "Babe, do you think you

could call Ms. Cornelia tomorrow to finally come in and fix that dishwasher?"

A pause. "Who?"

Raven shook her head, exasperated, and took a swallow of water. "The maintenance person. For the building."

"Oh. Yeah, sure."

Raven nodded slowly. They could do this. This could be done.

When her alarm went off the next morning and Raven began the daily choreography of trying to extricate herself from bed as silently as possible, she was surprised to see Akilah sit up beside her.

"I figured I'd get an early start on the day," Akilah said, leaning in to kiss Raven on the cheek. "I can finish unpacking so we can finally get out of all this cardboard chaos."

Raven grinned broadly. "Really? Wow. Thank you, boo."

Akilah winked. "Don't sound so surprised."

Raven was so engrossed in her microbiology textbook that she didn't hear the door chime when the woman came in. Raven registered her only when she was already at the counter, breathless, her forehead reflecting the overhead light with a thin sheen of sweat. She was beautiful, her eyes enormous, a mustard-yellow scarf setting off the rich brown of her skin.

"Hi, and welcome to Lotus. How can I help you?"

"I'm here for the two o'clock class," said the woman, wresting her jacket off. "I'm late."

She didn't want to look, but despite herself, Raven's eyes went instinctively to the large wall clock above the door to the studio: 2:01. A sign was posted beneath the clock: *We're sorry, but to avoid disruptions, absolutely no late arrivals. Please arrive 15 minutes early.* The woman's gaze followed Raven's, and she spoke quickly.

"Fuck. *Fuck.* I'm sorry, my friend got me a gift certificate to this place because— Well, I should have called ahead."

Raven walked out from behind the desk. She would deal with Katie's wrath later. And anyway, the afternoon restorative yoga class was filled with people in their sixties and seventies who mostly enjoyed falling asleep in child's pose. "I'll hang your jacket up," she told the woman. "Go on in. Do you need a mat?"

When the studio door was shut, Raven picked the book back up. She had two pages left in the assigned chapter, and then her weekly module quiz was due at three. They usually only took her about fifteen minutes, so she would be good as long as there were no other major interruptions.

The very moment the thought passed through Raven's mind, Jazmyne burst through the door with a pained look on her face, as if the reassurance itself had been some kind of jinx. Raven closed the book, sliding an envelope in to mark her page.

"Hey, hon. You okay?"

Jazmyne nodded, then shook her head, then burst into tears.

THE BUS WAS UNUSUALLY QUIET ON THE WAY HOME, WHICH suited Raven fine. She balled up her jacket and wedged it between the window and her head, curling against the glass and peering down at the notebook. It was a nice one, something European that Akilah's mom had gifted her for Christmas a couple of years prior. Raven had intended it to be for grand and transformative thoughts, and instead usually used it to take class notes when she was struggling to stay awake and wanted to appear focused and attentive. She clicked her pen twice, as though marking a ritual, and began to write.

- time —> commodity —> abundance over scarcity?

- time = ? money? Other things of value

- What if time were shareable as a resource?

    She paused and looked out the window, thinking of Jazmyne, who had cried on her shoulder until precisely 2:48 P.M. Raven had been watching the giant wall clock anxiously, thinking of both the quiz that was due and the elderly people who would stream out of the studio at 3:00, accompanied by the beautiful woman who would hopefully be relaxed because she had a great class and not ashamed because Katie had said something awful to her for being late, and Katie herself, who would not yell at Raven but would talk to her like she was a child, which was worse. All the while, she hoped that her heart rate wouldn't rise so severely that Jazmyne, crying in her arms, would notice, and look up and see her looking at the clock, and feel bad.

    Jazmyne was crying about nothing in particular, and everything in aggregate: being late for work again, the way a doctor had spoken to her, the bevy of new and possible and incomplete treatments they had offered her father today and when the hell was she supposed to research them, to get a second opinion, to call the patient advocate again and try to get a meeting, to look for a specialist, to look into the relief programs and discounts and support groups that everyone kept telling her were available but no one could tell her how to quickly access. She had cried over the cafeteria being closed before she could go down and grab the one soup that her father liked, because she was waiting for the doctor to come and was certain that the moment she stepped out the door someone would appear to answer all her questions, and she would miss it, miss it entirely. And she had cried over the embarrassment of crying at work, until at last something had come unhooked inside of Raven, and she began to cry too, and they sat that way, embracing, until Jazmyne had leaned away and gone into the bathroom to wash her face, and Raven had submitted her quiz with nineteen seconds to spare and guessed at random on the last two questions. And when the customers came wandering out at 3:00, their faces glowing and blissful and rested, they were greeted by the two women smiling prettily at them, offering chamomile tea with lemon and a sign-up option for a multiclass discount.

Raven read back over what she had written now. *Abundance.* She underlined that twice, then skipped a few lines and wrote something else.

TIMEBOX:
COMMUNITY PRINCIPLES
AND AGREEMENTS

Time is abundant, if we let it be.

The timebox is not a tool of theft; we do not use it to steal time for ourselves. We use the timebox to offer the gift of our time to others. Reallocating our time with this tool allows us to give more freely of our love, our creation, and our support to those in greatest need.

She paused. *Greatest need.* That would require a lot of thinking. Greatest according to whom? She chewed the end of her pen for a moment, then wrote *Advisers???*

When Raven got to the foyer of her building, she felt a new

brightness, a true joy she had not felt since . . . she wasn't sure when. She couldn't wait to talk to Akilah. She took the stairs two at a time. Something smelled delicious, something home-made and fragrant. Had Akilah cooked?

She almost collided with Ms. Cornelia in front of the apart-ment door. Raven waved politely. "Ms. Cornelia! Did Akilah call you about the dishwasher?"

Ms. Cornelia nodded, and to Raven's surprise, she reached out a hand as though to put it on her shoulder, then paused and pulled back. This was odd, but it was an oddity to be consid-ered later, beyond the urgency of this conversation with Akilah. Ms. Cornelia had not closed the door behind her, and Raven nodded curtly, said a simple "Thanks," and stepped past her into the apartment.

Kicking off her shoes, Raven immediately recognized the smell that flooded the apartment. *Coq au vin*. It was Akilah's only signature dish, one her father had taught her.

"Akilah!" Raven called out. "Ki! Where you at?"

She moved from room to room, gasping as she went. Ev-erything was impeccable. Gone were the piles of clothes, the dishes left everywhere, the random detritus thrown from boxes in the search for needed things. In the kitchen, the chicken sat simmering in its wine in a steaming slow cooker, next to what appeared to be a note. Raven reached for it, but when she heard a voice behind her, she jumped so fiercely that she almost knocked the Crock-Pot off the counter.

"I don't know if she's coming back, baby. Not right now."

Raven turned. It was Ms. Cornelia. How had she entered the apartment silently? Raven squinted up at her, not understanding, then backed away. Her eyes darted around the kitchen. A chef's knife was in a block in the corner to her right. The only other exit was the door to the back stairs. It was dead-bolted.

Seeing Raven's panic, Ms. Cornelia took a step back. Her face was mournful. "I'm sorry. I didn't mean to scare you. I just . . . I did everything she asked me to do." She was still walking, backward and out of the kitchen, her palms out and facing Raven as if to signify that she meant no harm.

Raven frowned. "You fixed the dishwasher?"

Ms. Cornelia nodded. She was in the dining room now, looking at Raven through the doorway. "Yes. And I did everything else she asked me. That's my job, you see. That's always been my job. I use my judgment as best as I can, but when folks come in here, they have to choose. They have to decide. I ain't here to hurt you, I swear. I just . . . In my experience, it's best to have someone with you when you get to this part."

"Which part?" Raven stepped forward. The smell of the coq au vin suddenly sickened her; it was too much, too sweet. Keeping her eyes on Ms. Cornelia, she reached over with one hand and deftly unplugged the Crock-Pot. "Ms. Cornelia, I'm sorry, but you're freaking me out a little bit. You're making me uncomfortable." She took another step forward, into the dining room.

"I know. I'm sorry for that. I thought I should be here. But I will go. I will go in a moment."

Raven felt like she was swimming, her vision hazy at the periphery, her body moving slowly as though against a fast current. "Yes," she said. Her voice sounded very far away. "Yes, please go. You're scaring me. It's scary to me, that you just—you just came in here, and . . ."

She felt something, something almost imperceptible, through the thin fabric of her sock. Something sharp and small. Raven lifted her leg, contorting her knee to look at the bottom of her foot. A tiny spiral of shaved wood clung to the white cotton— the remnant of something that had been drilled or bored. She plucked it away, and then her eyes fell on more of them, gathered in front of the door to the pantry. Thin curls of wood, and the slightest dusting of paint, pulverized into the air and settled on the floor.

"She asked me to," Cornelia was saying. The radiator was

hissing. "And it's my job, you see? It's my job. And when I met you all, I couldn't divine that it would turn out this way. Sometimes it do, but sometimes it don't. And you seemed so in love. So I just thought, you know . . ."

Ms. Cornelia's gaze never shifted from her as she reached down toward a box of tools that Raven had not even noticed was there. She closed the metal lid with finality and fastened the latch.

"But I got it wrong, Raven. I got it all wrong this time."

Raven's eyes moved from the wood spirals to the thin space beneath the pantry door. A light was on inside. Her gaze drifted up, up the heavy wood that had been painted and repainted over the years, its once-ornate carved ornamentation blurred and muted, and to the tarnished brass doorknob.

And beneath the doorknob, a newly installed lock.

Before she knew what she was doing, Raven was tugging at the doorknob, turning it and turning it uselessly, and then she was crying, and she was sitting on the floor. Ms. Cornelia laid a hand on her shoulder for a moment. Then she picked up her toolbox and walked heavily out of the apartment, closing the front door behind her.

SAVE CHANGES

12 HOURS

Early Sunday evening, Amber was already tired—and this cross-walk light was taking forever to change. With her arms wrapped around a full grocery bag, she blew a stray curl away from her face and watched it float back down to her sweaty forehead. That their mother couldn't do the grocery shopping was obvious, but when was the last time her sister had agreed to go?

These traffic lights were clearly designed for a different version of New York, one in which Broadway was crowded with vehicles. She counted ten—no, nine—people out on this street in Hamilton Heights. Though the signs were still there—for bodegas, pharmacies, and bars—most of the businesses were long gone, boarded up or steel-shuttered. Even the garbage cans were empty.

It did not help that Amber had forgotten to bring sunglasses, and that the tireless summer sun was burning her retinas and baking her face and arms, searing tan lines into the tops of her sandaled feet.

She craned her neck and peered down the street. It wasn't even like there were many cars around, just a few parked here and there and none at all passing on the street.

Still, the light blinked a cheerful DON'T WALK.

The seconds seemed endless. A fat drop of sweat made its way down Amber's temple. Only the thought of the pocket watch she'd been working on, an old timepiece with a shattered face and bent minute hand, attached to a silver chain, brightened her thoughts. Someone must have loved that watch before. Who was to say it couldn't mark time again? Amber had gathered all the parts she needed to fix it up, good as new, and they were waiting for her on the kitchen table.

Amber raised her arms a bit to air out her underarms and maneuvered the heavy, full grocery bag from one hip to the other. She would *make* Larry do the groceries next time, even if her sister always came back with all the wrong things (probably on purpose). Amber didn't care. Next week, it would be Larry's job to wander the near-empty produce aisles with a depressingly optimistic grocery list and return with shrink-wrapped chemical inventions that made their mother—even in her condition—wrinkle her nose.

As Amber settled the paper bag onto her hip, a sad-looking orange tumbled out onto the sidewalk and bounced adventurously into the street. Cursing under her breath, Amber did a quick check for NDRs and stepped out onto Broadway, scooped it up, and returned it to the grocery bag.

"Now, now. We don't cross the street against the light," said a pleasant, electronic woman's voice.

Amber straightened up fast to find the volleyball-size minder drone whirring in front of her at eye level. She fought the familiar urge to drop the bag and clutch at the necklace around her neck, hidden beneath the hem of her T-shirt.

Not for something as small as this, she thought.

"Identity check, please," said the pill, and Amber tilted her face up for scanning—not that the drone needed it. The muscles of her arms clenched around the groceries. After all these years of being careful, imagine getting arrested for jaywalking to save a pruney little orange.

You had to choose your battles, and Amber's policy was to not choose any at all.

She should have just waited for the light to change. The drone sent a few warm lasers across Amber's sweaty face, and, with a quick single pulse, read her left iris. "You're free to go. Be careful out there, Amber."

"Thanks," Amber said, "and sorry," even though the drone had already whirred away.

Because of the interaction, she had missed the crosswalk window, and had to wait in the hot sun another few minutes until she could finally get to the other side of Broadway.

As she jostled the bag up the steps to the family's brownstone, the curtains in the window of the house next door parted and she saw Mrs. Perez's gray little face peering out distrustfully. Amber offered her a wan smile, but Mrs. Perez immediately drew her head back and snapped the curtains closed.

This was what it was like now that they were pariahs.

Just beyond the front door, Larry happened to be running down the stairs, and Amber bodychecked her, pushing the groceries into her arms.

"Damn, hey to you too, sis!" Larry said as Amber gripped her by the shoulders, turned her around, and shoved her toward the kitchen, where they could see their mother's back at the counter.

"What's she doing now?" Amber whispered as she followed Larry across the small, dark living room, toward the bright white and pink of Diana's kitchen.

"You'll see," said Larry quietly. "Visiting hours."

New Dawn Surveillance Footage: House Arrest

Daily Visual Transcript Readout: 17:30

Facial recognition: confirmed. Inmate Diana Melo, age 43. She often smiles at the camera: friendly. Wears red lipstick and a neat full-skirt dress with pale pink apron. Subject hums to herself, a song not immediately identified in database scan. Nearest to the camera are a sink, a counter, and a stove. Behind the subject, a tidy kitchen table can be seen.

Typical behavior patterns noted. The subject is working on household tasks. Today, the subject is carefully transferring boiled oblong items into canning jars filled with blue brine. She seals each jar and holds it up to the camera. "For when you visit," she says, in a tone algorithms interpret as "pleasant."

Her daughters appear behind her and set a bag of groceries on the table. The subject ignores them, confirming repeated observations that she is minimally aware of her surroundings.

That the inmate's cleansing has resulted in warped function: confirmed. That the inmate poses no danger to the collective peace: confirmed.

End daily check-in.

"Oh god, Mom—is that window cleaner?"

Diana swiveled to look at them, smiling with all her teeth. The jar in her manicured hands contained a couple of indestructible Twinkies swimming in an electric-blue liquid. "Yes, honey?" Behind her, the camera light turned from red to green.

Larry looked at her watch and nodded at Amber. The daily mandatory check-in was done.

Diana added the blue jar to a cluster of four others, all identical and sickening, and smoothed her hands over the pale pink apron that nipped in at her waist. "Don't touch those," she said, winking, as if they were all in on some secret joke. "They're for our guests."

Amber sighed and sat down in front of her clock. Larry took the chair next to her at the table. This was how it was now with their mother, the ghost of the Diana Melo who raised them.

But whatever was wrong with Diana, it didn't seem to prevent her from seeing the groceries for what they really were: sad. She unpacked three puny oranges, the wilted vegetables, and pursed her lips.

"I really tried," Amber said. "The whole produce aisle was empty. You should have seen it."

"It's fine, honey," Diana said, fixing her eyes on Amber just long enough to make her uncomfortable, before she smiled. "Thank you for going. Take a seat. Rest a bit."

Her mother began bustling around the kitchen, putting everything away. Amber's and Larry's eyes kept drifting to the gleaming blue jars of Twinkies on the counter.

The doctors had told them that this sort of behavior appeared to be some fluke side effect of the Nevermind cleansing, which had not only wiped their mother of her unclean, rebellious instincts but also knocked out some essential part of her brain.

Diana had spent nearly a year training to become a Torch before her New Dawn supervisors let go of their dream of turning a dirty computer into a walking ad for Nevermind. The doctors scanned her brain and could find nothing wrong. She couldn't consistently execute even the most basic tasks. They had reluctantly let her come home just over a year ago. But the person who'd walked through the front door was a warped, cookie-cutter version of a mother from a children's storybook, a broken doll. The doctors said all the two sisters could do was be kind to her.

Even so, the image of the Diana Melo who had appeared in forced broadcasts across America, announcing the start of a revolution, did not fade in the memory of New Dawn, even after they decided she was useless. With the riots in New York, Diana had joined the pantheon of subversives, along with Mary Apple, Jane 57821—except that they had escaped and she had not.

No, Diana was put on house arrest instead, which she said suited her just fine, because all she wanted was to keep house for her girls. No one could know what Diana was thinking, or if she was thinking at all, and maybe that was for the best.

It didn't mean their lives were easy. Neighbors avoided Larry and Amber on the street, and the promise of a fresh start at school had shriveled up on Amber's first day at City College, when one by one, each of her professors made her sit in the front row of each class and read a statement from New Dawn, informing her classmates who she was and warning them that any decision to fraternize with her was one they made at their own risk. Larry, who started classes the next year, received the same treatment.

Amber had read about how sex offenders had to go door-to-door when they moved into a new neighborhood. She realized that was what was happening to her and Larry, except they were memory offenders.

Memory offender–adjacent, actually. Guilty by blood.

"I really tried," Amber said again as she sat down in front of her watch and Larry took the chair next to her at the table.

And so they were outcasts, all three of them, living in the shadow of the great revolutionary, always on probation, always on the edge of arrest. People were slow to forget the faces of the Melo family, which had featured so prominently in weeks of forced broadcasts of raids across the country. Here was Diana Melo, posing for a mug shot, her expression defiant, her hair wild. Here was footage of her afterward, hair neatly combed back, clutching a white slip of paper in her hands as if it would save her life.

Diana's days now revolved around a standing date with the New Dawn camera on the kitchen counter. When she'd first returned, her daughters had tried to coax her to spend more time in her bedroom or in the living room, but she resisted, logging hours making Technicolor, inedible chaos in the kitchen, as if it were her job.

It had been over a year of this, and somehow Amber hadn't broken.

Yet.

As if she could read her thoughts, Diana stopped and gave Amber a quick hug, wrapping her daughter in the floral perfume she always wore. It made Amber think that maybe part of her mother was still there. She blinked away the tears and turned to the organized mess before her.

The timepiece sat on the table, its tiny silver innards spread out on a piece of black velvet. It had taken Amber a few hours of tinkering to discover what ailed it, and then a full week to find the part she needed at one of the remaining legal rummage sales in Harlem. She could finally get to the work she had been look-ing forward to all week: replacing the oscillator and seeing if she could get it to "howl" at the right frequency and get the hands ticking again.

Normally Larry would mock her, but today she seemed dis-tracted and quiet. She watched their mother with the same hor-rified awe that Amber felt. This was how it was now, with their family: barely functioning, haunting each other like ghosts.

Amber turned to Larry. "Remember when there used to be fruit? Like mangoes and raspberries?"

Larry didn't say anything, so Amber nudged her. But her sis-ter slumped down in her chair, staring off into space, legs spread so that Amber felt hemmed in. When Larry raised a hand to brush back her hair, a golden gleam caught the light.

Was her sister actually wearing jewelry? Larry, who had dumped her father's last gift to her—a necklace with an amber bumblebee fossilized inside dangling from a shimmering gold chain—into a jewelry box and forgotten about it? Amber clasped

Larry's wrist midair and stared at the thin gold chain, noting the heart that dangled there.

It could mean only one thing. A wave of dread washed over her, but it was quickly replaced by an emotion that felt actionable: anger.

Upstairs, Amber mouthed.

Larry rolled her eyes but got up. Diana looked from one sister to the other and her eyes seemed to flash with understanding, but the moment was so brief that Amber was sure she had imagined it.

ONE OF THE FIRST FAMILY PORTRAITS THEY HAD TAKEN, LONG before their mother was detained, hung near the foot of the stairs and Amber had to pass it as she followed Larry.

Their father had saved up for a fancy camera, a heavy, clunky thing that Larry kept after he died. He had set it up on a tripod and the four of them had gathered around the couch, laughing. Here was Larry, dressed in a shirt buttoned all the way up, with a hideous bolo tie that made her look like she'd been plucked out of some old-timey 1990s movie and plopped onto the Melos' couch. She was sitting crisscross applesauce and her goofy smile revealed a missing front tooth. And here was Amber: standing behind the couch—on a stool, she remembered—eyebrows meeting over an anxious smile, her dark curls, barely restrained by a hair clip, casting a shadow on her face. She looked uncomfortable in her frilly dress, even though she herself had chosen it. Larry and Amber were miniature versions of who they would become: Amber could see that now.

But the real star of the photo was their mother, sitting on the couch next to Larry, with all three of them—Pablo, Amber, and Larry—unconsciously leaning toward her, like flowers tilting to sunlight. She wore a black sheath that showed the sinewy muscles in her arms, and her hair was a halo of wild golden curls.

Their mother leaned back against their father and looked relaxed and happy. She wasn't even smiling, but the serenity of her expression said it all. It seemed almost impossible that the same woman was in the kitchen behind them, at this moment baring her teeth and buzzing constantly around the kitchen like a trapped bee.

Once they'd taken a few shots with the timer, her father had hustled over to the camera and looked at the pictures on the tiny screen. "Let's bring Am-barr into the light. We can't have our prettiest girl in the shadows." But by then, their mother had gotten up and smoothed her dress. Larry had already slipped the bolo tie over her head and set about pushing Amber off her stool, while she clung to the back of the couch, squealing.

That photo was Amber's real favorite, the one in which their father was heading toward the camera, while their mother rose up, lost in thought, and Larry and Amber wrestled. She didn't think to look at it often, but she had it tucked into the mirror of her bedroom dresser.

And, anyway, there hadn't been many family photos after that. It was as if knowing the camera was there made it seem less important, somehow. This smiling photo, the one her father had chosen, had been hanging here for years and Amber rarely stopped to look at it. But even as she heard Larry's footsteps climbing toward the roof, something stopped Amber at the foot of the stairs and sent her hand up to her neck, to the comforting weight of the larimar stone against her sternum.

What if?

HER FATHER HADN'T TALKED ABOUT HIS CHILDHOOD MUCH, but Amber knew he'd grown up in the mountains of the Dominican Republic and that instead of going to school, he had been put to work in the vertical shafts of the larimar mines, digging for rare ocean blue the earth had hidden there, bright as anything. And maybe that was it: those who do the work are rewarded with magic.

But he had failed to use it when it mattered. They had seen their mother taken away in handcuffs, the pompified run-up, and the inevitable Nevermind cleansing of the group of rebels who had tried to incite a revolution. They all watched, even Pablo—that's all he had done. Watch.

Except, of course, when the live broadcast began of his wife in a white hospital gown, strapped in for cleansing. Then, he had left the room.

And who could blame him? Amber had stayed, but she didn't remember it herself. All she could recall was sitting down to watch it and feeling as if she were the one being erased—and wasn't it true? That by taking away a piece of her mother, New Dawn was erasing a part of Amber?

And, of course, then their mother stayed gone, because there were internments, reprogramming, Torch training—all of it televised as a warning to everyone else. She was hardly recognizable, their mother, in the footage. Artificially bright and co-operative. Here she was, processing paperwork at a Nevermind facility, cheerfully shredding militant contraband, escorting desperate-eyed people to their cleansings.

And all of it might have been prevented. It was so hard not to resent her father for waiting to give her the larimar until he was on his deathbed. He had waited until his own days were counted to tell her that it could rewind time.

Amber didn't believe him at first, assuming that this was near-death rambling, but Pablo was firm. "Use it wisely," he said. "You only get one."

11 HOURS

Up on the roof, the sisters sat leaning against the barriers and looking up at the sun, which showed no signs of waning. It was a small, bare roof, home only to a few highband network antennas. Before their mother had been erased, she had brought her daughters up here and told them that the New Dawn drones rarely buzzed up to the roofs of low buildings like theirs. Though the inside of the house was almost certainly bugged, the sisters weren't sure if the roof thing was still true. Still, they came here whenever they really wanted to talk in private.

Larry lit a cigarette.

"Disgusting," Amber said. "And it will kill you."

"My *mother* is downstairs, Am-barr," she said, drawing out the rolling *r* the way their father used to. "I don't need supervision."

"I think she might have something to say if she could see you."

"Good thing she can't come up here, then, huh," she said, taking a long drag.

"What's up with the bracelet?" Amber said.

"A gift from a friend."

"Still reckless and stupid. What's new?"

"Having a friend? What do you want me to do, Amber? Roll over and play dead, like you? Take up tinkering with little fucking *clocks*?"

"My clocks and watches don't get me in trouble. Remember the *last time* your love life almost got us all detained?"

"I was in high school, Amber! What did I know?"

"Right. And since that was so long ago, I'm assuming that you know what the rules are by now?"

"And what is it with the clocks, anyway?" Larry said, ignoring her and ashing into the empty street below. "I don't know what you and your little fetish are waiting for, but this is it. Look at our life: Our mother is fucked up *and* on house arrest. Papi is dead. Do you hear me? Dead. We are basically orphans. Nobody is coming to save us. This is the only life we get. Wake up, Amber, this is it."

Amber reached over and took a drag of Larry's cigarette. "Easy for you to say. You get to be carefree and have fun while I do all the worrying and clean up all your messes. You don't think I'd like to go on a date?"

Not that it mattered—no New Dawn–fearing family would let their offspring date a Melo sister. Amber had learned that the hard way. Whoever Larry was dating had to be outside the system.

Which made it all the more worrying.

Larry leaned back and pushed her shoulders against the wall so that she could look Amber in the eye and laugh. She lit another cigarette and took a long inhale.

"Her name is Natalie and—"

"Break it off."

Larry scoffed. "I'm seeing her tonight. Don't make such ugly faces," she said, switching into her impression of their mother. "One day your face will freeze like that."

"Do you hear yourself? You're going to get us all caught up and cleaned."

Larry laughed again, but this time the muscles in her jaw clenched. She stubbed out her cigarette and put it in her jeans pocket.

"I'm coming with you," Amber said.

"Hard pass. Don't be ridiculous." Larry put her palms on the concrete and pushed herself up.

Amber grabbed her sleeve and pulled her back down. "I have Papi's stone, remember?" She pulled the long gold chain out from under the collar of her T-shirt and held it up to Larry. It was an impossible blue-green, the crystalline shade of the Caribbean Sea, or so their father had told them. When Amber looked at it, she could almost see through the clear waters of it to a different world, a future wonderful beyond her imagination. "If anything happens, if we get caught, I can—"

"Oh god. This again." Larry glanced at the stone and gave Amber a long, pitying look. "That shit isn't real, Ambo. Look at our life. Look at what good it's done us."

"I won't make the same mistake Papi made," Amber said, almost pleading. "I won't wait."

Larry brought her head close to Amber's and squeezed her shoulder. "Do you really still think that's what he was doing? Holding out for something more important than saving his own wife?"

"Maybe he thought something might happen to us—to you and me—something worse than what was happening to her."

"Or maybe *it isn't real*. Maybe it's just a nice story and maybe it's just a pretty stone." Larry gently tapped the side of Amber's forehead with her index finger. "Ever think?"

"Papi believed," Amber insisted as she swatted Larry's hand away.

"Well, that's your problem," Larry said. She got up and extended her hand down to Amber again. "Both of you, really. Sitting around doing a lot of believing and not much else."

"That's bullshit and you know it," Amber said, taking Larry's hand, standing up, and then immediately snatching it back. "Somebody has to care about what happens to this family."

"Your believing and your larimar aren't doing shit for us, Amber." Larry leaned out on the barrier and looked down at the near-empty streets below. "Ever think about what New York used to look like?"

She had changed subjects again. Amber leaned out next to her. "I'm going with you."

"Just, like, people everywhere, you know? Crowds. Cars. Noise. *Life*." Larry turned to go inside, but not before punching Amber lightly on the shoulder.

"Fine, come along. That little stone won't do jack, but at least you'll get out of this depressing-ass house. Mom can babysit your clocks—but tell her not to cook them."

9 HOURS

Larry's room was on the second floor of the brownstone, right across from Amber's, but Amber couldn't remember spending any time in her sister's room since they'd started college. There were piles of clothes and textbooks everywhere and the walls were as bare as she remembered. Larry's drawings, all in black and white, were piled high in a corner by the dresser, surrounded by little nubs of charcoal. She had always been the most talented in her art classes and if it weren't for their family's reputation . . .

No use thinking about that, right?

It had taken some rummaging, but she had followed Larry's orders and dug up a pair of bell-bottom jeans, which would be the most likely to obscure their hover blades. She liked the way they looked, she decided, padding over to Larry's long mirror in her socks and doing a shy half turn to look at her own butt.

"They look good, Amber, you know they do. Stop being scared of your own reflection," said Larry. She was also wearing bell-bottoms, and a dark blue top tied at the midriff. Her hair was slicked back and she wore no jewelry except for Natalie's bracelet.

"Why don't you ever wear your amber? From Papi?"

Amber reached under the collar of her T-shirt, wrapped her fingers around the larimar and let it drop again.

"What does it matter?" Larry abruptly got up from her bed and headed to her open closet, which was bursting with rumpled clothes drooping from lopsided hangers.

"It's the last thing Papi gave us, isn't it?" But she could tell Larry wasn't paying attention. Amber sighed and sat down on the carpet to pick through Larry's makeup bag, which was spread out on the floor in front of the mirror. She didn't want to start a new fight. They'd reached an uneasy détente, and though Amber hated the circumstances, she sort of liked that they were doing something together, for once.

She was trying hard not to think too far ahead, though the images of New Dawn vans and the memory of their mother's arrest kept cycling through her mind. What were the chances that this would end well? She had even considered staying behind and letting Larry go on her own. Who knew how many times she'd gone out before and made it safely home? But could she ever forgive herself if something went wrong and she wasn't there?

Larry looked back at her for a moment, tilted her head to the side, and then swiveled back to her closet. "You look so good in yellow and I think I have a shirt—"

"Really, Larry, why don't you ever wear it?" Amber jumped up and started pawing through Larry's dresser. "Did you lose it?"

"Natalie wears the necklace," Larry said, gently pulling Amber back in order to hold up a mustard-yellow blouse with tiny flowers on it. "Groovy, baby."

Amber's jaw dropped. How serious was this relationship, that Larry had given Natalie something so precious, so full of memories? Amber did not know what to say, so she said nothing. She put on the blouse and it did look good. Larry nodded with satisfaction and then wandered back to her closet.

"Put some shimmer on," Larry said, her voice muffled as she rooted around on the floor underneath the racks of clothes. "Live a little. Better to look good if they catch us and put our mug shots out on the feed."

"Not funny," Amber said, but she dipped a brush in a shimmery powder and swiped it across her cheekbones, in part because she needed to do something with her hands and in part because she did look pretty when she turned her face to catch the light.

Amber smoothed on a bit of eye shadow and watched Larry's back in the mirror as she pushed aside racks of clothes, rummaged for something behind them, and emerged with their father's old camera.

"Got it! Remember, it does video too?" Larry pushed a button and the lens extended itself, as if stretching after a long night of sleep. "It still works!"

The sound reminded Amber of a rover. "Nope, nope, nope,"

she said, leaping up and reaching for the backpack before Larry had finished zipping it closed. "Are you trying to feed evidence directly to New Dawn?"

"It's just our own memories, for us," Larry said quietly, even as she let Amber put the camera back in the closet it had come out of.

"We're doing enough stupid risk-taking for one day, don't you think?"

Larry didn't have anything smart to say back, for once.

It took a few minutes to locate their mother, and when they did, they found that the door to her bedroom was locked. They listened for a moment and heard some muffled sounds they couldn't make sense of. Through the door, they told her they were going for a walk and she called out something about being careful, but she sounded so distracted that the sisters exchanged a glance as they walked to the front door.

"What's she doing in there, you think?" Larry asked.

"Who knows? Probably knitting a sweater out of barbed wire or something."

Larry snorted, but the sisters said nothing else until they were on the street in their hover blades, and Amber seemed to have sprouted eight legs, all rolling in different directions on the motorized wheels.

"You used to wear these all the time," said Larry, laughing. "I thought you remembered."

"I thought I did too," said Amber, careening into a parked car and setting off an alarm. Glancing back toward home, she caught a flash of movement from Mrs. Perez's window before the curtains snapped shut again.

"Okay, we can't start dealing with NDRs yet," Larry said urgently, grabbing her firmly by the arm. "I got you. Bring your feet parallel to each other—not too close—okay, and keep them there. I'll pull you until your muscles remember."

It took a few more minutes of spaghetti-legged panic, but

Amber's feet did remember how to skate. The adrenaline helped as she scanned the street signs and focused on following Larry.

Though there were no laws against going out at night, few people did. It simply wasn't worth the risk of an interaction with New Dawn. But there was some movement here and there, mostly people making their way to or from night shifts and the occasional patrolling rovers overhead. The city felt like a ghost of what it used to be, and though Amber had never seen it in her lifetime, she could somehow imagine it as Larry had on the roof: the people, the noise, the chaos.

The Riverside Drive Viaduct wasn't far from their house and Larry led them to it in lazy circles, with detours and slow zigzags down smaller streets. The worst thing you could do, Larry had explained, was lead a drone to an off-grid location.

The system worked because people gathered in the shady parts of the city, blighted places New Dawn didn't think worth regularly patrolling, and the goal was to avoid bringing attention to them. The lucky thing, Larry had said, was that Black and brown neighborhoods like Harlem and Hamilton Heights were full of blind spots, magical places where you could make all the noise you wanted.

Amber remained skeptical that any of this was true and her hand kept drifting up to the larimar against her sternum. Only a few blocks from home, they encountered the first NDR, planted in the middle of an empty street for routine checks. There was no one around, and the drone whirred hopefully from side to side to prevent anyone from making their way down the street uniden-tified. Larry grabbed her hand and pulled her down another side street and they continued their downhill descent, with Amber constantly looking over her shoulder for blinking red lights.

At the halfway point, Larry put out her arm and signaled Amber to a stop. She slung one backpack strap off and brought it against her stomach, taking out two full-face masks: a gold feathered one that she handed to Amber, and a leather one with cat ears for herself. Larry had explained that the masks confused the drone face readers, but that it was best to wait to put them on until they'd gotten away from their neighborhood.

Amber began to feel a bit more confident in her mask, and she was almost enjoying the speed and the balmy summer air as they glided smoothly down the hill toward the Hudson River. In the evening quiet the sound of distant music seemed to grow closer and louder, until at the bottom of the hill—where the street met Twelfth Avenue—two hazy figures appeared. Side by side, they didn't move. There was something monstrous about their heads that chilled Amber's heart, especially against the backdrop of the massive steel arches of the viaduct, which soared up behind the silhouettes in the darkness.

Though she could hear loud music and laughter from somewhere close, Amber started to brake, suddenly keenly aware that she did not belong here.

Larry squeezed her arm quickly and whispered, "It's their masks, you baby, don't stop." She pulled her toward the two figures and as they drew closer, they became two ordinary men, wearing jeans and hover blades themselves. One wore a mask shaped like a rat's head and the other a pigeon.

"Hey," said the pigeon in a muffled voice, the soft plastic twisting and contorting as he spoke.

"Hey. Thank you," said Larry as they parted to let them pass. She shook hands with each of them, in a gesture that seemed both oddly formal and naively trusting to Amber, but she followed suit. She was surprised when the pigeon put a second hand on top of hers and said, "Welcome."

She looked into the mask but could see nothing but the distorted plastic beak.

"Okay," she said, stupidly. The pigeon nodded back and the sisters skated to the bottom of the street.

Amber looked back at them. "Shouldn't they be asking for a special password? What if we're spies?"

"Everyone knows who we are, thanks to Mom, remember?" Larry said. "And besides, we want everyone to feel welcome."

"We," Amber said in a shrill little whisper. "*'We'*?"

Amber wanted to insist on an answer, but she went quiet as they rounded the corner and the viaduct expanded above them, the majestic lattice of steel arches darkening everything except the explosion of music and color before them.

There were at least a hundred people, dancing and mingling.

Somehow, it was like the city she always thought New York was meant to be.

8 Hours

Parked behind the crowd was a double-decker tour bus and people thronged there as well, swaying and laughing. A banner that read FREE LOVE & FUCK NEW DAWN in rainbow letters hung from a banister on the top deck. Someone had attached a fireman's pole there as well, and a giggling person dressed in a giant, round strawberry costume somehow managed to wrap two pink legs around it and hold on tight enough to slide down, to much celebratory hooting from the crowd.

The party spanned the width of the street beneath the viaduct, which was flanked by abandoned warehouses and deserted lots behind steel fences. Amber could see why this location had been chosen.

Larry took off her mask and rubbed her hands in the places where it had left ridge marks against her cheeks. Though she had told Amber masks weren't necessary in the off-grid areas, Amber kept hers on.

The heavy bass of the blaring soca thrummed in Amber's rib cage and she dug her nails into Larry's arm. "They have to turn this down. We'll get rounded up!"

Larry just smiled and kept on moving.

A group of people were gathered around a barbecue, and as far as she could tell, the cuts of sizzling meat were being passed around for free. Her stomach grumbled and she remembered the empty butcher's case at the supermarket.

There was a purple aircar hopping on hydraulics as a proud mechanic wiped his hands on a rag and stepped back, the torque wrench still in his pocket. A blow-up volleyball rolled where the car's wheels would have been, in the old days, and was kicked back toward the crowd.

A PARAchair glided across their path, a woman sitting on another woman's lap. They were dressed like 1940s burlesque dancers. Each briefly clasped hands with Larry and welcomed Amber before disappearing back into the crowd. Everyone seemed to know Larry.

Some people carried masks on sticks; others wore them on their heads like sunglasses. Amber had never seen so much bared flesh in one place. Feeling creepy, she averted her eyes from one couple making out only to land on another. She watched a pretty girl in a mod minidress dance by herself, her hips moving with serpentine ease to the beat, as if it was the most natural thing—and her heart jump-started when the girl suddenly turned and waved at Amber. She was about to raise her hand when she looked behind her and saw someone waving back at the girl. Amber's heart slowed, but it left her feeling quivery and un-settled. She crossed her arms over her chest.

"No way we don't get caught," she said, just to say something.

"Shut up," said Larry, her eyes scanning the crowd. If she'd witnessed what just happened, she was pretending not to notice. "This is why I can't bring you anywhere."

That stung. "Excuse me for—"

But Larry was already gliding off toward a group sitting in beach chairs. People around their age. One of them was a pretty girl with a candy-apple-red jacket, long locs, and a nose ring. She was wearing shorts and knee socks, flanked by two guys in bell-bottoms, one of whom was wearing a sweatband around his curly hair, the other wearing aviator sunglasses.

Amber suddenly couldn't remember the last time she'd approached a group of people in the hopes of making a friend. She didn't know what to do with her hands. She tucked her hair behind her ears.

Larry reached back and grabbed her hand. "Don't worry. They're nice," she said, looking back at Amber. "Like, *nice*-nice."

Larry skated up to them and hugged the girl in the red jacket tight. Then Larry kissed her on the nose, and the girl gave her a quick peck on the lips. They both giggled, as if they'd suddenly remembered where they were. And the two guys laughed. Clearly they'd seen this before.

"Get a room!" the one with the headband said. He turned out to be Franky, Natalie's brother. Her other brother was named Jay.

Larry took her hand and pulled her over.

"Amber, this is Natalie."

Natalie kissed her on the cheek and had such a sweet smile that Amber couldn't help but like her right away. She tried to draw on the well of anger she kept specifically for Larry, who always found a way to be carefree while Amber was stuck with the helpless anxiety of holding their family together through willpower and wishing. But in this moment, she couldn't quite remember what she had been so angry about.

When was the last time she'd seen Larry this happy?

Natalie poured something the color of an orange Creamsicle from a jug into two cups, added a healthy splash to each from a bottle of rum, and handed them to Larry and Amber. "Morir soñando."

Amber's eyes widened at the chunks of real orange in real milk, but she couldn't think of a way to ask Larry discreetly if these people were very rich.

"It's the other Melo sister!" Jay said. "Welcome! Y'all are famous around these parts."

"I'm sorry about what happened to your mom," Franky said. "And your dad."

"Thank you," Amber said, surprised at the catch in her own voice. "It's been a long time since anyone's said something like that to me."

In fact, when she thought about it, she was pretty sure no one ever really had.

AMBER FINISHED HER DRINK TOO FAST AND LET HER EYES roam. This party was like nothing she'd ever seen before. There was a wildness to this. An organic chaos. There were different kinds of music playing and though the crowd was composed of clusters, the people seemed to move as one. A gathering of sinners, worshipping the wrong things—and Amber belonged. A small, scared part of her was uncoiling to the beat. Someone pressed a fresh morir soñando into her hand and she drank it down, relishing the way the rum softened everything, including the sharpest points of her fear.

The crowd rippled and the booming bass of the music drowned out all her other thoughts. She allowed herself to just be, watching it all. After a few minutes, Jay wandered off and it had become clear that Larry and Natalie wanted to be alone.

A few feet away a group of break-dancers was clustered around an old boom box and a crowd cheered them on as they flipped over each other. Amber couldn't remember the last time she'd seen a boom box, but there it was, like something out of a history book, playing a song she'd never heard before but that everyone in the swaying crowd seemed to recognize. Franky asked her if she wanted to go watch them, and Amber nodded, feeling a wavy ease as she followed him, admiring the muscles in his shoulders.

The dancers were wearing black tights with bones printed on them. The incredible feats of grace and athleticism were only amplified by the fact that they were on hover blades. A boy did a backflip and the movement pushed his mask down over his face, and then they were all wearing their masks, showing off their double-jointedness and dancing together in a way that felt both choreographed and spontaneous, both collective and individual.

A girl glided up a makeshift ramp, a board leaning against a beat-up looking van, and twirled on the roof. Then, without so much as looking to make sure that her buddies were there to catch her, she somersaulted backward, taking Amber's breath with her as she turned slowly in the air, once, twice, and landed in a scrum of cheering skeletons.

As she clapped her hands along with the other spectators, Amber had to admit, if only to herself, that there was a sacred feeling to this whole thing, to a boisterous, trusting masquerade in the cathedral of the viaduct. There were people of all ages, and for a strange moment, Amber wished that she had an ark like Noah's so that she could take them all away when New Dawn inevitably flooded the underside of this bridge with its NDRs and white transports.

She snuck a sideways glance at Franky and found that he was already looking at her, as if he was trying to read her through the dark fringe of his eyelashes. Inhaling sharply, she took a quick step to the side to flee his gaze, forgetting all about the hover blades and tumbling down onto one knee.

"Yikes," said Franky, helping her up briskly, steadying her by the forearms. He didn't laugh at the raw red scrape on her knee. "I'll take you to someone who has a first aid kit."

Following Franky, she moved through the crowd, and it was like flipping through network channels, the music and the costumes changing every few seconds: a woman reading tarot cards, a group of musicians playing jazz, a group of people armed with spray paint creating a night sky on one of the steel awnings. Someone was serving Cuba libres from a bucket while half a dozen dancers twirled to a salsa song.

It was all too much and it was not enough. There wasn't enough time to enjoy all of it. Amber struggled to keep up with the red of Franky's headband in the crowd even as she tried to see as much as she could.

A drag queen dressed like Marie Antoinette glided by, long silver eyelashes brushing against the middle of her forehead, her pompadoured silver wig rising high above the crowd.

Amber, who had just caught up to Franky, whispered, "Beautiful," before she knew she'd said it. And the queen gave her arm a squeeze. "Thanks, baby."

Franky laughed. "Glad you like the scene."

"How could anyone not like it?" Amber said. "But it all seems like so much work to get here for just a few hours. Is it always like this?"

"Yes and no," Franky said, scanning the crowd. "What else is our time good for? But today is the summer solstice, the longest day of the year—and that's my boy with the Band-Aids," he shouted, grabbing Amber's hand. He pointed to a guy wearing a plush white costume as he put on a full rabbit head. "Follow the white rabbit!"

Several yards away, a pair of white ears loomed over the crowd, attached to a furry white body. As if on a mission, the rabbit was slicing quickly through the crowd, toward the river. Franky's friend was moving fast.

For a few minutes it was all a blur of color and music and laughter and Amber didn't have to admit to herself that she liked holding Franky's hand as they zipped through the crowd.

When the rabbit zoomed out of the border of the party and toward the Hudson, Amber assumed they would stop, but Franky only paused long enough to scan for pills in the air.

They glided out to the pier, where the rabbit was sitting on the ground and looking out into the Hudson. He took off his mask and shook out his hair, briefly exposing a tattoo of a nude, crucified woman on the side of his neck before his dark hair tumbled over it like a curtain.

"Wait, don't—"

"Oh, it's fine. I just wear it so I don't have to carry it," said the rabbit. He held out a hand to Amber. "I'm Eric. They've written this whole zone off."

Franky sat down next to him, leaving room for Amber between them, and pointed to Amber's raw knee. "You got any Band-Aids, man?"

Eric patted around in his pockets and drew out a small plastic first aid kit.

"But how can you be sure?" Amber said, sitting down carefully, still scanning the grounds for flashes of red.

"Can't," Eric admitted, with a shrug to indicate he didn't much care one way or the other. With deft fingers, he poured a bit of disinfectant onto a clean cotton ball and held it over the darkening crimson on her knee. "But look up. Look at the moon."

Amber's eyes had been trained on everything but the sky—on the skyline, on the water, on Franky, on Eric and his rabbit costume—but when she looked up, she gasped. The moon was round and full and seemed close enough to touch, and it was a deep pink. She barely felt the sting of the disinfectant on her cut.

"Do you like it?" Franky nudged her. "It's the strawberry moon."

Eric smoothed a new Band-Aid over her knee, then set about rummaging around in his costume again, which turned out to have a kangaroo-style pocket in the front, from which he pulled a half bottle of champagne and a small stack of plastic cups. "Magic," he said as he popped the cork and poured out three glasses.

"New moon beats New Dawn," Franky said, raising a glass.

"Oh, and wait!" Eric felt around in his strange pouch again, and from somewhere in the folds produced a paper bag. With a

flourish, he opened it and withdrew a small glass jar containing six beautiful, giant strawberries. "We are marking the occasion in style."

In reverent silence, they each had one. Swooning was something wispy heroines did in romance novels, but Amber couldn't help but lean her shoulder against Franky's. It was a shock to the system, all this forgotten sweetness.

They sat and watched the moon for a while, and Amber learned that Eric was studying to be a doctor, and that he did as much work off-grid as he did at the hospital where he was a resident.

"You make it sound like there's a whole world off-grid," Amber said. "Isn't it just a few pockets of people here and there?"

Both Franky and Eric laughed, and she was surprised at how pleased she was to be wrong.

"You got a piece of paper in there?" Franky said to Eric, who patted around for a few seconds and then came up empty, except for the brown paper bag that had held the strawberry jar.

Franky took it, patted his own pockets, and dug out a pen. Carefully, he tore the paper bag along the seams until it was flat and spread out on the pavement. Amber had the impossible memory of watching her father do this to make covers for her public-school textbooks. The tender exactness of his process, even though he had never been able to finish high school himself. She blinked it away, but not before Franky shot her a worried glance. "You good?"

She nodded.

He drew a quick outline of Manhattan island and began filling it with miniature versions of the Juan Duarte statue near Chinatown, the *Fearless Girl* at Wall Street, the Cloisters uptown.

"Wow," Amber said. "I can't believe you're just drawing this freehand."

"I want to be a cartographer someday," he said as he added some small skyscrapers to designate midtown.

Amber snorted and the bubbles tickled the inside of her nose. Franky glanced up at her and kept drawing. "Sorry, it's so cool," she said quickly, "but isn't the world mapped out already? Do we even need new maps anymore?"

"Do you really think maps are permanent? We are here," he said, drawing an X to mark the West Harlem Piers.

"The sun of New Dawn don't shine everywhere," Eric sang happily, taking a swig of champagne and beaming up at the moon.

Franky started adding little moon crescents all over the island, many of them along the Harlem shore, including one alongside a depiction of the Little Red Lighthouse. "All of these are either safe houses, farms, or off-grid zones."

Amber didn't know what to say, so she ran a finger over the indentations of the ballpoint pen on the brown paper. "All of these?"

"Yes and no." Franky shrugged. "Some spots get shut down and others pop up."

Eric tapped the map grandly. "Those strawberries we had are New York homegrown. We're doing it all off-grid."

Amber picked up the map carefully, studied it for a few stunned moments, then offered it back to Franky.

"Keep it," Franky said, waving it away. "It's time we got back to the group." He rose up and extended his hand to help her up, then Eric.

"Are you sure?"

Franky nodded as Eric stumbled to his feet behind him, trying several times before he finally righted himself on his hover blades and put his rabbit head back on.

"These maps are alive," Franky said. "The safe spots change all the time and there are old ones that we don't put on the maps at all. But if you get caught, get rid of it."

"I'll eat it," said Amber solemnly, and they all laughed. They took one last look at the strawberry moon and wended their way back to the party.

"Seems silly to hold a party for a moon in a place where you can't even see it," said Amber as they entered the cover of the viaduct again.

"Why?" said Franky. "Just because you can't see something doesn't mean it's not there." He bumped a shoulder against hers.

"Listen, I'm sorry for what I said before, about maps," Amber said as Eric waved a white furry arm and his ears disappeared in the crowd. "I get it. I mean, I love clocks. I'm teaching myself about them. If it was up to me, I'd be a clockmaker." She was talking too fast and saying too much, she could feel it.

"Clocks?" Franky said, turning and wheeling out to a stop in front of her.

"Yeah," Amber said as a flush crept up her cheeks.

"For real? Clocks?"

"You don't have to be mean about it. How is that any weirder than—"

"Come on," said Franky, raising his voice as they worked their way back into the crowd. "I have a clock for you to fix. People bring their talents here," he said, pointing to the bouncing purple Chevy convertible. "Whatever you're good at, there's someone out here who will appreciate it. Larry drew my picture the other day—like looking in a mirror."

"Anyone seen Mohammed?" he asked two women who were whispering excitedly; Amber couldn't quite make it out, but it sounded like they were discussing someone named Doc Young. In any case, they didn't know who Mohammed was and shook their heads.

They roved around between different groups until someone pointed them toward a cluster of guys playing a card game against a chain-link fence.

"I found your clockmaker!" Franky called out.

"Man, it's hard to get up fast with these things on, hold on," said Mohammed, and Franky skated over and extended a hand.

Mohammed took a bundle from a backpack nearby and

spread it out on the pavement, revealing an old-looking mahogany clock about a foot tall.

"Ooh," Amber said, dropping to the ground in front of it, completely forgetting about her scraped knee.

"It won't tick," Mohammed said, "and I opened up the box, but I don't want to risk messing it up by reaching in and taking it apart."

"Taking it apart is the only way to make it work," she said. "But you're right not to try it—you can break a finger if you don't do it properly and it's a spring clock."

Mohammed laughed and then stopped when he saw that she was serious.

"If you know what you're doing, have at it," he said, sitting down across from her and gesturing toward the clock.

"Let's see. I don't think this is the place to disassemble the whole movement, but maybe we can get a general idea of what's happening."

The boys gathered around her and she felt as though she were in an operating theater. The music drowned away as she examined the parts of the clock's heart.

"It's the deadbeat escapement," she finally said.

"That's what I've been saying," said Mohammed, and they all laughed.

"Okay, so for the clock to work, you need a pendulum, which swings side to side, right?"

"Right?"

"Right. Two things keep the pendulum swinging and swinging accurately: this toothy wheel right here, and this upside-down V-shaped part, which is called a deadbeat escapement. The deadbeat escapement catches the little teeth on the wheel to balance out the swing of the pendulum. Do you see?"

It was clear from everyone's vigorous nodding that they did not see, but Amber was already scanning her memory of the rummage sales for replacement wheels in this size.

Her family was in shambles. Her life was under constant surveillance. Her mother was a smiling stranger.

But this—this Amber could fix.

6 HOURS

A distant whistle pierced the air, followed by another.

"Down," Franky said. And everyone around them crouched.

A third whistle and the music stopped. The whistles kept coming in long, slow repetition.

"My sis—" Amber started to get up, but Franky pulled her down again. The whistles continued. She followed Franky's example and lay flat on the ground, the rough, cold pavement against the skin of her cheek as she watched Franky.

He took her hand and gave it a squeeze, mouthed, *Wait.*

Sweet gesture, but she couldn't wait. She wouldn't wait. She had seen footage of raids like this, of the phalanxes of dark uniforms descending on crowds, the red stripes flashing on their chests. Her heart was pounding hard enough to quake the earth. She put her palms down to push herself up, but then the alarm whistles stopped, as quickly as they'd started.

The chatter slowly resumed as everyone got up and dusted themselves off. A group of laughing revelers helped roll the strawberry back onto her feet and she curtsied grandly before wheeling off into the crowd.

"False alarm," Franky said as the music came back on, softer than before.

"I think the party's over," Amber said as she rose to her feet, furious with herself for having come in the first place. "I gotta go." She was already scanning the crowd for Larry.

"Keep the clock," Mohammed said. "Can you fix it and give it back to me when I see you next?"

"But will I see you again?" She swaddled the clock in the velvet cloth, relishing the weight of it, even as she handed it back to him.

"I have a feeling you will," said Mohammed.

"I'll bring the right tools next time," Amber said, to be polite.

"Thank you," Mohammed said, and for a moment Amber could imagine what it meant to be a regular girl, to have friends you could count on seeing again.

Amber turned to Franky and gave him a brisk hug. She didn't know how to say goodbye, so she didn't. She didn't say anything at all or think anything at all, but pressed her lips to his instead. He tasted like strawberries and his arms encircled her waist. She was steady on her blades when she backed away this time. Even if she wasn't brave enough to look Franky in the eye, she could see clearly now.

She heard him start to say something, but she was already darting away through the crowd, having spotted the red of Natalie's jacket. Larry and her girlfriend were sitting on the roof of a candy-pink Beetle, their legs swinging free. Each of them was wearing a single earbud and they pressed the sides of their heads together. From the way they were swaying, Amber guessed it was a sappy ballad. They reminded Amber of those old pictures of couples drinking from two straws in the same milkshake.

"Let's go," Amber said, wheeling up to the car. It came out like a half bark. The look in her eyes must have been enough, because instead of arguing, Larry turned back to Natalie and kissed both of the palms of her hands, and then they bowed their heads together, foreheads touching, and kissed while Amber made a show of jostling around in her backpack, searching for her mask.

When Larry and Natalie leaped down and Larry put her hover blades back on, their eyes were moist.

Without thinking, Amber reached past Larry and gave Natalie a quick, hard hug. "Stay safe," she said.

"You too."

Amber grabbed Larry's hand and squeezed it too hard. "Let's go, let's go, let's go."

The two sisters glided back up the hill, toward home. There were two new sentries at the entry point, this time a rooster and a frog.

New Dawn Surveillance Footage: Aerial view of Manhattan, two red dots swirling from the Viaduct and up to Broadway. At 135th Street, the dots stop abruptly, and suddenly change course, drifting up toward Amsterdam in stops and starts.

They began the uphill trip home, with Amber following Larry as she traced a zigzaggy route back to their brownstone. The city was quiet. It was always quiet, but after dark, the silence was something you could feel, especially after the cacophony of the party. Amber's ears picked up every sound that penetrated the stillness: a car here and there; a hunched, tired person walking to or from an evening shift; the quiet whir of an NDR in the distance.

They were only three blocks from home when a drone appeared from behind a corner and drifted lazily down toward them.

"Identification, please," it said, approaching their masked faces. "Please remove your face covering."

"Oh, shit," whispered Amber. She was frozen, but Larry hissed "Go!" and both sisters pivoted at once and zoomed down the street in the opposite direction, with the NDR in pursuit.

"Stop," it called out. "Identification, please."

For nearly half a mile, they managed to outpace the drone, only because it was an older model. Finally, Larry pulled Amber's arm and signaled her to stop. They turned into a side street, slipped behind the large plastic trash cans in front of a brownstone—and held their breath as the minder drone drifted past them, still calling out, "Wait, identification, please."

They clung to the metal bars, afraid to move, for a few long minutes, and then cautiously set out for home again. Amber toggled between adrenaline-fed trembling and churning rage. The trip seemed to take hours, even though they'd only had to backtrack a few blocks.

5 HOUrs

Anger vibrated in Amber's bones. She couldn't believe she'd embarked on an outing that dangerous with only a necklace—if it even worked—as protection.

Everything had turned out fine, but what if it hadn't? Larry had risked the entire family's lives, and for what?

At the door, the sisters stopped to take off their hover blades. Amber looked up at Mrs. Perez's window and saw only the slow swaying of the drapes, as if someone had just been there.

Never again, Amber mouthed to Larry. Larry opened her mouth to say something, then seemed to think better of it and clamped it shut. Instead, she picked up her hover blades and walked up the brownstone's stairs. She unlocked the door and left it ajar for Amber, who stomped up after her, determined to further make her point.

Larry walked toward the kitchen, but something stopped her at the doorway. Amber walked up behind her, intending to shove her, but the forced broadcast on the kitchen wall stopped her too. She leaned her chin on Larry's shoulder and whispered, "Oh, shit."

With a giant chef's knife, their mother was chopping at a dish rag on the cutting board, her eyes glazed and trained on the projection.

The raid on the Riverside Drive Viaduct had been fast and merciless and it must have begun mere minutes after they'd departed.

Amber's mouth went dry. Larry rushed up to the wall and Amber knew that if she could have walked directly into the screen and into the raid itself, she would have, just to find Natalie.

The New Dawn broadcast showed pills and black-clad authorities moving through a crowd in the dark, the red stripes of their uniforms glowing. She remembered all the strobe lights and spotlights that people had brought for the party. She could imagine them quickly turning them off to make things harder for authorities and for the minder drones to catch everyone as they fled in different directions. But a New Dawn spokesperson talked over the footage, proudly explaining that the forces had barricaded the crowd against the river.

People were desperately putting on masks and the Standards authorities were just as eagerly ripping them off amid the glowing red of pills whirling through the crowd, identifying and logging.

As the authorities shoved people into lines, the sisters watched in clenched panic, searching for familiar faces. The footage was fast-moving, pulled from NDRs as they flitted through the crowds like hungry mosquitoes, looking for identifiable faces as the cops wrangled the masked detainees into a convoy of transports. But even with such frantic panning, Amber recognized Mohammed, sitting on a curb looking sullen, his mask down around his neck, holding up his TriCard as his face was scanned.

A cut: Eric was being handcuffed against a parked car, the rabbit head of his costume rolling on its side in the street. Another cut: the pigeon who had welcomed Amber tore off his mask and waved it in the air, revealing a handsome, bearded face. Another: someone in a zombie mask was swinging a bat at the pills and managed to fell three of them before the uniforms were able to restrain him.

Amber and Larry watched in horror, while Diana continued, with a blank face, sawing away at her tattered dishcloth.

The footage cut out to show a man and a woman sitting behind a news desk. "These periodic disturbances are nothing to be concerned about," the woman said. "The order is always quick to respond and to set the disorderly aright. A good clean for these folks and they'll be sound as bells."

"I couldn't have said it better, Tammy. This is child's play. These networks are so fractured, it would be difficult to imagine an effective, organized resistance effort."

"That's right, Ron. There's no history to it," Tammy said. "Let's check back in on the live scene."

Smiling, their mother got out a mallet and began pounding it on the dish rag on the cutting board.

The footage showed Marie Antoinette, gliding, head held high, toward one of the detention transports, followed by ten minutes more of seizures and scuffles. Amber glanced over at Larry. Though her sister was stone still, she knew her eyes were scanning and rescanning the dark crowds for flashes of red.

Diana pounded away at the cutting board as if she wanted to smash it completely. And for once, Amber was grateful for her bizarre "cooking."

The mallet drowned out the pounding of their hearts.

4 Hours

Out on the roof, Amber sat on the cold concrete with her arms wrapped around her knees, turning the larimar over and over with clammy fingers while Larry paced a tight circle around her.

"Should I activate it? Should I use the necklace to reverse the raid?"

"We don't know if Natalie got picked up."

"But all those other people—"

"First of all, we don't know if that thing even does what Papi said it does," said Larry, her voice steel-edged. "Second of all, if it's real, we can't just use it at the drop of a hat."

"So what, then, we do nothing? Just like Papi?"

Larry ignored this last accusation and plopped down on the

ground next to Amber. "We stop and we assess the situation. We have a plan for this."

"'We'?"

"If Natalie's okay, she'll meet me at the Little Red Lighthouse in an hour. I'll leave in a few minutes."

"The fuck you will," said Amber. "Stop and think for once. It's past midnight."

"I am," Larry said. "Everyone is focused on the arrests at the viaduct, so that's where all the NDRs are."

"Do you think there are only, like, ten pills in New York?"

"You are free to continue being a coward, Amber. This is none of your business."

"None of my business? If you get caught—"

"What? I get wiped? Better than being afraid of my shadow all the damn time."

"That's not fair and you know it."

"Do I know it, Amber? Here are the things *I* know: I know our mother is canning Twinkies in Windex because our father didn't see fit to save her. And I know that at some point, you and I are going to have to make a decision for ourselves because no one—not even our parents—is going to take care of us."

"So you want to be selfish and only use the larimar to save Natalie."

"Correct," Larry said, rising to her feet and lighting a cigarette. "I have to find out if she made it out."

Amber scrambled up too. She rubbed her temples in hopes of soothing the headache that hammered away at her skull. "And what? If she's fine, we don't use it? What about all the other people you knew at the party? *Your* friends. Fuck them?"

"Yes," Larry said, squaring her shoulders and meeting Amber's eyes. "We have—at best, if that thing even works—one bullet in the chamber. These raids happen all the time and we can't save everyone, Amber."

"What makes you think you know more than me? That you're somehow smarter?" Amber snatched the cigarette out of Larry's hand and took a drag, and almost relished the wave of stomach-roiling nausea that followed. She deserved to suffer.

"This is how it's always been. You refuse to see the situation for what it is, and you want to be in charge at the same time." Larry walked up close to her, so that their foreheads were almost touching. "You're only a year older than me. Who do you think you are?"

"Well, if you're so wise to the ways of the world, then you know that what you do affects all of us," Amber said, pointing down, "including our mother, who can't even defend herself. It's pretty fucking selfish—you know that, right?"

"Okay, how's this for selfish: I'm going to end it with Natalie. You're right, it's dangerous. For her and for us. So if she's safe, you get what you always want. You lose nothing. You make no sacrifices and you fight no battles. Happy?" Larry's eyes moistened, but she quickly turned her back and leaned against the balcony, her cigarette smoke swirling around her.

Amber started to speak, wanting to disagree, but she stopped herself. Wasn't this what she had argued for?

There was no victory in it.

3 Hours

The trip to the Little Red Lighthouse was among the most stressful twenty minutes of Amber's life.

By then, she was comfortable on the hover blades, but not enough to keep up with Larry, who zoomed down one-way streets without checking for traffic, scooting in and out of the view of the NDRs.

By the time they reached Fort Washington Park, they were drenched in sweat—Larry from darting into traffic, and Amber from scrambling to catch up to her and herd her down less crowded streets and away from pill patrols. It was Amber who had to stop Larry and remind her to put on her mask when they'd gotten far enough away from home.

Even in its current state, with the waters of the Hudson swelling around it so that it was half-submerged, the Little Red Lighthouse was hardly so little. Its pointed turret loomed triumphant above them, unmoved by the rising, rushing river waters. In a few decades, it might be gone from view altogether.

The red made Natalie's jacket harder to spot on the lookout deck, but when she saw it, Amber expelled a breath she hadn't realized she'd been holding. Larry let out a loud whoop and swept Natalie up into a whirling hug.

Natalie and Franky had been near the edge of the party and had raced out through an alley just as the uniforms had descended on the viaduct. Amber felt an unaccountable relief when she heard that Franky had also made it out. But it was hard to celebrate anything with the raid footage still so fresh in their memories.

Larry gave her a meaningful look and Amber excused herself and sat on the grass nearby to wait while they talked. Franky was safe. She hugged herself. The part of her that would have been desperate to rush home was strangely absent. She could stare at the rippling waves of the Hudson forever. The strawberry moon was still out, but now it looked bloody to Amber. Could she really live with herself if she didn't use the larimar now, to save all those people? Could she really stand by and do nothing?

She looked over at Larry and Natalie, who were holding hands. For a moment, Amber thought Larry was going to drop down on one knee and propose—but then she remembered why they were here.

She reminded herself that Larry was doing the right thing, even as she fought the urge to barrel over there and tell her to forget it, to stay with Natalie. She could hardly believe her own thoughts.

She pulled the larimar over her head and held it in her palm. Could something this small really erase that entire raid? She looked at the place where the stone had been cleaved in two. Papi said all it took was turning the two halves of the stone in opposite directions . . .

IF SHE HAD BEEN GIVEN THE STONE WHEN SHE WAS A CHILD, Amber likely would have squandered it on something silly, like beating Larry in a game, or reversing the shattering of her mother's crystal vase. Now she was frozen in her tracks. People always said to listen to your gut, but what did her gut say?

No matter. Here was Larry, tears streaming down her face, her amber necklace bouncing oddly against her chest. She must have gotten it back from Natalie. It didn't suit her at all, Amber realized. It belonged with Natalie, just like Larry did. This was something her gut knew.

BEFORE HE DIED, PABLO GAVE A STONE NECKLACE TO EACH OF his daughters. Their mother was still in training to become a Torch then, to work at the Nevermind facilities, her face appearing on their kitchen wall nearly every day.

Between these broadcasts, Pablo had gathered his daughters at the kitchen table and offered them each a silk jewelry pouch, a blue one for Amber and a dark yellow for Larry.

To Larry, he had given the bee trapped in amber. "My restless Larissa," he said, closing her hand around the stone. "Remember that keeping time matters as much as rushing into the future."

"And to you, Amber, a larimar. The only way to change the future is to hold the past."

Larry had accepted her necklace with a barely concealed eye roll and later tossed it in a jewelry box in her room. But Amber had listened, clutching the gold chain as her father explained how he had come to possess the stone for the first time.

At sixteen, Pablo was essentially a professional miner, schooled in the dangerous work that had put his mountain village on the map. After one long, futile day of pickaxing at a rock face in search of glimmers of blue, he packed up his tools. The other workers wandered home, hungry and tired, but something slowed Pablo's legs and sent his eye roving, one last time, around the mine.

In one remote corner, he spotted a bright blue stone, bigger than any he had ever seen—so bright he thought he was hallucinating from exhaustion. But the stone seemed to ripple, and it was as if the mountain had swallowed live ocean.

The stone came loose easily in Pablo's hand, but he must have taken a wrong step because he tumbled down an unmarked vertical shaft, breaking both legs. For almost a full day, he clutched the stone and waited to be rescued, his broken body counting the passing of seconds with excruciating exactness as the muffled voices overhead figured out how to rescue him.

For a long time, Pablo had dismissed what happened to him in the mine shaft as a hallucination from the overwhelming pain searing through his legs—particularly his right, which had broken in three places and would never quite recover. In the hot darkness, he had turned the stone in his hands and found a cleft in the raw, unpolished rock, as if it had been sliced with a diamond-tipped saw.

To his surprise, part of the rock swiveled between his fingers and the dark cave was awash in a bright blue light. Next to him, a translucent blue woman appeared. She explained that the larimar would reverse time just once in his lifetime, before he passed it on to his eldest child. You could never be sure how much time the stone would erase, or how big its scope.

Would it erase his brother's new baby daughter? His cousin's newly issued visa to New York?

"That is the risk you take," the blue woman said. "Humans try to control time with numbers, but time does what it wants, and so does this stone. You may choose to never use the larimar, to save it for some other moment, Pablo, or you may choose to use it right now."

And this, Pablo knew—even through the blinding pain in his legs—was his first test. If he accepted the stone's gift now, his fall would be reversed and all the pain he was feeling would evaporate. It would be as if he had never found the stone.

For a few distressed moments, Pablo considered his options. His people, his brothers, his uncles were clamoring overhead. He could not understand what they were saying, but he could tell from the tone of their voices that they were trying to reassure him. He could trust them to hoist him out, no matter how much extra work it took.

So Pablo had gritted his teeth and turned the halves of the stone back to their original position. The blue woman disappeared, taking all her blue light with her and leaving him in the dark.

In the days after his rescue, Pablo began the work of convincing himself that he had imagined it all. His legs healed until the only memory of the fall was the stone he now carried as a lucky talisman, and the slightest limp.

When he presented the stone to Amber and told her its history, just before he died, she had simply stared at it. The argument that followed had been bitter and mostly one-sided. Did it really work? If yes, why had he not prevented any of the bad things? Why hadn't he stopped the ascent of New Dawn? She gulped for air. Why hadn't he saved their mother?

"What would you have done?"

"I would have saved Mom," Amber said. "I would have saved them all!"

"It can only be used once, and it's not simply turning back the hands on a clock," Pablo said—gently. "The larimar alone decides how its power flows."

He had waved all her other questions away, saying only, "For me, it's now a pretty rock, but for you, it's a source of power. And with power comes hard choices. You'll see."

"Bullshit," Amber said. "All of it is bullshit!" And she had wept for the last time in her father's arms, already grieving him. She would always regret that this had been one of their final conversations.

In the days after Pablo's funeral, Amber and Larry were alone in the brownstone. The broadcasts looped pictures and footage of their parents, announcing Pablo Melo's death as if it were something to be celebrated. The girls were just old enough to take care of themselves, the state had decided, and they mostly did—eating cheese out of canisters and walking around the house like zombies, both lonely and together in their mourning.

In her room, feral with grief, Amber had thrown herself across her bed and turned the stone's halves the way Pablo had shown her, and everything was suddenly a blindingly bright green-blue.

The blue woman really had appeared, translucent and dressed as if she were from some distant future. Amber instinctively patted her head and ears, though she knew she wasn't wearing a headset, then jumped back and knelt on the bed, jaw hanging open, as the woman approached.

Amber somehow knew not to be afraid, even though she could see her own bookshelves behind her. When she passed a trembling hand through the blue woman's chest, the woman only smiled, as if she found Amber entertaining.

"Do you wish to activate the stone?" The woman was holding a spinning cube in her hand. It stopped midair, one of its pointed corners hovering over the blue woman's palm.

"How much can you erase?"

The woman raised her palm an inch and the blue cube seemed to get bigger, until Amber could see that there were people inside of it. She peered into the box and saw herself and Larry, still dressed in black after their father's funeral, curled up together on the couch, under the family portrait. "This is it?"

"The larimar decides what she wants to offer you when you ask," the blue woman said.

Amber's mind raced through everything Pablo had said. If the stone could only erase a few hours, she couldn't save her father, and she couldn't save her mother. She shook her head no.

"I wouldn't call on me without reason if I were you," the woman said, and the blue cube began to spin again. "Every time you activate the stone without using it, you drain her power and she gives you less."

Amber tilted her head. "But wait—if my father never used it, wouldn't it have more power, rather than less?"

The blue woman tilted her head. "Oh, but your father did invoke the larimar. He *did* use it."

"When? For what?"

"That's not how this works." And the blue woman disappeared.

1 HOUr

The trip home was as uneventful as it could be, considering. The sisters listened for the mosquito-like whirring of NDRs as they made their way downtown, weaving down side streets parallel to Broadway. The night air was muggy, as if rain was coming, and Amber's blouse clung to her back.

The streets seemed eerie, quieter than usual—she wasn't sure how, but the silence seemed to deepen. It was probably because it was late and people were afraid to go out after the viaduct raids. But even in the heat, something about the quiet raised goose bumps on Amber's arms. Her senses seemed sharper too, picking up each distant car horn and closing door as if it were happening in front of her. The stench of garbage bags waiting for pickup filled her nostrils as they glided past.

Larry stopped sluggishly at every light to wipe her face.

Amber kept telling herself that this was the way things needed to be, that Larry had done the right thing, but her legs felt leaden. She looked up, hoping to catch a glimpse of the moon, but she couldn't see it.

Just because you can't see something doesn't mean it's not there.

When they turned onto their street, Amber's heart dropped down into her hover blades. The door to their house was wide open. The two sisters exchanged a terrified glance and moved in unison, kicking off their blades and sprinting up the stairs, through the living room, and into Diana's bright pink kitchen— where their beautiful mother sat at her kitchen table, surrounded by four bemused uniforms and a pill.

They watched her as if transfixed, as she, smiling radiantly, rolled an acid-green dough out with a rolling pin. As always, nothing about the way she moved showed that she was aware of what was happening, though there were dark stains forming where her sleeve creased underneath her arms, and there was an unusual sheen when her forehead caught the light.

Amber's hand drifted immediately to the necklace, but she knew not to wrap her fingers around it. She rested her palm on her chest.

"Larissa Melo," said one of the men, turning to the sisters. "We are taking you for scanning and diagnostics, regarding bugs that may have resulted in activities in violation of the New Dawn Standards of Moral Virtue."

Larry stepped forward, her eyes still red. The NDR approached and read her face.

One of the uniforms reached for his restraints, but another put out a hand to stop him. "We don't need those, do we?" he asked in a low voice. Because they all represented New Dawn, authorities did not wear identifying badges, but this one seemed like he might have been a decent person once.

Diana rose from her chair and gave Larry a long hug. "Going out for a walk? We'll see you in a few hours, honey." She kissed her daughter on the forehead. One of the uniforms tittered and another one elbowed him in the ribs.

Amber gave Larry a quick hug, then she and Diana watched the uniforms escort Larry to the back of a white transport and drive away, the NDR zipping along behind it.

It all happened so fast. Larry was gone. Gone.

Amber hoped Mrs. Perez had finally gotten the show she had been hoping for.

She closed the front door, leaned against it, and yanked the necklace from around her neck, breaking the chain. Her gut was finally talking. This was it.

In the kitchen, her mother was opening and slamming drawers. Had watching Larry get taken away somehow broken through to her? Was she having some sort of breakdown?

"I'm going to talk fast," Diana said, turning suddenly as Amber walked into the room. She was holding a roll of silver masking tape and a bottle marked SOUNDPROOFING CAULK in her crimson-manicured fingers. With quick, deft movements, she sprayed the caulk directly into the surveillance microphone and then bit off a piece of masking tape with her teeth to seal it, before moving on to the camera. "Because I know you're going to use the larimar, but there are several things you should know."

The shock stopped Amber in her tracks. Her mother, her real mother, was talking to her. There was no fake smile, no vacant stare. She was sealing the camera with tape as if she knew *exactly what she was doing.*

"Wait, wait. You can't do that!" Amber said, starting to peel back the tape on the microphone. "New Dawn will be back here in less than ten minutes! Remember when you accidentally draped a dishcloth over the camera last year?"

Diana laughed behind her and it scared Amber. When was the last time she had heard her mother *laugh?*

Amber's mind moved like lightning through the memory:

The authorities had stormed the brownstone and nearly taken her mother back into custody. The two sisters had huddled in terrified silence as Diana had refused to acknowledge the uniforms gathered around her. With steady hands, she'd poured batter into a piping bag, answering their questions with nonsensical small talk, and begun frosting smiley faces onto a tray of pink urinal cakes, which she had offered with an air of magnificent hospitality to the authorities.

After a few minutes, the uniforms had seemed as afraid as the sisters had been. They'd backed away slowly, murmuring in quiet, placating tones before effectively fleeing the kitchen.

Speaking as if their mother were not there, the uniforms had led Amber and Larry into the living room and warned them to keep Diana from touching the cameras. They understood that she was in a delicate condition, but she was also a high-profile detainee, and obscuring the cameras would trigger potentially stressful house visits. The sisters were old enough to hear the threat for what it was. When the authorities had turned to leave, Diana had smiled brightly and offered them pink frosted urinal cakes for the road. The humiliation and fear of that memory was slowly morphing into something else now as her mother leaned across the table, her eyes as bright and lucid as they had ever been.

This time they would arrest her, Amber just knew it. And the tape wasn't coming off fast enough.

"New Dawn'll be here in eleven," said Diana as she set a kitchen timer and placed it on the table, where it began to tick. "Come here, baby. You still have the larimar stone, right? You haven't used it." She said this as a statement and not a question. Amber wasn't sure if she should be offended, but the facts that her mother seemed to be speaking to her from the dead and that she remembered the larimar stone at all were shocking enough.

Dazed and mute, Amber followed her mother's orders and sat down, her fist tight around the larimar.

"We have an opening," Diana said, perching on the edge of her chair and reaching for Amber's hand. "The uniforms who arrested Larry, one of them is part of the resistance. If we leave now, we can meet him and—"

Amber snatched her hand back. "Wait, since when do you know anything about—"

Diana placed the heels of her palms on the table, as if she had lost patience and was about to rise and leave Amber there. She looked at the kitchen timer again (nine minutes and forty seconds). "It's me, Ambo-bambo. I've been here the whole time. I never left. This," she said, gesturing around the kitchen and down at her starched lilac dress, "is what I had to do to get home to keep you and Larr safe."

And just like that, Amber's mind went reeling back to the moment her mother had been returned to them in a white hospital gown. How the news coverage had been about how sweet and docile she was, and how apologetic her handlers had been. There were accidents in every technology, even the best of the best, they said as Diana sat primly on the couch, smiling, her eyes trained on the family portrait.

For the first few weeks Amber and Larry had tried. They had pulled her into the bathroom and showed her handwritten notes, about the larimar, about Pablo. They had shown her photo albums. She had been fiercely affectionate with them, but seemed to float away during these conversations, her eyes glassy. She would wander out of the room and leave them there, clutching photos of a young Diana and Pablo dancing on their wedding day. They would find her in the kitchen, making her inedible dishes, her smile tight and her eyes on the surveillance camera.

Amber looked at the kitchen timer. Nine minutes. Her mother got up and went into her bedroom. She returned with three small overnight bags.

"Pablo *used* the larimar, Amber. I was marched into a cleaning chamber, restrained, and left there. I was asked if I was ready to be cleansed and before I could answer, the procedure began. At the end, I was handed a signed white card that verified that I'd been wiped. And as I was being untied, this blue light washed over everything, and then I was standing in line to enter the room—but the card was still in my hand.

"For a long time, I told myself that I should keep the peace for you, whatever it took. But we're past keeping peace." She gestured at the kitchen and the sealed camera again. "It was never supposed to be permanent. This is not the life I want to leave you with.

"When I held up that card, people believed me. After that, it wasn't so hard to convince New Dawn that the cleansing had messed me up somehow, but they moved me through the reprogramming sequence anyway. It took some work to get them to send me home. Their dreams of publicity campaigns with Diana Melo as the lead Torch for the facility were hard to kill." She smiled. "But I managed."

Diana clutched two of the duffel bags and put one on the table in front of Amber. She rummaged through it and saw that it contained some of her favorite clothes, toiletries, all her clocks tucked into a sleek new mahogany carrying case, a photo of her and Larry at the zoo, and the family photo she kept tucked into her dresser mirror. "When did you—"

"I've been putting these together here and there since I got back," her mother said, almost shyly. "But I budgeted five minutes for you to grab anything else you can think of—"

"For what? I still don't understand. Where are we going?"

"Now that you girls are grown, it's time," Diana said, putting down the two duffel bags in the kitchen. She held up the timer. Seven minutes.

"Time for what? Are you suggesting that instead of using the stone we get ourselves *all* detained?"

Diana tilted her head back as if she hadn't anticipated any resistance from Amber.

"We can't save everyone," Amber said, remembering what Larry had said. "We can't be heroes if we're locked up ourselves."

Amber couldn't be sure, but wasn't that the sound of sirens in the distance?

"We don't have a lot of time," Diana said, glancing at the kitchen timer. "And I'm asking you to trust me."

"Trust you? When you've been lying to us this whole time? When we needed you the most?"

"You, of all people, Amber, should be able to understand what it means to lay low to keep safe. I'm suggesting that we keep the stone and use it to save more people, rather than fewer."

Amber shook her head. She backed away and found the split in the larimar, where the stone was cleaved in two. She turned the two halves in opposite directions.

NOTHING HAPPENED.

Amber's temples pounded. Over the sound of the ticking kitchen timer, her mother was still talking, fast and clear, about the networks she still had and the people who would help Larry escape the cleansing facility.

Then the room was awash in bright blue light and her mother froze midsentence. The blue woman appeared, holding her spinning cube. She glanced curiously at the kitchen timer, which had stopped its countdown, then at Diana, then at Amber. "Hello again," she said. "Are you ready to activate the larimar?"

"Yes," Amber croaked.

The spinning cube stopped turning. "Are you sure? Think, think."

In front of her, a large number 60 appeared next, and as Amber watched, it became a 59, and then 58.

"The stone will only offer its powers to you *once*," the blue woman said, bending a little at the knee to look again at Diana's frozen profile, as if she were trying to remember how she knew her. She turned back to Amber. "Then it will only work for your eldest child. Once."

Amber watched the seconds wind down, watched her mother, who was still motionless, one hand in the air. She noted the intensity in her eyes and how much she'd missed her real mother.

Forty seconds. The numbers seemed solid, but when she reached out to touch them, they dissolved.

"Can I see what the stone will erase, like last time?"

The blue woman seemed to think for a moment, glancing at the cube hovering over her palm. "No," she said.

Amber thought about all the good things she might be erasing, the time between Natalie and Larry, the summer solstice party, her fledgling friendship with Franky. They would all disappear. Would *she* even remember, and did she deserve to, if everyone else forgot?

What if the larimar didn't work?

She pictured Larry in some cold white-walled room, alone and scared.

"Are you *sure*?"

"Yes!" Amber shouted at the ten-second mark.

Her mother's earnest face disappeared and everything went pitch-black.

AMBER BLINKED AND SHE WAS STANDING AT A CROSSWALK ON Broadway, her arms wrapped around a bag of groceries, the stubborn evening sun overhead. Glancing at the red streetlight, she maneuvered the grocery bag from one hip to the other and caught the orange just before it tumbled out of the bag.

Amber smiled at the pill that turned onto Broadway and hovered over her suspiciously for a few minutes but did not engage. Could it really have worked? When the light changed,

Amber sprinted the rest of the way home, bounding up the stairs to the brownstone two at a time.

Larry was coming down the stairs, and Amber dropped the groceries on the floor near the door. She grabbed her sister and hugged her as tight as she could, even as Larry tried to push her off. "What are you doing, get off me, weirdo!"

But now Amber was crying. She held on until Larry stopped fighting and hugged back.

She pulled Larry into the kitchen, wanting to keep her close, and hugged her mother, who hugged her back, like she had always done, though she seemed as confused as Larry by the unusual display of affection.

Amber doubled back for the groceries and as Diana bustled about, unpacking them, she decided what she needed to do to keep her family safe.

With grim determination, she turned to Larry, plucked gently at the bracelet on her wrist and then mouthed *Upstairs*.

Larry rolled her eyes but trudged toward the stairs. Amber got up to follow her and took one last glance at Diana, who was staring off into the distance, wringing her red-manicured hands.

How long could she keep up the tightrope act before the rope snapped? Diana caught her looking and smiled.

She really didn't remember.

Amber turned to follow Larry out of the kitchen, through the living room, and up the stairs. She would tell Larry about the larimar and what she had done. She'd be able to prove it, to describe Natalie and Franky, whom she had never met. They might be able to safely stop the viaduct party from ever happening.

Maybe she would even lie a little and say that Natalie had been arrested; she knew Larry would do anything to protect her girlfriend, even if it meant never talking to her again. And she wouldn't say anything at all to her mother, because she was like a bomb waiting to explode their life in a thousand unpredictable directions. Amber was finally strong enough to hold them together, keep them all safe.

But there it was, the family portrait and her gut talking again.

Wake up, Amber, this is it.

She turned around.

Rushing past her mother, she started opening and closing drawers, until she found the caulking spray and the masking tape. Amber was clumsier at all this, but her mother gave her a single wide-eyed glance and immediately got to work, handing her a piece of masking tape and blocking off the lens of the surveillance camera. Amber grabbed the kitchen timer and set it to eleven minutes.

"Are you coming?" Larry called out from the stairs.

Amber dumped out the rest of the groceries. She cut the paper bag open and flattened it on the kitchen table, next to the old watch.

"What's happening?" Larry said, appearing in the kitchen. Diana took her hand and pulled her toward the table, where Amber was drawing a sloppy approximation of the island of Manhattan, adding dots to the safe spots she remembered from Franky's map. There were only a few she was sure about.

Larry watched, her mouth forming a small O.

Amber's memory wasn't perfect, but she had something better. She handed the pen to her mother.

"What am I missing?"

New Dawn Surveillance Footage: House Arrest

Daily Visual Transcript Readout: 17:30

Facial recognition: confirmed. Subject is humming, stirring something cooking on the stove. Per usual, she is dressed in a crisp, form-fitting dress, with a pristine apron tied around her waist. She raises a wooden ladle to her nose and smiles.

With a pair of tongs, she reaches into the pot and pulls out an old pocket watch, dripping with hot water. She smiles into the camera. "Time's up," she says.

Armed with a battering ram, the black-clad authorities swarmed the Melo family brownstone. The NDRs flitted about, collecting live footage for the detention broadcast. The images of the Melo house appeared on the kitchen and living room walls across the country.

Surprised to see a raid on what appeared to be a family home, people rose from their chairs to get a better look, following the drones as they hurtled through the house, weaving in and out of the rooms as the uniforms kicked doors open. One smashed the glass on a family portrait. As the frame hit the floor and shards of glass tumbled from it, a drone scanned the faces in the enclosed photograph.

The house was neat but empty, as if its residents had simply gone out for the day. In the kitchen, an old camera was playing Diana's video on loop. Drawn to the sound of a human voice, one of the drones buzzed over to it, beaming its footage live to the homes of northeastern America. Someone at New Dawn had taken too long to turn the broadcast off.

"Time's up," Diana kept saying, holding up the dead watch. "Time's up."

TIMEBOX ALTAR[ED]

They say you have reached the end of the road when you make it to Freewheel. It's like the edge of the world, no farther place to go. Bug and big brother Artis, Ola, and Trell all live in a commune near Freewheel's unmapped border, far beyond the wired sides of Sector Seven and Sector Nine. They reside on the periphery of the past and the future, where the crossroads of what was, what is, and what could be intersect, diverge, then join again.

Freewheel was the forgotten ghost town from another century, rusted railroads and battered signs far from Standards authorities and retinal scans, mostly unpatrolled by New Dawn's drones. There, the air all around glowed bright.

On that day, they walked until the shape of the language was no longer familiar, until they found what they were looking for: to be lost. The first child emerged, breathless, from shoulder-high blades of grass, walking as if wrapped in a blue aura. Their round, hairless head bobbed in the tall moss-colored weeds that nearly enveloped their small stature. Tears streamed from deep-set eyes, larger than most: Bug.

Later, the second child marched with her back straight up, dark eyes blinking through the pollen and the gnats. She stepped through the curtain of green, waved her long arms and slender hands as if she were swimming through the air, braids curled around her shoulders like two antennae: Ola.

Trell walked slowly, his gap-toothed smile passing as gentle, but his eyes were hard. They softened only at the sound of his best friend's name.

"Ol-a-gooooon-day!" he cried, exaggerating each syllable. "Ola, Ola, yay, Ola Ola yay!"

"Shut up, boy."

"Olagunde, you caught 'em?"

"Nope!" he heard from behind a swaybacked tree. Ola picked at the bark with dirty nails, peeling off the loose layers not yet stripped by the wind. "I don't know where Bug ran. Artis said they may have come out here."

Ola stepped from behind the tree, her blue shirt a bright burst of indigo among the black, brown, and green.

"For somebody so little, Bug sure know how to keep up a ruckus," Trell said. He nudged a large rock from the soil with his shoe. "Got to be the worst birthday party ever."

Ola wiped her hand on her pant leg and joined Trell, studying the rock warily, as if it would jump at her. "Of all the places to run, why run here? Feels a little sad to me," she said, staring straight off, wilderness all around her. "It's like you can feel the whole air full of what used to be."

Trell grunted, spun the rock onto its dirt side. Nothing exposed but dark black soil, moist and fragrant. "You know Bug. Little waterhead self. Let Artis tell it, that's all that child think they've got. They stay dreaming, talking about stuff they ain't never seen."

"Don't be mean, Trell. Everybody don't have it like you do."

"*Pfft*. And what I got? A daddy that stays on my back."

Ola was quiet. Bent down to retrieve Trell's rock. "Some people don't even have that." She studied the rock, turned it around in her hands and brushed away the wet soil, stroking it as if it were a talisman.

BUG IS THE CHILD WHO STANDS IN THEIR BARE FEET, OUTSIDE on the porch at night, nothing but hungry eyes staring up and through the stars. Bug was the child who never asks for more than what they have, and the one secret thing they most hoped for was stolen before the hope even had time to take root in their little heart.

Mama.

A number, a name, a face, the end—smooth river-stone skin the reflection of Bug's own. Mama was a faded holo, a dirty computer floating in the space between. She was more a sound than a fully fleshed memory, a voice that Bug imagined singing them to sleep. Mama occupied the fabric of Bug's dreams, and lived in the space between Grandpapa's peeling, low-slung ceiling and the cool sheets that separated Bug and big brother Artis from the dark.

But on that seventh birthday, Bug rose with a vision. Instead of waiting by the door, as they did every year, Bug spent the whole morning searching through the house, opening drawers, peeking behind furniture, and drawing frantically. Crumpled paper littered the floor. That afternoon, when they all sat together before the lopsided cake with too much frosting and only one candle because Grandpapa had misplaced the rest, Bug had filled their mind and cheeks with the same wish, and when they blew the lone candle out, Bug had decided to stop dreaming.

Dreaming wasn't going to bring their mother back, not from the hole they called Reassignment, not from the place that Grandpapa called prison. Not from the hole that was this heart that was the earliest memory, when Mama was with them in voice and flesh, when she placed her warm hands on Bug's head or shoulder or chest, every room in Grandpapa's house full of the sweet scent of her.

Mama.

Such a small word for the whole world.

There was never enough time for Bug to hold all the parts that were the best of her. The memory of laughter, the soundtrack of Bug's dreams; raised calluses on rough palms whose strength and touch even now Bug was starting to forget. Who needed a birthday full of presents when the only presence needed would not be there? Again.

So Bug ran. Stepped into a shadow cut from the night, cut from dark dreams that ended with the New Dawn rovers' descent. Some nights he could still hear the hovering whirs of the drones, his mother's screams as the Standards authorities came for her, Grandpapa and Artis holding Bug back, a recurring nightmare that always ended with a vanishing. The worst kind of dream.

Even chocolate cake couldn't make broken promises taste sweeter.

Tears shone in Bug's eyes. Heart stinging from the hurt and harsh chemicals swirling through the summer air, Bug had burst through the front door, painted haint blue to keep the bots and bad spirits out, and stomped down the porch steps, taking a tumble in the low-cut grass and skinning their knee.

"Bug!" Grandpapa cried. "She'll be home next year." But even with their back turned, running, running, running, Bug could hear the lie in the wind.

ARTIS KNEW THAT WHAT HE WAS CONTENT WITH WAS NOT ALways enough for somebody else. Not for Grandpapa, who fussed and worried over both him and Bug, and not for Bug, who longed for Mama, and not for Mama, who longed for something she said should be free but cost them all so very much.

Artis missed his mother too. At thirteen, he had more memories than his younger sibling. Sometimes he felt sorry for his Lil Bug, because Bug didn't have any memories of their father. Sometimes he felt envy and wondered if you can ever truly miss what you never really had. Their father was taken away when Artis was very small and Bug was still just an arm baby.

Some days Artis had to remind himself that his dad actually existed, that his mother was not a phantom. Remembering the dead was hard work.

Contrary to Grandpapa, Artis knew Bug needed more than back-in-the-day, when-you-were-little stories. Bug was getting older now. Asked questions to which no one knew the answers. The child needed the hardest story of all. Even an old soul, been-here-before child needed to be told the truth. It was a story that Artis rolled around in his own head, reworking and kneading the wet memories and the horror like clay. Some days it was easier than others. Some days he could dream with his little sibling, hold up the other tale Grandpapa had made in gold-streaked, hope-filled sunlight. But as each year passed, another birthday when their mother was not yet released, the gold tarnished and Artis was left with the rusted-out remnants of a darker truth: that Mama might never come back and if she was allowed to, she might not be the same Mama that any of them knew.

WEARY, SAD, DISORIENTED, BUG HAD RUN WEEPING FROM THE ramshackle house. Artis and Grandpapa calling, Ola and Trell—Bug's big brother's friends—running close behind them. At first it seemed like Bug had run straight into a wall of heat. The sun bore down, pummeling their face and neck. Heartbroken, Bug headed toward the tower, the grim obelisk that rose above the sector like a glowering gray fist.

Bug had heard the whispers, pieces of stories of what happened to those inside. People always hushed and stopped speaking when Bug walked in the room, but they heard things. Heard about the tower. Everyone in the communes called it the House of Dawn, but Bug knew there was no golden light there—unless being Torched lit you up. It was a monstrous place, a beast that had swallowed their mother whole.

Grandpapa said Mama had resisted. She refused to think of herself—her husband or anyone, certainly not their friends and neighbors—as unclean.

But the New Dawn rover droneys and the Standards authors had taken her away regardless, and no matter how many times Bug asked, Grandpapa said they weren't allowed to visit.

Bug missed Mama, the parts that could be remembered, the special moments fading from Bug's mind like disappearing light.

But longing could not cover the distance of fear. When the authors came for her, during Bug's birthday—an earlier one—Artis said Mama did not run. She held her children for one last time and then she told Grandpapa to hide. That day it seemed like the sky opened up, but instead of the sun parting the clouds, darkness descended upon them.

"Ava!" Grandpapa had cried, pulling his grandchildren to him. Artis said Mama ran out into the bright light of day, threw herself at the machinelike figures dressed in crimson and black, her arms flung out to fight. Somehow, she promised, she would come home again, somehow she would finish celebrating Bug's birthday.

She promised.

Artis didn't like to tell that tale, the story of a party interrupted, an impossible promise too long remembered. But Bug insisted. The promise was Bug's favorite part, the retelling something they could hold when memory wasn't always a choice.

Now, away from their family for the very first time, the world outside Grandpapa's porch looked different. The gray fist of New Dawn that held so many didn't look as approachable anymore. Or so close. Bug remembered Artis's anger, rare as the sun shining during rain. "She wasn't brave!" he'd mutter into his pillow, in the twin bunk bed of the back room they shared. In his sleep he'd cry out, "Nevermind!"—something about memories bagged like trash, then dumped. But Bug never wanted to forget, though Mama was more a story than a memory. Sometimes that's all that mattered. So in Bug's version of the tale, she was always brave, always kind, always loving.

"You've got your mama's eyes," Grandpapa would say. "Got her dreaming spirit too."

"She was a fool," Artis had said, mumbling on those nights when her absence became too much to bear, on the nights when he was tired of being strong, being hopeful, the only witness his wet pillow and the cool night air. "Should've run, not fought," Artis whispered, his voice choking on the pillowcase. "Maybe she would still be with us."

To be with her was all that Bug wanted, on this day more than ever. But nothing good could come from dancing in the flames or staring at the sun, and flinging one's self willingly into the authors' hands was something Bug was neither brave nor foolish enough to do. Bug had heard whispers about the civil unrest in some of the other communes, and Grandpapa was careful about where they traveled. Yet, like many living in the cluster, Grandpapa had to travel to work in the wired City of Light. Never knew when a protest might erupt or when the NDRs and authors might find a new target, and his wariness showed on his face and in the hunch of his shoulders. And Bug saw that. So they stared at the gray obelisk in the distance, shuddered and turned away, running in the opposite direction, racing down a path, not caring where it would go.

•—•

OLA AND TRELL FOUND BUG LYING BY THE TRACKS, WOBBLY head down, ear to the ground, listening to the rumbling sounds of ghost trains from long ago. A century before, Sectors Seven and Nine had been crisscrossed with iron. Once, the railroads connected all the small sectors and their surrounding ragtag communes to the rest of the nation, even the part where Ola, Trell, Bug, and Artis lived. But those days were gone, part of an industrial revolution that eventually became obsolete. After the Diesel Wars, when oil companies tried and failed to violently maintain global reliance on oil, the railroads had been ripped up, recycled, and redistributed—like everything else from the old world—all except the one set that Bug found down the winding dirt path that led deep into the woods, the one that was like something out of Grandpapa's old movie vids or his father's leather-bound storybooks.

Exhausted from running, embarrassed from the fuss, Bug welcomed the opportunity to escape disappointment. Bug didn't want to think about the gray obelisk anymore, his mama, or the stricken look of hurt in Artis's and Grandpapa's eyes. Instead, the child imagined the sound of phantom train whistles. Heard the rhythmic *clickety-clack* of iron horses galloping over shining new rails.

"Woohoo!" Bug cried, wiping away fresh tears. Sweat trickled down their back, the yellow jersey sticking as heat waves shimmered in the air. Bug spun around, imagining smokestacks and puffy clouds like in the old cartoons. Bells and headlamps, a rooster-red cowcatcher barreling down the track.

"Make way! Make waaaaay!" Bug cried. "Woohoo!" Arms flailing, the child ran smack into Trell's narrow chest.

"Dang!"

Startled, Bug's big eyes widened.

"You almost knocked the wind out of me. What you doing out here, anyway?" Trell asked, his voice filled with heat exhaustion and genuine curiosity. He carefully checked Bug's head for bumps and bruises, made Bug stick out their tongue, and looked the child up and down. Satisfied, Trell smacked a mosquito away from his arm and stared in wonder at the crossroads of rusted train tracks that seemed to stretch endlessly toward nowhere. Nowhere anyone had traveled since the advent of airships, not since combustible road vehicles had been abandoned years ago.

"We could've been eating now, all that special food your grandpapa made for your birthday," Trell said, "but instead, we're standing out here, in ole dusty Freewheel, burning up under the sun in a forgotten place nobody wants to be bothered with."

Bug's face rippled a bit, shifting from one emotion to the next: sadness, confusion, then back to sadness again. The child looked as if they wanted to cry.

They had not forgotten.

Seeing Bug's expression, Ola shot Trell a warning glance, and he mumbled a quick apology.

She placed her firm hand on Trell's shoulder, pressed down gently, then walked over to Bug. Her hands were so talented; she could fix anything. "It's okay. I don't like birthdays either," Ola said. "But that cake Grandpapa baked sure looked good. I would've loved to have a slice, wouldn't you?"

"What you said!" Trell laughed.

"Quiet, Trell. I wasn't talking to you," Ola said.

She didn't mention that having been homeless with her parents, she didn't get many birthday parties or presents.

Grandpapa worked as a cook and sometimes made extra servings to share with Ola and her family. Nothing special or too showy, just simple food that said *you're welcome* and not *you owe me*. He understood something about hunger and how it ate at more than the lining in the belly, how it ate at the heart and made it harder to concentrate and dream at night.

But Bug didn't seem interested in food right now. "My mama left me a present. I gotta find it," Bug said. The child stepped forward, awestruck, and stared at the railroad tracks, still imagining running far, far away. In Bug's mind the old tracks became a road made of wood and metal, of all God's promises, and at the end of that road, Bug's mama was standing on the porch, calling for them, Artis, and Grandpapa to come on in the house, because the streetlight was shining and it's time to eat.

Bug was hungry, could feel it gnawing at the pit of their belly, but wasn't ready to return home to Grandpapa just yet, so the child ducked and ran, balancing atop the nearest rail. Trell shouted and took after Bug. "You can't outrun me, grasshopper!" The air filled with their laughter as the three friends ran in circles, round and round, Bug leading them farther down the spiraling path until the sky was covered with a canopy of great leafy trees.

Here the air was cooler, quiet. Remnants of the old town lay scattered in the weeds and the rocks all around them.

"Where are we?"

IN THE RING OF COMMUNES OUTSIDE SECTORS SEVEN AND Nine, most everyone was a natural birth. Any talent they possessed came naturally. No access to enhancements or enrichment programs—only the highly privileged and the inherited rich could afford those.

But art was universal, something even the poorest among the communes could create on their own. They had to be resourceful, gleaning supplies from wherever they could be scavenged. Bug had been drawing since their chubby little fingers could hold a marker or a brush. Grandpapa and Artis had helped mount Bug's first show in the narrow hallway of their little house. They'd made the frames from wax pastels glued on cardboard, and Artis had even helped Bug write invitations. So when they emerged from the great trees' shadows and stepped into a wide, open clearing, Bug felt as if they'd stepped from the real world into one of their painted dreams.

An old-fashioned gas eater half-sunken in the earth rose, hood up, like a dinosaur. Bug ran to it, palms brushing away its reddish-brown metal flakes. Here, a strange scent filled the air, like steel mixed with honeysuckle. A dilapidated warehouse leaned over a battered boxcar covered in painted rainbows. A gentle wind carried the faint scent of rusted iron and melting rubber, offerings from an older day. Discarded refuse, repurposed and reimagined, adorned in all the colors Bug imagined in dreams.

The air was full of the scent of trees. They offered their great limbs as shelter to the children, a canopy of green that shielded them from the drones. Bug skipped around, delighted in what remained, spirit lost in the wild green clearing that someone had redesigned, it seemed, just for them.

"Look!" Bug ran over to a massive quartet of rugged faces, each distinctive, carved into concrete slabs. They stood facing away from each other, giant stone sentinels, wind-shaped under the sun.

"They have eyes," Ola said, puzzled. "Who would leave this here?"

"I don't know, but whoever it is," Trell said, shaking his head, "looks like they went clean off. There's more."

Tall figures made from scraps of wood, old signage, twisted bicycles, and traffic lights littered the area, remnants from another age. Someone had taken the time to sculpt a giant Tin Man. He peered down at the children with reflectors for eyes and oxidized gas-eater rims for a hat. It looked as if the Tin Man's hat and the pinwheels were meant to spin and the sculpture once lit up.

"*Fee fi fo fum!*" Trell yelled, looking around, amazed. "This looks like we walked onto the set of *Jack and the Beanstalk!* We gonna ease on down the road like *The Wiz!*"

"No," Bug said. "This is Mama's present she promised me! I thought I had to find it, but now I understand."

"Understand what?"

"We got to *build* it."

"Whatchu talking about, child?" Trell was only four years older than Bug, but he spoke as if that were eons.

"I know exactly what to do, just follow me. We're gonna need this," Bug said, picking up an OPEN 24 HOURS sign. They struggled to carry it, but no one argued. Bug pointed to the clearing where the four giant faces stood, staring off into the distance.

"North, south, east, west. Cardinal directions. We build here." They dragged the sign to the center of the stone diamond. Ola shook her head. "This is not the party you invited us to," she said, smirking.

"Don't worry, Ola," Bug said, patting her hand. "This is way better than cake! This is art! *Our* art, and can't nobody tell us what to do or how to do it."

Ola tilted her head, marveling at the little spirit in front of her. Bug was very special, and it was their birthday, after all.

Together the children lifted overturned wooden chairs covered in moss, carried bricks from the scattered piles, red dust staining their palms. Bug squealed each time they found an iron railroad spike, and held it overhead, almost as long as their forearm. Ola found a crate of old 78s with titles like *Joshua White and the Carolinas*. Trell rescued a box of old magazines, *Life* and *Ebony,* some pages crumbling at his touch. They uncovered old signs from stores that had long since been abandoned. Nothing was too old or dirty, too strange or broken, to be reimagined in Bug's eyes. All was art, all was beautiful.

They found a basket of ribbons, brightly colored, and wrapped them around the limbs of low-hanging trees and the scrubby bushes that sprang from the earth.

Played so long, even the sun grew tired. It went on behind a cloud to take a rest.

That's when they heard the singing, a strange tune none of them knew the lyrics to.

"*Around the world in a day*," the voice sang. It grew closer and closer. "*Swing low, sweet chariot. Let me . . . ride.*"

A tall robed figure emerged from the trees. Dressed in white folds that floated around them in the summer wind, a coppery scarf wrapped around their head, a golden gele. The children froze, unsure of what to do.

"Curiouser and curiouser," the elder said, waving a golden baton with bright streamers. "Well, traveler, looks like we got company. *Uninvited*," she muttered, and stomped her feet. She was wearing tall white boots with orange pompoms in the centers. "The name is Tangerine Waters, Mx. Tangee to you."

Trell looked over at Ola, Ola looked at Bug, but Bug was not afraid. Bug walked over to hold their hand, elated.

"Nice to meet you, Mx. Tangee!" Bug said. "Look what we built!"

Bug pulled away from Ola, who tried to hold them back, and clasped Mx. Tangee's many-ringed fingers, placing their chubby ones in her weathered hands.

"You are right on time," Bug said. "It's almost finished. What do you think?" the child asked, suddenly shy.

Mx. Tangee walked slowly over, the golden baton spinning the reemerged sunlight, to inspect the handiwork that stood before her: a tentlike structure built from everything imaginable. It rose from the center of the four carved stones as if it had sprung up from the earth, a wild blossom, a riot of color and textures, a haven for rescued, forgotten things.

"Looks to me like you built yourself an altar, a tent of miracles. Fitting for a place like this. You walking on ley lines, sacred land."

Ola's face finally lost its frown. The mention of ley lines intrigued her. She tugged at her shirt, the blue now stained with sweat and soil, and joined Bug at Mx. Tangee's side.

"You know, everywhere in the world there are ley lines, ancient spots of power, mystery, and intrigue, the places where our beautiful earth channels all of her energies," said Mx. Tangee. "These woods around you are sacred to the Wyandot, the Chickasaw, and the Choctaw. If you are lucky enough to find where these remarkable lines intersect—and you have the good sense to put down your shovel and just *feel*—child, there ain't nothing you can't build. You workin' deep mojo then!"

Trell looked skeptical. "If this is such a magical place, then why is everything so busted? Nobody has lived in Freewheel for well over a century. And when they were here, does anyone know if they ever prospered?"

Mx. Tangee smiled knowingly. "You the healer," she said. "Physician, heal thyself."

"What?" Trell asked, confused.

"If you know everything about all the things that's anything, you can answer your own question."

Bug and Ola giggled. Trell nodded, not sure if he understood.

Still, this strange woman was fun.

She untied her scarf, allowing loose locs to tumble out, then carefully adjusted and retied it. "Ain't just about prospering, it's about *progressing, connecting, tappin' into* something larger than yourself, so you can really see. Can't build nothing if you can't feel nothing. Community comes from feeling and feeling comes hand in hand with creation. What y'all out here creating now?"

"My present," Bug said. "My mama promised me, the last time I saw her. She said I would know it when I see it. I see."

"You sure do," said Mx. Tangee. She removed one of her earrings, shaped like a giant beetle. It carried a moon in its golden forelegs. "This is for you. To add to your altar."

"Why do you call it that? It looks like a clubhouse to me," Trell said. "'Altar' makes it sound like a church. Nothing wrong with that, I'm just saying."

"And maybe in a way it is like the spirit of a church. Together you have made something special, with *intention,* in a place on a day like no when else."

"No *wind?*" Bug said, puzzled.

"Naw, *when.* It ain't about the where or the who, it's the when. This is a Sirius matter, auspicious occasions. Constellations and stars move overhead, overstand?"

The children were saying *yeah* but shaking their heads *no.*

"It's all right, you will in time. Everything comes full circle. And time takes care of itself. Our work is the work of the living, of the present. The right now builds tomorrow. And while the when is important, it's also important to be mindful about the how. Like this right here," she said, and sang another tune. *"Souls look back and wonder, how I got ova!"* She guided them over to the first stone carving near her, the one facing north.

"Come, child, um . . ."

"Ola."

"Yes, come, Ola. Here is the north traveler. This spirit in stone is connected to the earth's energies that run in that direction." Mx. Tangee pulled out a ceremonial dagger, its blade riddled with beautiful markings, runes.

"Carve the first letter of your name. Do everything with *intention.* Think of how your heart beats and your blood flows. Whatever is truly in you, part of you, will flow freely."

Trell was behind Mx. Tangee's back, mouthing the word *Noooooo.* He giggled, but watched expectantly.

Ola took the blade. It was heavier than she thought. Purple gemstones and mother-of-pearl decorated the handle. Ola held the blade up, pointed at the stone, and carved, with some difficulty, a very wobbly *O.*

"Well done," Mx. Tangee said, pressing her palm against the stone flesh. She nodded approval. "Air, inception, a beginning. Well, it's getting started now."

"Do you live here?" Bug asked. Mx. Tangee just smiled. "I

wanna go next." They stood on their tippy-toes, tugging at the elder's bright robes.

Mx. Tangee laughed and ushered the child over to the stone carving that faced east. "I'm what you might call a fellow traveler. Most of my life I have lived on the edges of what everyone else proscribed for me. But somewhere along the way, I decided life had to be different."

Bug needed help to carve their *B*.

"Well done," Mx. Tangee said. "Sometimes good friends can help us see a vision through. Bug, your stone faces east, representing the earth and redemption."

Bug danced around as if they had won a prize.

Mx. Tangee passed the ceremonial dagger over to Trell, who dodged it, bobbing and weaving, shadowboxing. Finally he accepted the blade and held it up in the air. "I have the *powerrrrrr*!" he cried. Bug and Ola burst out laughing. Mx. Tangee just shook her head.

"You play too much," Ola said, grinning.

"Which stone, Mx. Tangee?" Trell asked. "Dirty South or the Wicked West?"

"South." Mx. Tangee pointed at the stone farthest from them. "Full of fire, the spark of life, love."

"Love!" Bug and Ola cried. Trell blushed.

"That's right, that's right," he quipped. "A lover not a fighter. I have nothing but love for all of you, so it is what it is." He carved a bold *T* into the stone and spun around two times before passing the dagger back to Mx. Tangee.

The dagger disappeared under one of her voluminous folds, and eyes closed, she whispered words that were carried away in the air.

"There's one left," Bug said.

"Yes, he'll be coming along soon."

The children blinked back surprise. "How she know that?" Trell whispered.

"Maybe she heard us talking about Artis?" Ola offered.

Bug followed Mx. Tangee as she walked over to one of the great leafy trees and whispered a prayer. "Thank you, old one, for the shelter you provide. Forgive me for borrowing this little piece of you," she whispered as she snapped off a thin branch. She gave it to Bug.

"Now, trace a big circle in the ground." Then she pointed her baton at Ola. It sparkled in the light. "You, create the rivers." The girl shook her head. "I already know you don't understand. That's all right, Ola, just draw what you think a river might do."

Ola thought for a moment, then taking the branch from Bug, created a series of wiggly lines streaming from Bug's big circle. "It looks like a giant sun," she said.

"A sunflower, a giant star," said Bug. "The sun is a giant star and guess what, guess what," they said, tugging on Mx. Tangee's robes. "Did you know seals and beetles navigate by stars? They be astro travelin'!"

"Whatchu know about *astro travelin'*?" Mx. Tangee asked, amused. "That music before your time."

"*Unh-unh*," Bug said. "Music made *of* time and that's why music is forever. Music's for everyone."

"That it is, that it is," Mx. Tangee said, beaming. "And now it is done. I like that good vision you added, little one. We surely need that." She stared at what the children had created. The structure looked like a child's joy personified, but her face changed, like the sky after rain.

"What's the matter, Mx. Tangee?" Bug asked, placing their palm in her hand.

She didn't speak at first, and her silence hung in the air to join undulating shimmers of heat. Sweat streamed down her brow, then Bug realized it was mixed with tears.

"How can they forget a future?" Mx. Tangee asked, turning her head as if questioning the air.

"Who?" asked Ola.

Bug stared at Mx. Tangee intently, as if trying to see something far off.

"Not they," Bug said. "*Us.*"

They stood there together, heads bowed as if in prayer, each one lost in their own thoughts. Then Bug grew restless, the disappointment and excitement from the day pulling their spirit in two different directions. Finally, excitement won, and before Ola or Trell could stop Bug, the child had scuttled off once more, like the golden scarab beetle Mx. Tangee had gifted them. It now hung over the opening to the altar that Bug had already claimed as their ark.

"It's like our own ship," Bug said, "but it's on land and it don't got no anchor and we not in no water, but that's all right. Like a spaceship that ain't yet reached the stars. We travelers, right, Mx. Tangee, travelers in an ark?"

"Sure enough, child."

"Arks are for protection, they keep you safe. And . . . and . . ." Bug searched for the right words. Sometimes the child could hear and see the thing, like the ark that they built, long before the words for it, or even the drawing, came. It was all inside them, the ideas and the images, the colors and the sounds. It all flowed.

"This is *our* protection. Can't no droneys and no authors come here and take none of us, none away. Okay?"

Ola and Trell exchanged a glance. So much was unspoken between them. Some things didn't need to be said. They knew how much Bug took promises to heart. Neither of the child's friends wanted to disappoint or harm Bug, so they kept silent.

Now the child stood before the ark—so named, so it was—the sunlight making it appear as if their little body eclipsed the opening, as if it were Bug's spirit that stood proudly before them and not just flesh. Every interesting thing they found that day, all of Bug's best discoveries, had been added with love and intention to the art they made together.

Standing vigil, Ola and Trell watched as Bug turned with a wave and ducked inside. No one followed at first, as if it was understood that the only thing required now was a witness.

Seated, palms down, Bug felt the ground vibrating beneath their fingertips. A sweet, musky, metallic scent, strange musical notes filled the air. Though their little body never moved, Bug felt as if they had been borne up and then their thoughts spread out into all the things around the ark. Bones became water, skin became tree, blood became air.

One moment Bug was there and then—not there.

Outside, Ola and Trell waited. They whispered quietly together, then called Bug's name. When the child did not answer, Ola ducked her head inside.

"Bug!" she gasped.

"What? What is it?" Trell asked, leaning in beside her.

"Gone!" they said in unison. Trell was so shocked, he nearly knocked the ark down trying to get himself in and then out.

"Where could they have gone?"

"Um! *Nowhere!*" Ola said with emphasis, fanning her hands. "There's no back door. There isn't a tunnel unless it's invisible. And we were both standing *right here.*"

Trell shook his head, long arms waving at the air. Nothing remained of Bug, and the only clue that the child had ever been there was the branch Mx. Tangee had given them. It rested in the spot where Bug had sat cross-legged.

"Why all the ruckus?" Mx. Tangee asked, walking over to them.

"Bug gone!" the children said in unison.

She quickly stepped around Trell and gently moved Ola aside. After studying the ark's empty interior, she retrieved the branch and backed out. "A traveler, indeed," she said, hope in her voice.

"What do you mean, a traveler? Artis is going to kill us if we lost Bug! Grandpapa is going to get us too. I don't know what's worse," Ola said, panic all in her voice.

"Calm down, child. What do you think you did all that work for? Sometimes when you make art, you never know where it'll lead you."

"How can you say that when *Bug. Is. Gone?* I mean, good and gone. Where did Bug go? *How?*"

"Mane, this is truly the worst birthday ever!" Trell said. "I knew I should've stayed home."

"Listen," Mx. Tangee said gently. "I know it's a lot to understand, to hold in at one time. But you've got to trust in the process. Bug put good, good intention in all of this beautiful work. It wouldn't lead the child noplace where they don't need to go. It's all up here," she said, her right palm resting on her heart, index finger on her temple. "Intention."

"All I know," Trell said, "is that we better bring Bug back with some *intention,* some prevention, and some intervention, or Artis is going to do something to us that I can't even mention."

Mx. Tangee threw back her head and laughed. "You are something else, child. Laughter sure is healing, and you know that all too well. That's your gift."

Trell covered his eyes. "I can't handle proverbs right now, Mx. Tangee. I don't know how we're going to go home without Bug with us. How're we supposed to explain all this?"

"Remember, trust in the process. It will explain itself."

WHEN BUG OPENED THEIR EYES, THEY FOUND THEMSELF seated at a great table, wide enough to stretch both arms and still have room. Bottles of colored water were arranged on it. And Bug could not contain their excitement when they saw the tubes, real *paint tubes* in shades of various pigments. Every shade that ever colored Bug's most vivid dreams.

At home, Grandpapa and Artis helped Bug make their paint, and they usually stored it in old egg crates. Whatever color they made was more water than pigment. But here—wherever here was—Bug had everything they needed. No painting on newspapers or the backs of packages pulled from trash cans at Grandpapa's sector job. Brown paper, white paper, stacks and reams of watercolor paper and canvases waited for Bug to map out the unseen, to make permanent their new memories.

It never occurred to Bug that all of this was not for them—after all, it was the ark that brought them here—and so Bug picked up a long brush and ran a fingertip over hairs so soft, they could have been sable. Bug had been intently drawing for a very long time when a wonderful scent filled the room. It was then that Bug finally realized they were not alone.

"Beauford Delany Dumas," a quiet voice said.

Bug turned. "Mama!"

They flung their arms wide open and knocked over an inkwell, the pink paint pooling on the table.

"I knew it! I knew you wouldn't break your promise, Mama. I found my gift, in the park, a funny park. There is this lady and these rocks and . . ."

Mama smiled and held Bug in her arms. "Looks like your gift found you," she said. They held each other for a long, long time—the best birthday ever.

"Hey, Bug! Ola, Trell!"

They could hear Artis hollering before he came down the path, his voice hoarse and very, very tired.

Trell froze, then turned to look at Ola, who shrugged her shoulders as if to say *Don't ask me.* Mx. Tangee twirled her baton, not seeming the least bit bothered.

Even the birds in the trees stopped their chatter. Every eye in Freewheel watched as Artis, Bug's big brother and main protector, came stomping through the field.

The three emerged from beside the ark, Ola looking everywhere but at Artis and Trellis with his head down so low, he didn't have no neck or chin.

"There you are! Whew! I've been calling out for y'all all day. Bug!" he said, and shook his head at the pinwheels and frenetic sculptures Mx. Tangee had scattered all around. Ola had fixed the Tin Man and now he was dancing robotically, all lit up, his hat of chrome rims spinning like Saturn's rings.

"Ola, Trell, what's wrong with you? I know Bug's here 'cuz *this*—whatever *this* is—has Bug's name all over it."

Trell nodded.

"Oh, excuse me, miss, I'm sorry. I'm Artis."

"Mx. Tangee, pleased to meet you."

"Likewise. I was looking for Bug, my little sib. It's their birthday and . . ." Artis wasn't sure how to describe heartbreak to a stranger. "It didn't go the way we hoped it would. They left their own party, you know, a bit disappointed, ran off to blow off some steam. Just up and disappeared, got my grandpapa all worried—"

"Well, since you put it that way," Trell said, trying to interrupt. "I need to show you something."

"What? Is Bug out here hiding, got y'all playing hide-and-seek in this heat? We'd never find them out here with all of this."

"See, that's what we're saying," Ola said, her eyes darting.

Artis froze. He didn't like the look on his friends' faces. He'd seen that panic, that powerlessness before. When Ola's parents lost their first home and she missed a lot of school. When Trell's dad had a health setback, and they weren't sure if he would wake again when he went to sleep. Something wasn't right.

"But I don't understand. You aren't saying anything. Where is Bug?"

"Bug gone," Mx. Tangee said, "but they'll be back."

"How you know, Mx. Tangee?" Trell asked, exasperated. "We've been waiting all day."

"Waiting for *what*?" Artis asked. It felt like a stone dropped in his chest.

When Ola tried to explain to him, and Mx. Tangee started speaking about the ley lines and the alignment of stars, Artis shut down. The one thing he never wanted, the nightmare that clouded his dreams. He couldn't face the idea that he'd lost his Lil Bug.

Couldn't lose them too.

Tears streamed down from his eyes, and then the hurt, the confusion, the anger. "A person can't just disappear. You sure Bug didn't just slip out the back and is somewhere hiding, lost, waiting on us to find them? You've just been standing out here, and no one even went to look?"

"Slip out where, Artis? Go in and look for yourself. There's nowhere for Bug to slip. We were *right here*. All of us. There's something very strange about this place. Something . . . like magic. I dunno," Ola said.

"How am I going to tell Grandpapa that Bug just magically disappeared?" Artis hung his head. "We need some help. We've got to find Bug. What if they're scared or thirsty or hungry? What if drones got them, an easy target all by themself? We might never . . ." Artis couldn't finish the thought, but something else replaced his fear.

Anger.

"How could you let this happen?" he asked, and turned to Mx. Tangee.

"Let? That's like asking how to stop the Earth from turning 'round."

"You crazy, and you don't even care! How could you leave a child like this? Leave them lost!"

A wind picked up, whirled off the river that peeked from

behind the trees on the border of the old railroad line. The birds that were listening had their fill, picked up their wings and took to the sky.

Mx. Tangee looked stricken, Artis's words pummeling her spirit.

"I never hurt a child in my life," Mx. Tangee said, her voice soft and quiet. "Never would, never could. But that didn't stop the world from trying to hurt me. I was the child that had to learn to travel alone. I was the child that had to watch every word, every expression, sight, sound, and speech. The world wasn't always kind, was never easy, but I stayed as strong as I could, for as long as I could. Nobody wanted to help me, so I helped myself. And later, when I got older, I decided I would be the help I never got."

Artis felt ashamed. He swallowed hard and wiped the tears from his cheeks. Ola and Trell stood beside him, tried to ease his grief. "I'm sorry . . ."

"Tangee," the three said.

"I'm trying to help you," she said. "I can try to explain it the best way I can, but it's better if you just . . . see for yourself." She pointed at the ark. They all did.

Artis stood in front of it, really looked at it for the first time. He took in the bright colors, the old signs, the antique records that had somehow managed not to break or melt all these years. The magazines with the vintage photos they'd hung up like wallpaper, somehow unaffected by moisture or sunlight. The spinning cans and tops, the red bricks laid out all in a neat row. And in the back, a wall that would have been impossible for Bug to move by themself or get through.

Something about the angle—in fact, something about the entire place—looked all too familiar. Artis reached into his pocket and pulled out a crumpled piece of paper, one of Bug's drawings they'd made that morning. "I've seen this before."

"Yes, you have," Mx. Tangee said. "Your Lil Bug is in there."

"But there's no one there!" Artis said, confused.

"There is and there ain't. Be patient. They'll be here before you—"

"Bug!" Artis cried.

As if they'd heard their name, the child emerged out of the ark, breathless, a big ole snaggle-toothed smile on their face.

Artis scooped Bug up and spun them around.

"Woohoo!" Bug cried. "Do it again, do it again!"

Mx. Tangee twirled her baton and smiled, relief brightening her face.

"Where have you been?" all of them shouted, speaking at once.

"And did you grow in there?" Artis asked, finally setting Bug down. Something was very strange. The top of Bug's head used to come only up to Artis's navel. Now his Lil Bug seemed taller.

And in a way they were. Bug had returned hopeful. If time had taken their mama, maybe time could bring her home again. Bug felt full, as if waking from a beautiful dream, their oldest secret wish really could come true.

Artis stepped back from Bug. He could smell the familiar scent of their mother, the scent taking him over and through his own memories. It was as if the scent had unlocked something precious inside him.

"I remember that," Artis said. "Where, Bug, where did you go?"

Bug tried to explain, but every word that came to mind moved them farther from where they wanted to be. How to explain what it meant to be so full of peace, to have Mama there and to just be able to sit and draw and laugh and talk with her?

When Bug thought about it, it wasn't like a grand adventure in Grandpapa's movie vids. They didn't climb a mountain or run with the wolves, or ride off in a starship to save the universe. How to explain all the time that Bug experienced, just waking each day, simply listening to their inner spirit, expressing themself fully, naturally, Mama encouraging Bug?

"I saw Mama," Bug said. "We painted and drew pictures, so many pictures. Did you know Mama wrote poems? She read some to me. I didn't understand them that much but they sounded real pretty. She says she loves my drawings, and that I should always make as much art as I want. She said something else . . ."

"How do you know it was Mama?" Artis asked. He studied Bug carefully. Trell had practically given him a medical checkup, asking him a million things that Bug really couldn't answer. All Bug knew was that it was definitely Mama and that they never felt so good. They'd spent so much time talking and painting and drawing together, it was like a million-million birthday parties.

"If you want to understand what your Lil Bug just experienced," Mx. Tangee said, "you all are going to have to try it yourself."

"I ain't going up in there," Trell said.

"You got to," Bug cried. "You all do."

"Why, Bug, just why?" Trell asked. He was shaking his head, *no-to-the-no-no*.

"Because you can't build a future if you don't dream it."

INSIDE THE ALTAR, THE AIR WAS HEAVY WITH HUMIDITY, THE weight of sticky heat. In the distance, the children could hear the drones darting through the skies like giant dragonflies. But the air was filled with a sense of mystery. They sat crowded together, pushing and shoving, each trying to find a corner where they could fit comfortably. They waited and waited but nothing happened, and finally, one by one, they ducked back out, defeated.

"Whatever happened to Bug, I don't think it's going to work anymore," Trell said sadly.

"How did it work the first time?" Artis asked.

"I went in by myself," Bug said, rearranging some of the art, adding to what Mx. Tangee kept calling the altar. "You just gonna have to be brave. Like me!" Bug said, raising their hands.

Ola, Trell, and Artis looked at each other. No one wanted to go first. Finally, Ola shrugged.

"I'll do it."

OLA EMERGED FROM THE SHADOWS AND THE HAZE AND FOUND blinding yellow sunlight, the sounds of aircars whizzing all around her. Someone blew a loud horn. Startled, she had to duck to dodge a brown delivery truck that raced just inches above her head. Ola dove to the ground, her shirt a blue blur, skinning her knee. Incredulous, she watched the delivery vehicle roll on its side, regain control, and then lower itself to the street.

But it wasn't the fact that the hand-me-down ark she helped build for Bug was gone, or that she could no longer see any of her friends or Mx. Tangee. It wasn't the fact that she was clearly no longer in the strange clearing full of old junk and rusted railroad tracks that Mx. Tangee called "found art" and Ola thought of as trash.

Nor was it the fact that the skyline looked completely different from anything she'd ever seen. The wired side of the sectors was all straight lines and edges, shiny cold glass and gray towers that looked like decaying teeth and dry bones. Here, the sky was full of trees, great Eden-like canopy tops adorned with organics, brightly lit round structures.

And yet even all that wasn't what made Ola's hand tremble. What shook her was something she could not explain. Inconceivable that it was her face that stared back at her own from a huge, illuminated sign, one that bore the words that would forever be sealed in her mind: WELCOME TO FREEWHEEL, WHERE EVERY CHILD HAS A HOME.

Ola sobbed. She would not have recognized herself at all if it weren't for the hope-filled eyes on the woman's face, the long, slender fingers on outstretched hands. Her own. And it *was* a woman, though she was unsure of the age. Ola could not remember when she had ever smiled that way, so full of uncomplicated joy, hope, confidence.

Before her, impossibly, was the evidence of a dream Ola didn't yet know she had. She held herself, crying quietly, thoughts racing, before she gulped and took a deep breath. Where was she?

Or better yet, *when*?

Ola propped herself up on her elbows, her braids curled around her shoulders. She watched a flying delivery truck back up and park on the opposite side of the street, right in front of what seemed to be a hundred-story grocery. Next to it were grass-topped housing structures. *Gardens growing on top of houses?* Ola's eyes widened at the sight. She had never seen so much food in all her life, not even on the vids.

A wide, short man emerged from a set of vanishing doors that opened on the side of the truck. He hopped to the ground, black hair sprouting like a bush from beneath his neat cap. Concern shone on his face as he looked both ways, then ran toward Ola.

"Miss, I am so sorry, ma'am. Are you all right?" He offered Ola a hand and pulled her to her feet. Ola looked confused and glanced at him suspiciously. She had never been called *ma'am* before. She was just going to tell him that she was all right when she realized the man's concern had turned from worry to something else she couldn't quite place.

"Ola?" he cried. "Of all the people I could have nearly clipped, it would have to be you!" He shook his head, embarrassed. "My daughter would never forgive me. She's a big fan of yours. Not going to believe this!"

Ola stood and stared, speechless and unable to believe much of anything herself, the lush, green city sprawling around her.

The air smelled cool and sweet. The driver was speaking, but Ola could not hear him. Her mind could not compute.

Finally, "Why are you talking to me like that? I'm just a kid." She didn't know what else to say.

"A kid?" He laughed. "Oh, so you have jokes, Mayor Ola, but you're right." He pointed at the billboard. "You can't be more than thirty-nine, but you've got the vision of an elder. You're just the right sight we need."

"Mayor?" Ola shook her head. "No, I'm eleven. I turn twelve in September."

"I'm sorry," he apologized again, his face radiating concern. "It's not every day I run into a legend—or almost run over one." He laughed awkwardly, but then lowered his voice, his eyes full of what Ola now realized was gratitude. "We are so very thankful for you, your team. We believe in what you have already done. What we will do together.

"The Power of Yet."

She had always wanted to leave the world that had forgotten her family and all the others abandoned on the outskirts of the Cities of Light. She'd imagined forgoing that world but had not yet imagined what might replace it. Being immersed in a place that had chosen with intention to forgo the grim worlds of silicon and carbon fiber and embrace something else left Ola feeling so light, as if her feet no longer fit in her shoes.

The old sectors and New Dawn, with their Torches and talk of light that hid dark shadows, had nothing on the blue-green sheen that pulsed on this city's strange streets.

To think that she could have had a hand in its creation planted a seed of hope in Ola she never wanted to forget.

"Where am I?" she asked shyly.

Puzzled, the driver stared at her, then waved his hand in the direction of the bright sign. "Freewheel, the city you created? Are you okay, Ms. Ola?"

He answered himself. "Of course not, how rude of me. Give

me a sec." He darted across the street as vehicles sped overhead. Ola watched as he raised his palm before the side paneling on his truck. He ran back with a brown grocery bag clutched against his chest. He reached inside and handed Ola a piece of fresh fruit, the most luscious, beautiful thing she had ever seen.

"My daughter loves tangerines. We gotta beg her to eat anything else. Figured you might like them too."

"I couldn't take that from you," Ola said. Fresh fruit, fresh anything was a very rare treat indeed.

"Consider it a gift. Because of you, my child has a home, and a good one, and a garden too. We grow most of our own food. And we're safe. That's all we ever wanted. To stay together and be safe. This is the least I could give you. Thank you, Ola."

Confused but excited, she accepted the offering and inhaled the citrusy fragrance, ran her thumb across the fruit's pebbly, uneven surface. She was digging a nail into it when a security drone swooped down from the gleaming ribbon of air, vehicles crisscrossing the sky. Ola panicked. Back stiff, she dropped the precious fruit, her hands trembling by her sides.

"Greetings, Olagunde 32917. We sense distress. Prepare for a courtesy health and well-being scan," the drone buzzed. No bigger than a helmet, the drone was a sleek green-and-gold creation, more mothlike than metallic. It hummed and soft lights flashed across the interface display screen. Ola was terrified.

A beam poured from the drone's smooth body and covered Ola in a cone of blue light that circled her head, an indigo crown. The drones she knew had frightening red lights.

She tensed up and prepared for the uncomfortable paralysis, the sense of violation, and the grief and shame that accompanied all of the drones' probings. Instead, Ola felt a warmth that seemed to calm her spirit. She smelled chamomile and lemongrass. It was a few more seconds before she realized that the drone's blue light had begun to mend the tiny breaks in her skinned knee.

"Health and wellness scan complete, Olagunde 32917. How do you feel?" the drone asked, its voice soft and comforting, not the brusque monotone of the drones whose every word was a command.

Ola was fascinated. "Better," she said politely. She wanted to touch the moth drone, to talk with it and discover how it was designed. But Ola just shook her head and wondered how many other things were upside-down right in this upside-down new world.

Intrigued by, well, everything, she watched in silence as the moth drone turned to the delivery truck driver and performed a similar scan. After the drone confirmed the driver's sense of wellness, it pulled back a little, as if to bring both Ola and the driver into its field of vision.

"Both of you need to be more careful. Traffic scans reveal that neither one of you was paying attention to your surroundings." The drone turned to the driver. "Do have a nice day, Daveed 29424," it chimed, then flew away, trailing a soft hum behind it.

The driver nodded and turned to Ola. "I'm Dave, by the way. I'm so glad you're okay. Thank you so much for being so kind about it. I don't know what I would have done if . . . Well . . ." He smiled, gratitude glimmering in his eyes. "Anyway, I wish you peace, and inner progress, the Power of Yet. We flow," he said. Then Dave saluted Ola with two fingers and dashed back to his delivery truck.

Ola had barely gathered her thoughts when a different, oddly shaped drone appeared from out of nowhere. It didn't look to be made out of silicon at all, or at least none Ola had ever seen. Black and white zebra-striped, its beautiful gossamer wings—a cross between a dragonfly's and the fins of a fish—undulated and pulsed as if moving in slow motion. Soothing flute and bell-like wind chimes sprinkled the air, growing slightly louder as it drew closer. The dragonfish drone gently buzzed around Ola's head as the delivery truck rose about three feet above its parking spot and sped on down the street.

"*Ola-Ola-ay!*" the dragonfish drone sang in a low voice that made Ola giggle in spite of herself. She had grown tense, but relaxed after the relatively benign experience with the first health-and-wellness drone. "Goodness! I have been searching everywhere for you." It did a shimmy dance in the air. "Scanning your itinerary and project files. Oh! You are late for your appointments, and remember, you are expected to attend tonight's artist reception."

Ola could see her reflection in the drone's rounded, mirror-like face. It was her and not her. The Ola she was and the Ola she might become. Curious, she decided to play along.

"And you are?"

"It hasn't been so long that you would forget me. But if you must ask, I am Lọwọ, your olùrànlọwọ, companion."

"My companion, like my assistant? A personal assistant?"

Lọwọ nodded. Ola squealed. "Of course," Lọwọ said. "You designed and named me yourself. Surely you recall?"

Surprise and pride filled Ola. She stared at her hands and then at the drone. She had only run from them before. Never imagined creating one of her own. Trell and Artis always said that she could fix or build anything. She never quite believed them, but here was proof—if a dream could be proof of anything.

She was starting to believe that was exactly what dreams could do.

"Where is the reception?" she asked.

"The Center for Art and Healing, of course. Are you all right, Ms. Ola? You don't seem to be." The drone tilted its wobbly head in a gesture Ola recognized—her own.

"Yes, I am, but tell me," Ola said. "Where is this . . . healing center?"

The dragonfish drone tsked like Ola's mother, its wings fluttering anxiously. *These drones are nice, but they can still be in their feelings,* Ola thought, and smiled. This one was adorable.

"Mayor Ola, you know better than anyone where it is. You helped conceive it. Right over there," Lọwọ said, pointing with the black tip of one of its right wings.

Ola turned to see an astonishing crystal cluster-shaped building, rising at an angle above lush, garden-topped homes. Amber and purple lights shone all around.

"It's spectacular!" Ola cried.

"That it is," the dragonfish drone said, seeming to smile at her. "But you are currently running late for your appointment with the civil planning and engineering envisioner and . . ." Lọwọ paused as if reading an internal list. "A quick hair appointment before the reception. Would you like for me to call you a ride? Or if you prefer I could just transport you there myself."

"Hair?" Olagunde said, touching her head self-consciously. "No, um, please reschedule all of that," she stammered. "Please send my apologies. I can walk to the reception."

"Are you sure?"

This is so overwhelming. "Yes," she said after taking a deep, calming breath. "I'll find my way."

"Yes, Ms. Olagunde," Lọwọ said, tilting its head in the other direction. For a moment, its tone sounded just like her mother. "It's right down that path, through the Children's Ark Park."

Ola smiled broadly. "Thank you, Lọwọ."

"Welcome, *Ola-Ola-ay!*"

As Ola walked, she took in all the sights and sounds of this wondrous new world she'd found. So different from the communes of Sector Seven and Sector Nine. But what struck her the most were the things she did not see. No dirty streets overflowed with weary, anxious, and hungry people. No pallets were piled in dangerous alleys. No one was unhoused, as she and her parents had been when Artis and Bug's mother and father had helped them. She noticed how the buildings shone in the shifting light, how the community was full of green growing things—not wall-to-wall shiny chrome or dull, pain-stained concrete. How the city radiated caring and compassion and not the fear and the great sense of lack that permeated the City of so-called Light with its terrible "Torches."

There were even actual public facilities, where anyone could wash their hands or shower and know that they could always be clean, safe. It was then that Ola realized, with some astonishment, that in all the blocks she'd walked in this new Freewheel, none of the folks she'd seen appeared hungry or looked as if they had no other home but the street.

More important, Ola began to notice the faces of the people she passed. People of all identities, nations, and ages, looking happy, sheltered, well fed, remembered. It was a marvelous thing to be seen, truly seen, and not walked over or peered through as if you did not exist, as if you should not exist. Here, Ola could sense the peace that came from those who moved with ease, who were more than tolerated, were respected, honored, loved.

Oh, to live in a world that saw and valued you!

Even the drones were different here, coded with algorithms, a sacred geometry that actually incorporated a person's dignity and humanity. The only drones she knew were the kind that disrupted and erased. Alerted the Standards authorities who escorted away the people she admired and loved in her community—like Bug and Artis's mom and dad. But not here, not in this place of greenness and gemstone-lit dreams.

She hoped to always remember such serenity and grace—a world where kindness flowed in streams.

She stopped inside a shop when a book cover caught her eye. It was a history of Freewheel. Ola flipped through the pages, reading rapidly. One passage stuck with her.

. . . grateful that the Age of Machine Disunion, a terrible time, is history and not our future. Since those dark days, autonomous systems and people have enjoyed decades of peace and unparalleled prosperity—for all. Blessings to those who fought for a new way of being. Many thanks to the contributors to ALTAR, the Age of Love Tech and Rejuvenation.

The list of the contributors made her drop the book and run, for there she saw her own name included prominently, as well as those of her dear friends.

Ola's thoughts spun, concentric circles of ideas and what-ifs. The more she thought she understood, the more she did not. The space in her chest tightened as unspoken hopes and images and voices rose inside her, scrambling from her heart to her brain. As she ran, she saw years of her life that she hadn't yet lived. *The Power of Yet*, the driver had said. She saw herself emerge from turmoil and the growing civic unrest caused by the constant security raids, detentions, and mass mind-cleanings—the Nevermind—at the House of Dawn. She saw herself graduating high school with Trell, mentoring Bug, moving into a college dorm, graduating with advanced degrees in cybersystem engineering and city planning, communal healing and psychiatry. The history book said that there was a new age of unparalleled cooperation between people and people, people and machines, and she saw how she had been—would be—a part of that.

Breathless, Ola found herself standing before the park Lọwọ had pointed out. A beautiful arched sign overhead read CHILDREN'S ARK PARK.

When Ola walked inside the old-fashioned wrought-iron gates that looked like signs and symbols, sigils from another time, she was greeted by children's laughter. Some played on merry-go-round–like structures; others bobbed and weaved in a colorful obstacle course. Still others climbed ladders that hoisted them into tree houses. Seesaws and something that looked like jet packs filled the open space. But it was the structure in the middle that caught her attention.

Shaking her head, Ola walked until she stood beside the first carved face. There, among the trees and the beautiful flower gardens, were the four mysterious sculptures Bug had discovered. When she saw the letter *B* carved in a childish hand, for the first time since she arrived, Ola knew exactly where she was.

"Look! It's Mayor Ola," a child whispered. A shout went up, and a small crowd gathered around her, sweetly singing a song she knew so well.

"*Ola-Ola-ay*," a familiar voice, Trell's, spoke from somewhere deep in the back of her mind.

"Ola, wake up. Can you hear me?" That little squenky voice sounded like Bug.

Then, in the blink of an eye, all the gemstone, lush, vine-covered buildings disappeared. The Children's Ark Park as well, but Ola could still hear the children's happy laughter, their lovely song. *Ola-Ola-ay!* In the blink of an eye the old Freewheel had replaced the new, and Ola found herself back inside the make-shift ark at the railroad crossing. With tall grass and the river at her back, the House of Dawn, a grim dragon, skulking in the distance, she emerged, determination in her eyes.

Her mind and body still throbbed and pulsed with disembodied voices, disconnected memories that pulled at the very center of her essence. The charged air parted around her shoulders.

Ola's body had not changed, not her hair or her nails, her eyes or her hands—those building, gifting, maker hands. But something in her spirit had. All that she had seen, all that she *would* see. She returned a body whole, a spirit split in two—a half that knew what she once was and a half that was brand new.

Two distinct people, like a shaft of hardwood cleaved down the grain.

As if in a daze, Ola looked around and found Bug and Artis standing on her right. Mx. Tangee peered over their shoulders.

"Dang, Ola, why you looking like that?" Trell said.

"It was so beautiful!" she said, and flung her arms around Bug. Trell and Artis looked at each other, then joined the group hug.

"I see you're back, journeyer." Mx. Tangee stroked her cheek. "Tell us what you saw."

Ola's braids swung as she waved her hands wildly, describing the wonders she had seen.

"I DON'T KNOW WHAT'S GOING ON UP IN HERE," SAID TRELL, HIS voice mimicking the one Grandpapa used whenever he caught the children up to no good, "but I guess I'm going to find out."

He stretched his long arms and bent to crawl inside the ark. He had put on a big performance, but the truth was, if the others weren't standing there, Trell would have backed right out.

"How did I let them talk me into this?" Trell grumbled, his eyes adjusting to the cramped darkness inside the ark. He tried to sit down like Bug had said, but Trell's legs were too long, and every time he tried to bend his knees, he got stuck, rubbing against the wall inside the ark. He winced and cursed under his breath—Trell hated being in the dark by himself.

"Don't worry, Trell," Ola said, as if she were reading his mind. His friend always had his back, like the sister he never had. Despite his humor and laughter, the extra height that some-times made others think he was older than he was, Trell carried a lot of fear inside him. Worry about the invisible target on his back, since drones tended to single him out for extra scrutiny and harassment, even when he was helping his father in and out of his wheelchair. Worry about being erased at school in certain classes, where his raised hand, let alone his voice, was not always welcomed. He loved science and biology, he liked the certainty of mathematics, the comfort it gave, knowing that some problems might actually have answers. Trell worried about the route home, wondering if that would be the day he couldn't avoid getting in a fight, having to defend himself from the older kids who saw him as easy prey, punching down for their own relief and entertainment.

But his biggest worry was about his father. Since the illness ravaged his father's immune system and rendered his once powerful, strong limbs incapable of holding his weight for long stretches of time, his unfulfilled dreams weighed heavily on Trell's young shoulders, just as the deadweight of holding his father up weighed on Trell's knees and back. Sometimes they would sit together after a meal, and his dad would flip through old vids of his youth. He'd tell Trell about the times when he'd persevered, had some personal victory. The far-off look his dad would get in his eyes brought a misty shine to Trell's own. Trell didn't want to get cut off in his youth, life slowed down by tiny white blood cells he could not see.

But it wasn't the fear about the disease being hereditary or about how his family never seemed to have enough points to cover even the most basic medical procedures his father needed. It was the time. The time that was stolen from not just his dad but his mother, Trell, and everyone else in the commune who suffered from physical or mental health issues and had nowhere, *nowhere* to turn. The horror of that made Trell so angry that sometimes he felt as if he could punch a hole through the whole world, but he knew he couldn't. Yet the anger sitting in his chest was sometimes so heavy it was as if he could not breathe, as if all the blood pumping in him was full of fire and poison, blasting like the brimstone in the old vids of cartoons.

So Trell laughed. He became the jokester, the wily trickster, the one always checkin' and regulatin', bringin' in the laughter and the wide, wide smile with all the don't-shoot-me, don't-punch-me, don't-erase-me teeth to make everyone else's day a little easier, to make them feel more comfortable in his presence, and feel safe—a feeling he lived most days without—when they saw him, to make the blows land softer, diminish the humiliation he felt when his raised hand was never seen, to make the anger that slept with him at night and rose in the morning when he woke simmer down, simmer it all down.

Trell grunted and tried to balance himself, squatting inside the ark. He leaned forward, but his foot slipped and he banged his forehead against something hard, something that appeared in the ever-darkening space, something he could not see. The force of the blow sent waves of brilliant colors flashing in front of his eyes, filling up the space with a blackness so dazzling, so omnipresent, it was as if he could reach out and hold it in his hand, capture it in a fist.

The pain hurt more than Trell expected. Though he was by himself, he still focused on holding back his tears. He was always holding back something. Some nights he wished he could just let go. Trell rubbed his eyes with the backs of two busted knuckles, expecting more darkness, but when he looked around, he wasn't in the ark anymore.

Trell found himself in the middle of the street, in front of his own house, but he wasn't standing, he was doubled over, leaning forward. It was an early morning. There seemed to be more trees lining the streets than Trell remembered and the house looked in better shape. The air smelled sweeter, like the end of spring or the beginning of summer. Trell heard a voice on his right that sounded familiar, but it was impossible, because his grandfather . . . it couldn't be . . . he was long . . .

"On your marks!" the familiar voice said.

"Granddaddy!" Trell cried.

"Get set!"

He looked to his left and nearly jumped out of his skin when he saw his father at his side, dressed in shorts and a loose jersey. He winked at Trell, his face full, the dark circles that once eclipsed his eyes like pale moons now gone. Dad was poised, strong, ready to sprint up the street and take flight.

"Go!" Granddaddy yelled from the sidewalk.

Muscles rippling in his arms and legs, Trell's father flashed a glowing smile, bright as a Sunday morning, before he took off. *What in the world?* Most days pain permeated his dad's joints and bones and kept him spending much of his day in bed, pretending to feel better than he actually did. But now all Trell could see were the backs of his heels, the bottoms of his feet. Dad was flatfoot rollin'!

"You better run, Tre-Tre! He'll be sipping in the shade while you're still catching up!" Granddaddy shouted.

Trell laughed. "I got something for him," he said, and took off like a shooting star. He had forgotten how much he loved to run, the way it felt to pump his arms, his knees rising and falling, cutting through space, flying high over the ground. When he ran he forgot his worries, forgot the disappointments, the anger, and the fear. It was like his body was burning through all the pent-up emotions, all the things he tried to hide when he moved through the world at *their* pace. When he ran he didn't have to be one way or the other, his long lanky legs and arms just doing exactly what they were made to do. He moved. Moved like gravity couldn't hold him, like he was part of the air and the air was part of him.

Running was something he and his dad loved to do together, but they hadn't done it at all since his dad got sick. Everything had changed when the disease began slowly but surely to remake his father's body into something neither one of them recognized.

But it wasn't running together that Trell missed, it was the time they lost. So much of his dad's days and nights were spent trying to navigate pain. It broke Trell's and his mother's hearts in a thousand pieces to see the person they loved suffering—and to be powerless to do anything about it. What made it worse was knowing that there was nowhere for them to go. Health care was unheard of in the communes. No one had enough points to even fix their teeth, let alone pay for a chronic illness. Only those who lived on the wired side of Sectors Seven and Nine even had a chance at such care.

What hurt the most was that Dad was struggling so hard for them not to see him struggling. He performed wellness every day he could, trying to look and sound as if he weren't managing the worst kind of pain.

But the dreams Dad once had for himself now fell to Trell. Every day Trell was told what was at stake, what he needed to do to be successful and have a chance to get out of the communes. But Trell never felt he could live up to those dreams. Now seeing his dad healthy again, moving as if nothing could stop him, made Trell curious about a world where that was even possible.

So Trell ran, putting everything he had into his arms and legs, thinking about how just moments before, the whole race would have been inconceivable.

When he made it to the end of the block, he discovered his dad was stretching, waiting on him.

"I told you I still got it," Trell's dad yelled in victory. "You know the people can fly! We always bring that fire!"

Trell was out of breath and could barely speak. He was surprised when his father practically lifted him up in the air, hugging him. It had been a long time since his dad was that affectionate.

But worry set in.

"Daddy, we shouldn't do too much. You might get dizzy and—"

His dad looked puzzled. "Dizzy? Did I miss something, Trellis? Young sir, you're the one that lost! We can try another day if you want to redeem yourself. I'm sure your grandfather and mother have something good cooking up on the grill by now."

Trell could remember the disease blowing through his dad's

body like a dangerous wind, shuddering through his lungs, gnawing at his muscles, making him too weak to even eat some days. Sometimes Trell and his mother took turns making his father soup, trying to season it a little, just enough to have a hint of flavor but not so much that he couldn't hold it down. He remembered the days when his mother locked herself in the bathroom, and her soft wails drifted under the door. The disease had taken more than time from all of them.

"You aren't sick anymore?" Trell asked carefully.

"Sick? Trell, you know we beat that a few years ago. I haven't had a relapse since."

"But how?" Trell asked. "Where did you go?"

Dad took his hand and peered into his eyes. "I think you must have heatstroke. Trell, you and your mama were right by my side. You know I had the best doctor you could ask for," he said with a wink. "And every day, I am grateful for you. Now come on, I'll race you back!"

Laughing, they ran until the sound of their running was like the rush of water, until the past was a distant memory that Trell had not yet lived. He ran, thinking he never wanted to stop, never wanted to stop being in this moment. He ran as fast as his long legs would take him, but he didn't think he could outrun the past, so he promised himself he would find a way to race toward the future.

"I KNOW WHO YOU SAW," OLA SAID. "I CAN SEE IT ALL OVER your face."

Trell looked calm, centered, as if he had received the answer to a question he was afraid to ask. He wasn't exactly sure how to explain what he had seen, or even how he was feeling, but he tried. The words tumbled out of him. When he finished, he nodded at Ola and walked over to Mx. Tangee, who waited.

"Thank you, Mx. Tangee."

"No need to thank me. Thank the land. Thank the sun and the stars. That river. You are standing in your truth."

"Artis, I know you don't want to, but I think you should give the ark a try," Trell said.

Artis looked away.

"You don't have to, if you don't want. The ark ain't a prison— it's an open door. You can walk through only if you truly want to. But if you do want it," Mx. Tangee said, "there's one thing left before you can. Come with me."

Artis and the children followed Mx. Tangee's flowing white robes to the four carved stones.

"West! West!" Bug cried. "Artis, you gotta carve your sign on the stone face."

"The first letter of your given name." Mx. Tangee handed him the ornamental blade. "Remember, whatever you create, do it with great intention. Put your heart in it. Nothing more, nothing less."

When Artis finished, he looked at his handiwork and laughed. "That's the easiest *A* I ever got!"

Trell and Ola chuckled while Bug walked around the stone carving, palms brushing across its face.

"It looks like an easel," Bug said.

"Yeah, it does. Come here, Bug," Artis said. The child outstretched their hand. "You know I would never leave you, right?"

Bug nodded their head. "You didn't have to say that," Bug said. "I already know."

DARKNESS AND HEAT PRESSING ALL AROUND, ARTIS wondered what he would find inside the ark. Part of him still wanted to believe that Bug was pulling his leg, Ola and Trell too. *Maybe they made the whole thing up*, Artis thought. *Maybe there was a hidden door inside.* But neither his eyes nor his heart had deceived him. Something marvelous did exist, something that took his little sibling and their friends out and away, if only for awhile, from the strain of the City of Light, the communes, and the endless drones and Standards authorities.

A fairy tale right out of his father's old books, the ones that got left behind when the authorities came and took him. Even though Artis wanted to believe that this was just another one of his made-up tales he told to comfort Bug on the nights when neither of them could go to sleep, he knew he couldn't be like one of those disbelieving characters in Grandpapa's vids. Unlike Ola and Trell, Artis had seen Bug's drawings, the ones he made long before this birthday. What they had discovered in old abandoned Freewheel, the stone faces with the strange carvings, the makeshift clubhouse they built together that Bug called "ark" and Mx. Tangee called "altar"—all of it could be found in bits and pieces in the art Bug had been drawing since he was very small. How could a little child have known that one day they'd all come out to this last railroad crossing?

Beads of sweat rolled down Artis's neck and made his T-shirt stick to his stomach. Artis didn't want to show his fear, and never wished to see it reflected in Bug's eyes. They had been through enough, suffered so much loss. Every day he and Grandpapa tried to help Bug believe that they could win. Artis wasn't sure if he still believed that, not until this day, when Bug found what Artis had long since stopped looking for: hope.

Grandpapa and even Artis's friends believed that New Dawn was the most dangerous thing in their world. But Artis knew that wasn't true. Hope was. Having too much, having too little. Trying to work out that invisible balance so you don't get crushed but also don't float away was labor Artis didn't always feel strong enough to do. It hurt too much to hope sometimes. Better to just *be,* take whatever comes as gracefully as you can, 'cuz it's coming anyway, whether you want it or not.

Artis wiped his neck with the back of his wide hand and adjusted his shirt on his belly. It was too dark in the ark. He looked around. Something had changed—he felt it humming in his bones. He could still hear the little kids running around the ark, whispering about what they had seen, what they witnessed. He heard Bug and Ola laughing, Trell rapping. Mx. Tangee freestyling—she actually had flow. He smiled. No matter what happened, somehow the younger kids always managed to stay up.

Artis imagined Trell dancing around the ark with Ola and Bug following his every move. Amused at the thought, wishing he could laugh and rap and just be with the rest of the kids, Artis leaned forward, pressed his ear against the warm, dark surface of the altar's interior, and then something inside him shifted, as if flipping a switch.

One moment he was crouched in Bug's ark, Mx. Tangee's altar; the next moment he was hearing soft murmuring and what sounded like—

Jazz.

The music his dad used to listen to on Sunday mornings. Memories flooded through Artis's mind, images of his dad quietly sipping a glass of wine. The time and joy he took in explaining the history and the special qualities of the rhythms and the instruments. How the drummer kept time, held them all together as the trumpet and the saxophone added their brassy voices to the mix and the piano moved to its own groove.

He remembered his father's intensity while creating his art, a painting that he worked on between shifts, listening to one of their mother's new poems.

Artis's chest tightened; his throat felt lumpy. Sadness filled his eyes, that and the longing for a life that wasn't snatched away just when Artis was starting to appreciate the music's beauty, just when he thought that maybe he'd be interested in art himself.

He flinched. Maybe that's why he never tried. Watching his parents, both artists, be taken away, needlessly, from their families, from Bug, from him, made Artis feel sometimes that creating was not worth the risk. But he couldn't take that joy from Bug, who poured their whole heart into their art.

The sound of the music grew louder. Artis rested his hands on the wall of the ark, not sure what was happening. The wall gave a little, which surprised him, because there was no door to the ark and the entrance was on the other side. A soft yellow light traced the outline of the opening in the dark in front of him. Now the voices and laughter grew louder.

Startled, Artis braced himself, moving as if in a dream. He crawled forward, then stood up, realizing that the space around him had expanded. Confusion and curiosity forced him forward, his eye tracking the sliver of yellow brilliance shining inside the darkness. Peeking through the crack, Artis saw a surprising scene unfolding before him.

Beautifully dressed people—men, women, and enbys, not to mention the children—chatted in small groups. Tall walls were covered in the most remarkable art, bold colors and wonderful forms, and something in the brushstrokes and the color palette seemed familiar. Nervous, Artis stepped out and discovered that the door was no longer behind him. The ark, the clearing, everything he knew was gone.

He passed through the sliding doors of a great lobby. The building, shaped like a giant gemstone, was impressive. On his left was a beautiful fountain with yellow and orange water shooting up into the air. TANGERINE WATERS, a sign read. He walked self-consciously, aware that he wasn't properly dressed, but the others around him only smiled and nodded their heads when they saw him. *As if they know me*, Artis thought. He wondered what they saw in him that he didn't see in himself.

Artis made his way to a floor-to-ceiling portrait, joy in his eyes as he took in the painting that could be no one but his mother.

"She's beautiful, isn't she?"

"Now, this is my favorite."

Artis turned to see the ark. Not the actual ark, but a painting of the ark. Artis would know it anywhere. The four stone faces rising up from the green earth, forming a diamond. The sacred circle with the rivers streaming all around.

Even when Bug was very small, it was clear how special a child they were. "I draw what's in my mind," Bug had said when they were finishing the ark. "Child, you draw things you haven't yet seen born in the world," Mx. Tangee had replied. Artis hadn't even been there then, and yet he remembered it clearly.

And how true those words were.

This work seemed to be a union between the real-life ark that Artis had witnessed and Bug's interpretation of what it could be. Artis could hardly believe what was happening. He was standing in the ark and staring at the ark at the same time. *Too meta for words,* he thought. The whole day had been.

He was suddenly tired, and part of him wanted to retreat, crawl back into the ark's dark interior, rewind the whole day, but the entrance behind him was sealed.

Bug had seen their mother. Ola had seen herself, and Trell had seen his father, healthy, even happier than his former self.

Was Artis afraid that if the ark delivered *his* father, he might not live up to Artis's dreams? Or that Artis might be the one to disappoint?

Part of Artis wanted to run into his father's arms, no matter how he turned out, hold him and never let go. If there would be a reunion, he didn't want to do it in front of everyone, even kind strangers like these. He didn't understand why the ark had brought him to such a formal occasion. Though he was proud of Bug, happy for them, their gifts were never what Artis questioned. He did feel some relief that there was a world where Bug could be their full, true self and be celebrated for it. Artis watched his sibling's friends, hugging each other, chatting with small children. Bug wasn't alone anymore. Bug had community, chosen family. Artis's lip trembled. That's really all he hoped for Bug. That Bug would be ensconced in a broader circle of safety and love.

The realization was like a burden lifted from Artis's shoulders. He didn't have to carry that worry anymore—here, he didn't need to. At least in this strange place, where the walls looked like amethyst crystals and the people walked as if they never had to fear drones or Standards authorities, he could set down his emotional sword and shield and bask in the knowledge that at least his vigilance was worth the effort. Bug was safe, might still be.

Tearing his eyes away from the ark on canvas, Artis was going to get a snack when he walked up on a group of people admiring another painting. They held wineglasses and nibbled on delicious hors d'oeuvres from plates no bigger than their palms. They all stared attentively at one person who was dressed in colorful robes. There was something about their spirit that invited people in, welcomed them to enter shared space.

The person wore their hair in a lavender shingle bob with one giant lock that jutted from the top of their crown, like a black unicorn. They waved their hands as they talked, wrists covered with nassarius and cowrie shells and semiprecious gems. They had a dark round face with fat cheeks that reminded Artis of his father. Artis's eyes went all wide and round with shock and the possibility of it all. In his heart he wondered if his dream had finally come true. The ark had returned Bug to their mother. *Now it's returning Daddy home to me.*

Then Artis noticed something. The eyes were wrong. Daddy's eyes were focused and dark with understanding and responsibility. These eyes were light and whimsical, dreamy like his mother's eyes. Like Bug's eyes. Artis walked closer to the gathering, squinting until he wasn't sure anymore.

"Artis?"

When they said his name, Artis knew. Their face lit up, revealing the little child that Artis had worked so hard to care for and nurture in the absence of both of their parents. The little one who loved to draw and stare at the sky until passing clouds turned into burning starlight. The child who believed that a field of broken dreams could be made whole. That magic was real.

Bug made Artis believe in hope and the Power of Yet.

They held each other as the soft, warm light from the crystal walls shone down on them.

"Now here's the real artist," Bug said, smiling at their big brother. "And I see you brought your little masterpieces with you. Trying to show me up at my own show." Bug laughed.

Little masterpieces? Artis was puzzled.

"Baba Bug!" a pair of voices shouted, one from each side of Artis.

Artis looked down and saw two children, standing on his left and his right. Bug crouched and embraced them. One child reminded Artis of his mother, the other of his father. Both had the Dumas smile.

"Y'all haven't been giving your daddy too much trouble, have you?" Bug raised one eyebrow and looked back and forth at both children.

"I've been good, Baba Bug, but he hasn't," the smaller one said.

"*Unh-unh,* I have been good, Baba Bug," the taller one pleaded before turning around and addressing Artis. "Tell Baba I've been good, Daddy."

"What about you, Daddy? Have you been behaving?" Bug smirked at Artis.

Artis didn't know how to answer that question or how to figure out the names of his own children without sounding like he'd bumped his head. And maybe he had. By the time he opened his mouth to ask Bug about the ark painting, he was struck by another sight.

"Dad?" His voice cracked. This time there was no mistaking the eyes.

"Hey, son, I see you made it through. Hello, Estelle; hello, Chip. Give your grandpapa some suga'."

Tears filled Artis's eyes. He could not speak.

"I know, Art. I feel the same way too. I'll never stop being surprised at how talented Bug is. And look at 'em, glad-handing, completely in their element. Hard to imagine how shy that child was, but you put a brush in their hand and leave them to it. When they finished painting the whole house, they'd be talking your ear off. And you were always so good with your Lil Bug. Wasn't the easiest mind to understand. But I couldn't be more proud of both of you. Our family has been truly blessed."

Artis searched for the right words, his mind pulled in the slow currents of a language made of feeling. He couldn't stop staring at his dad, marveling that he was really here. He wasn't as tall as Artis recalled, and his beard had gone all gray, but he still had that warm cinnamon scent that Artis remembered from when he was little, and that easy way about him, the humor that made Artis know that everything was everything and everything would be all right.

As he stood there, clasping his father's hand, watching his children—*he was a father now,* though a part of him knew he'd been like one for a lot longer—dance and play, Artis found the words that he'd been searching for.

Hope is greater than fear.

With the last musical riffs floating through the air, Artis found himself back at the railroad crossing with the ark behind him. Bug and his friends were speaking, but all he could hear was his father's voice. *I couldn't be more proud,* he'd said. Eyes shining, Artis held Bug to him, as if he would never let them go. It was better than any storybook ending he'd ever read.

• — •

The first sign was the silence of the birds, even the insects. Next, a terrifying hum filled the air. Trell shook, instinctively. *Drones.*

They couldn't see it yet, and that was part of its terror. You heard it, almost felt the malice first, before its black-and-crimson hull hovered into sight.

"Attention, Fugitive 11001 . . . 11011 . . . report to the House of Dawn!"

Unbothered, Mx. Tangee gathered herself. "That'll be for me."

Bug began to rock and moan. They'd already lost their parents. Mx. Tangee and Bug—they spoke the same language, shared a mother tongue, spirit to spirit. They were just beginning to understand each other. Now she'd be taken too.

Artis held Bug, trying to shield their eyes, but the child shook their head and pulled free.

"We've got to save her!" Bug cried, running to Mx. Tangee.

"Don't worry, Bug!" Ola said, and motioned for Trell to follow her. "Quick, help me with Tin Man."

The two ran over to the dancing sculpture. "Tin Man's got his own frequencies. He's used to jammin'," Ola said. "Now we're going to make him jam the drone's signal, buy some time, send it back to its port."

When Bug reached Mx. Tangee, she was about to duck into the ark. Bug grabbed her sleeve and tugged on the flowing white garment. She could see the desperation in the child's eyes.

"Mx. Tangee, you gotta go before they get you," Bug said, crying. "The ark will protect you, but I don't want you to leave us. Don't want us to be all alone."

Mx. Tangee held the child tightly.

"Never alone, Bug." She pointed at Artis, who hugged Bug close to him. She waved at Ola and Trell, busy working on the sculpture. "You'll always have each other." Mx. Tangee tapped her heart. "And I'll always have you."

"But why did you come if you were just going to leave?" Bug

asked, tears streaming as they stood near the ark's entrance, the drone barking orders overhead. "What do you want from us?"

"I want you to remember."

Mx. Tangee twirled her baton around the clearing and pointed up at the sky. As if on her signal, two birds dove from the trees and began to circle the drone. It suddenly began spinning, off-kilter. "*They* don't own the future. Remember."

Bug rose from the shadows, voice as quiet as the wind that rustled and curled around their shoulders. "I remember," Bug said. "My memory is full."

"Good. Carry it with you. Carry it forward," Mx. Tangee said. "You know which way our world must go."

She tightened the copper scarf around her head, tucked it behind her ears, and waved.

"Trell, don't lose your laughter or your light. One day you're going to burn brighter than the sun, heal us all." Trell waved his hand, smiled. "Ola, look at you. Already building something special. The future needs imagination like that. Artis, how can such a young body hold such a big heart? Your love travels space and time." She placed her palm on Bug's head.

"Traveler, your art is your ark. Always question, always seek to understand."

Bug's eyes lowered, thoughts and tears spinning in the dust. Fireflies blinked solemnly behind them.

"Will I see you again?"

"Listen, you see a bird, way up in the middle of the air, justa flyin'. When it's up there, it ain't studying nothing but the gift of flight, but when it gets ready to light, it has to come on back home to the ground, to rich green earth. Think on that when you see it flying so high, and know it will return." She placed her palm on Bug's little cheek.

"Not a promise, Bug. Fact." With that, she bent her head, the burnished fabric falling softly around her shoulders, and folded her tall frame into the ark.

The air felt electric. The drone hummed, sputtered, then collapsed.

Ola, Trell, and Artis cheered as Bug waited outside, standing on the rusted rail. Didn't need to look inside to know Mx. Tangee was gone.

A GREAT PLUMED BIRD, A RARE SIGHT, SHOT ACROSS THE SKY. A lone white feather floated in the air and landed at Bug's feet. Bug waited, but Mx. Tangee didn't return. A somber half hour, still as stone, passed before Trell stepped forward and stuck his head in the ark looking for her.

"What do you think's going on?" he asked. "None of us were gone this long. What's happening?"

All of the children watched Bug, but no one would speak their worst fears. Ola had the remains of the drone, studying it thoughtfully. Trell kept tracing the dark life lines of his palms. Artis stared at Bug as the child's changing monologue kaleidoscoped like colored glass.

"What if she don't come back?" Bug said, despair in their voice.

"This world so terrible, I wouldn't come back here either," Trell said. Ola nudged him.

"Let's hope she finds happiness wherever she goes," Ola said.

Bug thought about the day the drones had taken Mama. But the child also tried to remember what their mother had said when Bug had gone into the ark. Something about space and time being relatives, like a family. That neither was fixed, but depending how you thought about them, they could be changed.

Hope was in the child's heart, warring with the sadness, but mostly they felt relief and gratitude. Grateful that they weren't forced to watch the authorities take another person they cared for from them.

Artis couldn't bear to see his Lil Bug so distressed. This

was not the birthday he'd imagined for them. So many highs and lows, mind-blowing revelations, the realization that the world was more than any of them imagined when they rose that morning.

It was much too much for him, let alone a seven-year-old little kid.

"I'm the oldest," Artis said, choosing his words with care. He didn't want Bug to worry that he might not return too. "I'll go and see if it takes me where Mx. Tangee went."

Ola and Trell shook their heads. "Naw," Trell said. "You can't risk that. What if—" He let the unspoken thought hang in the air. "I can go."

"No, Trell," Ola said. "Your dad, he couldn't take it if . . ."

"If what?" Bug cried. "All you're doing is talking about leaving, about Mx. Tangee not coming back. About you not coming back. But what if we're not *supposed* to leave? What if we're supposed to *stay*?"

"But Mx. Tangee left," Ola said.

"I know," said Bug, "because her time isn't here yet . . ."

Ola nodded, almost understanding. Trell exhaled. Artis shook his head.

"Did you already forget what she said, what Mx. Tangee showed us?" Bug wiped their eyes.

They all stared at the youngest.

"She wants us to *remember*."

"I remember the day they took our father. I remember the day they took our mother. I don't want to have to remember this too. Ain't fair!" Artis said, his heart pounding. "They can't just keep taking and taking from us, from everybody, and making it impossible for us to breathe and live in our own skin. Mx. Tangee shouldn't have to *run*. Mx. Tangee shouldn't have to hide. She is! There is no such thing as unclean. That's just one of the lies they made to hide their own dirt."

"What are you saying?" Trell asked.

Artis turned to Trell and Ola, pleading. "I'm saying I remember what I saw. Y'all are too important to the future.

"A doctor—Mx. Tangee's healer. A city builder—an architect of dreams. An artist that changes hearts, inspires minds." Artis could barely breathe, but he pushed on. "Remember what you said when you came out, Ola, *the Power of Yet*. Whatever we build, I know in my heart it's going to start with each of you."

And then, before Bug or any of the other kids could protest, Artis crawled into the ark. He closed his eyes, stood with his arms stiff and his fingers twitching, but nothing happened. Confused, Artis opened his eyes and tensed his body. *Everything you do, you got to do it with great intention*, he could hear Mx. Tangee say. He concentrated, hard on what he hoped he would find on the other side, whatever side the ark chose to take him to.

Still, no shadows, no haze, no metallic sweet scent, no voices or music or change of scenery. Artis muttered, punched the air. He wrapped his arms around his stomach, the dirty shirt itchy against his skin, and screamed.

No one spoke when he finally dragged himself out of the ark and stumbled outside. Softly moaning, he held his forehead and let the tears shake his shoulders—tears he had held for many years, an ever-flowing stream of sorrow.

Trell and Ola knelt beside Artis. Bug held his hand.

"Artis?"

"Yes, Bug."

"Don't cry. You're important too."

One by one the others tried, entering the ark with great intention, but one by one they failed. They emerged from Mx. Tangee's empty altar and the ark remained silent, the world remained unchanged.

Though tears brimmed in their eyes, Bug's memory was full. They *promised*.

Though they would miss Mx. Tangee, Bug knew they all

would be forever grateful for the magic and the grace she had shown them.

Still, they waited until the stars traced circles in the night sky, and finally, they decided to return home.

"Thank you, Mx. Tangee," Bug whispered as they walked away, clouds forming overhead. "Thanks for helping to make my ark real."

Bug pulled out the drawing Artis had brought, one of the pieces Artis said Bug had been drawing almost since they were born. No one knew what it was before, but it was their ark all along. Bug stared at the bright colors, the dark circles that represented the 78s Ola found in the clearing, the great Tin Man standing in the background with his silver hat made from rims, and the four stone carvings, bravely facing a changing world, sending out love from the cardinal directions. Pride filled Bug's little chest, bursting from the corners of a wide smile that shone in their eyes.

The picture of Mx. Tangee grinning, standing next to the ark, spoke to Bug, filled the child with the same murmurs and whispers that led to this special place. In that moment, Bug didn't feel right taking the drawing home with them. Instead, Bug said a prayer, like Mx. Tangee had when she first borrowed the branch from the old tree. "Thank you, old one, for sheltering us," Bug said, and gently laid the drawing inside the ark.

THEY SPENT THE STORMY NIGHT FULL OF DREAMS, A QUILTED vision board composed of all the worlds they had witnessed.

In the morning, Bug and Artis gulped down Grandpapa's hotcakes.

"Whatchu up to?" he asked between bites. "You've been acting funny. Busier than two . . ."

When the siblings burst through the front door, Ola and Trell were already waiting outside.

Unlike their other visits, the trip to old Freewheel was quiet. No one wanted to speak the thoughts that had worried them in the night as they trudged through the wet grass. But when the children finished walking the winding path and returned to the railroad crossing, they found the ark in ruins.

The storm. Chaos covered the clearing and the railroad crossing. Their ark, Mx. Tangee's altar, was dismantled, with many of its decorations, their found art, scattered. The wind had turned the ark into a cluttered mess.

The world had taken so much from them. Some things they would never get back. They didn't know how they would live if it had taken the magic too.

Dejected, they walked out of Freewheel, moving as if their limbs had lost their—

"Music?"

A song pierced the air. Bug pulled away from Artis and began to run, little legs pumping like pistons. The others hurried after Bug's grasshopper legs, Trell's square knees rising and falling, Ola scissoring along, her thin frame slicing through the air, with Artis rolling after. Fear and excitement rippled through their weary, dream-dusted bodies, their minds filled with the knowledge of the stolen years time had taken and then returned to them, the memories still moving through their consciousness like molten gold.

Bug was the first to see the new child. They stared in astonishment. The boy, not much taller than Bug, stood in the grassy field, dressed in oversize white majorette boots with bright orange pompoms, spinning a railroad spike.

The mysterious child beckoned, pulled a crumpled piece of paper from his pocket. He smiled when he offered Bug the gift. Bug recognized it instantly. It was the drawing left in the ark, Mx. Tangee's altar, but there was a new message scrawled on the other side of it, in a handwriting Bug had memorized from old birthday cards and folded-up poems.

Great loops in the *e*'s, the *s*'s like music notes.

Mama.

"What the note say?"

Bug passed the drawing to Artis. Artis's hands shook as he read aloud:

Happy birthday, Bug. Artis, I am so proud of you. Return whole, my children, your eyes a constellation of stars. Full of the knowledge that I love you, that we are what we carry—the years, the nights, and the seconds, and all the spaces in between. It flows through us, flows from within us. This love cannot be stopped. It grows—and it must be free. The time to dream is a sacred thing, Trell. It heals, lifts us up. Ola, every child, not just my own, needs it. Our world demands it. You've got to dream a future before you can build a future. Together, let us begin this dreaming awake.

On cue, the child spun, dipped, and danced, pointed as he sang each of their names, whole notes floating in the air. "Bug, *Arrrrr-tis,* Trell, *Ola-Ola-ay!*"

"Whaaaaaaat?" Trell cried, hand over his mouth.

Ola punched him playfully. Bug clapped their hands. Artis shook his head as they laughed and followed the child back down the wild path toward the park, a boisterous, joyful, magical parade. Bug holding Artis's hand, they ran past a faded sign that read STAR CORE METRO, past the broken gas eaters and the rusted heaters too. They marched across the path together, the railroad spike pinwheeling in the shimmering light.

The ark was gone, but the power remained.

We remember, Bug thought.

Then they ducked under the canopy of forest, the others following, and let the dark green radiance embrace them.

ACKNOWLEDGMENTS

To all the fandroids, F.A.M. (free azz muthafuckas), time travelers, and dirty computers, I cannot thank you enough for supporting this expansion of the *Dirty Computer* universe. You MAKE ME FEEL seen and heard, so in return I hope you can see some of yourselves inside this book. I hope that you felt me thinking of our community and wrapping my arms around you as we navigate our way into the future.

Thank you to my creative copilots, N8 "Rocket" Wonder and Chuck Lightning, for your encouragement at the beginning of this new endeavor for me. As I fought through anxiety and feeling SO AFRAID for humanity, you guys reminded me that we are the creators of beauty and that our imaginations have the power to inspire nations. It was an honor developing the world of the *Dirty Computer* emotion picture screenplay with you, which then gave me a conceptual base for these stories. None of this would have been possible without your hearts and our conversations under the PYNK sunsets.

Thank you, mama, for always encouraging my love of science fiction reading and writing as a lil' DJANGO JANE.

To my late grandmother Bessie, thank you for sparking my love of sci-fi by making chicken and dumplings for us to eat as we watched *The Twilight Zone* MANY MOONS.

Thank you to my entire Wondaland Arts Society family. To my management team—especially Kelli Andrews and Mikael Moore—thank you for your constant support of each new vision I have. Thank you to my editor, Kyle Dargan, for being the cosmic glue and devoting so much love and time into making sure these stories got out and on time! Thank you to Eve Attermann and everyone at the William Morris Agency. Thank you to David Pomerico at Harper Voyager for presenting this opportunity and holding it wide open for us to creatively swim in waters untouched!

Thank you, Octavia Butler. Thank you, Greg Tate.

And finally, and most importantly, I must thank all of the writers who decided to TAKE A BYTE with me. Thank you for taking ownership of this world in a way that I have always wanted. As a community of storytellers, thank you for using your light in ways that our future needs. Not only did you all say "yes" at a time that was very hectic for the world, you all made the adventure, the sexiness, and the stakes of these stories bigger than I would have just on my own. Alaya, Danny, Eve, Sheree, and Yohanca—I am so happy to have had the opportunity to collaborate with you, and I look forward to the brilliance you all will continue to bring into this CRAZY, CLASSIC, LIFE.

ABOUT
THE AUTHOR

JANELLE MONÁE is widely celebrated as an American singer/songwriter, actress, producer, fashion icon, and futurist whose globally successful career spans over a decade. With her highly theatrical and stylized concept albums, she has garnered eight Grammy nominations and has developed her own label imprint, Wondaland Arts Society. Monáe has also earned great success as an actor, starring in critically acclaimed films, including *Moonlight*, *Hidden Figures*, *Harriet*, *The Glorias*, and the 2020 horror film *Antebellum*. She will star in the highly anticipated sequel *Knives Out 2*. *The Memory Librarian* is her debut book.

ABOUT THE COLLABORATORS

YOHANCA DELGADO is a 2021–2023 Wallace Stegner Fellow at Stanford University. Her writing has appeared in *Best American Science Fiction and Fantasy*, *Nightmare*, *One Story*, *A Public Space*, *The Paris Review*, and elsewhere. She holds an MFA in creative writing from American University, and is a graduate of the Clarion workshop.

EVE L. EWING is an author and a sociologist of education whose research is focused on racism, social inequality, urban policy, and the impact of these forces on American public schools and the lives of young people. Her works include *Ghosts in the Schoolyard: Racism and School Closings on Chicago's South Side*, the poetry collections *Electric Arches* and *1919*, and the middle-grade text *Maya and the Robot* (illustrated by Christine Almeda). She has written for the Champions series, the Ironheart series, and other Marvel projects. Along with the award-winning author and poet Nate Marshall, Ewing wrote the play *No Blue Memories: The Life of Gwendolyn Brooks*, commissioned by the Poetry Foundation. Ewing is currently an assistant professor at the University of Chicago Crown Family School of Social Work, Policy, and Practice and an instructor for the Prison + Neighborhood Arts Project, a visual arts and humanities project that connects teaching artists and scholars to men at Stateville Maximum Security Prison through classes, workshops, and guest lectures.

ALAYA DAWN JOHNSON is the author of seven novels for adults and young adults. Her most recent novel for adults is *Trouble the Saints*, winner of the 2021 World Fantasy Award for Best Novel. Her young adult novel *The Summer Prince* was longlisted for the National Book Award, and *Love Is the Drug* won the Norton Award. Her short stories have appeared in many magazines and anthologies, including *Best American Science Fiction and Fantasy*. She lives in Mexico, where she received a master's degree with honors in Mesoamerican studies at the Universidad Nacional Autónoma de México for her thesis on pre-Columbian fermented food and its role in the religious-agricultural calendar.

DANNY LORE is a queer black writer/editor raised in Harlem and currently based in the Bronx. Their contemporary speculative fiction and science fiction has been published in *FIYAH*, *PodCastle*, *Fireside*, *Nightlight*, EFNIKS.com, and other venues. Their comics work includes *Queen of Bad Dreams* for Vault Comics, *Quarter Killer* for Comixology, *James Bond* for Dynamite Comics, and *Star Wars Adventures* for IDW Publishing. They have short comics in *Dead Beats* and *The Good Fight*, and have also edited *The Good Fight* anthology and *The Wilds* from Black

Mask comics. Their work is included in the YA prose anthology *A Phoenix First Must Burn* from Viking Books.

SHEREE RENÉE THOMAS's first all-fiction collection, *Nine Bar Blues: Stories from an Ancient Future*, was a best collection finalist for the Locus Awards and the World Fantasy Awards. Her work also appears in *The Big Book of Modern Fantasy* (1945–2010) edited by Ann and Jeff VanderMeer from Vintage Anchor. She is also the author of two multi-genre/hybrid collections, *Sleeping Under the Tree of Life*, longlisted for the 2016 Otherwise Award, and *Shotgun Lullabies*. A Cave Canem Fellow honored with residencies at the Millay Colony for the Arts, VCCA, Bread Loaf Environmental, Blue Mountain, and Art Omi/Ledig House, her stories and poems are widely anthologized and her essays have appeared in venues such as the *New York Times*. Thomas edited the two-volume World Fantasy Award–winning *Dark Matter* (2000, 2004), which first introduced W.E.B. Du Bois's work as science fiction, and coedited the anthology *Trouble the Waters*. She was the first Black author to be honored with the World Fantasy Award since its inception in 1975. She serves as the Associate Editor of the award-winning journal *Obsidian: Literature & Arts in the African Diaspora* and as the Editor of *The Magazine of Fantasy & Science Fiction*, founded in 1949. Thomas was recently honored as a 2020 World Fantasy Award Finalist in the Special Award—Professional category for her contributions to the genre. She lives in Memphis, Tennessee, near a mighty river and a pyramid.